The Wishing Tree:
Love, Lies, and Spies on Chincoteague Island

by

M. S. Spencer

The Wishing Tree: Love, Lies, and Spies on Chincoteague Island

COPYRIGHT © 2023 by Meredith Ellsworth

Cover Art by *Tina Lynn Stout*

The Wild Rose Press, Inc.
PO Box 708
Adams Basin, NY 14410-0708
Visit us at www.thewildrosepress.com

Publishing History
First Edition, 2023
Trade Paperback ISBN 978-1-5092-5010-3
Digital ISBN 978-1-5092-5011-0

Published in the United States of America

Addison circled the oak. Sure enough, the small strip of canvas still fluttered in the cold wind. She touched it, then drew her hand back and walked down to the water. Her eyes danced with the waves, searching, imagining what it would feel like to see Seth's head pop up and watch his long arms battling the current to get to the shore. And to her.

"Surely Hurricane Thomas would have taken it."

She jumped and whirled around. A man leaned against the wind-washed trunk. He was tall and thin, his hair a glossy espresso, his eyes the inky blue of a stormy ocean. He reminded her of the portrait of her great-great-grandfather which hung in her family's Chincoteague house. "Taken what?"

"Whatever you left on the tree." He peered at her. "Isn't that what you wished for? To have your token carried off by the wind? Or is my guidebook wrong?"

She shook her head slowly. "No, it's not wrong."

He waited, his lean body bent slightly forward, his eyes attentive. She found herself wanting to tell him everything—about the boat and Seth and the accident. She opened her mouth, but he spoke before she could get a word out.

"Forgive me, you looked so lost that I had to try to cheer you up, and suddenly that seemed stupid and then it got all awkward and here I am apologizing before I've even asked your name."

Praise for M. S. Spencer

Spencer's last release, *Hidden Gem: The Secret of St. Augustine*, earned a Silver at the Florida Writers Association's Royal Palm Literary Awards, 2022. It was also named Best Mystery Book of 2022 by N. N. Light's Book Heaven.

"Real-life mystery meets fiction in this delightful tale, and a dash of romance is sprinkled in."
~*Shelly H., NetGalley reviewer*

"The hunt for the treasure was intricate, well-plotted, and unpredictable. A great read if you're looking for a unique romance."
~*Michelle Godard-Richer, Bookbub reviewer*

The Penhallow Train Incident: "I suggest carving out some time before you start reading. Stockpile food, tell the family they're on their own, and lock the door."
~*Rochelle Weber, reviewer, author, and editor*

Lapses of Memory: "Mark my words, you will laugh, grumble, and then laugh some more. This book was memorable, and I'm not likely to forget about it anytime soon."
~*Romance Authors at Large*

Flotsam & Jetsam: The Amelia Island Affair: "This book has it all. A smidgen of romance. A murder or two or more…Entertaining, amusing, and page turning."
~*Barbara T., NetGalley reviewer*

Dedication

To my mother,
whose ashes lie just offshore.

Chapter One

Three grand essentials to happiness in this life are something to do, something to love, and something to hope for.

~Joseph Addison

Assateague beach, Saturday, March 15

"But Mama, I don' wanna give up my shell!" The little girl held her razor clam shell, chipped and white with age, close to her breast. "I *wuv* it!"

The large woman in an unforgivingly tight tube top threw her cigarette away and bent down to the toddler. "S'okay, honey belle. If y'all don't wanna get your mostest biggest wish—like, say, goin' to Six Flags— you don't hafta put yer shell up onna wishin' tree. Fine by me." She straightened, her purple capris making ominous sounds.

The little girl gave her mother a suspicious look and took a step toward the gnarly oak tree, its branches crooked in various directions, its barkless trunk a sinewy mass of beetle highways.

"That's it. Go on, Starlyn. Put it right there on that branch."

The girl stopped, her hand stretched halfway to the tree, the clam shell clutched in a desperate grip. "Tell it to me again, Mama?"

1

The woman sighed and pulled another cigarette from her voluminous tote bag. "See, Starlyn, this here's a wishing tree—"

"Does every island have one, Mama?"

"What? No, um…um. Ony Shincoteague. Why, honey, people come from miles around—even from as far away as Nassawadox, to hang their hopes on this here tree. It's been a…er…*special* tree for ages. Your grammy left her shell here, and that's how she found Grandpa, you know."

The little girl frowned. "But Grammy says she found Grandpa on the internet."

"Internet?" The woman took a long pull on the cigarette and hitched her pants back up over her belly. "Star baby, she's too old to use the internet…Oh, wait a minute. No, darlin'. Grammy said she caught Grandpa 'in her net.' She pulled him up in her *fishing* net. See, it was in the bad storm of eighty-two, and Dad had gone on one of his binges…I mean, er, he hadn't been able to go out fishin' for three days and had found, er, other pursoots. The way Ma tells it, Dad was a-walkin' by the ditch where it pours inta Swan Cove pool and fell in. A coupla minutes later, Grammy came by and threw her seine in to catch somethin' for dinner. Instead of a fish, she pulled out the man o' her dreams."

"Mama?"

"Enough questions, hon. Jes' stick yer shell there behind that toy truck." She pointed at a miniature Tonka pickup speared on a twig. "Time to get home and start supper."

Little Starlyn shyly set her treasure in the spot her mother had indicated. Then she scrunched up her eyes and balled her little hands into fists.

"Did you make your wish?"

"Uh-huh."

Her mother waited until the girl had turned her back, then pushed the token a little deeper into the crevice. "All set?"

"Uh-huh." Starlyn's lower lip trembled. "G'bye, shell." Her mother took her daughter's hand, and together they waddled down the beach toward the parking lot.

Addison watched them go. It had been all she could do to keep from laughing as she listened to the exchange between the two. *I don't want them to know I was eavesdropping.* Even more, she didn't want her cheerful mood to be dispelled, leaving her with only the sadness she came with. The child's hopeful expression, the mother's cynical affection, took Addison's mind off her grief, if only for a short while.

When the pair had gone far enough down the beach, Addison emerged from the forest of loblolly pines and cypress that defended the march between the shore and the wetlands. Keeping her head down, she walked crab-like toward the old sand live oak, covered with the flotsam and jetsam of human desire. If she didn't know better, she'd think it had been tossed ashore in the throes of a great gale, shards of a wrecked ship clinging to its boughs. In fact, its roots went down as far as the Pleistocene era.

This tree, so Chincoteague lore went, welcomed the first Spaniards to its shores. The conquistadors tethered their horses to it, horses that would evolve into the Chincoteague salt hay ponies that roam the marsh today. This tree had seen hurricanes, naval battles, gun runners, pirates, poachers...and lovers. From the early

1700s on, a young maiden of the Eastern Shore would hang her token—a kerchief, a ribbon, an earring—on the ancient oak. It was said that if a high wind caught the token and blew it away across the ocean, her true love would reveal himself. The girl would visit the tree every chance she had, hoping to find her precious trinket gone. Of course, she usually had a true love already in mind and, to get the ball rolling, would sometimes contrive to draw the object of her affection's attention to the tree. He would dutifully collect the trophy, keeping it hidden until the day he proposed.

Addison remembered her grandmother relating the legend as they huddled around the fire in the big old house on Alder Island, the wind whistling through the pines outside. She closed her eyes, visualizing the old woman in her rocking chair, her back ramrod straight, while the children sat cross-legged on the floor.

"Your parents will be back soon, but I think we have time for a story or two. Shall I tell you about the wishing tree, young'uns?"

"Yes, yes!"

Addison's brother Bertie yelled above the rest. "First tell us about Jennie, Nana. I want to hear about Jennie Hill."

"All right, Bertie."

Addison said crossly, "But then you'll tell us about the wishing tree, won't you? Promise?"

"I promise." She rocked for a minute before beginning. "Jennie Hill's family was one of the earliest to settle on Chincoteague. Her grandfather, Captain Timothy Hill, built the oldest house on the island."

Bertie raised his hand. "I know all about it, Nana! It's this little wooden shack up North Main Street. A guy from the mainland moved it there to renovate it. Used to be a bicycle shed. Pop says it's...it's—"

"Unique!" shouted Addison. "Pop says it's one of only two houses with wooden chimneys in all of Virginia."

Her cousin Phoebe—just shy of six—snorted. "A wooden chimbly? No way. You light a fire innit, the whole thing'd go up in flames."

Nana signaled for quiet. "Well, for one thing, the chimney wasn't attached to the house, so they could pull it away if a fire got out of hand. Plus they lined the inside with a kind of homemade cement called chink that protected the wood. And for your information, small fry, they made little kids climb inside to slap the stuff on." She regarded Phoebe over the top of her glasses. "So mind your manners or I'll send you up the *chimbly*."

She went on. "Now, Timothy's son, Timothy Junior, was a wealthy man, so he moved to a fancy white house on the other side of the island—at the end of Deep Hole Road. He and his wife Zipporah had one child, a daughter. Even at thirteen, Jennie was a beauty, and many of the local boys admired her. One young man—Tom Freeman—not only admired her; he fell madly in love with her. He couldn't eat; he couldn't sleep. He wrote reams of letters professing his love." Here Nana leaned toward her audience, and her voice dropped. "*But he never sent them.*" The children sucked in a communal breath.

She straightened. "When he asked Jennie's father for her hand in marriage, Timothy brushed him off. 'She's too young,' he said. And 'I won't have her marrying beneath her station.' See, Tom was a handyman, an odd-jobber. He had no money and no fixed address."

"Was he a bum, Nana?" Addison had read about bums. They ate some kind of canned stew and rode around the country in cattle cars.

"No, no. He was a hard worker, but the Hills were landowners, pretty high up in Chincoteague society. It wouldn't do for their daughter to go with a common laborer."

"That seems awful snobby to me." The little girl sniffed. She had lately been studying Carry A. Nation's visit to Chincoteague. After considering and discarding temperance as a cause, she had settled on the abolition of class warfare.

"Tom Freeman thought it was unfair too, little Addy. He kept after Jennie, wooing her constantly."

"But he didn't get her, did he?" said Phoebe with satisfaction. "He blowed his brains out, didn't he?"

"Shush, child. Who's telling the story?"

"Yeah, pipe down, kid." Bertie gave Phoebe a noogie. She yelped.

When order was restored, the old lady resumed. "One fateful day, Tom decided to take one last stab at winning Jennie's heart. He met Jennie and her mother as they were walking into town. When Zipporah angrily thrust him aside, he pulled out a pistol and shot her."

At this point, the listeners always gasped. Then giggled.

"And then, he turned to Jennie. Jennie, whom he loved desperately—whom he couldn't have—and shot her dead."

Bertie cried, "No! That's not how it happened. You're forgetting, Nana. She didn't die right away. She lingered"—he said it with relish—"*all* night in *horrible* agony before she bit the dust as the sun came up."

"That's right. Thank you for clarifying that, Bertram." Nana winked at the boy. "So, while she...lingered, he pointed the gun at his head. This time the bullet did its job, and he died instantly." She rose.

"It's so dumb, Nana. How could someone kill the one he loves? It doesn't make sense." Bertie always asked the same question.

"Ah, you see, Bertram, love does peculiar things to people—especially to men. You'll find out when you grow up."

Bertie muttered, "I ain't loving any *girl*. And I ain't gonna kill anyone."

At this point, Phoebe would always cry, "Tell us another one, Nana."

"It's getting late, children. It's time you were all in bed."

"Pretty please?"

"Yes, Nana—pretty please?" Addison recalled her grandmother's promise. "A story about the wishing tree."

Nana heaved a theatrical sigh and sat down again. She pulled a gold pocket watch from her waistband and checked it. "We have ten minutes before your parents arrive. Let's see..." She tapped her chin. "The wishing tree, eh? Would you like to hear about Elmira Hopkins?"

"Yes, yes!" This was a new one, and the children sat up straight, eyes bright. Would there be bloodshed? Romance? Revenge?

The old lady settled back and in a crooning voice began. "It was not long after the tragedy of Jennie Hill that Elmira Hopkins came to live on Chincoteague. Even though she had turned thirty, she was still a striking woman. Tall she was, with lustrous nut-brown eyes and high cheekbones. Her hair was jet black, and she had a widow's peak."

Phoebe raised her hand. "What's a widow's peak, Nana? Did her husband fall off a cliff?"

The old lady chuckled. "No, Phoebe. It's the way her hair grows." She touched Addison's forehead. "See how it comes down to a point? Folks used to say that was a mark of high breeding. The Steeles are a very distinguished family."

Bertie frowned. "Pop says we're nothing special. He says"—he blushed—"we puts our pants on one leg at a time like everyone else."

"True, but your ancestor Richard Steele was a famous writer in England almost three hundred years ago. He and his friend Joseph Addison were part of a group of London intellectuals who molded the English language and literature we use and study today."

Addison asked, "Is that why Mom and Dad named me after them?"

Nana laughed. "Yes, you got the short straw, I'm afraid, Addy."

Phoebe chirped in her squeaky voice. "What about the Lambs?"

"Your family was noteworthy as well, Phoebe. Charles Lamb flourished just a few years after Addison and Steele. He helped define English romantic poetry and authored a wonderful children's book of tales from Shakespeare." She pointed at the bookcase. "It's right there on the bottom shelf."

Phoebe pinned a gratified smirk on her face. "I

knew it."

"All right, children, do you want to hear about Elmira or not?"

"Yes! Yes! Please go on, Nana."

"Very well." She resumed. "Her glistening ebony hair was so long she could sit on it. Straight, too. Young Luke Tarr says his grandpappy swore Elmira's mother was an Indian, descended from Pocahontas herself. Elmira laughed at that, she did. But there was no denying that her almond-shaped eyes and her ivory skin—smooth and clear as a vernal pool—could have belonged to the Powhatan maiden."

"Was she nice, Nana?" Addison hoped the answer would be yes.

"Nice?" The old woman let her head shake, releasing it for a moment's rest from her rigid posture. "It was hard to tell. Townsfolk described her as aloof. Above us all. Hoity-toity."

Bertie sniggered at the word and elbowed his sister.

The old lady gave him a sharp look. "That means she was a bit of a prig, Bertram."

"Oops. Sorry, Nana."

After a minute, she continued. "Elmira had a chin like an eagle's beak—sharp and curved. Regal. People called her Queen Elmira behind her back."

"And was she very rich, Nana?"

"Oh yes. Her father owned the dry goods store and had aspirations."

At this, the children's eyes grew large, for they thought aspirations must be a terrible, evil, or possibly wonderful thing.

"Elmira had attended the Atlantic Female College in Onancock and deemed herself highly educated.

Although she didn't bother to apply, she expected to be appointed schoolmistress of the one-room school up at the end of Main Street. But a strange thing happened. Another woman, name of"—Nana tapped her chin—"Little Dutch Smith, that's it. She arrived from Accomac and announced she'd been hired to run the school. Well, you can imagine the uproar"—here Nana squeezed her eyes shut—"but what could anyone do? The county had chosen Smith, and Elmira had no recourse. She did the only thing left for a young woman of the time to do—she asked her father to find her a husband."

Tommy Bunting raised his hand. "I bet nobody on Chincoteague would take her, on account-a she was so mean, right, Mrs. Steele?"

Phoebe pinched his arm. "Naw, it was because she was so beautiful. The boys were all a-scared-a her. That's the truth, ain't it, Nana?"

"I don't know, child. The fact is, no one came forward, even though her father offered a half stake in his business to anyone who would marry his daughter. Years went by, and Elmira's chin grew sharper and her figure thinner. She acquired a pinched look, like she'd swallowed a tadpole."

"What happened next? Did she die?"

Nana stopped and stared at the questioner. "Die? Everyone dies. But no, Elmira lived a long life. And a happy one."

"How did that happen? She lost her job and never found true love."

"You haven't let me finish." Nana pulled out her pocket watch and checked it. "You children have pestered me with so many questions, our time is almost up. Perhaps we should stop for now."

The chorus of no's that met this announcement brought on the crack of a smile. "All right, but you'll have to be quiet as sleepy kittens if we're to finish before your bedtime. Where was I?"

"Elmira not dying."

"Oh, yes. Although she probably wished to at that point. Little Dutch Smith not only captured the schoolhouse job, but the heart of the only man Elmira had ever judged to be matrimonial material: Jonah Blake. She had even begun to think of moving away—perhaps to Salisbury.

"One cold spring day, she rowed a boat from her home on South Main around to Tom's Cove and beached it where the refuge parking lot is today. She climbed over the dunes and emerged onto an empty, wind-driven landscape. The waves were high, and black skimmers rode the whitecaps, dipping down to snag a fish now and then. Blowing sand covered her delicate lace-up boots. She wrapped her raccoon coat closer and started to walk north. As she rounded a high bluff, a sudden freshet blew her off balance, and she fetched up against a dead oak. Its bark had been stripped by the wind, and it stood at an odd angle. But when she pushed the trunk, it held firm. Stuck in nooks and crannies among the branches were snippets of cloth. She noticed one colorful scrap and pulled at it. It came loose in her hand. She recognized the shred of coral silk that came from a particularly becoming frock Little Dutch wore the day she arrived."

"Did she spit on it?"

"Spit on it? Why would she do that?"

"I would have," said Phoebe. She wrinkled her

nose. "Nasty old Dutch, stealing Elmira's boyfriend."

Nana tittered. "Why, Phoebe, aren't you the vindictive little thing! No, she didn't spit on it. But its presence gave her pause. How did it get there?"

A little boy raised his hand. "I know, I know! She put it there to find her true love! That was the wishing tree, wasn't it?"

"Yes, Tommy, it was indeed the wishing tree—the very same one your mothers and fathers left their tokens on. But in this case it didn't work for Dutch. Can anyone tell me why?"

Addison stared at her grandmother. "Because the token was still on the tree, right? You only find your true love when the wind carries it away. So Jonah wasn't Dutch's soul mate after all?"

The old lady clapped her hands. "Good for you, Addy! Yes. Later that week, the children found Little Dutch in the schoolhouse, badly beaten. Jonah had taken her savings and skipped town."

Phoebe asked, her eyes wide, "If her token had blown away, that wouldn't have happened?"

"It may well have happened, but Little Dutch, being from away, didn't know how the wishing tree worked."

Addison was gleeful. "And Elmira did know. When she saw Little Dutch's offering on the tree, she realized that Little Dutch had made a mistake. Did she laugh spitefully?" She cackled like the Wicked Witch of the West. Or so she hoped.

"Not at all. She helped nurse Little Dutch back to health, and they became fast friends. Then one day, a few months later, Elmira took her own token out to the wishing tree."

"And did the wind take it?"

"Yes, indeedy. The next day a stranger came to town, a dark-haired man with azure eyes. He took one look at Elmira and went down on one knee. A year later, my grandfather was born."

Addison cried, "Elmira was your great-grandmother?"

"She was."

A sigh of delight rippled through the audience. Phoebe went up on her knees. "Tell it again, Nana."

The old lady laughed. "Maybe next week, dear ones. Your parents will be here any minute." She rose and straightened her skirt. The neighbor children got their things and went out on the porch to wait.

Addison and Bertie's mother beckoned them from the hall. "Time for bed, children. Up you go."

Bertie took the stairs two at a time, but Addison lagged behind. She tugged her grandmother's sleeve. "Nana, does the wishing tree still work?"

The old lady stopped and gave her granddaughter a long, speculative look. "There's only one way to find out."

Chapter Two

And pleased the Almighty's orders to perform / Rides in the whirlwind and directs the storm.

~Joseph Addison

Assateague beach, Saturday, March 15

Addison circled the oak. Sure enough, the small strip of canvas still fluttered in the cold wind. She touched it, then drew her hand back and walked down to the water. Her eyes danced with the waves, searching, imagining what it would feel like to see Seth's head pop up and watch his long arms battling the current to get to the shore. And to her.

"Surely Hurricane Thomas would have taken it."

She jumped and whirled around. A man leaned against the wind-washed trunk. He was tall and thin, his hair a glossy espresso, his eyes the inky blue of a stormy ocean. He reminded her of the portrait of her great-great-grandfather which hung in her family's Chincoteague house. "Taken what?"

"Whatever you left on the tree." He peered at her. "Isn't that what you wished for? To have your token carried off by the wind? Or is my guidebook wrong?"

She shook her head slowly. "No, it's not wrong. I mean, the legend of the wishing tree says that if your offering blows away, you will find your true love.

Or…he'll come back to you." She thought of little Starlyn. "Some folks think it just means your greatest wish will be granted."

He took a step toward her. In the waning light, his eyes took on an even darker hue. His mobile face showed distress. "Which one are you hoping for: a new love…or that your lover will return to you?"

"What? No. I mean…Yes…I—"

He waited, his lean body bent slightly forward, his eyes attentive. She found herself wanting to tell him everything—about the boat and Seth and the accident. She opened her mouth, but he spoke before she could get a word out.

"Forgive me. I'm being impertinent. You just looked so lost that I had to try to cheer you up, and suddenly that seemed stupid and then it got all awkward and here I am apologizing before I've even asked your name."

Addison shot a quick glance to see if he were laughing at her, but his expression was unreadable. Embarrassed? Indifferent? "It's all right. You just startled me. I'm Addison Steele." She removed a mitten and stuck out her hand. He took it in a very large one of his own. She could feel the calluses on his palm. *A carpenter? Maybe a sailor?*

"Nick. Nick Savage."

"Nick?" *Oh dear. Maybe the resemblance to great-great-grandfather Nicholas isn't so far-fetched.* "Is it…is it short for Nicholas?"

His face twisted with chagrin. "No. My given name is Nicodemus."

Whew. Nicholas was a name that had been saddled on at least one Steele boy in every generation.

According to the family narrative, it was meant to serve as a cautionary reminder of an ancestor's scandalous fling with a Greek sea captain. Her mother, on the other hand, insisted that everybody just liked the name, and once it was established in the family tree it became a tradition. Addison preferred the more romantic version.

She took stock of Nick's chiseled features. With his coppery skin, straight nose, and wavy hair—not to mention those striking blue eyes—he could certainly pass as Alexander the Great's brother. A thought came unbidden to her mind. *Since his name isn't Nicholas, at least I don't have to worry about any kinship issues.* She gulped. *Addison! How could you? I'm ashamed of you.* "Um, so…Nicodemus. Is it a family name?"

"No. My father was a populist."

"Huh?"

Nick chuckled. " 'Nico' means 'victory' and 'demos' means 'of the people.' "

Now Addison was totally confused. "I'm sorry?"

"Oops, my bad. That was a pun, and a poor one at that. Actually, my parents were devout Christians and named all their kids after obscure Biblical characters. Nicodemus was a Pharisee who came secretly to Jesus just before his arrest and asked him if he was truly the Messiah."

"I…uh…see."

He fiddled with a razor clam shell stuck in a crook of the tree. Addison recognized the one little Starlyn had put there. A piece broke off in his hand. "Oh dear, have I destroyed some damsel's dream?"

She took the piece and slid it behind the shell. "Don't worry, she's young. She'll have more and better dreams."

He gave her a bemused look. "I'll take your word for it." A flock of willets flushed, flying in an arc out to sea and back. "Do you live here on Chincoteague?"

"No, but my family has had a house here going back four generations. How about you?" She blinked, thinking how odd it was to be exchanging pleasantries in the wind and cold, standing on a lonely beach, with only a dead oak for ambience.

"I'm visiting the area for a few weeks. The waitress at Jim's Restaurant told me about this tree, and I figured I could use a destination for my walk." He contemplated it. About seven feet tall, its rough, knobby burls and serrated limbs held numerous shells, scraps of cloth, even matchbox cars. He bent closer and plucked an object from a twig. "What do we have here? Gumby?" He held the tiny green rubber man up for Addison's perusal.

She giggled. "Well, the rules require you to put something on the tree that has significance for you."

"Maybe Gumby sacrificed himself to bring Pokey back." He carefully set the toy back on the branch. When he turned to her, his white teeth flashed in the setting sun. One black tendril fell over his brow, veiling the sea-bright eyes. Addison gulped. He held out a hand. "It's getting dark. May I escort you back to your car?"

"That would be nice. Thanks, Mr. Savage."

"Please. Nick."

"Oh, okay. You may call me Addison."

He gave her a long, lazy smile, leaving her with the impression that he already knew her well. Addison fell into step beside him. As they walked, she stole a glance at him and had to stifle the sudden urge to invite him home. *It's only been a year. It's too soon to get involved with another man.* She stopped short. *Addison girl, what are you thinking? Seth hasn't even been declared officially dead yet.* The notion that he might never come back hurtled through her mind, but without the usual pangs. Could the man tramping alongside her be the cause of this sudden admission? *After five minutes' conversation? I don't think so.*

They reached her Subaru. Next to it crouched a vehicle that resembled one of those huge containers that oceangoing freighters transport: black, big, and boxy. Its door handle sat at eye-level. Its headlights loomed over her head.

"I hope you don't disapprove of my Hummer." Nick patted the tank. "Isabel is my baby."

Addison was at a loss for words.

He gestured at the passenger's side door. "May I offer you a drink? I thought I'd head to that place on Main Street for something to raise my temperature."

"You mean Dobie's?"

"That's the one. The upstairs bar is called something else though."

"Cheyenne's Lounge. Cheyenne is Dobie's mare."

"Mare? Isn't that a little chauvinist?"

"What? No, he sponsors her. He…" She petered out.

He grinned. "I knew what you meant. Cheyenne is one of the salt hay ponies that locals can sponsor, right?"

She nodded, relieved. "Yes."

"So, how about that drink?" When Addison looked pointedly at her car, he held up a palm. "Oh, I see. Well, you can leave it here, and I'll bring you back."

Did he just wink? Despite her attraction, her mother's voice rang in her ear. *Never get in a car with a stranger.* She cleared her throat. "No...urk...no, thanks. The refuge closes at dusk. The entrance is barred."

"I see. I could drop you off at your house then."

Oh, and never let him know where you live. "Then I'd have to find a ride back to the refuge in the morning. So...sorry."

His friendly optimism dissipated. "Oh. Well. Then I guess I'll see you around the 'hood."

"No! I meant...I'll meet you there." She smirked. "A hot toddy would be nice."

His eyes narrowed. "What's so funny?"

"Oh, it's a standing joke around here. The bartender at Dobie's is nicknamed Toddy."

"I see. Does he entertain?"

"Huh?"

"You know..." He wiggled his hips. "Do a pole dance or strip?"

"God, no." She envisioned the squat old man with the pug nose. "God. No."

"Well, let's hope he knows how to make a good hot toddy, then."

He fired up the tank and rumbled over the sand to the refuge road. Addison's Subaru felt like a wind-up toy trundling along behind him. They'd almost reached the ticket booth at the entrance to the refuge when she remembered that she hadn't made her usual prayer to the storm gods to take her token and bring her husband back.

****

Cheyenne's Lounge, Saturday night

Nick shouted over the cracks of pool cues hitting

19

balls and the nonstop swearing of the players. "What's your pleasure?"

Addison started to say "the usual" but caught herself. It wouldn't do to have Nick think she was a regular in Cheyenne's. "Something toasty...I'll have a Rusty Nail."

" 'Rusty nail'? Sounds painful, but okay." Nick turned to the little man behind the bar. "I understand you're known for your hot toddies."

The bartender started and glared at Addison. "I'll be glad to make one for *you*, sir."

Nick carried the drinks to a small booth as far from the pool table as possible. Addison shed her down jacket and mittens. He grinned. "I was wondering what you looked like under all that cold weather gear." He framed her with his fingers. "Not bad. Not bad at all."

"Um." *Do I thank him? Simper? Either way he'll think I'm an ass.*

When she didn't respond, he continued. "I bet those golden curls bounce when you dance." He wound a short ringlet around his finger, then let it loose. Sure enough, it sprang back like a coiled spring. "Frames your face like a mane. *Hmm.* Together with your eyes—how would you describe them? Amber?—you remind me of a lion cub: all cuddly and playful on the surface." He raised an eyebrow. "But perhaps with a fierce, untamed wildfire simmering just underneath?"

Great. Now I have no *idea how to answer.* Addison sipped her cocktail and tried to evade Nick's eyes, which bored into hers. She focused on his hands. Broad, with long, thick fingers. Fine black hairs crisscrossed a thin white scar across the back of his right hand. It brought to mind the calluses she'd felt on his palms.

"Do you sail?"

"Me? I used to. Where I grew up in Rhode Island, boats were the principal form of transportation. My brother used to race."

"Really? So did Seth." Addison clapped a hand to her mouth. She couldn't believe his name slipped out so easily. She hadn't been able to speak it for months. What was it about this man that made her so garrulous? And why was she sorry she'd mentioned her missing groom?

"Seth?"

"He is…was…my husband. He was…lost at sea."

"Ah, so he's the one you left the token for." He put a leathery hand over her small, soft one. "I'm so sorry. How long were you married?"

This was always the worst part. "Three days."

His eyes widened. "Only three days?"

Addison swallowed a large gulp of alcohol and almost choked on it. *You've gotten this far. Spit it out.* "We were on our honeymoon, sailing from Washington down the coast to the Bahamas on Seth's blue water boat—a Whitby 42 ketch. A…a squall came up just off Hatteras. We capsized. The Coast Guard rescued me, but…"

"But they never found Seth."

"No. Not yet."

Nick hailed the bartender. "Two more please." He swung back to Addison. "Wait. 'Not yet'? So you believe he's still alive?"

Until that point, Addison had truly believed Seth would come back, riding a dolphin or an albatross or something, joking that he'd found his way to Atlantis and had returned to take her there. "I…don't know."

Nick was silent. Just as Addison began to feel she should change the subject he said gruffly, "I suppose my story can wait."

"No, please. Tell me why you're in Chincoteague."

"Believe it or not, it has to do with someone lost at sea." At her stunned look, he said hastily, "My brother, Daniel. He came down here a few weeks ago to go deep sea fishing."

"On a head boat?"

"No, he hired the whole kit and kaboodle. He was the only passenger, aside from the captain and the first mate. According to the report, he hooked a big marlin but refused help. Typical of Dan, really. The crew was in the stern working on some gear when they heard a shout and a splash. Coast Guard determined the fish pulled Dan over the bow. They searched for two days, then gave up."

"And you think *he's* still alive?"

"I don't know either." He smiled at her. "I was in DC when I heard about the accident and thought it was worth a shot to come see for myself. I came down to talk to the captain—hoping he could shed more light on what happened. And pay the poor guy for his trouble."

Addison reflected that Nick sounded remarkably composed considering his tragic story. *It's probably not polite to ask if they were on good terms.* She rose. "I'd best be getting home. Thanks for the drink."

"My pleasure." He jumped up. "I'll walk you out."

In the darkened parking lot, he stepped close to her. A tangy scent of clove and citrus wafted from him. "Addison, I…uh…I'd like to see you again. It's just…well, I'm a little lonely, being a stranger here."

"Um."

"It would be nice to have someone to talk to—maybe catch a meal. That is, if you don't think that's inappropriate under the...under the circumstances?"

She almost laughed. Their circumstances were about as romantic as ham and eggs. When she didn't say anything, he whispered, "I promise, we'll stay on dry land."

Now she did laugh. "All right. Call me—my cell is 202-555-1204. Good night."

As she pulled out, he tooted the Hummer's horn—creating a seismic wave that rumbled through the town, rattling windows.

She made her way back up Maddox Boulevard, turning right on Chicken City Road and left on East Side Road. Her family's house lay on an island—really more a spit of land that breached the grassy marshlands between Chincoteague and Assateague Islands. The building had been added onto with each generation and now sprawled over half an acre. Every level had a balcony or bay window with a view of the lighthouse. Addison walked into the semicircular, glassed-in living room as the sun set in a glorious riot of reds and oranges, spotted here and there with the black silhouettes of hunting marsh hawks. She thought about her day and the insertion of a new character in her little world. What part would Nicodemus Savage play in it?

The telephone rang. "Hello?"

"Ms. Steele? Ms. Addison Steele?"

Damn, another solicitor. "May I ask who's calling?"

"This is Agent Robert Peel of the FBI. You were seen in conversation with Mr. Nicodemus Savage today."

What is this? "I beg your pardon?"

"You are acquainted with Nicodemus Savage, are you not?"

"Um…"

"Ma'am? Are you there? We'd like to ask you a few questions. Would it be possible for me to come to your house this evening?"

Addison almost dropped the receiver. "Oh, dear. Yes, I suppose so. My address is—"

"Thanks, we have your address. I'll be there in ten minutes."

Chapter Three

If we hope for what we are not likely to possess, we act and think in vain, and make life a greater dream and shadow than it really is.

~Joseph Addison

Addison's house, Saturday, March 15

An unmarked white sedan came to a stop on the gravel circle in front of Addison's house. A man of medium height and weight got out of it. The porch light revealed bland features above a monochromatic tie and a plain gray suit. He had colorless hair cut close to his scalp and opaque eyes.

"Ms. Steele?"

"Yes?"

He flipped his lapel to reveal a badge. "Agent Robert Peel. May I come in?"

She led the way to the kitchen and indicated one of the hard wooden chairs. *No reason to make him too comfortable.* She noted his glance at the coffee pot but determined not to offer him any.

He regarded her for a minute, then shrugged and sat down. When she took the other chair, he barked, "How long have you known Mr. Savage?"

Addison refilled her cup from the pot on the counter before answering. "Let's see…three hours?"

Agent Peel bestowed a less than gracious stare upon the openly defiant Addison. "Ms. Steele, my informant told me you seemed on quite intimate terms—"

"Informant? Let me guess. You talked to Toddy Smollett, the bartender at Cheyenne's. Who moonlights as the local matchmaker."

"According to his file, Mr. Smollett is a respected member of the commercial establishment," returned Agent Peel stiffly.

"Toddy has a file? As far as I know, he's never been farther than Salisbury in his life. He's not so much as filched a candy bar. Why, he even pays his parking tickets."

The agent produced a cold smile. "Everyone has a file."

Addison sucked in a breath. She asked in a small voice, "Do I?"

Instead of answering the question, he indicated the urn. "May I have a cup of coffee?"

She poured another mug and handed it to him. He hesitated a minute. Addison hoped he was waiting for an offer of sugar or cream, which wasn't in the cards. He finally mumbled, "Thanks, I'll take it black."

After a sip of her own, she'd recovered enough to say lightly, "Sure, Toddy makes a mean mai tai, but his views on romance are based mainly on the bodice rippers he sneaks from his wife's night table." Before the agent could object, she went on firmly, "I met Mr. Savage this afternoon. We both happened to be taking a stroll on the beach. It being a chilly day—as you no doubt noticed—we agreed to meet for a drink at Dobie's. We drove in separate cars. I returned home alone." *Chalk one up for Ma.*

The agent rose. "I see. Well, thank you for your time, Ms. Steele."

As she showed him the door, it occurred to her that he had revealed nothing of his purpose. "Wait. You haven't said what this is all about, Agent Peel. Why are you interested in Mr. Savage's movements, anyway?"

"We're merely following leads." He paused. "Look, will you be seeing him again?"

With any luck. "I don't know. He's visiting the island, so there's a good chance I'll run into him."

"If he mentions his brother, Daniel Savage, would you let me know? Here's my card."

"His brother? In fact, he did tell me about him."

"Yes?" Peel's eager face loomed close.

"He said he'd gone overboard while deep-sea fishing. He came here to find him, or at least learn more of the circumstances of his disappearance."

The man blinked. "Oh, really? Interesting."

"Why?"

"Because, Ms. Steele, Nick Savage is lying."

The news shook her, yet on another level it didn't surprise her. There was something not quite authentic about Nick's story—something missing from it. Still, she wasn't about to show any doubts in front of this cop. "Why on earth would he lie? He doesn't know me from Adam."

"We are investigating the theft of highly classified documents from Wallops Island Flight Facility. We believe Daniel Savage, a biologist and grantee there, is complicit."

"What does that have to do with his brother?"

"Nick Savage is aware of what his brother did.

Daniel Savage has disappeared indeed, but not from a fishing boat."

****

Addison's house, Sunday morning

"What's that expression? Red sky in the morning, sailors take warning…"

"Red sky at night, sailors' delight."

"Yes, that's it."

Addison squinted at the sky. It was still cool on her deck, but the sun peeked through the long, gray ribbons of cloud, lacing them with scarlet. "So, you're predicting a late spring blizzard, Phoebe?"

Her companion dropped a second tablespoon of sugar into her coffee. "Me? No, but Lois Merkel on Channel 8 is. And she's got the software to prove it. She claims we're in for an inch of sleet—maybe even marble-sized hail."

Addison sighed. "I'll have to dig out the shovel. It must be somewhere in the garage."

Phoebe drained her coffee and got up to refill it. "I brought doughnuts."

"Cream-filled?"

"Of course." She handed Addison the box and sat down. "How long are you staying this time?"

"A month. The Senate is renovating the library, and while it's closed, a number of the staff were given the time off."

"Not all of them? It doesn't gall you to be considered dispensable?"

"Actually, I don't mind. The head librarian could only finagle this minuscule space in the basement of the Dirksen Senate Office Building for our temporary use, and all thirty of us could hardly fit in it. They even had to rent a couple of rooms in the old VFW building to store the collections in."

"Then why not work remotely from your townhouse? Unless of course this is your excuse to spend a little quality time with your cousin."

"That's the main reason, yes." Addison smiled at Phoebe. "But our kind of reference work requires a physical presence. The members expect personal service. Plus a lot of our materials are the only copies extant, so I can't retrieve them online." She hesitated, then blurted out, "It's also an opportunity to do some research on my book."

Phoebe's eyebrows went up. "*Your* book? You're writing a book?"

"Don't sound so surprised. I'm compiling a bibliography on the French and Indian War for the Library. The Government Printing Office is going to publish it."

"And you can work on it here?"

"Uh-huh, although I may have to go up to Alexandria for a few days at some point."

Phoebe bit into her doughnut and chewed quietly for a minute. "You don't always have to come to Chincoteague, you know. Not that I don't enjoy your company. You could take a road trip. Or go on a cruise—oh!" Her eyes grew big. "I'm sorry. I wasn't thinking."

Addison patted her arm. "It's all right. This is home to me. I love coming back. Plus, I have to keep up family relations—I promised Mother I'd look after you. You're the only cousin I have left, Phoebe."

"Second cousin, once removed. The Lambs were only promoted because your grandfather disinherited his second son, the dastardly Nicholas. Admit it: you're just here to make sure I don't make off with the family silver."

"I thought you already had it all."

"Not yet." She looked Addison over. "Maybe…maybe this is a safe haven for you? From certain memories?"

Addison knew she was referring to Seth. She nodded. "You caught me."

"You never know. He could come waltzing in any day now." She gestured at the interior. Through the sliding glass doors, Addison glimpsed the living room, every surface of which was piled with books and papers. "You might want to clean up a bit. Just in case."

"Hey, I'm workin' heah." Her melancholy evaporated. "Phoebe, you always know how to cheer me up."

Phoebe grinned. Her short bob of flaming red hair bounced up and down, and her gray eyes glinted. "Now, tell me about the FBI man. Was he cute?"

The question caught Addison off guard. "Not at all. He was…well, the most apt adjective for him would be 'drab.' "

"I see. I suppose they cultivate that look at the FBI. And he claimed that this new beau of yours—"

"Just an acquaintance, Phoebe."

"—has a brother on the run?"

"That's what he said. But Nick—"

"Nick? Short for Nicholas?" Phoebe looked suddenly anxious.

"No. It's short for Nicodemus."

"*Hmm.* That's still Greek, though, isn't it? Is he a sailor by any chance?"

"As a matter of fact, yes." Addison laughed at Phoebe's shocked face. "He's no relation, if that's what you're worried about."

The girl seemed unconvinced. "All right. What does he look like?"

"I thought we were talking about the FBI agent."

"After you tell me about Nick. Hair? Eyes? Build?"

"Quit changing the subject, Phoebe. Even though Nick told me that his brother had gone deep sea fishing—"

"The G-man says he's a spy? Well, one of them's lying, and I think they frown on that at the FBI. That leaves your boyfriend."

Addison shook her head. "He doesn't seem the type to lie."

"The only men who don't lie are asleep. I repeat, what does he look like?"

Her mug at her lips, Addison gazed out at the marsh. The sky had cleared, turning a deep cobalt blue, but she knew from experience that the fluffy little clouds on the horizon would soon wade across the water, bringing wind and snow. She shivered. A great blue heron broke ground and flew past them, squawking angrily. "Nick? He reminds me of the portrait of great-great-grandpapa that hangs upstairs. Dark chocolate hair with a touch of wave, eyes the color of that London topaz Mother used to wear on her birthday. Deep greenish-blue."

"Tall? Short? Hefty, brawny? Winsome?"

"Thin. Tall—maybe six feet." She held one hand over her head. "About your height." She thought back. "Big hands. Callused. I forgot to ask him what he does for a living."

"A sailor, you said."

"I don't think as a profession. He said he came down from Washington. He has an urban air about him."

"And what's that?" asked Phoebe, amused. "The scent of smog?"

"Don't be silly; there's no smog in DC—just a lot of hot air." Addison conjured up the man who inexplicably made her heart flutter, discomfiting her. "He smelled of spice—clove, I think. Or allspice. Something manly."

"Ooh, the pheromones are working overtime here. Clove, huh. I used to love those clove drops. Too bad they don't make them anymore." She picked another doughnut out of the box and held it up. "Is cinnamon a manly scent?"

"Nah. Too sweet."

Phoebe ate the pastry in two bites. "They say musk is very masculine."

Addison wrinkled her nose. "Musk makes me think of one of those animals that spray you—a weasel or beaver or something."

"I sure hope Nick doesn't spray people." Phoebe rose. "I've got to get my materials ready for school tomorrow. We're going to paint wooden eggs for Easter and put up a big banner with the alphabet at the entrance to the school. I must say, kindergartners are a hoot—much more enthusiastic than the second-graders I had last year. What are you doing today? Does Mr. FBI want to interrogate you again?"

"I doubt it. I think I made it pretty clear I hardly know his target." Addison picked up her mug and followed Phoebe inside. "I thought I'd walk the wildlife loop up to the service road. See what's dabbling in the impoundments."

Phoebe pulled her car keys from her pocket. "Have fun. I still don't understand this addiction to bird watching. Once you've seen a 'life bird,' what do you do with it?"

"Savor it, dear. Savor it. What can I say? It's in the blood."

"Only on your side of the family." She turned at the door. "Are we still on for the trip to Norfolk?"

"Oh, I'd forgotten about that. I really don't have time, Phoebe."

"Saving yourself in case Mr. Greek Seafarer shows up again?"

"Not at all. I've work to do. I can't take a whole day off."

"Stick with that alibi, cuz. As long as you can."

Addison put the breakfast dishes away, musing on the new developments. She hadn't heard from Nick. *Of course, it's only been a day.* Did he know the FBI was lurking? If he did, did he know they'd talk to her and that she would find out he had lied to her? What would be his reaction? To run away or double down on the lie? *If he runs, I might never see him again.* She dropped the dish towel on the floor and stood staring out the kitchen window.

Heaving a sigh, she picked the towel up and started drying the coffee cups. *So what? What difference does it make?* Granted, Nick was handsome and a good listener. He probably only made her heart go pitty-pat because she'd been without male companionship for more than a year. *Admit it, Addy. You're just plain horny.*

A few hours later, she grabbed her hiking vest and binoculars and headed out the door. The clouds had rolled in while she'd been pondering her feelings, and a chill breeze had sprung up. She went back inside, got her hat and gloves, and drove out to the refuge.

The ticket booth was closed, and no one shared the road with her. She parked at the entrance to the wildlife loop, a three-mile paved road that encircled Snow Goose Pool. She started to turn right onto the asphalt, then changed her mind and took the path that meandered through the marshes. Where the trail curved to go back to the road, an observation post had been built.

She climbed the steps to the small platform and surveyed the pool. The water was high this morning, and whitecaps showed. A band of northern shovelers escorted by a phalanx of black ducks scooted around, nibbling on grasses. Overhead, a vee of Canada geese honked raucously, reminding her of harried commuters on a jammed highway. Most of the migrating waterfowl would be coming through in the next week or so, but for now the wide water seemed awfully barren. In the mud flats by the shore, a lone dowitcher sowed a line of test holes looking for snails. She climbed down and, following the path to the loop road, turned right. At that moment the sun—pale and wan—broke through the gray billows.

I think I'll go up the service road for a bit. She headed toward a swing gate. From here, a seven-and-a-half-mile gravel road led to the northern tip of the island. The first mile or so was surrounded by dense pine woods. Sheltered from the wind, Addison began to warm up. She came to a large area of dead and dying stumps on her left. A decade before, a fearsome army of pine bark beetles had invaded Assateague, killing off most of the forest. Some parts of the island had recovered, but it would take years for the more slow-growing trees to come back. She switched her gaze to her right, where a series of small freshwater impoundments had been constructed for dabbling ducks. A quarter of a mile to the east lay the dunes and the ocean. Waves crashed in the distance.

She stopped to photograph a family of red-breasted mergansers. As she fiddled with the shutter to get a better bead on them, a white blotch hit and clung to her camera lens. She looked up. Snowflakes drifted down softly. *They're not going to amount to much.* She had started to walk north again when the flakes suddenly mutated into sharp little spikes of ice and began slicing and dicing her coat. *I guess Lois Merkel at Channel 8 was right about the hail.* She smashed her hat down on her head, turned around, and plodded back toward the loop road.

She paused to catch her breath at the pool. Beside it, a narrow path led through the sea grasses toward the sandhills that overlooked the ocean. In the driving sleet, she could barely make out a man standing on the top of the dune, his pale jacket blending with the flurries. He faced away from her, holding binoculars up to his eyes. *Tall, black-haired—that's Nick.* She shouted his name, but the wind whisked her voice off into the ether. Hesitating only a moment, she started down the path toward him. She had reached the halfway point when he turned. She drew off her hat and waved it, but instead of waving back, he slung the binoculars over his shoulder and slid down the sand bank to the ocean side.

By the time she had climbed up to the crest, he was only a distant shape marching swiftly down the beach.

Chapter Four

When love's well-timed 'tis not a fault to love; the strong, the brave, the virtuous, and the wise, sink in the soft captivity together.

~*Joseph Addison*

Assateague beach, Sunday, March 16

The sleet turned back into snow. Great gobs of soft, wet flakes landed on Addison's head and back. She could barely see the water, much less the rapidly fading figure. She tried not to feel snubbed. *He must not have recognized me.* She wished he'd told her where he was staying. *I could, like, just* happen *to wander by. Maybe just* happen *to run into him.* Depending on how he reacted, she'd know whether he'd seen her or not. Whether he cared or not. *Oh,* real *mature, Addy. You're acting like Phoebe. Why don't you just go all out psycho and stalk him?*

Will I ever see him again?

She trudged back to the service road, head down, and somehow made it to the wildlife loop. It was another half mile to the parking lot, so if Nick had walked down the beach, he would likely have left the refuge by the time she reached her car. Out of the blue, the image of Seth rose before her, that wide grin she so loved plastered across his tanned face. *Oh, Seth.* She

37

missed him then, with a blinding, searing ache. Bent double, she let the agony flood through her. Tears mixed with snow washed over her frozen cheeks. Her throat clogged, and her lungs screamed for air. With an effort, she stood up. *I'm going to get pneumonia if I stay here.* She stumbled down the road, reaching the loop parking area at last. Her car sat, the sole vehicle in the lot, looking as friendless as she felt.

She crossed the Assateague channel bridge. At the edge of the wide belt of grasslands separating the two islands sat a McDonalds. The sight always buoyed her, harking back to the inglorious battle waged between the townspeople and the tourists. The mainlanders—outraged at the prospect of a fast-food joint situated at the entrance to one of the premier refuges in the country—organized petition campaigns and wrote strongly-worded letters to the local paper. Phoebe called it NIYBY—Not In Your Back Yard. The locals won. *As well they should have.* She felt a little better.

A block down, the café across from the Refuge Motel beckoned. Addison found a seat at the bar and ordered hot buttered rum. A basketball game was playing on the big screen television. The Turkish owner's eyes were glued to the play. "Is this some kind of tournament, Emin?"

He pivoted toward her. "Yes, yes! This is March Madness, Addison. Very exciting."

"March Madness? Sounds bacchanalian."

"Excuse me?"

Addison reminded herself that English was not his native tongue. "Is it college or professional?"

"It's the NCAA—the national college tournament. Sixty-eight teams play rounds in brackets through

March and April, eventually whittling down to two teams. We're at what's called the Sweet Sixteen."

"Sixteen teams, as in eight against eight?"

"Correct. After that we go to the Elite Eight, then the Final Four, and finally the championship."

Addison pointed at the screen. "Who's playing now?"

Emin swelled with pride. "The ones in green are from George Mason University—my daughter's school. They were totally...how you say? Underdogs. Not even ranked in the top twenty—and look at them! They're whipping Connecticut's butt!" He gestured at the television, on which a tall young man had just lobbed a three-pointer.

"That's...er...nice." She sipped her drink, feeling its warmth spread to her fingers and toes. The door opened, letting in a rush of freezing air. Nick entered, shaking snowflakes off his brown mackintosh. He stopped when he saw her.

"Hey there, Addison. What are you doing out on a wintry day like this?"

I could ask you the same question. "I could ask you the same question."

"Me? I've been inside. Just checked out the museum. Interesting."

"You didn't go to the beach?"

"In this weather?" He held up a finger. "Emin, old man, could I get a whiskey—no, wait, an Irish coffee. That's the ticket." Addison's bewilderment must have been written on her face, for he said jauntily, "Oh, Emin and I go way back. I was in here for breakfast only this morning."

The Turk clapped him on the back. "With his

appetite, I should be able to pay off my mortgage in six months."

Addison inspected Nick. He didn't seem wet or chilled the way he would be after a cold walk on the beach. *Maybe he went home and changed.*

Nick checked his watch. "Almost four already. That museum took longer than I thought."

Four? So it had been forty minutes. *Possible.*

Nick began talking basketball with Emin and Addison finished her drink. As she rose, he touched her elbow. "Um, Addison?"

"Yes?" Could he hear her heart going *blam, blam, blam*? Could Emin hear it too?

"Are you free for dinner?"

"I…I think so."

"Great. Pick you up at seven?"

Addison made a quick calculation—wash hair, dry hair, shave legs, find the makeup she'd put away after Seth's death, figure out which of her two nice outfits to wear…three hours should be enough. "Sure."

She had reached the door before he called her back. "It would probably help to have your address."

Oops. "Twenty-two twenty-two Alder Branch Lane. It's off East Side Drive."

Two hours later, sitting atop a heap of discarded clothes, she suddenly remembered the FBI agent. *Should I confront Nick with his accusation?*

****

Riptide restaurant, Sunday evening

"Isn't the snow lovely?" Addison stared dreamily out the window at Chincoteague Bay. The restaurant was currently empty except for a trio of businessmen and the waitress, Ginny. The floodlights on the building illuminated the fens hemming in the channel on either side.

"*Mmm*, yes." He held his hands as though framing a photograph. "It's like tinsel tossed over the black water and red-gold grasses. Rather Christmasy."

She sighed. "I love Chincoteague. If I'm away too long, I get homesick. There's something about it—hardscrabble, rough, enduring, clinging to its roots with all its might in the face of an implacable Mother Nature."

Ginny dropped off two glasses and opened the bottle of Pinot Grigio for them. "Ready to order?"

"I'll have the rockfish tacos, please, and a green salad after."

"After the tacos?" Ginny seemed surprised.

"Yes." She touched her lips. "It cleanses the palate."

"I agree. That's how the French do it, and they know a thing or two about palates." Nick handed the menus back to Ginny. "I'll have the same." When she was gone, he leaned forward, moving his glass to one side. "Are there other families like yours, ones that have been here for generations?"

"Oh, yes. The Merritts, the Thorntons, the Whealtons, and others. If you go to the cemeteries, you'll see the same names over and over on the headstones."

"When were the islands settled?"

"Chincoteague has been claimed by patent since 1650, but until the beginning of the nineteenth century, it was mainly used to graze livestock. Only a hardy few lived here."

Ginny brought their meals. They ate quietly for a

few minutes. Addison scoured her brain for some way to bring up Agent Peel, but it was preoccupied with Nick's strong fingers as they squeezed the taco together. She woke up when the contents spewed out either side of his mouth. "Oh dear."

"Oh dear is right." He dropped the mess on his plate and wiped his hands on a napkin. "Think maybe I'll use a fork."

Addison picked up her own. "Sounds like a plan."

He took a bite, chewed, and swallowed. "You mentioned cemeteries just now. The other day I passed the Red Men's cemetery. I was curious about the name."

Addison laughed, relieved to find a neutral topic to discuss. "I bet you thought it held Indian burials. There *were* Indians on the Eastern Shore, but they didn't establish any settlements on Chincoteague. In fact, the Improved Order of Red Men is a fraternal organization, like the Elks and the Moose. They trace their origins back to the Sons of Liberty."

Nick laughed with her. "Sons of Liberty? As I recall, Sam Adams and his friends painted themselves red and masqueraded as Indians when they threw the English tea overboard. Never knew their gang became a permanent club. I don't suppose they've continued their illicit practices."

"You mean vandalism?" She snickered. "Unless you count buying lottery tickets by the thousands and round-the-clock poker games. The Red Men have had a lodge here since 1891. In the early years of the twentieth century, Chincoteague boasted more than seven fraternal lodges. That big brick building on Main Street next to the hardware store? That was the Masonic temple."

"Huh." He poured the last of the wine into their glasses. "I'd love to hear more about Chincoteague's colorful history, but"—he signaled for the check—"it's getting late. I'd better take you home."

They drove through the darkened town and out to Alder Island. He went around the car and let Addison out. She took a step toward the front door. *Do I want to invite him inside? Ulp, maybe not.* Instead, she walked past the house and out to the dock. Nick followed her. They stood together, staring up at the Milky Way. After a minute, he shook himself. "It's a bit damp for stargazing. Do you mind if we go in?"

No! I'm not ready. I hardly know the man. Seth... "Okay." Addison led the way to her living room. "Nightcap?"

"Don't mind if I do."

"Jack Daniels?"

"Perfect." Nick busied himself with rebuilding the fire, and Addison filled two glasses with ice and whiskey.

She set them down on the coffee table while he poked at the logs. Her anxiety began to ebb in the flickering light. *I feel so comfortable with him. It's as though I've known him forever.* She didn't find herself comparing him to Seth as she had expected. *Could it be because I'm in my childhood home?* She had never shared it with Seth. When they came down to Chincoteague, they'd always rented a place nearby. Of course, her newfound tranquility might be due to the fact that Nick hadn't made any sudden moves and seemed content to talk about idle things.

They sat down on the couch facing the fire, and

Nick wrapped a languid arm around her. Addison's skin prickled, and she wiggled on the seat, trying to ignore the heated signals pinging from her lower regions. As the silence lengthened, the urge to jump on his lap grew almost unbearable. What to do? *He'd surely be appalled to know what's running through my head—or rather another part of my body—right now.* Better start a conversation quick. Nothing safe sprang to mind, and Addison said the first thing that popped into her head. "So, what were you doing on the beach today?"

"Me? I wasn't on the beach. Perhaps you didn't notice the inclement weather?"

"But—"

He turned to face her. His hands went to either side of her face, and he drew her to him. Gently, his lips brushed hers. "*Shh.* Addison, are you…are you thinking what I'm thinking?"

She stood up, only to shimmy onto his lap. "I am."

****

Addison's house, Monday morning

The *craaack* as something smacked into the bay window woke her. Addison shot up. The fur throw she'd pulled over them some time in the night fell to the floor. "What the hell was that?" Outside on the deck, a juvenile mallard fluffed his feathers and tottered over to the water. He tipped himself back in and swam away. "Poor old duck—he must have struck the glass. Looks like he survived."

Nick rolled over, his eyes still shut, and fell off the couch. "Ow! Tell me again why we couldn't go upstairs last night?"

Addison didn't want to have to justify the wreckage left in her bedroom by her preparations for their date. They wouldn't have been able to find the bed, let alone use it. "You were in too much of a hurry, that's why."

He reached up and pulled her down. "Oh, and you weren't, little firecracker? Tell me, how long has this sexual abandon been pent up inside you?"

Addison reared back. *Seth. Oh my God.* Guilt surged through her veins. How could she have jumped into bed—or onto a couch—with a total stranger so soon after Seth...*What if he's still alive and comes back?* What would she tell him? *Of course, I'd have to be honest. He'd understand, but...would I want him to?*

She examined the man lying on the floor wrapped in fur. His hair was mussed, and a slight five o'clock shadow roughened his strong chin. She gave a little hiccup. He raised himself on an elbow to gaze at her, and the vise of doubt clamped on her heart was suddenly loosened. She took a deep, shuddering breath.

"Addison, I swear you're more beautiful this morning than you were last night." He grinned. "Of course, last night you were caterwauling like a Pictish princess in heat."

She huffed but stopped when something on his arm caught her eye—blue lines on the skin. She bent closer. "Is that a tattoo?"

Quick as lightning, Nick pulled the throw up over his shoulder. "Er...could you hand me my jeans?"

Addison regarded him, a scintilla of mirth lurking around her eyes. "Nick, will I see you again?"

He stared at her open-mouthed. "Of course you will. You don't think—"

"Well, then, do you really believe you can hide a tattoo from me?"

He hesitated, then bared his wrist, exposing a two-inch-square image of a man flying an open-cockpit, single-engine plane. Underneath were the letters DMB. "What does it mean?"

"Did you ever hear the song 'Daniel' by Elton John?"

The tune immediately began playing from memory. "Yes—and now it'll be stuck in my head all day. Wait a minute—Daniel, as in your brother? DMB is Daniel My Brother?"

"Yes."

"But why the plane?"

"You know the lyrics, don't you? Elton John's Daniel goes to Spain on an airplane. When my brother left home for Europe, I had this tattoo done to remember him by."

"Did he reciprocate?"

A spasm of pain rippled over Nick's face. "No."

"No? What happened?"

He closed his eyes. "Later. Maybe." He opened them and attempted a smile. "I'm too hungry."

Addison got the message: sensitive subject, back off. She pulled the rug off Nick and twisted it around her waist.

"Hey!"

Stopping for a minute to admire his broad chest and manly parts, she swept toward the door, calling over her shoulder. "Breakfast?"

"Sheesh, Addison."

"I'll take that as a yes." On the threshold, she turned, tossed her head, and dropped the throw. "I'll be back in a jiff." Leaving the gasp of admiration in her wake, she went upstairs to dress.

Chapter Five

The world is grown so full of dissimulation and compliment, that men's words are hardly any signification of their thoughts.

~Richard Steele

Addison's house, Monday, March 17

Half an hour later, Addison entered the kitchen to find Nick, barefoot, attired in jeans and flannel shirt. He was cracking eggs into a bowl. "Omelet?"

"You can cook, too?"

"On all four burners."

"Or at least two." She winked impishly.

He arched an eyebrow. "I'm not just a boy toy, you know."

Addison pulled a bowl of fresh melon chunks out of the refrigerator. Nick finished the omelet with a quick flip of the wrist, split it, and slid half onto each plate. "Coffee?"

"Why, thank you. You are quite…domestic. Are you available nights?"

He kissed the top of her head. "Possibly. Is it salaried or do I have to depend on tips?"

"Don't worry: you'll do just fine."

He took a bite and gazed at her as he chewed. "Your turn."

"My turn?"

"Your story. Why are you here? What do you do?"

She debated whether to observe that he had so far avoided providing details of his own life but figured she'd wheedle them out of him at some juncture. Setting her mug down, she waved a hand at the walls covered in pictures of her family. There were daguerreotypes of great-great-uncles and -aunts, family reunion photographs, and, over the fireplace, an oil painting of an eighteenth-century ancestor, a rather pudgy man in a long, curled wig.

"As I told you, this house has been in my family for several generations. These are portraits of kin going back as far as our pre-American roots in England. We were one of the first to run cattle here, eventually settling on Assateague. We moved to Alder Island during the Civil War to get away from the gunrunners. Did you know Chincoteague was the only town in Virginia that remained in the Union? We were not welcome on the mainland."

"I did not know that. I trust no interfamily feuds were ignited by the conflict? Any Capulets and Montagues on the Eastern Shore?"

"Not that I'm aware of. Everyone pretty much got along, except for the Jennie Hill tragedy, but that was due to unrequited love."

"I did read about her. Very sad."

"It's interesting…" She hesitated, unsure whether to spring her hypothesis on him. *He'll think I'm just a silly romantic.* "I've always thought the truth may have been more complicated than what was handed down."

"Really?"

"Uh-huh." She took a carton of juice from the

refrigerator and poured two glasses. "The Hill house still stands at the end of Deep Hole Road. Next to it is the family cemetery. Jennie is buried there."

"What about her killer, Tom something?"

"Freeman. I believe he was laid to rest on the mainland next to his mother. Anyway, I was rambling among the gravestones one day and found Jennie's. It's white marble and has a dove carved at the top, with the name E. Virginia Hill." She gazed at Nick. "But on the back side, someone had scratched a heart and the words My Eternal Love. Under it were the initials J. B."

"J. B., huh? Not T. F. A love triangle perhaps?"

"Not exactly. Jennie had lots of admirers." Addison rose and pulled a battered notebook out of a drawer in the pantry. "This was my grandmother's. When we were kids, she used to tell us tales of Chincoteague. We finally persuaded her to write them down." She flipped through some pages. "Here we are. 'Around the time of the shooting, a man named Jonah Blake, a salesman from Salisbury, lived on the island. He was one of Jennie Hill's suitors, but her father was adamant that Jennie was too young for courting.' " She looked up. "J. B. could be him."

Nick raised his eyebrows but said nothing.

"See, as Nana told it, when Tom Freeman accosted Jennie and her mother, he waved his gun around and shot wildly into the air. She said it was amazing that he hit anything at all, much less the two women in front of him."

Nick said slowly, "You're postulating he didn't shoot them after all? That this Jonah Blake killed Jennie Hill?"

"My theory is, he saw her with Tom, misconstrued

the situation, and shot her in a jealous rage."

"Leaving Tom to take the heat?"

"Yes, but Tom must have believed he struck the women, since he killed himself on the spot." She ran through Nana's stories in her mind. "It would fit Jonah's character. He was known as a ladies' man. He chatted up several local women, including an ancestor of mine. The one he married he beat up, then stole all her money and skipped town."

"Heavens, not your ancestor?"

"No, thank God. Blake chose a woman named Little Dutch Smith over Elmira Hopkins. Elmira was later happily married to my great-great-grandfather Nicholas."

Nick gave a start. "Nicholas? Oh, so that's why…" He grinned. "Boy, Chincoteague isn't some sleepy little backwater, is it? You've all kinds of adventurers, secret brotherhoods, scoundrels…maybe pirates?" He raised his chin at the portrait. "Like the cavalier there. He looks like a real swashbuckler. Might he be the dread buccaneer Henry Morgan?"

"No, that's Sir Richard Steele, the eighteenth-century writer. I'm a direct descendent." She examined the picture critically. "He always appeared a bit foppish to me."

"So *that's* why your name seemed so familiar! I couldn't put my finger on it until now. Richard Steele. *The Spectator*. Only two years of circulation and yet one of the most influential tabloids in the annals of English literature."

"You know your history. I was named after his best friend and collaborator, Joseph Addison."

As Nick buttered a slice of toast, he muttered, "An

ancestor of mine, Richard Savage, knew them both."

"Really? Who was he?"

"A poet, immortalized by Samuel Johnson in his *Lives of the Poets*." He regarded the portrait. "Our family has a story too—one that does not present Steele in a very felicitous light. In fact, Richard Savage's heirs swore to exact revenge on the Steeles for his untimely demise."

Addison gulped. "Oh dear, are you planning to exact that revenge on me?"

Nick burst into laughter. "Heavens, no. It's water under the bridge—specifically, the Blackfriars bridge in London. The events occurred almost three hundred years ago, Addison."

"But…what happened? What is Sir Richard supposed to have done?"

He shook his head. "It's not important. The feud has vanished into the mists of memory." He kissed her hand. "If it will ease your mind, I shall call you Juliet and you may call me Romeo. Or, since we are here on Chincoteague, bastion of Union sympathies, I shall be Tom and thee Jennie."

"That didn't turn out well for either of them."

"We'll make this a comedy then. They always have happy endings." He went to the sink and started to scrub out the pan. "But enough about me. So…you don't live here year-round?"

What the hell? Why the reticence? Or did the subject bore him? Addison decided it wasn't worth pursuing. *For now.* "No. We close it up during the winter. My brother Bertie stays here with his wife and kids in the fall for the migrations. I get it in the spring for the nesting."

His brow wrinkled. "Are you nomads?"

"Huh? Why would you say that?"

" 'Nesting'? 'Migrations'?"

"Not humans. Birds." She handed him the juice glasses to wash. "I'm talking about birds. Chincoteague is a major rest stop on the Atlantic Flyway. In the fall, the refuge hosts thousands of snow geese, brants, and ducks on their way south. In the spring, they land here to rest and breed before heading north. During the months of March and April, more than three hundred species may pass through."

"Ah. And where does the winter find you?"

"I'm a librarian in Washington, DC."

He handed her a glass to dry. "So…are you on sabbatical?"

"No. I'm laid off while they renovate. I'll be here a month."

"That's good news." He blew her a kiss. "Any more coffee?"

"It's in the pot." When he returned to the table with his cup, Addison took one more stab at probing his mysterious behavior at the beach. "Er, so what did you do yesterday?"

"Other than the museum? And a very delightful soiree?"

"Yes."

"Lessee. I did some correspondence, checked with my broker and my publisher…"

"Publisher? You're an author?"

He blinked, then said quickly, "I thought you'd never ask!"

Addison wasn't about to tell him that last night she could have cared less what he did out of bed, and so far this morning he'd avoided divulging any personal information. "Well?"

"Yes, I'm a writer. I…uh…write travel books."

"Guidebooks?"

"Guidebooks? What do you take me for, a hack? No, I write stories about traveling. The last one regaled my fans with my adventures in the Peruvian rain forest."

"So, it's sort of like the difference between a food writer and a recipe writer?"

"Precisely. Have you read Bill Bryson? My books are in the same genre—amusing tales of travel adventures, not tiresome lists of cheap hotels and places where you can get American food. I'm down here doing research for a book on the Delmarva Peninsula."

"Oh, really? So where can I find—"

Nick rose abruptly. Setting his mug in the sink, he said lightly, "Will you look at the time? I didn't realize it was so late." He retrieved his raincoat from the hook. Shrugging it on, he kissed her. "Thank you for putting up with me. If you don't mind, I really have to get back to work—I have a deadline." He said it with a grin, but it was clearly a rebuff.

"Fine. I have things to do *too*, you know." She stomped up the stairs, went into the bathroom, and slammed the door.

She didn't hear him leave the house, but as she sat stewing on the edge of the tub, she heard gravel crunching outside, then a car horn toot. She ran to the bedroom window in time to see the Hummer backing out of the driveway. He raised an arm in salute when he saw her.

Addison turned away and dropped down on the

bed, deep in thought. *The night I met him, Nick said he was here looking for his brother. And now he claims to be doing research for a book. Did he lie then, or now? Could he be doing both? Why not say so?* That FBI agent said Nick's brother had stolen classified material, but he didn't actually say Nick was involved. Well, to be clear, he said Nick was lying, so at the very least Nick knew what his brother had done. *What did Peel ask me?* To let him know if she saw Nick again. Why? So he could arrest him? She blinked rapidly to clear her head. *I'm wading into deep waters here, and that's beyond foolish. I can't assume Peel is telling the whole truth either. The Feds never do. No, I have to wait before I make a judgment—see if Nick comes clean.* She wasn't sure which she hoped for more: to see Nick again…or not to.

She rose and looked again out the window toward the road. He had waved goodbye so guilelessly—it was difficult to believe he wasn't the genuine article. *Wait a minute.* He waved. What was it about that arm? She thought back to the walk on the beach and the man in the snow. She squeezed her eyes tight, trying to latch onto it. Something was different…but what?

Chapter Six

Our real blessings often appear to us in the shape of pains, losses and disappointments; but let us have patience and we soon shall see them in their proper figures.

~Joseph Addison

Chincoteague Elementary School, Tuesday, March 18

"Come on, Addy. You *promised* to help me chaperone. You'll see. It'll be fun!"

Addison sized up the clot of five-year-olds and sighed. "All right, Phoebe. Can I drive separately or do I have to take the school bus with you?"

Phoebe tossed her a look that did not augur well for the birthday present Addison had asked for. "Fine. Take your car. But don't be late."

Fifteen minutes later, Addison found her cousin arguing with the security guard at the entrance gate to the main base of the Wallops Island Flight Facility.

"Why do we need to do anything else? As I've told you now *twice*, this is a special tour arranged by my former boss—perhaps you've heard of Horace Greeley? He happens to be the chairman of the Virginia Senate's Committee on Local Government. That means he oversees relations between the Accomack County government and"—she pointed an exasperated hand at the gate—"*you*." She fixed the man with a steely-eyed glare. "Would you like me to give him a call *now*?"

"I understand, miss. You've made quite clear your special relationship with the senator. Twice. But as I explained to *you*, miss, you still have to have a pass. You were supposed to pick it up, as well as a tour guide, at the Visitors Center. I cannot permit"—he contemplated the mob of tiny potential terrorists hanging onto Phoebe's skirt—"minors to rove around freely in our facility without an official escort."

The standoff continued as the racket issuing from childish throats grew exponentially. Finally, Phoebe sniffed. "Well, nobody *told me* we'd have to stop back there." She checked her watch. "It'll take *at least* twenty minutes to drive the bus back to the center, pick up a guide, go through reams of red tape, and come back here. The kids have to return to school by noon. Can't you make an exception?"

As the guard began to shake his head, she gave him a dazzling smile and ostentatiously checked his name tag. "Walter Pope? I'm sure you know all about this facility and those big white balloon thingies. Who needs some dumb old guide from the Visitor's Center? Why, I bet you'd be *marvelous*. Could you maybe, possibly, escort us?" She bent to wipe a little boy's nose with a dirty tissue and stuffed it back in her pocket. When Walter cringed, she remarked gaily, "I can see you're great with children."

Addison approached them. "Phoebe, why don't I run back to the visitor center and collect the guide and pass? It won't take but a few minutes. I'm sure this nice man can find something for the kids to do to pass the time."

Walter allowed a smidgen of relief to cross his features. "All right, but you'll have to move the bus away from the gate. You can park it back there on the shoulder."

Phoebe gave one last imploring look at Walter's impassive face. "Quick like a bunny then, Addy! Oh, and tell the driver where to go. Come on, children. I see a path over there to the woods. We *are* allowed to walk on the *public* sidewalk, aren't we, Officer?" This had no effect on Walter.

Addison secured the pass and the guide in record time. The children were already boarding the bus, so she parked her car behind it and got on with them. As they neared the main gate, they were dismayed to see that a long line of cars had built up in front of them. Several people were shouting and gesticulating at Walter, whose inscrutable expression would have made him an ideal candidate for royal guardsman at Buckingham Palace.

"Let me go find out what's going on." Addison passed an open convertible with several gentlemen shaking their fists and jabbering in French and a minibus filled with swarthy Arabs in pristine white thobes. As she approached the gate, she realized Walter's blank face was due to more than just soldierly reserve. The crowd around him were bellowing in yet another foreign language—this one full of unfamiliar syllables and diphthongs. She marched past them and stuck her pass under Walter's nose. "Walter? Can you let us through now?"

He cast her an agonized look. "I can't deal with you right now, miss. These fellows claim to be visiting scientists, but they're not on the roster. I'm waiting for the director to come down and verify their identities. You'll have to wait a little longer."

Phoebe came up behind her. "Walter! You *promised*."

The poor man threw his hands up. "I wish I could help. I really do." As he gazed at Phoebe, his face softened and began to glow. Phoebe opened her mouth to retort but subsided suddenly. Addison turned to find her cousin equally soft and pink.

Do I sense a warming trend? She opted for a conciliatory tone. "Look, Phoebe, why don't we give it up for today? It's almost time to take the kids back for their snack and nap anyway, isn't it? I'll drive the guide back to the visitor center. You can set up a new appointment later."

Phoebe reluctantly unpinned her eyes from Walter. "Yeah, I guess so. What days are you on duty, Walter? I mean"—she blushed—"to ensure the next visit goes off without a hitch."

His face lit up, and Addison was surprised at how good-looking he was when he smiled. To be sure, he was quite a bit older than the twenty-four-year-old Phoebe, but his brown hair flecked with silver shone in the morning light and his taupe-colored eyes sparkled with humor. She gauged his height at about six two. *It's nice for once that Phoebe isn't towering over a guy.* The uniform definitely helped. "I'm here Monday through Friday, miss."

"Please, call me Phoebe." Addison's cousin dimpled.

At that moment, a short fellow, tie askew, khakis bulging with belly, lumbered toward the unruly throng. A paper fluttered in his hand. Walter sighed in relief.

"Here comes Director Klopman."

As the facility administrator approached, one of the newcomers extricated himself from the group and headed toward him. Pale-faced, with just a sprinkle of artificially blackened hair, he spoke in heavily accented English. "Finally, you haff come, Mister Klopman. This…this apparatchik"—he wrinkled his nose at Walter—"would not let us through until you arrived. Please inform him who we are."

Klopman wiped his brow, pushing back the one remaining strand of yellowish hair. "You must be Grigory Andreyevich Vasilinak. Yes, I'm *Director* Friedrich Klopman. I apologize for keeping you waiting. I was held up by…er…discord between our resident Turkish virologist, Dr. Arslan, and his colleague from Armenia, Dr. Hanessian. It took a tricky bit of diplomatic maneuvering to settle them down." He wiped his brow again. "This facility is dedicated to pure science. Why must these people bring their politics with them? So unnecessary." For a moment he seemed to have lost his thread. "Um…er…oh, yes. Welcome to the Wallops Island Flight Facility."

"Sank you." Vasilinak introduced him to the others. The ten men could have been brothers—each had a similar stocky build, heavy black mustache, and wore a slightly shaggy brown suit. When the last man had ardently pumped his hand, Klopman turned to Walter. "This is the delegation from the International University in Minsk, Pope. They are Belarusian microbiologists, here to develop an experiment to go as payload on our Small Launch Vehicle Research project. You should have been expecting them. Didn't you get the memo?"

Walter glared at him. "No, I didn't get the memo. Did you ask your assistant *Eric* if he sent it out?"

"I'm sure he did, Walter. Eric has proven to be much more efficient than my last assistant."

Walter sneered. "Not in this case, he hasn't." He held up his clipboard. "Do you see a memo about these guys? *Do you?*"

Addison and Phoebe exchanged looks. *Woo-hoo, do we have a new subplot in the Wallops Island soap opera?* For locals, the closed facility—with its constant stream of foreigners and practitioners of obscure, esoteric disciplines—was a rich source of conspiracy theories and gossip.

Phoebe whispered, "I have to go back to the children. Keep your ears open!" She winked.

Addison studied the security guard, whose face was still contorted with resentment. *This Eric must be horning in on established territory. I sense a disruption in the pecking order.*

Klopman pushed the clipboard away from his face. "Give it a rest, Pope. I'll take these men off your hands and get them set up with their paperwork and assignments. They'll be here for six months, so you'd better get used to them."

"Where are they staying?"

The director grimaced. "I tried to get rooms at the Chincoteague Bay Field Station, but they were booked, so they're bunking in the Exchange and Morale Association housing here on the main base." He shook his head. "They're not usually allowed to lodge there, since they're supposed to be escorted while on base, but I managed to sweet-talk the manager into taking most of them. I owe him a case of his favorite Pinot Noir."

"Most? They're not all staying there?"

"No. Vasilinak—he's the leader—has a room at the Assateague Inn."

Walter raised an eyebrow. "How did he swing that?"

"You'll have to ask Vasilinak. He specifically requested the inn. I believe he reserved two rooms." He leered, a disconcerting sight in the rather frowsy face. "I understand a lady friend will be joining him."

"Does that mean the others won't leave the main base?"

"No, no. At certain phases of the project, they'll be utilizing the assembly building at the launch facility."

"So they'll be coming and going every day." Walter ground his teeth.

"Don't worry. You won't have to check them in separately. Those housed on the base will be traveling in a group—we've procured a school bus for them."

"A school bus! Isn't that a bit unprofessional?"

Klopman shrugged. "Evidently their government didn't trust us to use military transport. The school bus is cheaper anyway." He pulled out a note pad. "Let's see: is there anything else you need to know?" He flipped a page. "Oh yes. The university informed me they will be accompanied by a...chaperone. She arrives today." He blinked. "I didn't put two and two together until now. She must be the lady friend. *Hmm*." The thought seemed to disturb him.

Walter said sharply, "Chaperone? You mean, a handler? As in KGB?"

Klopman fiddled with his watch. "I don't know about KGB—isn't that Russian intelligence? She's...uh...listed as university staff—I assume she's simply an escort to facilitate communications while they're in the United States." He gestured at the Belarusians, now bunched in a tight, apprehensive pack. "I don't think their English is very good."

"What's her name?"

"Something unpronounceable. Begins with a *Z*. Why?"

Walter clicked his pen on. "Just doing my job. Have to get their names. Since I didn't get the *memo*."

Klopman ignored the jab. "Eric has the complete list. Get a copy from him." He grasped Vasilinak's elbow.

As they passed Addison, the scientist stopped and peered at her. She fidgeted under his serious stare and finally asked, "Do I know you?"

He shook himself. "Perhaps. You are Ms. Steele?"

"Y…yes." *How on earth does a foreign microbiologist know who I am?*

"Ah." He turned without another word and followed Klopman. The rest trailed after them. Two of the men were whispering. The sounds were susurrant and guttural—incoherent babble—but as she turned away, she caught one word: "Savage."

Savage? Could they be talking about Nick? Or were they denigrating those barbaric Americans? No—they weren't speaking English. *They have to be referring to a person*. On a whim, Addison caught up with Walter, who was heading with some deliberation in the direction of Phoebe, currently herding her toddlers back onto the bus. "Walter?"

He slowed only slightly. "Yes?"

"You're required to recognize everyone, right? Both visitors and staff?"

"Uh-huh. I'm supposed to memorize all the photos. Don't want any unauthorized persons trespassing on the base."

"Good. Does someone named Savage work here?"

Walter halted. "Savage? Why do you ask?"

What do I say? "I…uh…overheard those foreigners talking about a person called Savage."

The guard squinted at the departing group of men. "Huh. That's odd."

"Why?"

"A Daniel Savage *was* assigned here. He came from the University of Chicago."

"Daniel? Daniel Savage? He worked *here*?" *Nick implied his brother was on vacation. He said nothing about him living in the area. Could this be a different Daniel Savage?*

"Yeah. Had a grant from NASA. He was some kind of biologist, but he's been gone for weeks. The Belarusians couldn't possibly be acquainted with him."

"What about you?"

"I was hired after Savage left. Never met him."

Addison grasped the last straw. "Well, the scientific world is pretty small. They might know him by reputation."

He shook his head. "I think he worked in management—not in the labs. Unless…" He cocked his head. "They might have heard the rumors."

"What rumors?"

"That he stole classified material and sold it to a foreign entity. He went off the grid in February. No one's seen him since."

Chapter Seven

Whether a pretty woman grants or withholds her favors, she always likes to be asked for them.

~*Richard Steele*

Addison's house, Wednesday, March 19

Addison put the telephone down for the fifth time. The first two calls had been dead ends. Since she'd neglected to ask Nick where he was staying, she had first tried Cora Anne at the Assateague Inn and then Heidi at the Refuge. When those didn't pan out, she contacted the newer hotels up Main Street. No Nick Savage. Could he be renting a house? Staying on the mainland? She slammed a palm on the table. *Why didn't I ask for his phone number?* She snorted. *Why? Because I had no idea that, one, I'd want to call him, and two, I'd have to call him.*

First of all, she needed to hear his response to Peel's accusations. Were Daniel Savage the brother and Daniel Savage the scientist one and the same? If so, was Nick aware that Daniel had stolen documents? Peel said he was, but Nick hadn't mentioned it. Could the FBI be way out in left field? *It's possible that Nick knows nothing of Daniel's history with the Wallops facility—only that he drowned while fishing. After all, he said he hadn't seen him in a long time.*

According to Walter, Daniel Savage was a biologist. Nick hadn't specified what his brother did for a living. *What* did *he tell me?* They were from Rhode Island. Daniel raced sailboats. He'd gone to Europe. They'd had some sort of falling-out that he didn't want to talk about. Begging the question: then why did he come looking for Daniel? She picked up the phone again, then put it back down. *On the other hand, do I really want to get mixed up in this?*

Instead of giving up, she flipped the pages of the phone book. Maybe Island Vacations had a listing. She had begun to dial when the phone rang.

"Addy? I'm on a break, and I only have a minute. Can you talk?"

Damn. "Sure, Phoebe." *I bet it's about Walter.*

"It's about Walter. Walter Pope? The security guard at Wallops Island?"

"Yes, I remember him." *Only too well.*

"He…uh…called to apologize about yesterday. He wants to make it up to me. He…Addy, he asked me out. What do you think?"

Addison recalled the tender looks that had passed between the two. "I think you should take him up on it. He does owe you—and the children." *The children…* "On second thought, ask him to arrange a special tour for them instead."

"But what about the date?" Phoebe's wail petered out quickly, but her point was made.

"Okay, okay. Just insist he does it before you go out with him." She smirked into the receiver.

"I can hear your lips smacking, Addy. Are you smirking? It's not polite. Walter is…well, he seems rather nice. For a security guard. Don't you think?"

"I'm sure he could bear a little more scrutiny." *Wait a minute.* "You could ask him about Daniel Savage."

"Who?"

"Daniel—look, can you come over for coffee after school? I want to bounce something off you."

"I'll be off at noon—it's early release day. Let's get some lunch instead, and you can give me advice."

"Okay, but I want to go to the Rusty Scupper." Addison didn't fancy having inquisitive locals listening in on them.

"All the way out to Lankford Highway? Why so far?"

She didn't have to tell Phoebe that talking about espionage or the goings-on at the secretive NASA facility was perfectly acceptable. Discuss a budding romance in public, and you'll find yourself outed by the town crier, an office currently held by the proprietor of the Assateague Inn. "In a word: Cora Anne Jester."

"Ah. Okay."

"I'll swing by at twelve and pick you up."

They chose a corner booth in the empty restaurant. The waitress came over. "Anything to start, ladies?"

"Yeah." Phoebe stuck a finger on the menu. "I'll have the loaded fries and a Bud Light. You got any burgers?"

"How about the Super Deck Burger? Two kinds of cheese, pickled jalapenos, bacon, and our *secret* sauce." She pretended to look furtively around.

"What's it come with?"

"Fries."

"I'll have that, but hold the fries. Lemme get…coleslaw?…No, applesauce. Addy?"

"Phoebe, I've been looking around this place and you know what I noticed? It's a *seafood* restaurant. Fancy that."

"Seafood?" Addison's cousin gave a little shiver. "Never touch the stuff."

"What? You don't like blue crabs? Fish? Not even salt oysters?"

Phoebe recoiled in horror. "Ew. Islanders don't eat squiggly, slippery things that live in the water. No, sir. We like food that doesn't look up at you from the plate. Preferably brown."

"You've been living here too long, cuz." Addison tapped the menu. "I'll have the crab cakes and a Caesar salad. And iced tea. Thanks."

When the waitress had dropped off their orders, Phoebe leaned forward. "So, what did you want to talk about?"

"It's about Nick."

Phoebe scrutinized her, one eye closed. "You slept with him, didn't you?"

The blush started around her toes and worked its way up. "That's neither here nor there."

"It's about time, that's what I say. You've been mooning over Seth way too long. It's been—what—a year?" She sprinkled hot sauce over her fries. "When do I meet him?"

"Nick? I don't know." Addison tried to keep the agitation out of her voice. "I have no way to reach him, and I haven't heard from him in two days."

"You think he's the kind to love you and leave you?"

Addison paused. A rugged face suffused with desire rose before her. As she watched, his expression morphed to laughter, his sapphirine eyes twinkling from some private joke. "I...I don't know. But"—she rallied—"this isn't about him. It's really about his brother. If he *has* a brother."

"What are you talking about? Didn't Nick tell you his brother went overboard and that he had come to town for answers?" Phoebe took a bite from her hamburger. The cheese oozed out onto the plate, carrying with it a pile of sliced jalapenos. She scooped them up and chucked them in her mouth.

"Yes. But then, after we...after that...well, he told me a different story. He says he's writing a travel book on the Eastern Shore."

"Huh. So his credibility is in question. You're thinking the brother is a figment of his imagination?"

"Well...not exactly. It's kind of complicated." Addison didn't think now was the right time to tell her cousin of her rather fanciful theory. "See, when the FBI agent—Robert Peel—came to the house the evening I met Nick, he told me Daniel Savage is wanted for selling classified information."

"Wait." Phoebe ticked her fingers off. "Nick's brother—the brother lost at sea—is Daniel Savage, the spy on the run?"

"Yes. At least I think so."

Phoebe dropped her spoon. "You're kidding! And Mr. FBI says Nick is in cahoots with him."

Addison considered. "He didn't actually state that. He only claimed that Nick knows about the crime."

"*Hmm.*"

"That's not all. I've just found out that he actually worked at Wallops."

"Who, Nick?"

"No. Daniel Savage. He's a biologist. A grantee from the University of Chicago."

"How did you find that out?"

"Walter."

"My Walter?"

"Yes." Addison told her cousin about the Belarusian scientists' name-dropping and what Walter said about Daniel. "That FBI agent is snooping around. Before he arrests Nick or does something stupid, I need you to find out what else Walter knows about Daniel Savage."

Phoebe drew back. "This will be our first date. I don't necessarily want it to be our last."

"You can just say you'd heard some buzz about trouble at the facility or something. Get him talking. Don't say anything about the FBI."

"What will you be doing?"

Addison set her salad aside. "Trying to find Nick."

Phoebe called for the check. "What happens if he doesn't want to be found?"

****

Addison's deck, Thursday, late afternoon

"Looks like you've got a nibble."

Phoebe pulled her fishing rod out and checked the empty hook. "It's gone! Damned crabs—they snatch my bait every time."

"You shouldn't use chicken wings then. They love them."

"Really? I didn't know that. I'm sure as hell not torturing a cute little earthworm instead."

"Suit yourself." Addison pulled up her line, neatly unhooked the thrashing rockfish and dropped it into her bucket. "That's enough for an early supper. Why don't you stay? You haven't told me about your date with Walter yet."

Phoebe checked her watch. "Sure, why not?" She reeled in her line and laid the pole on the deck.

Addison picked it up and stashed the creel and rods under her porch. Lugging the bucket over to the cleaning table, she began scaling and gutting the fish.

Phoebe watched, her nose wrinkled in distaste. "I don't know how you can do that without gagging. Ugh."

"You have to be willing to do the yucky jobs if you want to eat."

"You know I can't stomach fish, even if someone else takes care of the yucky jobs." She followed Addison to the kitchen. "You got any of that fried chicken left? I'll have that."

Phoebe made a salad of baby lettuce and early radishes while Addison set a big skillet over the flame and melted a large lump of butter. When the fish started to sizzle, she went to the refrigerator. "Wine?"

"You got any diet cola?"

"Phoebe!"

"Okay, okay—how about a Bud?" She held up a pinkie. "It will pair nicely with chicken *à la Colonel*."

Addison gave it to her and poured a glass of Chablis for herself. She handed Phoebe the box of chicken pieces, slipped the crispy browned fish on her plate, and sat down. "So?"

Phoebe tonged salad from the bowl, then carefully chose a leg from the box. "First things first. Have you located Lover Boy?"

Addison's mood dipped. "No. I thought I glimpsed him down on Main by the Roxie, but I couldn't catch up with him." *How can such a big man be so hard to find on an island that's only nine square miles?* "We were talking about your date."

Phoebe took a long gulp from the can. "It was okay."

"Just okay."

"Well, a little better than okay. See, I didn't expect much. I mean, Walter's a security guard for Chrissakes. I figured he'd be all macho and martinet. You know—all hat, no cattle. And no sense of humor." Phoebe sipped her beer, avoiding Addison's eyes. She whispered, "I was kinda, sorta wrong."

Addison waited.

"First off, he brought me flowers. And not just any flowers—my favorites: tulips. He claimed it was just serendipity, that they were the perkiest blooms in the store. Ha. Then"—she put the beer down—"get this! He opened the car door for me—like any of the Tickell boys would ever think of that. And you know what he drives? A Morgan. It's this little English sports car with a leather belt across the hood and wire wheels. *Super* cool."

"A Morgan? Those aren't just super cool; they're super expensive."

"Yeah, I was wondering about that, but he said he'd inherited this one from his dad. It's an antique." Her cheeks rosy, she said, "He only uses it for special occasions. He drives a clunker to work."

"Okay, so he gave you flowers and drives a neat sports car. What about the actual date?" *I'll bring up Daniel later, once she's wound down.*

"I'm getting there." Phoebe ripped the skin off the chicken leg, ate that, then began to tear the meat off in strips. "I figured he'd drive too fast and try to show off, but he didn't. We went to Ruby's. He'd reserved the best table—the one in the corner on the deck. We were the only ones out there, but it wasn't all that cold. I wore that Irish fisherman's sweater you gave me last Christmas. He said the color matched my eyes, which was pretty funny since it's gray. I mean, it's not like it's hard to match gray with gray—as opposed to say, blues, or greens. You know?"

Addison took a bite of fish. Wrangling over the color palette would only slow up the process. She knew her cousin would eventually get there; she just had to be patient. *Besides, I can always distract her with a question about the menu.* "What did you have?"

"Ooh, you won't believe this, Addy. He let me order a *sirloin*—and with none of the judgy crap I get from *some* people—plus a really nice Chianti. That's that Italian wine that comes inside a basket. Ruby let me take the bottle home. I'm going to make one of those drippy candle things." She raised her eyes to the ceiling. "For those romantic dinners we'll have outside under the stars."

"Be sure to wear your parka and ski mask. Anything else?" Addison loved the way Phoebe—at six feet tall, all of a hundred and thirty pounds—talked about food.

"And death-by-chocolate cake. Ruby's is the absolute yummiest." She lapsed into happy memories.

Addison ate the last bite of fish. *I can see I'm going to have to drag it out of her.* "Did you get a chance to ask about Daniel?"

"What? Oh, yeah, I did. As you instructed, I didn't disclose names. I just casually dropped a remark about an incident at the facility. He said—in this really official tone—that he could confirm the reports."

"Really? He told you about the missing material?"

"Huh? No." Phoebe leaned forward. "Get this: there's been a rash of ethnic clashes lately. Klopman mistakenly put this Turkish guy in the same office with an Armenian, and they've been at each other's throats. Then these two Asian guys got into it. One's a communist from China, and the other's from Taiwan. The Chinese man is insisting the Taiwanese is spying on his research. Threw him out of the lab. Bodily."

"Wow. Sounds awfully physical for a nerdy scientist."

"Yup. Evidently there's a bunch of communist Chinese there and only the one guy from Taiwan. Klopman recognized the potential for controversy and found space in another building for the poor sap." Phoebe chugged her beer. "So much for the land of liberty."

"They're sure the Chinese guy didn't just want to have his lab to himself?"

"Who knows? China keeps threatening to take over Taiwan, doesn't it? You'd think he'd want to keep an eye on his enemy. You know—keep your friends close and your enemies closer."

"Huh. So Walter didn't have anything to say about Daniel Savage?"

"Oh, I almost forgot. Yes, he did. I wrote it down. Hang on." She pulled a small notebook out of her purse. Licking the grease off her finger, she turned some pages. "Here it is. Walter said a Daniel Savage had been working on the management team for the Small Launch project." She looked up. "Not sure what a small launch is—a tiny rocket? Anyway, he vanished a month ago, and right after that the FBI showed up. They were investigating the theft of documents."

"What sort of documents?"

"Walter had no idea—but they were classified."

Addison chuckled. "You don't suppose Daniel's disappearance and the FBI arrival could have been coincidental?"

Phoebe didn't take the bait. "The chatter was that he'd sold secrets to an Eastern European state, but the director claimed that was hearsay. Walter thinks he's covering it up to protect his behind. Anyway, there haven't been any new developments in weeks. That's about it."

"Those foreign scientists who were at the gate last Friday were East Europeans. Could they be involved?"

"Dunno, but they'd just arrived, hadn't they? They would have missed Savage by a fortnight."

"That doesn't mean anything. They could have received the documents, passed them on, then reappeared as innocent scientists to continue the espionage."

"Too dangerous. Anyway, our government keeps close tabs on foreign visitors to our secure facilities. At least that's what Walter says."

Addison thought of the leader. "One of them knew my name, Phoebe."

Chapter Eight

Many take pleasure in spreading abroad the weakness of an exalted character.

~Richard Steele

Addison's House, Thursday, March 20

Her cousin put down her beer. "One of the foreigners knew your name? How?"

"That's another thing I'd like to find out."

Phoebe finished a second chicken leg. "So, did I do good?"

"Not bad. Thanks." *Now, if I could only find Nick.*

"That wasn't the end of our date, though." She giggled, looking more like a pixie than ever.

"Oh?"

Phoebe rose and slid her dish into the dishwasher and tossed the can in the recycle bin. Over her shoulder she lilted, "Let's just say, he's macho when he's supposed to be." Before Addison could ask for the succulent details, her cousin picked up her purse and sailed out the door. At her car, she stopped and yelled, "I'm meeting him at Dobie's when he gets off work. Thanks for the grub!"

Addison stared after the retreating car. A sunbeam hit the rear window and bounced back in her eyes. She checked her watch. Only five thirty. It wouldn't get dark for another hour. *Might as well take a walk.*

But where? It would take too long to get to the refuge, and East Side Road didn't have any sidewalks. Memorial Park? Too muddy. *I know—I'll try that new nature walk over by the high school.* From Church Street, she took Chicken City Road to Deep Hole. She hung a left on Hallie Whealton Smith Drive and parked at the head of the Island Nature Trail.

Addison struck out on a marshy path past small vernal ponds already stocked with mallards. The snow had melted, leaving the ground soggy. Uprooted trees had fallen willy-nilly, dragging the vines festooning them across the path. The pungent smell of peaty earth and rotting vegetation made her nose itch. A crash to her right signaled a whitetail deer spooked by her presence. Over her head, a Delmarva squirrel chattered at her, his long fluffy tail jerking back and forth. Sunlight filtered through the loblolly pines, picking out the delicate spring hepaticas and bloodroot poking through the winter leaves.

Addison sighed. Even more than the beach, walking the woods of Chincoteague never failed to calm her. So much life snuggled here! Little things— frogs, snakes, voles. Big things—hawks and owls— hunting the little things. Death and life continued with or without her consent. A blue jay squawked in the black tupelo over her head. She looked up, trying to spot him among the crinkly brown foliage, and stepped into a puddle. "Shit!" She shook off the water, but black muck clung to her new hiking boots. Picking up a stick, she sat down on a dead log and began to scrape it off.

"Here I leave you alone for a mere couple of days, and you take up mud wrestling."

Addison jumped. Her feet slid out from under her, and she landed heavily in the puddle. "Nick! What the hell are you doing here?"

"Staying dry. Which is more than I can say about you." He helped her up.

"Where have you been?" The words were out of her mouth before she could stop them.

"Me? Doing research for the book. I took a tour of Delmarva—quite a lot of quaint little towns once you get off Route 13. Have you ever been to Eyre Hall?"

"Is that near Eastville?"

"Closer to Cheriton. A beautiful historic plantation. The Hall was built in 1760 by Littleton Eyre, and Eyres have owned it ever since, going on now twelve generations. Even this early in the spring, the formal gardens are spectacular. I was lucky—the caretaker was there, and he took me on a grand tour." He pulled out a small notebook and jotted something down. "I believe I'll devote a whole section of the book to it."

"I see. What about your brother?"

"Daniel? What about him?"

"I thought you were in Chincoteague to find out more about his accident?"

Nick peered up at the sky. "It's going to get dark soon. Let's go, shall we?" He took her hand, and they walked down the path.

By the time they reached the parking lot, twilight had descended. Nick clicked his keys. The Hummer's engine roared, and the headlights came on. "Pretty nifty, huh? I can do this from thirty thousand feet up."

"Great, so the car thief can steal it before you've even retrieved your luggage."

"What? Oh. *Hmm*. I hadn't thought of that."

"Yes, well." Addison unlocked her door the old-fashioned way and settled on the nubby leather-like seats of her Subaru. "I hope you had a productive week." As she began to back out, a hulking figure blocked the way. She braked.

Nick called from behind her. "Addison, are you by any chance pissed at me?"

No way she'd show him anything but indifference. "Why should I be? I barely know you."

He took a step back at that. "I think you know me better than most. Or have you forgotten last Sunday night?"

The jab stung like an angry red ant. "I…I…"

Nick came up to her window and leaned in. "Look, I told you I'm here doing research on the peninsula. I arranged this trip a month ago." When she didn't answer, he reached in and touched her hand. "I gather you didn't get my message. I left a text on your cell. An interview I'd been requesting came through unexpectedly, and I had to get down to Cape Charles on the double. After that, I arranged for a guide to take me around all the hamlets." He gazed at her anxiously. "I'm really sorry."

The defrosting process had gotten as far as her left aorta when Addison caught herself. "It's not that. In fact"—*gulp*—"I didn't even notice you were gone. It's this habit of not telling the truth I have a problem with. First you claim you're searching for your brother, then that you're writing a book. And all the while you had the FBI on your tail. You need to get your stories straight, Mr. Savage. Get back to me when you've settled on a line." She flicked his fingers off the sill, rolled up the window, put the car in gear, and drove away, leaving Nick open-mouthed.

She pulled into her driveway behind a white sedan. The ever-lovable Agent Peel emerged from it. "Do you have a minute, Ms. Steele?"

This is turning into a stellar day. "Sure." Hoping Nick hadn't come after her—*or do I?*—she led the way up the steps. Peel followed her into the living room. She sat on the sofa and, ignoring the massage chair, indicated the wooden desk chair. He remained standing.

She sighed. "What can I do for you?"

"We understand you visited the Wallops facility and tried to force your way in."

"What! I did nothing of the sort. What a ridiculous thing to say."

Peel stared down at her, his eyes expressionless. "I have fairly decent sources."

"Well, they're wrong," Addison said crossly. "If they'd bothered to check with Walter Pope, the security guard on duty"—*ha! It pays to be on a first-name basis with the staff*—"they'd know that I was there with my cousin's kindergarten class for a special tour. We were stopped because we'd forgotten to bring our guide. It was all perfectly innocent."

"I heard there was a fracas. How do you account for that?"

A fracas? This G-man has an unusual grasp of vocabulary. "No." *Wait a minute.* "Your source may have been confused. A group of foreign scientists had a bit of a dustup at the same time that we were trying to enter through the gate. I'm not sure what the problem was, but the director had to come out and take them in personally."

"Foreign? Were they by any chance from

Belarus?"

Addison's retort died on her lips. "I don't know, but I heard them say something about Daniel Savage."

Peel jerked, his eyes alert. "They did? What did they say?"

"I only heard the name. They were speaking some Slavic tongue. Very harsh."

The agent rose. "That is very helpful, Ms. Steele. The FBI appreciates your continued vigilance."

So now I'm a snitch? Addison rose too. "His brother says Daniel fell off a boat, Agent Peel. Do you think he's still alive?"

Peel's eyes closed to slits. "We don't know, Ms. Steele, but if he is, he'd better not be looking forward to a long and happy life."

She accompanied him to the door. "You mentioned stolen documents. Is he a foreign spy?"

He didn't look at her. "That information is not yet verified."

Typical closed-mouth public servant. "This is a small town, Mr. Peel. Very little goes unnoticed, and us locals are quite good at ferreting out news of what goes on in the facility. If Savage wasn't under suspicion, you wouldn't be after him, would you?" She put a hand on his arm. "But what do you want with his brother? Even if Nick Savage knew about Daniel's activities, that doesn't make him complicit."

"On the contrary. We have reason to believe he was instrumental in Daniel's escape." And with that the agent loped down the stairs to his car and drove off.

****

Addison's house, Friday

Addison stewed over Nick for the rest of the

evening and over Peel for most of the next day. Too many unanswered questions. *They're all hiding stuff, and it's really annoying.* She tried to work on her assignment, but suddenly a list of sources on an obscure pre-revolutionary war seemed awfully tame compared to the espionage going on under her nose.

Phoebe was busy—"We have to finish the banner before school lets out for Easter vacation"—and the fish weren't biting. She sat at her laptop idly googling, watching the clock till it was cocktail time. An article discussing Samuel Johnson and his pronouncements (negative) on the upstart American revolutionaries led her to his social set, of which Joseph Addison and Richard Steele were prominent members. "Johnson must have known my namesakes well." She read on. A footnote referred to reports of a dalliance between the married Steele and a woman named Eliza Haywood. *Was my ancestor a lecher?* Her grandmother had always spoken of Richard Steele in such respectful terms. Was this Haywood person one of those women who try to smear a man's reputation after she's rebuffed? Or was Richard in fact a cad, a stain on his family's reputation? Addison typed "Eliza Haywood" into the search box.

Several links appeared. She clicked on a biography. Eliza Haywood, along with two other women who formed the "naughty triumvirate," was a writer of what the author called "amatory fiction." Not as benign as it sounded, the snippets were quite ribald, even pornographic. As for Haywood's personal life, she was apparently as promiscuous as her heroines. Addison was reminded of the old adage: Write what you know. The tale about an affair with her ancestor was unsubstantiated—*that's a relief!*—but instead was thought to be a creation of a notorious grifter and womanizer named…She looked closer at the small print. "Richard Savage."

She sat back. Savage?

****

Addison's house, Saturday morning

"I won't be more than three, four days, Phoebe. You won't forget to feed Mopsy?"

"Only if I'm allowed to call him Pussy."

"Suit yourself. He won't come unless you call him Mopsy though." Addison put her overnight bag in the back of the car and hugged her cousin.

"I think you're making a mistake, m'dear. You've been mooning over that Nick fellow for days. You should at least find him so you can ask him about his brother."

"You forget—I have no address and no phone number for him. Not even an email. He'd have to find me, and he hasn't made any attempt to."

"What do you mean? You saw him last Wednesday at the park."

"We happened to cross paths there. He gave me some lame excuse about touring the countryside." She fought back the tear. "It was really pathetic, Phoebe."

"He did apologize."

"Sort of. But he clammed up when I told him the FBI was watching him. I think he realized I'd cottoned to his web of lies and has crept off to some gopher's burrow."

"Clammed up? Did you even give him a chance to answer?"

"I'm not going to dignify that with a reply." *How*

did she guess?

Phoebe put a hand on the car window. "All right, take care. Are you going to stop by the Dirksen building?"

"I'll check in for any messages, yes, but my plan is to do some research at the Library of Congress."

"Oh? They let peons in? Cool."

"I have a referral from the Senate librarian. Like I told you, I've been working on the bibliography of the French and Indian War. But Phoebe?" She looked up at her cousin. "I was messing around on the internet and came across a very provocative clique of women writers from the mid-seventeen-hundreds. They were contemporaries of my Steele ancestors." She hesitated. "There were rumors...Anyway, I want to see what the Library has on them, maybe do a separate monograph on my own."

"Provocative?"

"Women who were writing X-rated romance novels before novels were even recognized as a literary form."

"Even before—who was that guy—Tom Jones? I thought that was supposed to be the first real novel."

Addison shook her head. "Twenty years before Henry Fielding wrote *Tom Jones*, a woman named Eliza Haywood published a novel called *Love in Excess*. Over the next thirty-odd years, she churned out seventy more. The early ones were super racy, filled with pirates and kidnappings and wild sex."

"Wow! Who knew? I say dump the bibliography. Stick with the sex goddess. At least it'll keep you busy and off the streets." Phoebe winked. "If I see your Nick, I'll blow him a kiss." She waved the car off.

Addison checked her rearview mirror and, when Phoebe was far enough behind, muttered, "He's not my Nick."

****

Alexandria, Virginia, Saturday noon

Three hours later, Addison pulled up in front of her townhouse in Alexandria. She loved Old Town, with its cobblestone streets and miniature houses squeezed into each block like so many crayons in a box. Her house on Lee Street overlooked a park. Beyond it lay the Potomac River, wide and busy. Watercraft plied the water—taxis ferrying patrons to the National Harbor complex on the Maryland side, sightseeing tour boats zipping up to the Kennedy Center and down to Mount Vernon, the sternwheeler *Cherry Belle* hosting a wedding party out on the water, giving the passengers a welcome sense of freedom from the discipline of dry land.

The house smelled of the roses and carnations she'd bought herself for Valentine's Day, albeit a little musty. She found the withered stems in a vase and threw them out. As she bustled about the kitchen, she became gradually aware that her fingers were icy cold. *What the heck?* She checked the thermostat. Sixty degrees! *Damn, the heat's out.* Shivering, she dragged her winter coat from the back of the closet and put it on. Flipping through her address book, she found AAAA Heating and Air and dialed the number.

"I'm sorry, Miss Steele. All our repairmen are out. I can't fit you in until tomorrow. Will you be all right? How cold is it in the house?"

Addison drew her jacket closer. "Sixties. I'll survive. Tomorrow between ten and twelve, then."

"Oh, by the way, since it's a Sunday, there's a surcharge."

"How much?"

"It's double our usual hundred dollars for a house call, plus any materials and time over half an hour. Are you okay with that?"

"Do I have a choice?"

"I'll take that as a yes." She rang off.

Addison checked her watch. One o'clock. *Might as well find a restaurant. I'll hit the library this afternoon.* Maybe she'd pick up some brandy—and an electric blanket—to keep her warm through the long night.

She walked down the Strand to Chadwick's. A few people sat at the long bar watching basketball. *Oh, yeah, March Madness. Wonder if Emin's daughter's school won?* She didn't see anyone to ask, so she found an empty booth and ordered the Arrogant Bastard ale and the black and blue steak. The waiter wrote it down. "Good choices. The ale's our most popular, and the steak is my favorite. It was the chef's idea: blackened with melted blue cheese. It's even better than a blue cheeseburger."

"I agree."

"So do I."

Addison jumped, and she and the waiter looked over the back of the bench.

Nick grinned. "Hello, Addison. Mind if I join you?"

Chapter Nine

Fire and swords are slow engines of destruction, compared to the tongue of a Gossip.

~Richard Steele

Chadwick's, Saturday, March 22

Blinded by the brilliance of his smile and his scintillating indigo eyes, Addison forgot that she was angry with Nick. He didn't wait for her consent but plopped down opposite her. "I'll have what she's having, plus whatever lager's on draft." He waved the waiter off, keeping his eyes on Addison. "What brings you to Old Town?"

Addison toyed with reminding him of their last frosty encounter but wanted to keep the warmish, glowing-ish, snug feeling in the pit of her stomach just a wee bit longer. "I'm doing research at the Library of Congress."

"Really! Working at the greatest library in the world? You must be at the pinnacle of your career."

"No, no. I'm not on staff there—I just have stack privileges. I'm a reference librarian in the Senate Library."

The waiter brought a frothing mug, an empty glass, and a colossal brown bottle. He set the glass and bottle before Addison. Nick's eyebrows went up. "I see you went with the beer bomber. I'm impressed."

She tapped his mug with her glass. "I inherited the bottomless pit from my mother."

He took a sip and put the mug down. "Wait. Did you just say the Senate Library? You've totally lost me. Isn't the Library of Congress the Senate's library?"

"No. I mean, yes. You're right—the Library of Congress is technically the library for the US Congress and not a national library like other countries have. It's open to the public—"

"Congress is so gracious, isn't it? After all, we *do* pay for it."

Addison caught the remains of a twinkle in his eye. "Actually, the core of its original collection were books owned by the founding fathers, and when they were destroyed in the War of 1812, Congress bought Jefferson's personal library. Politics aside, it's a hassle for anyone—even a congressman—to use the LC, so we maintain a small library in the Russell Senate Office Building for quick reference."

"So...do I have this straight? You're working *in* the Library of Congress, but you work *at* the Senate Library."

"Bingo."

The steaks came, sizzling and redolent of buttery blue cheese. Addison took a long pull on her ale.

Nick watched her with amusement. "I want to see you finish all twenty-two ounces."

For answer, Addison took another long gulp. Pretending that the burp was really a ladylike cough, she put the bottle down carefully. "Do not underestimate a thirsty librarian."

He chuckled. "Consider me enlightened." He

swallowed half his beer. "I'd always heard the Library of Congress doesn't permit you to go look for books on your own. You said you had stack privileges. What exactly does that mean?"

"If you're an accredited researcher, you can get passes for certain floors. Stack privileges are like golden tickets to hungry academics."

"And which floors are you honored to stand on?"

"C and D. I'm compiling a bibliography of writings on the French and Indian War."

"A bibliography, huh? Does it keep you awake nights? I mean, wondering what the next plot twist will be?"

"Ha-ha." Nick hadn't struck her as the caustic type before. The joke grated. "Actually, bibliographies and other compilations serve an essential function for historians. They combine many different links in a single document, allowing the scholar to skip a lot of authentication steps and save valuable research time."

He drew back. "*Whew*. I stand corrected."

She took another sip of ale. "Being a librarian is really quite gratifying. I have to be intimately familiar with all kinds of reference books, so I can quickly provide any scrap of information a senator asks for. They expect us to fill a request before they've even hung up the phone."

Nick leaned across and took her hand. "I didn't mean to be flippant. It's just…well, I confess I find librarians intimidating."

She couldn't discern any glimmer of sarcasm on his earnest features, so she let him continue to apologize. And hold her hand. She only wished he'd squeeze it a little tighter. "Why?"

"You have to know so much. Librarians have prodigious memories, filing away facts and figures, and even more awe-inspiring, retrieving them at a moment's notice. Me, if I don't write my phone number on my wrist, I have to call the telephone company."

Addison laughed. "You should exercise your memory like any other muscle. Besides, I love following the trail of some obscure reference through volume after volume, only to suddenly arrive at the primary source. It's like a scavenger hunt." She picked up a french fry and chewed on it. "In fact, I came across a tantalizing tidbit of English scandal the other day."

He sobered. "And what is that?"

"Oh, something to do with my ancestor Richard Steele and a woman named Eliza Haywood."

"Haywood?" He leaned forward, his eyes burning. "What about them?"

She hesitated. *Why does he suddenly look so intense?* "Um, I expect it was merely a spat between members of a literary circle. Nothing special." She took another gulp of beer. "Tell me, what are *you* doing in Alexandria?"

Nick finished his ale and signaled the waiter. "Seeing my...er...a colleague. Say, where are you staying?"

"I have a house in Old Town. "

"I thought you lived on Chincoteague."

"The family summer house is on the island—it's a bit of a commute from there to the Capitol."

"I see." He handed the check and a pile of bills to the waiter. Pointing at Addison's plate, he said, "It's on me."

"Oh, no. You don't have to. I'm—"

He rose and plucked a white jacket from the hook. "May I drop you somewhere?"

Addison hadn't known how much she missed Nick until now. The prospect of a few hours of sweet refreshment beckoned, and she dropped her plans to go to the library without a second thought. "Home would be great." She batted her eyes.

It wasn't until they reached her door that Addison recalled the state of her furnace. "Oh dear, I forgot. The heat's off. It's freezing in the house." She cast her eyes at the street, hoping irrationally that she'd find a large billboard telling her what to do.

Nick took her arm. "There's no reason for you to stay in this drafty place then. Tell you what, why don't you come back to the hotel with me? You can at least stay warm until the repairman comes tomorrow." He gave her a little tug.

It was too simple. Something was wrong. His invitation came out too glibly. *Wait a minute. How did he know the repairman wasn't coming until tomorrow?* She studied him from under her lashes. What was different about him today? *Something is slightly out of whack—the pieces don't fit.* "I'll be fine—I've got to go to the library anyway."

He drew back, his displeasure barely concealed. "All right. Well, er…how long will you be in town?"

"A few days. How about you?"

"Just overnight. Maybe I'll see you back in Chincoteague." He backed away, stumbling over the curb.

Addison unlocked her door and went straight to the window to watch him walk to his car. *Wait, that's not the Hummer.* She hadn't paid any attention when they drove from the restaurant, her thoughts absorbed with the imminent tryst. Now doubts assailed her. *You're being silly. It's probably just a rental car.* After all, a Hummer would be impossible to navigate through Alexandria's narrow streets. *Could it be his town car? No, he's staying in a hotel. But didn't he say he came down from DC to look for Dan?* She bit her lip. *That doesn't have to mean he lives here.* He also said something about Rhode Island. And that he was only here for a day, to meet a colleague. *So our encounter was completely fortuitous, and I'd better stop thinking about him right now.* Addison stuffed her notebook into her bag and headed to Capitol Hill.

She showed her pass to the guard at the back entrance of the Jefferson Building and went to her assigned carrel. Other than the ancient professor who'd been working on a history of Ethiopia for the last twenty years, the work room was empty.

"Let's see, shall I go back to Benedict Arnold's role in the French and Indian War? Or see what I can find on the dirty girls?" She turned on her laptop and clicked on the Library of Congress catalogue. "Ooh, I'm in luck—their books are on one of my floors."

She took the elevator up to D level and walked along the narrow corridor between the dusty stacks. Halfway down, she found three shelves filled with works by Eliza Haywood and her sister writers, Delirivier Manley and Aphra Behn, known as the "fair" and sometimes the "naughty triumvirate." Most of the books were by Haywood, and Addison pulled one out entitled *Idalia, Or, the Unfortunate Mistress.* The frontispiece displayed an engraving of an aristocratic woman, a Mona Lisa smile hovering on her lips. *Almost as though she were thinking titillating thoughts.*

Addison settled on the ground and began to read. Only the jingling keys of the security guard roused her. "Closing time, Ms. Steele."

"Is it that late? Oh my." She put the volume back on the shelf, resisting the urge to dog-ear the page. She grinned at the guard. "I've been reading a romance novel from the eighteenth century, George."

The old man rolled his eyes. "Whatever turns you on, miss."

Addison picked up her briefcase and left the building. She stopped first at the vet to reclaim Mopsy's sister, Flopsy. As she opened the door to her house, the cat jumped from her arms, rolled on her side, and stretched to her full length, all the while eyeing Addison with undisguised reproach. "I'll play with you for a minute, Flopsy, then I have to work." Flopsy stalked into the kitchen, swishing her tail, and plunked down next to her bowl. Addison fed her, then went to her study.

Huddled over her computer, a rug wrapped around her knees and her fleece bathrobe over her shoulders, Addison resumed her search for information on Eliza Haywood. There wasn't much. She finally found an entry in an online encyclopedia. Haywood had written erotica, but—in an ironic twist—also guides to marriage and raising children. She even produced a literary magazine. "Miss Eliza was a very busy lady."

The cat perked up her ears. *Oops, I guess I spoke out loud.* She read on. The periodical was called *The Female Spectator*. *I wonder…*Addison clicked on several other links. Sure enough, Haywood's journal was founded as a rival to the *Spectator*, published by

Joseph Addison and Richard Steele, her ancestor. A footnote caught her eye. "It was rumored that Haywood had an unhappy love affair with Sir Richard Steele, and that it was to exact revenge when they broke up that she launched her tabloid."

I thought the affair had been debunked. Hmm. The cat yowled, and Addison went to the kitchen. "You hungry again? Flopsy, you are definitely getting fat. If the vet's going to insist on feeding you wet food, I may have to take you back with me to Chincoteague."

Watching Flopsy gulp down her meal reminded her that she hadn't eaten in eight hours. She opened a can of tomato soup and dumped it into a small saucepan, adding milk to dilute it. As it simmered, she slathered butter and chopped garlic over a thick slice of bread and stuck it under the broiler. The only chilled wine was a bottle of inexpensive champagne, so she poured herself a glass and went back to the computer. *Let's see if this story has any legs.* Was Richard Savage really at the bottom of it?

She skipped all the *Wikipedia* articles and found a monograph on Eliza Haywood from the *Britannica*. It described whispers of an affair with Sir Richard Steele but opined that it was circulated by that inveterate tattletale, the poet Richard Savage. *Aha.* In fact, the article maintained it was *Savage* who had fathered a child by Haywood.

Oh, really? So did Savage savage Steele? She grinned to herself. *Let's see…Richard Savage…Ah.* He claimed to be the illegitimate son of the fourth Earl Rivers. His father had himself been—according to a history of Parliament—"one of the greatest rakes in England," so it was entirely possible.

What about my ancestor, Sir Richard Steele? Nothing in her family annals implied a brush with impropriety. She looked through several articles, but other than a tendency to gout and a willingness to rack up debt, he seemed to have been fairly reputable.

The smoke alarm buzzed. "Oh my God, the soup!" She ran to the kitchen. The pot was spitting and gurgling. She reached it just as it boiled over and spent the next hour cleaning red slop off all the kitchen surfaces. When she'd thrown the last dish towel into the washer, she opened the oven. A small black chunk was all that was left of the bread. "That's it. I'm going to bed," she told an indifferent cat.

Not until she lay facing the ceiling did it occur to her that the Steele-Savage-Haywood saga might not be of only historical interest. Nick said he was a descendant of Richard Savage. *If so, could he be as big a charlatan as his ancestor?*

Chapter Ten

It is a secret known but to few, yet of no small use in the conduct of life, that when you fall into a man's conversation, the first thing you should consider is, whether he has a greater inclination to hear you, or that you should hear him.

~Richard Steele

Alexandria, Sunday, March 23

"Thanks for coming out on a Sunday, Mr. Bigelow."

"Not a problem. To show you how much I appreciate a good customer, I'll only charge you time-and-a-half instead of our usual double the weekday rate."

Addison wasn't about to suggest he ask for the boss's approval. She buttoned up her heavy cardigan. "How long before it feels any warmer?"

"Probably take an hour or so."

She paid him and, after he'd left, got her coat and went out in search of a cozy lair. She took the bus to the Library of Congress, only to find it was closed to visitors on Sunday. What to do? A beer at the Tune Inn sounded good. *Let's hope they have a fire. Or at least a space heater.* She walked down to the intersection and was about to cross Independence Avenue when she noticed a familiar silhouette hunched against the cold, leaning on the library wall. *Nick? Didn't he say he was leaving today?* She called, but he didn't seem to hear. She started toward him. Just as she broke into a trot, he melted around the side of the building. By the time she reached the corner, he was nowhere to be seen.

Maybe he's still sulking because I brushed him off. She started back to the bar, but a steamy, smoky tavern filled with rowdy customers no longer seemed attractive. She took the bus back to her townhouse.

****

Alexandria, Sunday to Monday

Addison moped through Sunday. What had Nick told her in the restaurant? That he was staying overnight before returning to Chincoteague. So he could have been on his way to Union Station when she saw him. The idea lifted her spirits.

By Monday, she was bored enough to go back to Eliza. The exploits of the novelist kept her glued to the pages. The woman had lived a very romantic life. Her origins were somewhat obscure, but her exploits in the bedroom were worthy of George Sand or Anaïs Nin. Her earliest works were nothing short of raunchy. She lived with a fellow writer and actor, William Hatchett, for twenty-five years but was believed to have had children by other men. Her life with Hatchett must have softened her earlier dim view of males, for her final treatises were guides on being the perfect wife.

On the other hand, Richard Savage—purported sire of one of Eliza's children—lived primarily off the generosity of others, including the eminent Samuel Johnson, who had written his biography. Savage was a prolific fabricator and con artist but also—oddly enough—a distinguished poet. Despite enjoying an inflated view of himself, he died in debtor's prison. Addison thought again of Nick. *One day he's straightforward and sweet, the next...let's face it...he's kind of slippery. Did he inherit Richard's character flaws?*

Her ruminations continued as she packed her bag Monday night for the drive to Chincoteague. If Richard Steele and Richard Savage were rivals for the affections of the enticing Eliza—was that the blood feud Nick talked about? Should she avoid the current Savage? *That may be a moot point since he seems to be avoiding me. Accept it, Addy, it was a one-night stand. Move on.* But as she clicked the suitcase closed, she again felt his ardent eyes, a mere few days before gazing at her with an intensity that could only be described as passion.

****

Chincoteague, Tuesday afternoon

She reached Chincoteague at two o'clock. *I should be just in time to pick Phoebe up.* Her cousin was shooing the last kindergartner onto the bus when Addison pulled up at the school entrance.

Phoebe walked over to the car. "Oh, great, you got my text. I left my car at your place. Can you give me a ride?"

"That's why I'm here. Do you want to go get it now or have something to eat first?"

"No, thanks, I ate with the kids. Nothing like a meal from the four food groups: gummy bears, Cheetos, and celery stuffed with peanut butter. I just want to go home and take a nap." Phoebe put Addison's briefcase on the car floor and sat down. "So, what did you learn in school today, young lady?"

Addison described her findings as they drove to Alder Island. "Richard Savage's personality reminds me distressingly of Nick."

Phoebe took Addison's suitcase from the trunk. "You've certainly cooled on the man. What's he done now? Did he get in touch with you in Alexandria?"

"I ran across him, yes. He acted...I dunno, different. Less...warm."

"You mean not as affectionate? Like he was no longer interested?"

"No..." She thought of Nick's invitation to return to his hotel. "More...calculating, I guess." Addison picked up Mopsy, who purred happily until he smelled Flopsy on her and struggled out of her arms, taking care to use his claws. "I got the impression he had something on his mind."

"Well, he's here in Chincoteague. I saw him yesterday in front of the bank."

"*Humph.* No skin off my nose. I'm done with him." She climbed the steps to the front door. "And anyway, how did you know it was he? You've never met him."

"You described him, remember?" She smacked her lips. "Dreamy—tall, shimmering hair, rippling biceps, six-pack abs, deep blue eyes. No one else in Chincoteague fits that description."

"Who knows? Maybe it was his brother, back from the dead."

"Yeah, right." Phoebe pointed a finger at Addison. "I know you, Addy. You do this with every guy you're attracted to—you feign indifference, if not outright hostility. You really like him. Admit it." She lugged the case up the steps and dropped it with a thud in the hall.

"You're not going to be happy until you work this out."

Addison sighed. "By the way, how is Walter? Have you gone out again?"

Phoebe's face fell. "We haven't had a chance. He's been run ragged by this new crop of visiting scientists. They're from this country that boasts it's the last bastion of Stalinist communism, with a dictator to boot. Walter says they're going wild—they keep sneaking off campus to eat at the Sonic or buy toiletries at the dollar store."

"That doesn't sound so wicked."

"No, but Walter's responsible for making sure they stay on the reservation." She lowered her voice. "He says one of the group shadows the others and is constantly eavesdropping on them. She's this great hulking creature. They claim she's from the university, but he's sure she's KGB. He says she gives him the creeps."

"Well, the KGB can't do anything to us, or to Walter. The worst that can happen is the scientists are sent home. Or put on a diet." Addison started up to her bedroom. "You don't seem upset. Are you off Walter too?"

"Not at all. I—" Behind her, Phoebe's phone buzzed. "Hang on." A minute later, she called up from the bottom of the stairs. "Walter finally has an evening off. We're taking *Little Dutch* out for an evening sail."

"You'd better not have purloined my last bottle of wine."

"Who, me?"

Addison heard a distinctive clink. *Sigh.* "Have fun. Thanks for taking care of Mopsy."

Addison unpacked, then spent a couple of hours

answering emails and paying bills. At five thirty, she closed the laptop and went to the kitchen. *At least my dear cousin left the whiskey.* She made herself a drink and went out on her deck. It was warmer here than in Alexandria. A light breeze whispered as the sun curtsied to the pine trees on Assateague. The trees bowed gracefully in return. A cormorant popped up, swallowed a fish, and dove under again. The resident kingfisher whipped past her, shrieking his indignation at her intrusion into his territory. Addison sighed. It would be a beautiful evening for Phoebe and Walter's sail.

She sat back and sipped her drink. The smoky aroma of bourbon mingled with the sharp, mineral scent of oyster shells blowing from the old shucking barn down the way. Darkness had begun to settle when the image of Nick rose before her, his ebony hair tousled and his lips reddened with desire as he made love to her. *Where is he? Why did he act so...so alien, so disconnected, in Alexandria? Did I see more than was there?* He said he would be in Chincoteague for just a little while—to work on his book. *Will I ever see him again?*

Only a loon answered her questions, and its lilting moan did nothing to lighten the mood.

Her cell phone rang.

"Addy? Are you out on your deck?"

"Is that you, Phoebe? Was your date cancelled?"

"Not at all. I'm on *Little Dutch* with Walter. I repeat, are you on your deck?"

"Yes, Phoebe. Why?"

"Get your binoculars and look across to Assateague."

Addison did as she was told. "Okay, the lighthouse just started beaming."

"Now turn them south down the channel. Can you see Assateague Point?"

She swung her glasses to the right. "Yes."

"Okay. Look beyond the point—out into Tom's Cove." Phoebe paused. "See anything?"

Addison held her binoculars to her face with one hand and spoke into the phone. "No...What am I looking for? Wait! A light just flashed. Who could be out there this late? Can you see anyone?"

"Not a soul besides us. Too cold for fishing." Phoebe's voice was grim. "We were sailing in Tom's Cove and just passed the old Coast Guard station when Walter saw a light winking on and off. It seems to be coming from the end of the Hook."

"Could it be a distress signal?"

"Maybe. But Walter says a light that bright could be seen as far away as the Wallops launch grounds. And—get this, Addy. Walter says it's in Morse code."

****

Addison's house, Wednesday afternoon

"All right, can you show me on the map exactly where you think the light originated?"

Walter leaned over the marine map Agent Peel held spread out on the table. He made a great show of perusing the entire area from Chincoteague to the mainland, including the NASA launch facility clearly marked on Wallops Island. "We were in the boat about here in Tom's Cove—"

"No, we weren't, Walter. We were much farther west than that," interrupted Phoebe. "I remember 'cause we'd already passed Orville Beebe's duck blind."

"Duck blind? That bushy shed on stilts? Okay, yeah." He pointed. "We were right over this abandoned oyster farm—"

Phoebe broke in again, to Walter's obvious irritation. "You forget. We had passed Orville Beebe's blind *and* Noah Merritt's oyster shack...and—"

Addison intervened. "Walter may not know the cove as well as you do, Phoebe. He's not a native."

Walter huffed. "I'm not an islander, but I'm no city rube. I was born and raised in New Church."

"*Huh.*" Phoebe was unimpressed.

"Look, I'm really sorry that the FBI didn't provide me with a map pinpointing all the duck blinds and oyster beds in the area." Peel's tone bordered on treacly. "Why don't *you* show me where you think you were, Ms. Lamb?"

"Okey doke." Phoebe didn't hesitate but stuck her finger on a spot just south of Assateague Channel. "Right about there, midway between Assateague Point and the end of the Hook, tacking north."

"I'm sure we were farther south—here, behind Fishing Point." Walter didn't want to let it go.

Phoebe shook her head. "Nope. If that were so, you couldn't have seen the buildings on Wallops Island. The flashes came from our port side—I'd say about here." She moved her finger to the channel between Wallops Island and Chincoteague.

They all pored over the chart.

Peel sighed. "In that case, the signals could have come from anywhere—even the mainland."

Walter was still fuming. "They *must* have been launched from the tip of the Hook. That's where the actual equipment has to be."

"How about you, Ms. Steele?" Peel turned to Addison. "You say you could see the lights from your house?"

"Yes, but I don't know Morse code so they just appeared as random flickering." She closed her eyes. "They could have been merely reflections on the water. It was impossible to tell what direction they were coming from."

"See?" Walter apparently thought this vindicated his position.

Peel folded the map. "It looks as though we're going to have to explore all those little islets and spits of land. There might be evidence on the…what did you call that peninsula, Miss Lamb?"

"Assateague Point."

"Or the Hook." Walter's voice rose over Phoebe's. For a split second, they glared at each other, wisps of smoke issuing from their flaring nostrils. Walter won. "The Hook's all sand, built up over the last hundred and fifty years. Most of it's closed except to off-road vehicles, and even those can't get all the way to the end because of the piping plovers."

"Piping…what?" Peel blinked.

"Plovers. Birds. They have a nesting area at the tip. Fish and Wildlife designated it a protected area. Someone could easily set up some kind of transmitting device there without anyone knowing."

"Yes, but the only way he could get to that part is by boat."

Walter was not deterred. "So? You have to take a boat to Assateague Point as well."

"That's where you're wrong." Phoebe preened. "A path that branches off from the Woodland Trail leads to the beach. You can walk all the way around the point. Easy peasy."

"Alternatively, an enterprising fellow could get to either place by air."

The others stared at Peel. "Huh? He'd need a landing strip, wouldn't he?"

"Not if he were wearing a jetpack."

Addison barely caught a sardonic tilt of his lip before it faded, leaving Peel's face as vacuous as ever.

He stuck the map in his briefcase and rose. "Thank you all for your cooperation."

Walter said, "I'll alert the base security about the lights."

"No need. The fewer people in the loop the better. I shall report it to Director Klopman myself."

Addison walked the agent to the door. "You'll keep us informed, though, won't you?"

Peel looked at her, his face unreadable. "It's on a need-to-know basis, ma'am. Sorry."

Chapter Eleven

There is not any present moment that is unconnected with some future one. The life of every man is a continued chain of incidents, each link of which hangs upon the former.

~*Joseph Addison*

Addison's house, Wednesday, March 26

Addison returned to the living room to find Walter and Phoebe bickering. "You expect me to believe that your Morse code is so perfect you should have been able to understand exactly what they were saying? Hogwash. When did you last use Morse code? In the Cub Scouts?"

Walter stood his ground. "In my former job, we had a workshop on all kinds of spy techniques: short-wave radio operation and invisible writing; codes and ciphers—*including* the use of encrypted Morse code messages."

Phoebe's jaw dropped. "Wow, Walter." She sat on his lap, her eyes bright with curiosity. "Tell me more."

Walter eyed her. "Do you really want to know?"

She kissed the top of his head. "Yes. What was this job?"

"Security guard at the Spy Museum in Washington."

Phoebe visibly deflated. "Night watchman at a dinky museum? Here I thought you were going to say the CIA or the Foreign Legion—something really exciting."

"Phoebe!" Addison was shocked.

Walter said calmly, "For your information, the Spy Museum is one of the most popular destinations in DC—which, last I checked, contained at least a hundred museums." Without warning, he threw out his legs and Phoebe bumped down them to the ground.

"Walter!"

The two combatants stared at Addison, then burst out laughing. Phoebe went so far as to roll around on the floor with her eyes squeezed shut, giggling till tears leaked out of them.

Addison took the opportunity to make herself a cup of coffee while the two recovered. She came back in carrying a steaming mug and sat down. "Now, what were you two squabbling about?"

Walter interjected before Phoebe could speak. "I was telling Phoebe that—though it was definitely Morse code—when I spelled out the message, I couldn't make head nor tail of it. The words were all gobbledygook."

"Did you give it to Peel?"

"Yes. He said he'd send it to the CSI lab to see if they could decipher it."

"If *they* can read it, you'd better be prepared to admit you don't know jack about Morse code." Phoebe stuck her tongue out at Walter.

"I don't care, as long as he tells us what they find."

Addison thought of Peel's tightly controlled face. "Fat chance of that."

Phoebe picked up her keys. "I'm going home. I need a break."

"Er, Phoebe?" Walter edged closer to her. "You *are* going to give me a lift back to my car, right?"

She gave him a critical once-over. "All right, but you have to ride in the back."

When the two had gone, pushing and shoving to get out the door first, Addison went out on her deck. The sun beat down from the top of the sky, toasting her shoulders. It was low tide, and the mud flats spread from the saltgrass to the middle of the channel. Far out in the shallow water, an old man poled his punt, his head bobbing up and down as he searched for the tell-tale indentations in the mud where crabs lay waiting for summer. She felt antsy, as though she were standing on the edge of a precipice. *Why am I so nervous? Spring fever?* The small hairs at the back of her neck tickled. She resisted the urge to swing around. *Don't be ridiculous. There's no one there, Addy. You're acting like a weenie.*

"Didn't you hear me knock?"

Addison tripped and almost fell forward into the muck.

Nick caught her elbow and pulled her back. "There's no call to run away. If you're still sore at me, I'll just skedaddle." He gave her arm a tentative squeeze.

"What are you talking about?"

"You weren't in a very friendly mood last time we met."

"*Me*? What about you?"

Nick drew back, clearly mystified. "I don't know what you're talking about. Wait...I wonder..." He studied her face. "It might behoove us to forget the past and start afresh. What say you?"

Go with the flow, Addy. "All right."

He looked back through the glass doors to the living room. "Could I interest you in some liquid refreshment?"

"I thought you'd never ask."

She poured two iced teas and took them back out to the deck. They sat quietly, enjoying the peace. After a while, the sun began to tilt, as though contemplating the hour of his slow descent to oblivion. Addison shivered in the faint stirrings of the evening breeze.

Nick rubbed her arm. "Still a bit chilly, I guess."

"Yes. March can be very impetuous around here."

"Shall we go inside?"

She didn't really want him to answer, but she had to ask. "Don't you have work to do?"

"I took the day off. We writers need breaks as much as anyone, you know." He led the way, and they sat next to each other on the couch.

"By the way, have you found out any more about your brother's accident?"

His eyes lit up. "As a matter of fact, yes. I finally ran Captain Frank to ground." He wrinkled his nose. "Not the most affable of men."

"Frank? You mean Frank Reed? Daniel rented the boat from him?" She thought of the crusty old fisherman. He'd never adjusted to running a head boat for city slickers and was disinclined to be sociable. "Yeah, he's pretty typical for islanders. So he was the one who informed you of the accident?"

"Er…Yes. Yes." Nick paused. "It *is* odd, now I think about it. Reed called me because Dan had listed me as an emergency contact." He broke off, frowning.

"Well, if he'd been abroad, maybe that was the only contact he had."

Nick looked as though he were going to debate the point, then thought better of it. "Anyway, Frank admitted that he hadn't actually seen Dan go overboard."

Addison puzzled over this. "Well, he would have known if Dan *didn't* fall, wouldn't he?"

"Of course. I'm not making myself clear. Dan vanished from the boat, so it's safe to assume he fell into the water. What the good captain didn't know is what condition he was in at the time."

"You don't think...you're not suggesting Frank Reed did him in? I've known the man all my life! His son used to mow our lawn. He doesn't have a mean bone in his body."

"Of course not. He says he heard a clunk coming from the bow. The wheelhouse hid Dan from view, so Reed couldn't see what actually happened. It could have been Dan hitting his head on a bulkhead...or hitting the side of the boat as he went over." He paused. "Frank says they weren't that far from shore."

"Where were they?"

"They'd just passed a duck blind belonging to a guy named Beebe."

Addison snickered. "Good thing it's not hunting season. Orville Beebe's blind as a bat. He might've bagged a Homo sapiens thinking it was a competition-sized snow goose."

"Huh?"

"Never mind."

He stared at her for a minute. "Anyway, if Dan

were unconscious when he went over, he would have drowned, but if he were merely injured, he might have been able to swim to the beach. According to Reed."

"What beach? It's mainly marsh along Assateague Point."

"I'm sure he said beach. He mentioned something about a canal."

"The Canal? That would mean they were beyond the channel, heading back to the marina."

Nick frowned. "What's the Canal?"

"It's a sea lane that separates Chincoteague Point from Chincoteague. Years back, a storm smashed through, cutting off the point from the main island. It's part of the Intracoastal Waterway now, maintained by the Army Corps of Engineers."

"Okay, so if the boat was in the canal when he went overboard, could Daniel have made it to shore?"

Addison put down her tea. "Most likely. It's not very wide. Anyone at the marina might have noticed him swimming."

"Depends which way he swam, doesn't it?" Nick shook his head. "Maybe he's been lying in some underbrush on the point all this time."

"You said this happened a couple of weeks ago. If he were near the beach, someone would have come across him by now. A birder or a fisherman. Someone." Addison went to the kitchen to refill their glasses. When she returned, he'd moved a little closer to the center of the couch. She pretended not to notice. "On the other hand, if Captain Frank were farther east, back in Tom's Cove, your brother would have been closer to the Hook. In that case—if he made it there—it could be a long time before anyone finds him."

"The Hook?"

"The peninsula that wraps around the southern end of Tom's Cove. There used to be a fish-processing factory there, and a Coast Guard station. Now it's Fish and Wildlife property, and they've closed it to human traffic."

"*Hmm*. I guess it's worth a shot. I'll go tomorrow."

Addison was surprised. "Tomorrow! What if your brother is lying somewhere slowly bleeding to death? There's no time to waste!"

"Wherever he is, he's already been there for two weeks. It's unlikely an extra night will make a difference. I'll go out on a limb and assume there are no man-eating beasts roaming the point."

"Still..."

Nick peered up at the sky. "Plus, if I started out now, someone would have to rescue me as well. It's not like I'm familiar with these parts. It makes more sense to get a search party up when it's daylight. I'll need a boat, won't I?"

"Yes, I suppose."

"I'll check at the Curtis Merritt marina in the morning." Nick drew her down onto his lap. "For now I need sustenance."

Addison checked her watch. "It's only four o'clock. Nowhere near dinner time."

"Dinner? Who said anything about dinner?"

"But—"

He stopped her words with a hungry kiss. They broke apart, staring at each other.

"I...really missed you, Addison."

Where did that come from?

He took her in his arms again, and this time the

kiss was gentle. Brushing a wisp of golden hair from her brow, he whispered, "It's been way too long since our last…meeting."

"But—"

He picked her up and carried her toward the stairs.

I guess my questions can wait.

****

Addison's house, Thursday morning

"Why *can't* I go with you?" She'd begun to whine, and from the look of disgust on Mopsy's face, it was clear that he didn't approve. She didn't care.

Nick remained patient. "I told you. Bud Ferris—he runs a boat-rental business in the marina—only had a small launch available. Everything else is either still winterized or in storage. He's piloting the boat, so if we do find Dan, and he's injured or incapacitated, we won't have room for you."

"I can handle the boat."

For a second, Nick seemed at a loss for words, then he spoke quickly. "Ferris won't let anyone else take it out. Something about no insurance."

"Well, if you're going to leave the boat on the shore while you two search, someone should keep an eye on it."

He shook his head. "He'll stay with the launch. He says it's nothing but sandy beach there. It'll be hard to miss a body or any evidence of Daniel's presence."

Addison took a deep breath and opened her mouth to press her case but shut it again quickly. "Okay. Good luck."

Nick shot her a suspicious look but went off to his Hummer without another word.

She waved him off. It had been on the tip of her

tongue to tell Nick about the Morse code, but something held her back. *He's definitely hiding something. Why did he insist on going alone?* A terrible thought crossed her mind. Could *he* be the one behind the flashing light? And he didn't want her along because he intended to remove the fixture, or whatever he used. *That would mean...could only mean—he's the spy.* It would explain his mysterious absences and his volatile changes in attitude. And *that* meant...She slapped her forehead. *I was right! Nick is Daniel! There is no Daniel—there never was.*

She reviewed the timeline. According to Nick, his brother was last seen a few weeks ago, but Walter had said Daniel Savage disappeared in early February. Nick arrived here March 15 or thereabouts—six weeks later. *It fits.* She gulped. *Oh dear, what have I gotten myself into?* Her mind a hodgepodge of jumbled thoughts, she went out on the deck. Clouds had rolled in but headed south, leaving a swath of blue sky behind. The water glimmered in the clear light, and the air smelled of sprouting pine needles. On the berm across the channel, a pair of mated Canada geese sat like statues near their nest.

She stared at them, forcing her mind to relax. *Okay. Walter said the flashes were in Morse code, but he couldn't decipher the dots and dashes. Dots and dashes...Maybe he couldn't translate it because it wasn't in English—it was in a code.* "The code was a code. *Hmm.*" Peel had taken Walter's rendition back to the lab to examine. *Even if they decipher it, I'm betting they won't tell us what it says.*

Addison ran up the stairs to her study, booted up the computer, and clicked on the Search box. "Morse code…Morse code." She found an article on the history and development of the code but nothing on its current use. "Wait a minute—Walter said he learned it at the Spy Museum. There may be an online course offered somewhere." A few minutes later, she had found a gold mine of information. She called Phoebe.

"Phoebe, isn't this your day off school? Can you come over?"

"Sure, what's up?"

"Walter believes those light flashes we saw were in Morse code, right?"

"Walter believes in all kinds of things—Loch Ness, ghosts, the Yeti. He's crazy in a lovable sort of way."

"He did say he'd learned Morse code when he worked for the Spy Museum though, and that means it's still in use somewhere. I've been researching it, and I've come across something very interesting."

"Hold that thought." *Click.*

Chapter Twelve

There are many more shining qualities in the mind of man, but there is none so useful as discretion.

~Joseph Addison

Addison's house, Thursday, March 27

Addison went into the kitchen and poured herself a second cup of coffee. Five minutes later, Phoebe's ancient Toyota belched and coughed up the drive. As Addison carried her mug up to her study, the front door opened.

"Addison?"

"I'm up here."

Phoebe trudged up the stairs, a lidded cup marked Ivan II Shore's Best Gas & Coffee in one hand and an envelope in the other. She dropped the envelope on the desk. "This was shoved under your door."

"That's weird. No one rang the bell, and I've been here all morning." She ripped the end open. A single sheet fell out. The scrawl was barely legible. She read it aloud. "Please to meet me at one of the clock today at Assateague Inn. Sank you. Grigory V." She looked at Phoebe. "Who the hell is Grigory V?"

Phoebe took the paper from her. "No idea. Do you suppose he means Gregory the Fifth—like the Pope or something?"

"Don't be silly. It's not a Roman numeral. It's a capital V—the first initial of his last name. But why not write his whole name out?" Addison tapped it thoughtfully. "Wait—I think he may be the leader of that group of microbiologists who blocked our way into the Wallops flight facility. The NASA director called him Vasilinak." She dropped the paper on her desk. "Phoebe, he's the one who knew my name."

"The guy who talked to you at the gate? What exactly did he say to you?"

"He just said, 'You are Miss Steele.' Then he went off with Klopman."

"Klopman. That reminds me. Walter still hasn't rescheduled the kids' tour. I'm going to have a thing or two to say to him tonight."

Addison was busy with her own thoughts. "Vasilinak...it sounds Russian, doesn't it? They were Slavic looking. Could they be Russians?"

"No...What did Walter say they were? Boborussian? Bobblehead?" Phoebe scrunched up her nose. "Belgravian?"

"You said they came from a communist country. There aren't many of those left. Hang on." Addison typed Communist Nations Today on her phone. "Ah, here's a list. Cuba? No. North Korea? A big no. How about Belarus? Does that sound familiar?"

"Yes, that's it—Belarus. Some tiny country in the middle of Europe—like Luxembourg or that other one."

"But this one's communist. Says here it's the last remnant of the Soviet empire, still very repressed." Addison slipped the sheet into the drawer of her desk. "Maybe that's why he didn't identify himself— consorting with the enemy would get him in serious trouble."

"And why he dropped the note off rather than mailing it."

"I wonder what he wants? Could he be behind the flashing lights?"

Phoebe frowned. "They're supposed to be locked up tight at night. How could this Vasilinak guy get hold of a boat, take it out to the Hook, set up a flashing light, and—"

"And get home before curfew? *Hmm.* How about this? He's the one *receiving* the signal."

Phoebe sat down in the armchair next to the desk. "Before we go all tin hat and see spies everywhere, what other purpose could he have?"

Addison mused. "A scientific experiment?"

Phoebe thought this over. "Possible. We have no idea what these guys are doing here. It could be perfectly legit. What do microbiologists study, anyway?"

"Another item to look up. Maybe the signal wasn't a coded message. Maybe it was some kind of scientific notation."

"If so, Agent Peel is wasting his time. I'll bet he hasn't bothered to check with NASA about experiments they're conducting." Phoebe pulled her chair closer to Addison. "So, what is it you found out about Morse code?"

"I almost forgot!" Addison clicked on the link. A news item popped up. "Three years ago, some Russian spies were arrested in North Carolina. They were sending proprietary information stolen from this artificial intelligence company in Raleigh. Guess what their method of reporting to Moscow was?"

"Morse code?"

"Morse code." Addison nodded. "So it's still possible that these so-called scientists are spies."

"Wait a minute. I thought we'd concluded they were doing science stuff."

"Somehow, I doubt Peel would be so exercised if there wasn't *something* going on at the facility. He's looking for Nick's brother after all. Who he believes is a spy." She sucked in a breath. *Time to share my hypothesis.* "Phoebe, I've been thinking."

"That's never good."

"Nick took a boat out to Tom's Cove today. He said he was going to look for Daniel on the Hook. He wouldn't let me go with him."

"So?"

"Phoebe, I'm beginning to wonder if Daniel exists."

Phoebe said indignantly, "Well, if Daniel doesn't exist, then Agent Peel is an even bigger fool than I thought."

"No, no. I'm saying…suggesting…that maybe Nick *is* Daniel."

"I'm not following you."

"That Nick and Daniel are the same person. He's the one who's been signaling to Wallops. He went to the Hook without me in order to get rid of the evidence."

"Where'd he score a boat?"

"It's Bud Ferris's, but Bud's staying by the water while Nick explores."

Phoebe mulled this over. "Okay. Why would he be sending information *to* Wallops Island? It doesn't make any sense. Wouldn't a foreign spy want to extract secrets *from* the facility?"

Addison had the answer. "You and Walter only saw the answering flashes...you know, like 'Roger. Message received.' If the lights originated from the mainland, they would have been too far away for you to observe."

Phoebe threw up her hands. "Maybe Dan and Nick are in it together—one at either end."

"Together?" A little spark of hope stirred in her. *Would I rather Nick and Dan be two people or just one? Definitely two.* "That begs the question: what does this Grigory Vasilinak want with *me*? And how did he know who I was? And where do the Belarusians fit in?"

"Nowhere...Didn't we just establish that they aren't allowed to leave the facility after dark?"

"In the note, Grigory asks me to meet him at the Assateague Inn, so he must be able to...hang on a minute. That's it. When I arrived at the gate with the guide for your tour, the Belarusians were waiting to be escorted in. The NASA director—"

Phoebe giggled. "His name's Friedrich, but Walter says the staff all call him Klippety Klopman behind his back."

Addison wagged her finger at Phoebe. "Name calling is beneath you. Anyway, he said something about putting two of them up at the Assateague Inn. He named Vasilinak."

"Yes, but we must assume the same rules still apply. They're not supposed to leave their quarters after curfew."

"How do we know they follow the rules?"

Phoebe was not persuaded. "They have to; they're under surveillance. I told you this Schwarzeneggersized woman watches them. Walter says she's KGB. Walter says you don't mess with the KGB."

"Well, she can't be in two places at once—watching both the main group and this Grigory person. That's why he insisted on staying on the island instead of at the main base. He has an accomplice who is using Morse code to contact him."

"Someone from outside. Someone in hiding."

"And we're back to Nick."

"Or Dan."

"He must be the one who gave Vasilinak my name." Addison bit her lip. "Nick's been using me."

"Again, what for? Last I checked, you were a lowly librarian, not Mata Hari."

Addison shook her head, trying not to cry. "I...I don't know."

Phoebe must have seen her cousin's eyes well up, for she said briskly, "Getting back to the signal. What did it say? If we could translate it, we'd have a better idea of who's behind it."

"Could it be a code—a cipher using the dots and dashes? That would explain why the translation made no sense to Walter."

"The FBI could figure that out, couldn't they? Don't they have expert code breakers?"

"They do." Addison thought about that. "But say it's *not* in some code. Nick would have used English."

"Nick, or Dan."

"Why couldn't Walter decipher the message then?"

"Incompetence? Or maybe...maybe the message was in—" Phoebe stopped and stared at Addison. "What language do Belarusians speak?"

"I dunno...Russian?"

"Ha." Phoebe crumpled her coffee cup and threw it in the trash. "So all we need to do now is find someone who knows Russian and can translate the message."

"*That* should be easy on Chincoteague." The two women regarded each other in consternation.

"Ulp."

Addison slapped her forehead. "Damn. Walter gave the paper with the code to Agent Peel, didn't he? So even if we found a translator, we don't have anything to translate."

"Not to worry. Walter's no dummy. He saved a copy." Phoebe rose. "I'm going to go get it."

Addison caught her elbow. "Is it wise to tell him our suspicions? I mean, what if we're wrong? If he gets caught helping us, it could cause an international incident."

"Walter can keep a secret." Phoebe cocked an eyebrow. "After all, he trained at the Spy Museum." She started toward the door. "Say, speaking of Nick, did you hear from him yesterday? I saw him at the post office, and he asked about you."

"How did you know it was Nick? You still haven't met him."

"Like I said before, he fit your description to a T." She pointed at the portrait over the bookcase. "You were right—he looks exactly like great-great-grandfather."

"Did you introduce yourself?"

"Uh-huh. I told him I was your cousin." She rolled her eyes. "I can see why you swooned over him. He's a doll. So…did he find you?"

Addison turned away to hide her flushed face. "Er, yes, he did…find me."

"Good. Gotta run. I'll let you know what Walter says."

****

Assateague Inn, Thursday afternoon

At one o'clock, Addison walked into the lobby of the Assateague Inn. No one was about. It was still too cold for all but the hardiest of bird watchers, and Cora Anne, the manager, usually stayed in her double-wide on the inn grounds unless renters were arriving. She wandered out the back door. A marsh lay before her, beyond it the partially hidden tents and RVs of the old Maddox Family Campground, now a KOA. To the north was Maddox Boulevard, flanked by video stores and food stands. A creek ran through the fens, meandering toward the south. At the end of a long wooden walkway, she spied a stocky figure standing on a small platform. She started toward him. He must have heard her footsteps echoing on the weathered planks, for he turned and waved.

Two Adirondack chairs took up most of the space on the little dock. He indicated the one to his right and sat down in the other. It occurred to Addison that he wanted to face away from the road and any potential witnesses. She caught herself. *Stop being so suspicious, Addy. He probably only wants tips on where to eat.*

"Miss Steele?"

"Mr. Grigory…er…?"

"Grigory Andreyevich Vasilinak. We met at Wallops." He pronounced it *vallops*. "I am visiting scientist there. We are microbiologists."

"Yes, I remember. You called me by name. How did you know who I was?"

He blanched and looked furtively around him. "A

friend…a man I know. He tell me you can help."

Walter? "Does he work at the facility?"

He shook his head. "No. Yes. Sort of."

He was obviously lying. Either that, or his English wasn't good enough for the job. She decided to let it go. *If he wants information, it couldn't be Dan or Nick. They know I'm no spy. Yes, it's most likely Walter. I'll ask him myself later.* "You say you need help. What kind of help?"

He blinked. "We are microbiologists. We are from Belarus. It is in Europe."

"Yes, I know. What kind of help do you need?"

"Eastern Europe. You know it? Near Lithuania? Poland?"

She gave up. *He'll tell me when he's ready.* "Belarus borders on Russia too, doesn't it?"

His eyes narrowed. "Yes, on the east." His mouth snapped shut.

Addison had the impression he was not thinking kindly thoughts. Inspiration clicked. *Maybe he can settle the Morse code question.* "Do you speak Russian?"

"Belarusian." He tapped his chest proudly. "Is different from Russian. We are not Russians." Vasilinak took a moment to survey their surroundings, even though the only other living thing within fifty yards was a great blue heron standing silently in the water. The bird watched them with interest. Addison wondered idly if one could attach a listening device to a waterfowl.

Grigory's voice dropped. "However, the Russians, they control us. Our president—dictator-for-life Lubashenkov—works for the Russians, even while he claims to care only for his people." He spat into the water, flushing the heron.

Time to get this show on the road. "Um, Mr. Vasi…Vasi—"

"Vasilinak."

"Mr. Vasilinak, you must tell me why you asked to meet."

He froze, and his voice dropped even lower. "We understand you have a bot. A large bot."

"A bot?"

"Yes…" He scrunched up his nose. "A bot that goes on the water?"

"Oh, a *boat*! Yes, my family owns a cabin cruiser that sleeps six." Light began to dawn. "I'm afraid it's still in winter storage though. Do you…do you need it for something?"

He rose and twisted his shoulders to look toward the inn.

As Addison's gaze followed his, she caught sight of a figure stepping back into the shadows of a second-floor balcony. A woman. Klopman had said a second member of the Belarus delegation—a female—was staying at the Assateague Inn. *She must be the KGB minder.* And she'd seen them.

Vasilinak was trembling and chewing on his lip. He said quickly, "Fishing. Bot for fishing. Yes. My colleagues and I would like to go…fishing." He leapt out of the chair. "So nice to meet you, Ms. Steele. We'll be in touch." He sprinted up the boardwalk and disappeared into the building.

By the time Addison reached the lobby, it was empty. She heard a shout, then a car engine started up. She ran outside. A green SUV, its side door crushed in, skidded out of the back parking lot and bumped over the rutted gravel lane leading to Chicken City Road. There was no sign of Vasilinak. Cora Anne was standing in her doorway, a phone pressed to her ear.

Addison waited a few minutes. When he didn't reappear, she decided to go home. She found Nick sitting on her doorstep. He did not look happy. In fact, he looked rather damp. "What happened?"

He stood up, and water sloshed off his pants, dribbling into his soaked tennis shoes. "Fell in."

That seemed to cover it, so Addison unlocked the door and ushered him into the foyer. "Wait here," she ordered, and ran for a towel. She unbuttoned his shirt and dragged the sopping jeans down, forgetting to take his shoes off first. Nick bent down and pulled the sneakers off, knocking them to one side. Addison found herself nose to nose with a somewhat bedraggled if awfully handsome face.

He kissed her forehead. "I feel better already." He wrapped the towel around his middle, which did nothing to obscure the significant effect she'd had on more than his mood.

She pushed off the floor. "Coffee?"

"Maybe later." He picked her up and bounded up the stairs.

Chapter Thirteen

No oppression is so heavy or lasting as that which is inflicted by the perversion and exorbitance of legal authority.

~Joseph Addison

Addison's house, Thursday, March 27

Two hours later, Nick sat at the kitchen table, steaming mug in one hand, the other holding Addison's pink flannel bathrobe tightly across his chest. "Check them again. I'm sure they're dry by now."

Addison dutifully opened the dryer door and felt the jeans. "Still damp."

Nick checked his watch. "It'll have to do. I've got to go. I've an appointment at five thirty."

"Hold on just a minute." *Keep it offhand, Addy. Let's just see what he says.* "You haven't told me what happened today. I take it you didn't find Dan?"

"We didn't get far enough. I...uh...fell off the boat as we were untying it at the dock." He refused to look at her, although she was sure he could hear her muffled titter.

"Not much of a sailor, are you?"

Nick bristled. "In my defense, the skipper doesn't exactly run a tight ship. He had lines and tools and crap scattered all over the deck. I tripped on a rope."

"Doesn't sound like Bud Ferris."

"It wasn't. Turns out his outboard motor was on the fritz."

"So whose boat was it?"

"Captain Funt's Funtime Excursions." He said glumly, "First name's gotta be 'Allen.' "

"Oh dear, not old Jedediah Funt's wreck! I would have warned you. That tub spends more time under the water than on it."

"At any rate, we didn't make it out of the marina. I paid him half what he asked. He didn't complain." Nick got up and went to the dryer. "I hate to run, but I have to find another boat for tomorrow." He pulled on the jeans and his shoes. As she buttoned his shirt, he drew Addison to his chest and kissed her.

He's suddenly in an awful hurry. Her hand flew to her mouth. *I can't believe I let him make love to me when...*"Okay."

He gave her a funny look. "See you soon?"

"Um..." She had her hand on the knob when the door swung toward her. She jumped back. "Oh my God! Phoebe! How long have you been standing there?"

"Only a second. I just arrived." She peered over Addison's shoulder. "You aren't alone?"

Nick stepped to Addison's side. "Hello there, I'm Nick Savage. And you are?"

Phoebe stared from one to the other as her cheeks turned progressively pinker and pinker. "We...uh...met yesterday. At the post office?"

He looked her up and down. "My bad. We did meet yesterday. I apologize. You're Addison's cousin, right?"

"Phoebe. Phoebe Lamb." Phoebe's eyelashes fluttered wildly. "I…uh…hope I'm not interrupting anything. I—"

"Not at all!" Nick pushed past Addison, smiled at Phoebe, and legged it to the driveway.

Addison let Phoebe in. "What are you doing here?"

"Gawd, he's so gorgeous!" Phoebe watched the Hummer chug down the road. "Your Nick seems to be popping up everywhere. I thought I saw him at the marina a little while ago."

"You probably did. I told you he was going to take a boat out—ostensibly to look for his brother—but it…didn't work out."

"I guess not. He must have made it here from the marina in record time."

"He…uh…fell in. Had to return to shore."

Phoebe pointed at the trail of wet footprints going up to the bedroom. "By the looks of it, he spent a bit of quality time here before I arrived though. Have you decided to give him the benefit of the doubt?"

Addison wiped her face with a towel. "I won't dignify that remark with a response. Have you seen Walter?"

"Not yet. We have a date at seven. But I did talk to him. He says Belarusian is not the same as Russian, although they're both Slavic languages."

"That's what Mr. Vasilinak said."

"*But* Walter says Russian is the second official language of Belarus, so Belarusians understand it."

"Damn. That means the code could be in either Russian or Belarusian."

"So we need a translator who knows both."

"Neither of which is in great supply on the

Delmarva peninsula. I suppose we could check if there's a Slavic language department at Salisbury State. Want some coffee?"

"Love some."

They went into the kitchen, where Addison filled two cups, adding cream and two tablespoons of sugar to Phoebe's. She sat down across from her cousin. "I suppose it's not really our problem anyway."

"What do you mean?"

"The FBI is handling it. It's not our job to translate the code, or even get involved."

Phoebe tossed her head. "Tough. This is too juicy a scoop. Besides, Peel wouldn't even have the message if Walter and I hadn't seen the signal."

"Has the good G-man been in touch with you?"

"No, and it's really insulting. We should be kept in the loop."

"Sweetie, I doubt if the FBI would agree. If this is a case of espionage, it's better to leave it to the professionals." Addison thought about Nick and the boat. *I should have challenged him. I should have demanded he come clean, but...*Best to set it aside for now. "Phoebe, Nick is going out again tomorrow."

Phoebe made air quotes. "To look for his brother?"

"So he says, but if I'm right, he could be trying to cover his tracks. I have to find a way to follow him."

"If he *is* the bad guy, that could be dangerous."

Addison conjured up their recent erotic coupling. "I don't believe he would harm me."

"Unless he were desperate." In the face of Addison's stubborn expression, Phoebe said, "Okay, here's a question. What will you do if you catch him?"

Addison opened her mouth and shut it again. "I

guess I could call the police…"

Phoebe gave her a sympathetic pat. "Look, hon, didn't you just tell *me* to butt out?"

"But…"

"Tell you what: I'll lay off if you promise to do likewise."

Addison didn't answer.

"I'll take that as a yes." Phoebe dropped their cups in the sink and led the way into the living room. "So?"

"So what?"

"Weren't you supposed to meet the spy or whatever he is? Grigory something?"

Addison gasped. "Oh my gosh, it completely slipped my mind."

Phoebe grinned. "Something big and sexy distract you? You did go, didn't you?"

"Oh, yes."

"Okay, spill." She sank down on the sofa.

Addison leaned forward and lowered her voice. "It was very cloak and dagger. We met at the end of the dock at the inn. He was nervous and shifty-eyed."

"Shifty-eyed? Like he was going to mug you? Or…" Phoebe clutched her throat. "*Kidnap* you?"

Addison drew back. "No, no. I guess 'shifty-eyed' isn't really accurate. He was more frightened. Maybe even terrified."

"Ah. So what did he want with you?"

"He wanted to borrow the Aspen 32. He said he and his colleagues were going fishing."

"Huh? That's it?"

"Yup. Then he saw someone on the second floor and took off."

Phoebe sank her chin in her palm. "Fishing, huh?

So why the cryptic message and covert rendezvous? Just games?"

"I don't know. He didn't get a chance to clarify, but I got the feeling they wanted to do more than fish."

"Like what?"

"Like—" Addison's cell phone rang. "Hey, Leonard, what's up?" She listened for a minute. "Me? What for?" Eyes wide, she stared at Phoebe. "All right, I'll be down right away." She stuck the phone in her pocket.

"Leonard? As in Chief Hogarth?"

"Yup."

"Well? Why did he call?"

Addison rose slowly. She spoke, her voice dazed. "He wants me to come down to the police station. Grigory Vasilinak has been arrested."

"Your new Belarusian friend? Do you think it has to do with your confab?"

"It must be."

Phoebe picked up her purse. "I'm coming with you."

Addison didn't argue.

****

Chincoteague police station, Thursday, early evening

Addison and Phoebe walked into the police station on Community Street to find the chief of police in a standoff with the ubiquitous Agent Peel.

"Look, this man's not going anywhere until his court-appointed lawyer gets here."

Peel's face had turned an unbecoming maroon. "Vasilinak is not an American citizen, Chief Hogarth. The FBI wants him for questioning in a matter of national security."

131

Hogarth stood his ground, taking up quite a bit of it, Addison thought uncharitably. He stuck out his considerable belly and poked a fat finger in the agent's chest. "Nevertheless, he deserves a lawyer present, at least until we can get hold of his embassy."

Phoebe piped up. "He has diplomatic immunity, doesn't he?"

The two men turned to the women. Hogarth opened his mouth and closed it again. It was obvious he didn't know the answer.

Peel's eyes flicked from Addison to Phoebe. "What are you two doing here?"

"Leonard"—Addison nodded at the chief—"asked us to come down."

Peel bristled. "I didn't authorize that. And I don't appreciate interference in this issue. Please leave."

Addison knew these were fighting words to her cousin, and Phoebe didn't disappoint. She put her hands on her hips and cried shrilly, "We most certainly will not. We are American citizens. You have no right to order us around."

Leonard intervened. "I want them here, Peel. Last I checked, this is my beat, not yours." He called into the other room. "Darlene! While you're on the phone, find out if the prisoner has diplomatic immunity."

Peel said gruffly, "He's not a diplomat. He's here on a temporary visa. No immunity."

Addison volunteered, "I think for police matters, you go to the consulate, not the embassy, Leonard. Have you checked if there's a consulate nearer than Washington?"

Leonard bellowed over his shoulder. "Darlene?"

A petite woman with a mop of frizzy brown hair

came to the door. "Sheesh, Leonard, I'm working as fast as I can. I have Nancy at the library looking up the bit about diplomatic immunity."

"Never mind that. We already have an answer. What about a consulate?"

"It looks like they only have an embassy, and that's in Washington."

"Have they called you back?"

"Not yet."

"So." Leonard turned back to Peel and grinned. "I guess we'll just have to wait."

Addison touched the chief's elbow. "Why *did* you ask us to come, Leonard?"

"Huh? Oh, yeah." He glanced at Phoebe. "As I recall, I only invited *you*, Addison. The prisoner refuses to talk to anyone but you." He patted her shoulder. "I trust you can explain to him about the public defender. I don't think he understood what I was saying. His English isn't great."

Robert Peel cast an accusatory eye at Addison. "You know of any reason why he specifically requested *you*, Ms. Steele?"

Whoa, buster. This from the guy who keeps his cards so close to his chest they leave an imprint? She saw no reason to share her theories about the boat and the scientists with Peel. At least not yet. Like she'd told Phoebe, the Belarusian had impressed her as more frightened than furtive. *I don't have proof that Grigory and his friends wanted to do anything besides fish.* "I have no idea. We met at the entrance to the Wallops Facility when the Belarusians were just arriving."

"Oh, yes. The fracas." He said it grimly.

"So maybe I'm the only one he knows outside of

the base. Leonard, may I speak to him?"

Phoebe tried to follow Addison, but Darlene barred the way. "Only authorized personnel beyond this point." She shaded her eyes to look up the foot or so to Phoebe's face. "Have some coffee, Phoebe."

"Phooey." Phoebe sat down on the hard plastic seat with a thump.

Agent Peel paced the room.

Addison passed through the door Leonard opened and found herself in a room with two jail cells. Grigory sat, head in hands, in one. Leonard let her in and left, turning the key in the door. Addison suffered a twinge of claustrophobia at being locked in but suppressed it. She sat down next to Vasilinak. "Grigory, it's Addison Steele. What can I do for you?"

When he lifted his face, she saw a well-developed purple bruise on his temple and a black eye. "You are the only one I can trust, Ms. Steele. You didn't tell the policeman about the boat?"

She shook her head. "What did you want it for really?"

He peered at the door. "Can they see us? Or hear us? Is it—how you say—beetled?"

Addison almost laughed. "You mean bugged? I don't think so. Not much need for surveillance cameras on Chincoteague. We already know each other's business."

"All right, then." He lowered his voice to a bare whisper. "We want to defect."

Chapter Fourteen

A day, an hour, of virtuous liberty is worth a whole eternity in bondage.

~*Joseph Addison*

Chincoteague police station, Thursday, March 27

"What!"

Vasilinak was perplexed by her obvious shock. "Why you surprised? We want freedom as much as any other pipple. Belarus very sad place to live. No money, too many Russians. We can't do our work with government watching every move."

"But what about your families?"

"Only Vladimir Stepanovich has family left in Minsk. He has said his goodbyes to his mother. He is ready for a new life."

"I...see." *Whew, who could have predicted I'd be running an underground railroad for a bunch of refugees from communism when I woke up this morning?* "What is your plan?"

He said eagerly, "We use your boat to escape from Olga Ilyich and go to Washington, DC, to plead for asylum."

"All of you?"

"Yes. We make pact before we left Belarus that we would find a way to stay in United States."

"I see. First though, who gave you my name? And why?"

His eyes swept the cell. He whispered, "I told you. An American. A friend."

"Was it Walter Pope? The security guard?"

He shook his head. "I promised not to tell. He thought you would help with boat."

Addison went with a different tack. "You said you want to escape from Olga. Who is Olga?"

He spat on the floor. "Olga Ilyich Zhuk. KGB. Our handler."

"Is she a…er…large woman?"

"Very large. Like gorilla." He hunched his shoulders. "How you say? A bully."

So Walter was right. "Was she at the Assateague Inn this morning? Did she see us talking?"

He touched his face gingerly. "Yes. She already suspects we're planning to escape, and when she see you and me together at hotel, she guessed it would be soon." He blinked. Addison had a feeling he was about to serve her with a large fib. "I…uh…tried to leave, but she came after me in her car and almost ran me down."

Addison gasped. "She didn't hit you with it, did she?"

"No, no. She hit tree. Put big dent in side."

"Was her car by any chance a green SUV?"

He nodded. "It is rented. University will not be happy they must pay for damages."

"Tell me what happened."

"She was waiting for me in lobby. She threatened to put us on plane back to Belarus." He took a deep breath. "To tell the truth, I…I fear I lost my temper. We grappled, and I ran outside. She came after me, and we had a—how you say?—an altercation in the parking lot."

"Wait—you confronted her? Was that wise?"

He glared at Addison. "No, of course not!" He touched his face again. "She's much stronger than me."

Addison was puzzled. "So if Olga hit you and tried to run you over, how come you were the one arrested?"

He closed his eyes. "This woman—the manager—she come out of that house nearby. She saw us. I think she call the police."

Cora Anne. She must have thought Grigory was roughing up a woman. "Did you describe what really happened to the police?"

"I tried to…but then I think to myself, this may give us—how you say—lucky break." He indicated the cell bars. "I'm safe from Olga Ilyich in here. I will insist we wait to see representative from my embassy. That gives us time."

"But what about your colleagues?"

"She won't touch them while all eyes are upon us. However, we must find a way to protect them."

"How about putting them in jail with you?" Addison was half jesting.

"Most excellent idea!" Grigory jumped up. "Once we are all under police protection, we can ask for sanctuary." He sat down again, breathing heavily. "Ah, but how to accomplish that?"

Addison indicated Grigory's bruises. "They would be arrested if they started a brawl or a bar fight."

He turned to Addison, his eyes alight. "Perfect! Can you arrange?"

What the hell am I getting myself into? "What could I possibly do?"

In an instant, Grigory's expression went from animated to dismal. "I don't suppose you are heavy drinker?"

Addison raised a shoulder. "I do enjoy a nice glass of vodka now and then."

"Of course!" Grigory leapt up again. Addison's neck started to ache from all the vaulting up and down. It was like watching whack-a-mole without a mallet. "We have some good Belarusian vodka. We'll have a party and—"

"Er, Grigory, you *are* incarcerated, you know. I don't think they allow parties in here."

"Yes, yes, I understand. *They* have the party. With you. And then—"

"Grigory," she interrupted again, gently. "I don't know any of them. It would come across as somewhat peculiar were I to waltz into the building hefting a bottle of Stolichnaya and offering to share it with any Belarusians who happened to be around."

"No Stolichnaya. Vodka Belaruska only." He wrinkled his nose. "Hokay, but we must find a way to get my colleagues into custody..." He held up a finger. "Aha! There's a pub near their dormitory where we drink. They could meet you there."

"You must mean the Rocket Club. That's where the NASA folks all congregate." She tapped her lip. "It's inside the main base though, so locals are prohibited. Especially ones who want to throw boisterous drinking parties." She sighed. "Are your friends allowed off campus?"

Vasilinak nodded. "We have permission to travel to certain places. We can visit private laboratories outside the facility and some commercial establishments."

"The dollar store."

His eyes lit up. "Yes! A delightful emporium! And there is this small restaurant that sells hamburgers and as much—what is it called?—soda pop as you can drink." He rubbed his stomach.

"You mean the Sonic drive-in." She clucked her tongue. "Neither place would be appropriate for a brawl, I'm afraid, especially if drinking vodka is involved. Anywhere else?"

"There is local tavern we have been to. We must go in a group, and Olga always accompanies us. But still, we are off the base. No security. Except for Olga."

"Local tavern…you're referring to Ray's Shanty?"

"That's it. So, we organize an outing to this Ray's Shanty."

"How will you do that?"

He thought. "I'll tell Sergey Pavlovich to ask Olga. She likes him. She has sweet spot for him." He grinned.

"Okay, so then what?"

"Once there, my colleagues could pretend to drink too much"—he raised an imaginary glass to his lips—"and start ruckus."

"What happens if no one wants to fight with them?"

"*Hmm*. They could argue amongst themselves. Pavel Fyodorvich and Vladimir Stepanovich often disagree over experimental procedures. Sometimes the disagreement can—how you say it—devolve into fisticuffs."

"I'm not sure…"

He looked at her with big, brown, puppy dog eyes. "Could you please to arrange it? Without an American ally, we have no chance."

Sigh. "What do you want me to do?"

He wiggled happily. "I write plan down, and you smuggle it to them. Then you meet them at the bar. When they come to blows, you call police and keep other patrons out of the way."

Damn. Just when I thought my life couldn't get more interesting..."I—"

The door opened, and Leonard peeked around it. "You finished, Addy? The lawyer is here."

She rose. "Yes, I am." She turned to the Belarusian, who was trying to wipe the panic off his face. "Let me think about it. I'll get back to you when I've worked it out."

"You are our savior." The absolute trust in his eyes unnerved her.

Phoebe stood in the center of the lobby, arms and legs akimbo. "Come on." She grabbed Addison and led her out to her Toyota, ignoring the FBI agent's calls. As they drove off, he came storming out of the building waving his arms. Phoebe stepped on the gas and did a wheelie around the corner.

"Phoebe!"

"Never mind him. He can't do anything to us. Now, what the heck is going on?"

Addison—arms braced on the dashboard—looked at the clock. "Phoebe, it's almost seven—didn't you have a date with Walter?"

Phoebe slammed the brakes on. "Oh, shit, I forgot all about it. Look, I'll drop you off, but I'm coming back tomorrow and I expect to hear the whole saga."

"Phoebe, do me a favor. Ask Walter how well he knows Grigory Vasilinak."

"Huh? Why?"

"Just do it."

****

Addison's house, Thursday afternoon

For once, only a cat waited at home for Addison. "At least I have you for company, Mopsy." She picked him up, which did not please him, and hugged him, which he disliked even more. She let him down and went to fix herself a drink. "I think, yes, a vodka tonic will hit the spot." She giggled.

She checked her messages. Nothing. A little finger of disappointment poked her breast. *I'll just take my drink to the deck then.* A red-winged blackbird cheeped defiantly from a swaying stalk of cordgrass. Dark gray clouds massed overhead. She prayed the crisp breeze would push them past the island to the mainland.

Why doesn't he call? On the other hand, do I want him to? Nick was so mercurial—warm and affectionate one day, then brusque and a little flinty the next. Perhaps that was normal for an undercover operative. *If he is one. Damn! I don't need mysteries. Why can't I have a nice, comfy, mundane, predictable romance?* The sun set and blackness filled the sky. *Looks like the clouds are here for the night.* She went inside.

A slice of cold pizza and a glass of chianti later, she settled down with the latest mystery by her favorite author. *"Artful Dodging*...clever title." She didn't realize she'd fallen asleep on the second page until a gentle knocking at the door woke her up.

Yawning, she stumbled to the foyer. "Who is it?"

"Um. Nick."

She opened the door. He stood in the darkness on the porch. "I...lost your phone number. Sorry to come by so late, but I wanted to see if we could get together Saturday night."

"Why don't you come in?" Addison peered at the figure.

"I…uh…can't right now. I have someone waiting."

"Did you rent another boat?" She snickered. "I suppose you fell in again and want to bypass the ridicule."

"No, that's not it. Gotta run. Saturday at eight, okay?"

"That's awfully late—what did you have in mind?"

"I'll bring dinner—we need to talk."

His somber tone made her uneasy. *What is going on? Is Phoebe right? Could I be in danger?* "I guess so."

Nick turned and loped down the steps. "Great. See you then."

****

Addison's house, Friday afternoon

"All right, my dear. School's over. Time to cough up. I want to hear all about the Belarusian drama."

Addison held the phone to her ear while she dried her face. "You up for a late lunch? I'm buying."

"All right, just this once." Would that were true. Phoebe was an unrepentant sponge. "Can you pick me up at home?"

"Okay."

Phoebe waited outside her house on North Main and hopped in. They drove down the causeway to the mainland. Addison turned left on Atlantic Road and then left again onto a dirt road next to a large billboard announcing This Way to Wrigley's Seafood Restaurant. "It'll be empty on a Friday. We can talk." They bumped down the lane to a long, low building that knelt next to Watt's Bay.

The hostess greeted them as old acquaintances. Phoebe pointed to a table in the corner that looked out over the marsh. "Can we sit there, Bessie?"

She nodded and led the way, the stub of a cigarillo hanging onto her lower lip for dear life. "What brings you gals out here today?"

After a momentary pause, in which Addison realized neither of them had concocted a suitable excuse, Phoebe announced, "We're planning a surprise birthday party for…Cora Anne Jester. You know, over at the Assateague Inn? She's Chincoteague's biggest busybody, see…So we had to get out of town or—"

Addison finished up. "Or she'd know all about it before we had our coffee."

That seemed to satisfy Bessie, although Addison's anxiety level spiked when she saw the hostess pull out her cell phone and start tapping. She whispered, "Tell me Cora Anne's birthday is sometime soon."

"As a matter of fact, it's next month." At Addison's look, Phoebe huffed, "I'm not a complete nincompoop, you know."

Bessie came over, a sly look on her face. "Moira's out today, so I'll take your order. Okay, how you gonna surprise Cora Anne, Phoebe?"

"Never you mind, Bessie. I want the pork chop please, with baked sweet potato and green beans. And gimme a draft beer. Addy?"

Addison ordered the stuffed flounder and iced tea. When Bessie had reluctantly moved off, she quickly related the Belarusians' intentions.

"So, they want to defect, huh? Stands to reason—I

read up on Belarus after Walter spouted off about it. It won independence from the Soviet Union in 1991, but it's been run since '94 by this Stalinist dictator, Luka-something. Soviet troops remained in the country, and a lot of former KGB agents transferred their affections from Moscow to Minsk. So, basically, Russia still rules it. It's hardly the Heaven on Earth the state travel agency claims in its brochure."

Bessie brought their plates and lingered.

"Thanks, Bessie. We'll be fine. Really. We'll call you if we need anything else."

She shrugged and moved off. Phoebe giggled. "I suppose we'll *have* to throw Cora Anne a party now."

"And have it here." Addison dug into the enormous whole fish—belly stuffed with crabmeat—which was the specialty of the house. After a couple of bites, she scoped out the room for signs of Bessie, then whispered, "Grigory asked for our assistance."

"What? How on earth can you help a Belarusian dissident win asylum?"

"We, Phoebe, we. See, the idea is we stage a barroom brawl and get all the Belarusians—except Olga, of course—taken into custody. Once they're behind bars, she won't be able to do anything when they declare their desire to defect."

"Who's Olga?"

"The KGB agent assigned to them."

"Oh, right. Walter calls her the Elephant Woman." Phoebe shivered. "Was she the one who hit poor little Grigory?"

"Yes."

"So how come he was the one arrested?"

"Cora Anne saw them struggling and called the

144

police."

"And she and the cops just assumed it was the man's fault. Huh." She slathered butter on her potato. "Okay, we need Walter then."

Chapter Fifteen

You see, among men who are honored with the common appellation of gentleman, many contradictions to that character.

~Richard Steele

Wrigley's Seafood Restaurant, Friday, March 28

"Walter! I forgot. Grigory said he'd gotten my name from an American friend. He said he promised not to tell who it was, but it's got to be Walter."

"So that's why you asked me how well Walter knows Vasilinak." Phoebe wrinkled her brow. "It can't be him. He only met the Belarusians the day we took the kids to the facility. That was the first time Vasilinak spoke to you. The timing's off."

"But Phoebe, that was ten days ago. They've had all this time to get acquainted. Grigory must have told Walter about their plans, and Walter suggested he ask me for my boat."

She shook her head. "The boat idea may have come from Walter, but again...who gave Vasilinak your name?"

"*Hmm.*" An idea pinged. "The Belarusians probably flew into Dulles. Olga didn't arrive until a day later, so someone else would have escorted them to Wallops."

"If it were a taxi driver, he wouldn't be from around here. He's likely long gone back to the airport."

"Someone from the embassy?"

"How would a Belarusian diplomat stationed in Washington, DC, know who you are, let alone about your boat?"

Addison was stumped. "Maybe he read about me online?"

"*Online*? What are you? A closet celebrity? Or on the Ten Most Wanted list?"

"Everybody has a social media presence, Phoebe. Aren't you on MeWe? Gab? My Space?"

"No way. Dabbled in Facebook a couple of times but then decided I didn't want the world to know my blood type and what I had for breakfast." She stuck a green bean into her mouth and chewed. "And anyway, even if it was a secret, Walter would have told *me*—or dropped a hint or something."

Addison said mildly, "You haven't known him that long, Phoebe."

Her cousin remained undeterred. "Whether or not he's already involved, we should still bring him in now. He can be our inside man." She bobbed her head with conviction.

Addison pursed her lips. "Do we really want that many people in the loop? If Walter's implicated in our little scheme, he could lose his job, couldn't he?"

"But he'd be a hero! The white knight who delivers innocent civilians from an evil regime!" Phoebe's eyes gleamed and her cheeks colored.

Romance moves from bud to bloom? "Well, maybe he could initiate the hostilities."

She drew back. "Now that would *definitely* get him

canned. What I meant was, how about we sound him out? There's bound to be a better way to get these guys asylum than disturbing the peace."

The image of a colorless face popped into Addison's head. "I could ask Agent Peel."

"Peel?" Phoebe raised her eyebrows. "Isn't he the enemy?"

"The FBI is in the business of protecting people, isn't it? If he facilitated the Belarusian defection, it could get him an award or commendation or something."

Phoebe swigged her beer. "You may be right. Plus it would take his mind off Dan."

"Dan…or Nick."

"Whatever."

They asked Bessie for doggie bags and drove back to the island. At Phoebe's door, Addison said, "Okay, you work on Walter, and I'll find Peel."

"It's a plan."

****

Salisbury, Friday afternoon

Finding Robert Peel turned out to be more difficult than Addison had expected. He always cropped up when she didn't want him, but now he seemed to have fallen off the face of the earth. Walter had contacted him before, but she didn't have his number either, and Phoebe didn't answer her phone. *Wait a minute—the first time he visited the house, he gave me a card, didn't he?* After searching every drawer in the house, she tried the closet. It was in the pocket of her parka. She called the cell number, noting the area code was 202—*that's Washington, DC*. "Agent Peel?"

"Yes." Guarded tone. "Ms. Steele?"

"Where are you?"

"Why do you ask?"

"Because you're not on Chincoteague."

"No, I'm in Salisbury. Why?"

"When will you be back?"

"Not for a couple of days. I have a lead here. Again, why?"

Damn. "Could I come up to town? I'd really like to talk to you. I have some information."

"I won't be back in DC for a while."

"I meant Salisbury."

His vexed sigh was a little too loud. "All right. Meet me at 900 North Salisbury Avenue at four o'clock."

"Great." Addison checked her watch. Two thirty. It took about an hour to get to Salisbury, the closest major city to Chincoteague. She started the car and drove down Church Street. As she turned right on Main, headed toward the causeway that crossed Chincoteague Bay, a movement caught her eye. On the sidewalk a block away, Nick ambled past Miss Molly's Inn. She thought about turning around. *I don't have time.*

She found the address easily. No sign or any kind of insignia indicated it was an FBI building. The receptionist—a dowdy woman in her fifties with a gray complexion and soft, white hands—didn't refer to Peel as an agent. In fact, she only said two words: "In there."

Addison shrugged off the thought that maybe Robert Peel wasn't what he said he was. *That would be silly. What would be the point in impersonating an FBI agent?* All she had to do was ask for identification.

Peel sat at a battered desk, a laptop open before him. He did not rise when Addison entered. "What is it?"

Ooh, not too happy to see me. She guessed he hadn't forgotten Phoebe's cavalier treatment of him at the police station. "Er, Mr. Peel, would you mind showing me your badge again?"

He sat straighter. "I beg your pardon?"

"I don't see any evidence that this is an FBI office. So, I'd like to see your ID. Please."

He got up, closed the door, and indicated a chair. Standing before her, he pulled a badge from his inside pocket and held it out.

She scanned it quickly, a bit embarrassed by her overcaution. It certainly looked genuine. She transferred her gaze to him, the obvious question in her eyes.

"Yes, I'm under cover. The receptionist knows who I am, but the landlord thinks I run a software company." He paused and almost chuckled. "My other employees work from home."

"You must not be very deep under cover, since everyone on Chincoteague knows who you are."

"Only you and your chief of police. That became necessary when he arrested Vasilinak."

You go ahead and enjoy that little fantasy, mister.

He returned to his desk. "Now, why are you here?"

"I have come to tell you what Grigory Vasilinak told me yesterday."

Peel's eyes opened wide. "He confessed?"

"He told me that he and his colleagues are seeking asylum."

"They want to defect? Huh." To Addison's surprise, the news didn't seem to shake him. "Why tell you?"

"They hoped to borrow my boat to escape, but Olga saw us talking and attacked Grigory."

"Olga?"

"She's their KGB handler."

He nodded knowingly. "The full-figured gal."

"Uh...yes. Anyway, she's the one who gave Grigory a black eye."

"The version the witness gave was that *Vasilinak* attacked *Olga*."

Addison tried not to laugh. "You've seen them both. What do *you* think happened?"

"I see your point." Peel typed something quickly on his computer. "And why did you come to me?"

This was unexpected. "I'm just a private citizen. You're a federal agent. Aren't you the proper one to assist them?"

"Look, Miss Steele, I've got my own problems right now. We'd been going on the assumption that Vasilinak was a spy, working with Daniel Savage. If what you say is true, that can't be the case."

Addison stared at him, flummoxed. "Okay, do you believe the Belarusians are connected to Savage or not?"

"Given current evidence—including yours—I'd say no. This is where the case stands, Ms. Steele. We know Daniel Savage sold documents to someone. We don't know who. A crowd of foreign scientists from the last remaining Iron Curtain country appears at Wallops Island six weeks after Savage takes off. Sure looks suspicious. We're investigating their backgrounds— trying to get a bead on which one might be Savage's contact. To be honest, I haven't found anything incriminating on any of the scientists yet, except one."

He closed the laptop. "If they're honestly looking to defect, they're hardly going to be plundering classified material. We may have to widen the field."

"You said, 'except one.' So you *do* have a suspect. Is it Vasilinak?"

"Could be, but there's another one who's been seen in odd parts of the campus—like, close to the perimeter."

"Which one?"

He gave her a wry look. "You seriously expect me to disclose that information?"

Worth a try. "Okay, so if you're right, there could be just the one bad apple in the Belarusian bowl, and the others are true scientists. Scientists who only want to be left alone to do their work. I'm sure it's very important work too. Why should they have to suffer because of one wormy Macintosh?"

"Agreed."

"Then you'll help them?"

Peel shook his head. "Nope. It's not in my bailiwick. My focus is on the document thief. I'm after the inside man. Since Savage is gone, I'm guessing he left a cohort behind."

"But—"

He cut her off. "I can let the State Department know of their request, but I've got my hands full." He waved in dismissal. "You know your way out."

Addison stood rigid, fuming. "Well, if you won't lift a finger to facilitate the escape of desperate people from an evil communist state, then I won't tell you my other news."

"Other news? What's that?"

"I'll leave you with this: have you ever seen Daniel

and Nicodemus Savage in the same room?" And with that she stalked out. The receptionist didn't say a word.

Addison stomped to her car, lobbing impolite descriptions of Peel at the sidewalk. *So what if I don't have proof that Dan and Nick are one and the same? It'll at least give that...that heel something to think about.* Halfway back to Chincoteague, she gripped the steering wheel and spoke to the windshield. "If the federal government won't do it, by golly, we'll do it ourselves."

Chapter Sixteen

Vanity makes people ridiculous, pride odious, and ambition terrible.

~Richard Steele

Addison's house, Friday, March 28

"Phoebe? Why haven't you answered your phone? Did you get in touch with Walter?"

Addison heard some rustling, then a rather breathless voice saying, "Oh, er. Hi, Addy. Yes, I did." Her voice faded. "Stop that! C'mon, Wally." She came back. "Walter is with us, but he has to work behind the scenes. He'll lose his job if Klopman thinks he's gone rogue—even if it's to save the scientists."

"Okay, we need to get together and plan. Can you come over for lunch tomorrow?"

"Walter is on duty, and I'm tutoring at school till one. How about if you and I meet at Jim's after that? Next week's Easter vacation. I can really dive in with both feet then."

"All right, just so long as you don't do a belly flop."

****

Addison's house, Saturday morning

Addison was pulling on a sweater, readying herself for a pleasant hike on the Woodland Trail, when the phone rang. It was Darlene, the police chief's secretary. "Addison? Can you hold for a prisoner?"

"A prisoner? Who?"

"The Russian guy—Greg something."

"You mean Grigory Vasilinak. He's not Russian. He's from Belarus."

"Huh." Darlene chewed her gum for a minute. "So, do you want to speak to him or not?"

Sigh. "Yes. Put him on."

"Miss Steele?"

"Yes, Grigory? Don't worry, we have things well in hand. The ideas we discussed? I think we can work it out. You stay put—"

His voice broke through her well-ordered speech. "I can't!" He wailed. "Director Klopman—he has come to bail me out of jail. What do I do?"

"What!" Addison blurted, "Tell him you don't want him to spring you. You don't want to be free. Tell him"—she gulped—"you feel you must atone for beating up a woman."

He snorted. "I don't think that would work. Please come, Miss Steele. He is finishing the paperwork now. I...Excuse me." She could hear him snapping at someone in the room. "Just a minute. It's—" The line went dead.

Addison was in her car and roaring toward the police station five minutes later.

When she reached the parking lot, the director of the Wallops Flight Facility was holding the door open while a thin young man dragged a protesting Vasilinak out of the building.

Red-faced, Klopman shouted, "Why are you complaining, Grigory? You should be thanking me."

The Belarusian saw Addison and shook off the young man's hand. "She—she will make it all clear. Wait!"

Klopman's eyebrows went up, but he did pause. When the young man started pulling Vasilinak again, he held up a hand. "Just a minute, Eric." He addressed Addison. "Who are you?"

"I'm Addison Steele—a friend of Grigory's."

A bewildered expression replaced the frown. "How could you be his friend? He's only been in the country a few days."

"Nonetheless." She looked up and down the empty street, then lowered her voice. "Mr. Klopman, he wants to defect."

"What!"

"*Shh*. Yes. If he stays in jail he's safe from his KGB handler. The plan was to ask for asylum from his cell."

His brow wrinkled. "His KGB handler?"

Grigory swatted Klopman's elbow. "Olga Ilyich Zhuk. Our escort. You didn't know she is KGB?"

"Of course I knew. We have an agreement: she doesn't interfere with your research, and we don't interfere with her…chaperoning."

Addison said sharply, "You don't worry that she's doing a bit of spying on her own?"

Klopman shook his head. "We keep an eye on her at all times. She is under surveillance twenty-four-seven."

"By whom?"

He eyed the young man, Eric. "Security. Monitoring foreign scientists detailed here is a function of the Office of Security."

"While they're at the lab. What about at their lodgings?"

Klopman was growing restive under her questions. "The Belarusian biologists are quartered on the main base in the dormitories maintained by the Wallops Exchange and Morale Association. They can't get into any trouble there. And if you must know, women and men have separate facilities. Miss Zhuk is isolated from her charges."

He clearly wasn't aware that Addison knew better. "She's isolated all right. She's living at the Assateague Inn. Next to Grigory."

The director blinked, then rallied. In the voice he probably used in the lecture hall, he trumpeted, "*Suffice it to say*, we have full knowledge of all her activities."

"So you're aware she tried to run Grigory over with her car."

"We discussed that. She informed us she was avoiding a Sika elk in the road and didn't see Vasilinak in the dark."

"It was one thirty in the afternoon."

"He was in the woods…" He suddenly seemed to recognize he was losing the debate and held up an imperious hand. "That's enough, Miss Steele."

Grigory had been quietly mumbling during this exchange. "My colleagues, Director Klopman. They also want to defect. So you see, I cannot go back to the research station. Olga Ilyich will suspect the truth. It would be bad for us all." A tear welled up in his eye. "She will force us to return to Minsk. We will be punished."

"Return to—?" Klopman rubbed his neck. "Look. We can't talk about this here. Come with me, both of you."

The three of them got in the back of a gray limousine with the NASA emblem on its door. Klopman leaned over the front seat. "Eric, take us to the base."

They drove in silence until they'd gone through the security gates. Klopman's driver left the car with an attendant and followed them to the director's office. He stood, arms folded, leaning against the door. Addison studied him. *He hasn't said a word this whole time.* Klopman called him Eric. *He must be the newcomer Walter mentioned.* Walter had implied there was some history between them. *He doesn't look all that threatening.* Slender and short, he sported a filmy goatee and a man bun, both of which heightened the slightly feminine aura.

Klopman sat down and steepled his fingers. "Now, what's this about defecting?"

Grigory was nonplussed. "Um. Defect. Means stay in United States. Is correct word?" When Klopman didn't answer, he said resolutely, "We don't like communist dictator. We like America. You understand?"

While both Addison and Grigory thought this was more than enough justification, apparently Klopman did not. "Um. I hope you'll reconsider."

Grigory looked at Addison. She asked, "Reconsider?"

"Yes. You see, if I let your group seek asylum, it would cause an international incident. Our program has had to strike a very delicate balance between national security and the need for scientific cooperation. It took years of negotiations. The Belarusians have our word that we won't let you stay in the US when your project is complete."

Addison spluttered, "But that's preposterous. Are you saying you're comfortable ignoring the petition of these long-suffering men?" She stood and held her arms out. "Men who are on their *knees*, begging you to liberate them from subjugation, to fling aside the last obstacle to their freedom?" She sat down, out of breath but proud of herself.

Klopman was unmoved. "My hands are tied." He stood up. "Mr. Vasilinak, your colleagues await you in the lab. Miss Steele, allow me to see you out."

"But—"

Eric stepped forward. "I'll escort her."

The young man hustled her toward the front gate. She wrestled out of his grasp. "How do you expect me to get home? I don't have a car."

He held up a set of keys. "I'll drive you back to the police station." He opened the rear door for her.

She got in the back seat. With an effort, she calmed down. *I'll probably get further with Eric if I cozy up to him.* "So, how long have you worked for Director Klopman?"

"I was assigned to him a month ago."

"Are you a scientist?"

"No."

"Oh." She tried again. "Where were you before?"

"DC."

"With NASA?"

He pulled over onto the verge and turned his head. "I would remind you, Miss Steele, that you are a private citizen. It would be healthier if you kept your mouth shut and your idle hands busy with whatever it is you normally do. Am I making myself clear?"

She said meekly, "Yes."

He dropped her off. She watched the official limo drive away, her thoughts tumbling over and over. Eric had most assuredly threatened her. *But why? Who is he really?*

****

Jim's restaurant, Saturday lunch

It was a depressed Addison that looked up from her menu to see Phoebe. "It's a no-go."

"What? Our riot? Our daring plan to free the oppressed and be cited in high school history books?" Phoebe unbuttoned her coat and hung it on a hook by their booth. She sat with a plop on the opposite bench.

Addison nodded glumly. "Klopman says he doesn't want what he calls 'an incident.' Evidently the US made a promise to the Belarusian government. He sent Grigory back to the lab."

"I know all about it. Walter told me. Thanks, Kitty." She took the menu from the waitress. "I'll have the turkey club and a cup of cocoa."

Addison threw the menu down. "Nothing sounds good. I guess I'm just not hungry." The shadowy figure of last Thursday came to mind. "Anyway, Nick's bringing dinner over tonight at eight."

"Eight? A trifle late, isn't it?"

"I thought so too, but maybe he has something else to do. Or maybe he's worried about Peel catching him."

"That's silly. He's been seen in public all over the island. If Peel wanted to nab him, it wouldn't be hard."

"True." It occurred to Addison that maybe Nick didn't want to wait too long for the after-dinner party. She smiled. "He could have an alternative motive."

Phoebe smacked her lips. "Woo-hoo."

****

Addison's house, Saturday night

Addison would have splashed cold water on her face to keep awake if she hadn't spent the last hour carefully applying makeup for her date with Nick. Her stomach—used to eating at seven—grumbled. She wished for the second time that she'd ordered something at Jim's. *I hope Nick finds bleary-eyed women with iffy gastric issues attractive, because that's what he's going to get if he doesn't get here soon.* She checked the clock again. Eight thirty-five. *He's awfully late.*

The sun had gone down through a haze of moisture-laden clouds, and now the sky was pitch black. Addison sat gazing out the sliding door to the deck, waiting for the lighthouse beam to come back around. The doorbell rang. *At last.*

Nick stood on the front stoop, his face obscured by a stack of Styrofoam boxes. When she opened the screen door, he walked past her and stopped. "Where's the kitchen?"

"Right where it's always been."

"Oh…er…right. Can't see around these boxes." He moved carefully across the floor, stumbled once over the threshold, and dropped them on the counter. Then he turned around.

Addison closed her eyes, expecting him to come to her, take her in his arms, and kiss her. Instead, nothing happened. She opened her eyes. He was staring at her. "What's the matter?"

He pressed his lips together. "Addison? I have to tell you something."

161

Here it comes. Addy, my dear, you've been a chump. "Let's sit down."

"I'd better stand." He took off his heavy jacket and hung it on the banister, then faced her. "I'm not who you think I am."

"You're not a travel writer?" *Already figured that out, fellah.*

"Huh?" He looked momentarily surprised. "No, I'm not. Is that what you thought?"

"That's what you told me." *Why does he seem confused?* "What's the matter? Can't keep your stories straight?"

"Oh, uh. Sure. See...no. I'm not a...travel writer."

Okay. "And I suppose you're not looking for your long-lost brother either?"

"No...Well...In a way, I am."

Muddled, Addison couldn't think of anything to say. *What is going on? Is* everything *a lie? Including...including us?* "Look, Nick, if you don't want to be with me, that's fine. Just say it, and...and leave." Her voice broke on the last word.

His face fell. "That's not what I...I mean, I don't...I can't..." His tense expression cleared. "Oh, golly, that must be it! Hang on." He turned his back on her and fiddled with his face. Then he pivoted toward her and opened his eyes wide.

"You look like you've seen a ghost."

"Look again. Look closely at me, Addison."

Addison was even more muddled. "What are you trying to say?"

"Look hard."

She did. She saw the same old Nick of the jet-black hair and thick biceps. His nose was the same aquiline appendage standing proudly in the center of his tanned face. The high cheekbones reminded her of the portrait of Sitting Bull in the Senate library. His eyes—those beautiful indigo eyes...*Hold your horses.* "What happened to your eyes?"

He held out his hand. She couldn't see anything until he picked something off his palm. A contact lens. He held it up to the light. It was tinted blue. She transferred her gaze to his face again. Eyes the color of rich mahogany gazed back at her. "You're not Nick."

Chapter Seventeen

How is it possible for those who are men of honor in their persons, thus to become notorious liars in their party?

~Joseph Addison

Addison's house, Saturday, March 29

"That's what I've been trying to tell you. I'm Daniel."

She took a step back, her hand over her mouth. "Daniel? Are you…are you…"

"I'm not going to hurt you. I came here to explain. I know Nick's searching for me—"

"Not to mention the FBI."

"Yeah, them too. But they're after the wrong person. They're obstructing my…mission." He held a hand out in supplication. "Addison, I need you to get hold of Nick for me."

"What for?"

"I have to speak with him—in a neutral place. It's urgent."

"I—" A pounding on the front door drowned out the question.

"Miss Steele? It's Robert Peel. Open the door."

Daniel held a finger to his lips. Addison was torn, but barring additional information, she had to break

164

Daniel's way. She silently pointed toward the deck. Daniel slipped out into the darkness. She gave him two minutes, then went to the front door. "This had jolly well be important, Agent Peel. It's almost nine o'clock."

The agent strode past her. "Is someone upstairs?"

His arrogant tone made up her mind for her. She pulled him around to face her. "*Excuse* me? You can't just barge in here. Aren't you supposed to have a warrant? Who the hell do you think you are?"

He paused. She could tell he was trying to wrestle his anger under control. Finally, he growled, "Is Daniel Savage here?"

Addison was elated that she didn't have to lie. If she had, her face would have turned scarlet and a childhood tic in her cheek would most certainly reignite. She would have blinked rapidly and, if pressed, probably fallen down in a full faint. As Phoebe often said, particularly when Addison was trying to get out of doing something, *You, Addy, are the worst liar the world has ever known.* "No, he's not."

"*Was* he here?"

Shoot. Okay, okay. Think. At that moment her eyes swept the room for any sign of Daniel's visit, and fastened on the white jacket that hung from the banister. *Uh oh, that's his.* Something about it…She pivoted to stand in the kitchen door to draw Peel's attention away from the coat. "What makes you think he was?"

"He's been seen in the vicinity."

She pointed at the boxes in the kitchen. "A man delivered my dinner. You probably saw him drive away."

"Oh."

She took advantage of his hesitation. "What's all this about? I should remind you that I don't know Daniel Savage. I only know his brother, Nick."

He grunted. "Seems to me just yesterday you hinted they were the same person."

"Well, they're not."

He cocked his head. "May I ask what changed your mind?"

Damn. "I was just messing with you, Agent Peel. I…uh…it was a wild guess. Like I said, I only know Nick." *After all, I just met Daniel. It's not like I* know *him.* "Now, would you mind leaving? My dinner is getting cold."

He stood his ground. "We have uncovered evidence that Daniel has not left the area."

"What evidence?"

"You remember the lights directed at the Wallops facility?"

"Of course I do. We reported it to you."

He twitched impatiently. "Our expert linguist broke the code."

"So it was definitely Morse code?" Addison sat down hard.

Peel remained standing, his glance darting around the room. "Yes. That guard—Pope—couldn't decipher it because it was in Russian."

"Not in some kind of code?"

"Huh?" His eyes flickered as though this were a new idea for him. Then his lips tightened. "No."

"What did it say?"

"I am not at liberty to tell you, but we're entertaining the possibility that Daniel Savage is communicating with someone at the facility—most likely the spy embedded with the Belarusian biologists."

"I told you yesterday—they all want to defect. Why would they jeopardize their chances?"

"That's the line Grigory Vasilinak gave you. We at the FBI are less gullible." He paused. "Even if *some* of the scientists want to defect, it doesn't mean they *all* do."

"Do you have your sights set on the bad apple?"

"Back to the fruit metaphors, are we? No, we haven't identified who it is yet, but we're sure it's one of the Belarusians."

"On what basis? There are professionals assigned from other countries at Wallops." She thought back to the line of cars at the main gate when she and Phoebe tried to enter. "I've seen Arabs at the base. Why couldn't one of them be the spy?"

"Arabs?" His eyebrows went up. "Did you notice something?"

"No. I saw Frenchmen too. Even our allies spy on us, you know." *Who was Klopman concerned about that day?* "Or it could be an Armenian operative."

"Last I checked, Armenians don't speak Russian. And neither do the French." Peel's words were determined, but Addison thought he seemed momentarily disconcerted.

"Huh. So, what's your plan? Once you figure out who it is, move in and arrest him?"

"Not immediately. We want to monitor their exchanges awhile longer."

Addison recollected her recent conversation with Vasilinak. "Belarusians don't speak Russian either. They speak Belarusian."

"Yes, but Russian is their second official language. They would be conversant in it. In fact"—he rubbed his jaw—"they could be using Russian to avert suspicion."

Addison thought of Grigory's earnest, frightened face. "Nonsense." She went to the door. "Good night, Mr. Peel."

He walked down to his car without another word. Addison had just opened one of the Styrofoam containers when she heard a movement from the living room. "Agent Peel, I told you to go."

"Was that who just roared off in the unmarked car? Friend of yours?"

"Daniel? You came back? That's probably not a good idea."

A man came into the kitchen. Raven hair, powerful build, Roman nose. She peered closer. *Cobalt blue* eyes. "Nick?"

He shook the droplets off his brown raincoat and dropped it over Daniel's jacket.

Addison picked it up and began to hang it on the hook. *Wait! That's it! That's what was different! The man I saw on the dunes wore a white jacket. It was Daniel. That's why he ignored me!* For a second, she was distracted by the revelation. *Nick didn't ignore me after all!*

His voice broke into her happy thoughts. "Was he here?"

"Who? And hello to you too."

"Daniel. *Was he here?*" Nick loomed over her, his eyes glittering.

Addison felt a frisson of fear. *Who can I trust? Are they all bad guys?* "Yes, he was here."

"Did he tell you anything?"

"He didn't have a chance to. Agent Peel showed up."

Nick visibly relaxed. "I take it Agent Peel is the FBI man on my brother's track."

"Yes. You didn't know?"

"I haven't been fortunate enough to meet him face to face." He pursed his lips. "Blast. I thought I could catch Daniel."

Addison sat down on the kitchen chair. "All right, let me get this straight. When we first met, you claimed your brother had drowned at sea. Apparently, you are currently aware that Daniel is alive. Or were you lying before?"

He hung his head. "I was lying."

Well, that was easy. Now what? "Why?"

"Why did I lie to you? I'd only just met you. I doubted it would go over well to tell you I think my brother's in trouble—maybe of his own making—and I'm trying to stay one step ahead of the law."

"Or keep one step between him and the law? Peel tells me you're interfering with his investigation. He says the FBI believes you helped Daniel escape."

He drew back. "Peel told you that? Huh." He peered into the container. "Spaghetti and meatballs. Good choice." He stuck a fork in a meatball and ate it standing up. "You want some?"

The words brought her down to earth. "Nick Savage, tell me the truth. Are you working with your brother?"

"Open the salad container, would you?" He collected two soup plates and spooned some of the spaghetti into each. "Got any wine?"

She tried to stand firm, but she was too hungry.

She gathered glasses, cutlery, and a bottle of Bordeaux and sat down across from Nick. They ate quietly for a few minutes. Addison didn't mind; it gave her time to think of how to phrase her questions. Nick was hiding something. *No—he's hiding a* lot. Was he a bad guy? A good guy? In her experience, congenital liars were generally not good guys. *But he's so good-looking. And warm. And funny.* "Daniel has brown eyes."

"I know."

"He's been wearing tinted contact lenses."

"Ah, that explains it."

"Explains what?"

"Why I keep getting in trouble with you."

Addison stopped, a slice of tomato halfway to her mouth. "What do you mean? Has he been—" *Oh my God—Alexandria?* "Was he the one I…uh…talked to in Alexandria?"

Nick cocked his head. "He was in Alexandria? I suppose he was checking in with his organization." He peered at her. "You met him?"

"We…uh…had lunch. I thought he was you."

"And he didn't disabuse you. He didn't try anything, did he?"

She visualized Daniel's disappointed face when she refused his invitation to go back to his hotel with him. "No." She took a big swallow of wine.

"I wouldn't put it past him. He's never been able to resist a beautiful woman. I wish I knew if he was aware of our…relationship." He reddened.

Addison resisted the impulse to ask, "Oh, do we have a relationship?" and instead observed, "If he's been tracking us, he probably does. Why else disguise his eye color?" She frowned. "Does he often impersonate you to meet women?"

He chortled. "He doesn't need any tricks to acquire lovers, if that's what you mean. It's more likely he wanted to pass as me to put off the FBI."

"That wouldn't help him, since Peel's after you too." She inspected him. "You are twins, aren't you?"

"Fraternal. Hence the variation in eye color. We are very much alike, as proven by your failure to distinguish the superior one."

This was going nowhere. She didn't want to be an accessory to whatever he and Daniel were up to. She dabbed a napkin on her lips. "It's time you came clean."

"I can't. Not yet. First, I need to find Daniel."

"Well, you're in luck. He wants to find you too."

His eyes narrowed. "Really?"

Chapter Eighteen

*If men would consider not so much wherein they differ,
as wherein they agree, there would be far less of
uncharitableness and angry feeling in the world.*

                                                    ~Joseph Addison

Addison's house, Saturday, March 29

"Are you surprised?"

"That Daniel wants to talk to me? Yes. I've been
assuming he's on the lam." Nick's brow furrowed.
"Maybe he *does* want my help."

*Now we're getting somewhere. That means Nick
isn't already involved.* "He only said he wanted to talk
to you—he didn't say anything about needing help."

"And this occurred before Peel arrived?"

She nodded. "Dan ran out the back way."

He sipped from his wine glass. "Do we have my
brother to thank for the feast?"

"The spaghetti? Yes. I provided the wine."

Nick scooped up another meatball. "Too bad he
had to make himself scarce. Guess he'll go hungry
tonight."

"He can always get more food."

"I don't think so. I'm betting he's back in his
hiding place by now."

"And where is that?"

"I'm pretty sure it's the Hook. When I took the boat out yesterday, I found the remains of a fire a few yards from the shore. Next to it was an indentation in the sand—marks of a sleeping bag. My guess is he's been camping out there."

"Do you think he'll go back to the same spot, though? Peel is on his trail. He knows the messages are originating from somewhere around Tom's Cove. He's working on the theory that one of the Belarusians is receiving them."

"Messages?"

She put her fork down. "You don't know about the flashing lights?"

He shook his head. "First I've heard. I admit I hadn't the foggiest why Daniel has stayed in the area. If his job was to lift the documents, he should have cleared out once he got hold of them. But he stuck around—why?"

"He—or someone—has been sending Morse code messages in Russian to the Wallops facility."

"How do you know?"

"We saw them." Addison had a moment's hesitation. "To be honest, I only saw the reflection on the water. The others disagree as to the source, as well as to whom they're directed."

"We?"

"Phoebe, Walter, and I."

"So where does the FBI agent come in?"

"We reported it to him. He sent the code to his forensics people. They say it's in Russian."

Nick rubbed his jaw. "If Daniel's the one sending the signals, he'll continue to use his camp site. If it's not him, that means his mission is over."

173

"Mission?"

"The documents."

"But he stole those weeks ago! Like you say, he's still around. What could he be doing now?"

Nick poured more wine into each glass. "Maybe he's arranging a ride back to Belarus...or to Russia."

She sucked in a breath. "You're accusing your brother of being a Russian agent?"

Grief washed over Nick's craggy features. "It's the only explanation. Look, I love my brother. But we haven't spoken in five years. We had a...falling-out."

"What happened?"

He put his glass down. "A difference of opinion. He'd taken up with some extreme leftists. They advocated insurrection to take down America and transform it into a communist state." He grimaced. "They had secret enclaves set up around the country and were stockpiling weapons and training their recruits in urban warfare. How to blend in with protesters and start a riot, or encourage looting—that sort of thing."

"Oh dear."

Nick's gaze went blank, as though he were going back in time. "Daniel seemed to harden before my eyes. If I tried to talk to him, he'd spout some drivel from their pamphlets about establishing a new world order once the privileged elite was destroyed." He shook his head. "Where do they get this tripe? It never crossed his mind that if the wealthy were gone, there wouldn't be anybody left to pay for all the free stuff he wants. And nobody to produce it. Finally, I gave up. He took off for Europe soon after that." He rubbed his temple. "We lost touch."

"How did you find him again? Did he contact

you?"

Nick shook his head. "No. I…learned about the theft of the files and that he was suspected. When I came down here, I tried to find him—to convince him to turn himself in."

Addison examined his face. "You…learned. About the files. Nick, *who are you really?*"

He slurped up some spaghetti and wiped his mouth with a napkin. "A concerned citizen."

"All right then." She decided to circle around. "Why does *Daniel* want to see *you?*"

At that he threw up his hands, flinging a dollop of tomato sauce onto her shirt.

"Nick!"

"Oops. Sorry."

He tried to sop up the stain, but she brushed his hand away angrily. "I think you should go."

His eyes pleaded. "But…"

"No. Until you can tell me the truth, we're done. Go do whatever it is you plan to do and leave me out of it."

He rose. "For the record, that was the truth. In fact, almost everything I've told you is the truth. I thought Daniel was dead. When I discovered that he might be alive, I hoped to reconnect, get him to do the right thing. And I *am* a travel writer." His stare was steady.

She rose too. "Telling me the truth is not the same as telling me the *whole* truth. Goodbye, Nick."

****

Addison's house, Sunday morning

Addison didn't want to answer the phone, but it wouldn't stop ringing. When it finally went to voicemail, Phoebe's soprano blared, "Addy, I know you're there. Your car's in front. Plus, I can see you on the couch."

Addison rose on an elbow. Sure enough, Phoebe's face was pasted to the glass door. A phone was stuck to her ear.

"Let me in!"

Addison sat up. The room whirled around her. She waited until her head stopped spinning, then stood. Something wet trickled down her leg. She pulled her sock off and smelled it. *Whiskey. Now where?* The empty tumbler lay on its side on the floor. She picked it up and shambled to the sliding door.

Her cousin's nose wrinkled. "P U. Smells like a tacky bar in here." She went to the kitchen, filled a glass with water, and brought it back to Addison. "Let me guess. You had a tiff with lover boy."

"Oh, Phoebe." The tears began to fall again. "It's over."

"There, there." Phoebe sat carefully on a chair. "It had hardly begun."

"I...I know. It's just..." Addison lowered her hands from a mournful face. "I really liked him."

"So what's the problem?"

"I don't trust him."

"Is that all?" Phoebe settled back on the cushion and said comfortably, "You can't trust any man. You think I trust Walter?"

"You don't?"

"Of course not. He'll say anything to get into my pants. He even offered to give my class a VIP tour behind the scenes at the launch facility. Like he didn't already owe me one. And I know he's only agreed to lend a hand with the defectors to gain brownie points with me."

Addison giggled. "Are you going to reward him?"

Phoebe winked. "Some day soon. Now, why don't you go upstairs and wipe the mascara off your nose?"

Addison rose. She put a hand on the banister and noticed Daniel's jacket was gone. Did Nick take it? *Or did Daniel come back while I was asleep?* To stave off fresh tears, she squeaked, "You free for lunch?"

"Aren't I always?"

Thank God. "Let's get Sonic burgers and go out to the beach."

"Uh-uh. The food will be cold by the time we get to the refuge. Sonic has a picnic table in the parking lot. We can eat there."

"Okay. A bit romantic for my blood, but why not."

****

Sonic drive-in, T's Corner, Sunday midday

They were sitting in the sun at an old wooden picnic table when the sirens started up. As the women watched, police cruisers, cherry lights spinning, careened in and out among the cars on Route 13. Behind them roared an ambulance and behind that a fire truck.

"Must be an accident." Phoebe sipped her soda.

"They're turning down Chincoteague Road."

"Really? It's gotta be big if the Chincoteague Fire Department can't handle it." Phoebe was dunking a fry in a puddle of ketchup on the burger wrapping when her cell phone tinkled. "Hello? Oh, hi, Walter...Slow down. What? *What?* We'll be right there! What? Oh, come *on.*" Her tone turned wheedling. "We won't get in the way. It would be so exciting...well, thanks a *lot.* Why'd you bother calling me?" She jabbed at the talk button.

Addison assumed Phoebe would elucidate, but the girl just sat there, tapping a nail in staccato time on the table. "Phoebe?"

She huffed. "That was Walter."

"I know."

"There's been a murder at the base."

"A murder! Who?" A picture of Daniel rose before her. "Not…not someone we know?"

"Uh-huh."

Addison resisted the urge to shake her cousin. "Who?"

"One of the Belarusians. Their leader."

"Grigory Vasilinak? The man I talked to?"

"That's him. These Slavic names all sound alike, don't they?"

One. Two. Three. "What else did Walter say?"

"Besides that we can't go and view the corpse? He was found in a storeroom. Stabbed with a penknife." She licked her lips. "The knife was still sticking in him when the janitor found him."

Addison slammed her palms down, knocking her cup over. Syrupy liquid dripped onto the pavement. "Olga. The KGB agent. She killed him."

Phoebe pressed her lips together. "I'm sure a KGB officer would have no qualms about murder, but isn't that a bit obvious? And would she use a penknife? You'd think she'd have a gun."

"A gun!"

Phoebe ignored Addison's shocked face. "Yeah—a tiny folding pistol. Three-D plastic. The kind the metal detectors can't spot. Or maybe a poison vial. One of those rings that hold poison, like the Borgias used." Her

178

eyes widened with enthusiasm. "Or a lethal shoe."

"Are you done?"

"For now. But I'll have more after I tackle Walter tonight."

"Don't encourage him."

Chapter Nineteen

Though her mien carries much more invitation than command, to behold her is an immediate check to loose behaviour; to love her was a liberal education.
                                        ~Richard Steele

Addison's house, Monday, March 31

"What's the scoop? Did you get anything out of Walter?"

"*Mmph, mmph.*"

"Phoebe? Are you still eating?"

The earpiece filled with the sound of swallowing. "I'm on vacation, Addy. It's spring break. And it's only nine o'clock."

"Is Walter there?"

"Of course not. And no, he didn't just leave. I told you—we're going slow. I want to see how much groveling he'll do before I bestow my favors."

"You're a hard woman. Did he at least give you the skinny on Grigory?"

"He did indeed."

"I'm coming over." Addison reached Phoebe's house on North Main in record time. "Well?"

Phoebe was putting the last dish in the dishwater. She wiped her hands on a dish towel. "Coffee?"

"Yes, thanks."

"Let's go out on the deck."

They sat down on splintery Adirondack chairs and gazed out over Chincoteague Bay. The marsh flats shone golden in the cold sun. A fisherman putt-putted by, his empty crab traps piled in the bow of his Sinepuxent Bay skiff. Oystercatchers delicately picked their way among the muddy shells exposed by the low tide, poking at oysters with their long orange bills. A loon called. The traffic behind them on Main Street was light for a Monday, and the kind of peace you feel when snow is softly falling descended on the two women.

Addison didn't let it last long. She took a sip of coffee from her mug. "Okay, give."

Phoebe sighed. "Poor Walter, he so wants to impress me. He must have read somewhere that the way to a woman's bed is through her friend."

"Meaning me?"

"Yup. See, he spent Friday and Saturday encouraging the Belarusian fellow to go for it. The two of them concocted the whole scheme."

"Scheme? What did it entail?"

"Walter's assignment was to find a getaway car."

"Getaway car. Are they going to rob a bank before they leave?"

"No, silly. Let me finish." Phoebe giggled. "They needed a car no one would recognize, one that could be ditched later."

"Huh." Addison kept her impatience reined in by holding her breath and counting to ten.

"So—Walter actually snagged one! You remember that old Ford truck Jedediah Funt's had on blocks for years? He was willing to let Walter take it off his hands for fifty bucks."

"Is it drivable?"

"It wasn't. Walter had it towed to the Graffitti brothers' garage, and they tinkered with it until they got it running. After all, it only had to get the men as far as Salisbury. They'd stash it there and board a Greyhound bus for Washington."

"I see. So when was all this supposed to go off?"

"It did go off. Well, almost. Yesterday. First, Walter picked up the leader—"

"Vasilinak."

"—At the Assateague Inn at three a.m. on Sunday morning. They drove to the main base, then around to the back door of the men's dorm. While Vasilinak snuck in to collect the others, Walter stayed with the car, ready to jump out when they arrived."

"Leaving the foreigners to drive off?"

"Right, and eventually make their way to the embassy in DC."

"Okay, but these guys probably don't have American driver's licenses and they've only been in the country a few weeks. How would they know where to go? Why wouldn't Walter drive them himself?"

Phoebe gave her a superior smile. "Because this way he wouldn't be linked to them. He'd stroll in for his shift at eight, act surprised, and enthusiastically join in the search for the defectors."

Addison checked her cousin's face. "But something went wrong."

"Right. Walter dropped Vasilinak off as per the plan, but then he waited and waited. Nobody came. About four a.m. he figured they'd gotten cold feet, and he left. He couldn't risk being seen by the early shift."

"And when he came back later, there was indeed a

search going on."

"Nope."

"Why not?"

" 'Cause Vasilinak wasn't supposed to be there. As far as the staff was concerned, he was still at the Assateague Inn, sleeping. It was only when the janitor found the body that they knew he had entered the base."

"Oh dear. What about the other scientists?"

"I think they're being kept in their rooms." Phoebe made a face. "Vasilinak—against Walter's wishes—informed them of the plan ahead of time, so now they're in hot water too. Walter is furious that Grigory leaked it."

"He's right. I'll bet someone heard them talking and took matters into his own hands." Addison took a sip from her mug. "So what's the status now?"

"They're investigating the crime scene, but Walter says they're zeroing in on Elephant Woman."

"The KGB agent. Olga Zhuk."

"That's her." Phoebe snorted. "The police must not go by Agatha Christie rules."

"It's never the most obvious one?"

"Yeah."

"Will they arrest her?"

"No idea." She frowned. "Can they? Arrest her?"

"I don't know. I guess we'll find out." Addison's mood darkened. Even though she had barely known the Belarusian, she felt responsible for him and his colleagues. "I wish we could have come through for them."

"Yeah, well, we did our best. It isn't Walter's fault Vasilinak was bumped off." Phoebe got up. "I've got to drive to Pocomoke City for some art supplies for the class. You wanna come?"

"I don't think so. I'm going to go home and work on Eliza."

"Eliza?"

"Eliza Haywood, the erotica authoress."

"Let me get this straight. You're into pornography now? Nick not enough for you?"

"I told you. It's over between us." Addison sighed.

"I see." Phoebe rolled her eyes.

"It's just…just really interesting. See, there was a whole coterie of female scriveners who wrote quite unladylike books long before George Eliot and the Brontës upset the literary world. They were independent, they didn't use male pseudonyms, and they promoted an adventurous sexual life for women."

"*Hmm.* I'll have to look her up. Or should I wait for your blockbuster exposé to come out?"

"It'll be a while. I have to do it on my own time. Then I'll have to find a publisher."

"The Government Printing Office won't do it? They're printing your bibliography, aren't they?"

"They only publish work products—and even then, they're pretty choosy." Addison gazed unseeing at the water.

Phoebe paused. "Penny for your thoughts?"

"Huh? Oh, it's just…well, there was a persistent rumor that Eliza Haywood had an affair with Sir Richard Steele. He was—"

"I know who he was. I had to listen to the agonizing epic narration of the family tree every Christmas just like you did."

"Oh, right. Well, anyway, the scuttlebutt was that she'd had a child by him. But—"

Phoebe squealed. "I never heard that! I wonder if Nana was aware of it…Or she was and didn't think it appropriate for tender little ears?" Her eyes sparkled. "So…is it true?"

Addison shook herself irritably. "It was never proven. Most contemporaries of the two asserted it was a smear campaign launched by the poet Richard Savage, and that her child was in fact sired by Savage, not Steele."

Phoebe whistled. "Savage? As in—"

Addison cut her off. "I have no idea. It's a…common name." *Phoebe doesn't need any more arrows for her gossip quiver.*

"Kinda makes you shiver though, doesn't it?" Phoebe checked her watch. "I gotta go."

Addison followed her cousin out and drove home. Her day seemed suddenly bleak. The thought that she might have made a mistake sending Nick away intruded. She pushed it away.

****

Addison's house, Monday afternoon

"That's it. I'm done with Eliza. I swear her love life was umpteen times more impressive than mine." Addison closed the book. "*Love in Excess* will have to wait until I'm in a more…amatory mood." She checked her watch. A perfect time for a ramble.

She pulled on her hiking boots and drove across the bridge to the refuge. The temperature had gradually risen during the day, but the clouds were heavy with moisture. *It'll rain tonight for sure.* The parking lots at most of the trail heads were full, so she kept on until she reached the ocean. The visitor center and beaches were deserted. *Better weather for bird watching than basking, I imagine.* The mist rising from the ocean as the warm air hit the cold water made visibility pretty poor but lent a Scottish Highland feel to the scene. She crossed the dune and headed north. *Might as well take a gander at the wishing tree.*

By the time she reached the scraggy oak, the mist had thickened into fog, erasing the line between the ground and the air. She checked for her token. *Yup, still there. That settles it: Seth's never coming back.* Loneliness struck her like a brick to the head. *I'm never going to be happy, never find love again.* But then the familiar anger returned. *Why did you do this to me, Seth? Why did you abandon me? We had such wonderful plans—a life of travel, adventure, and romance ahead of us. Years and years of bliss.* All at the bottom of the sea. She reached a hand out to rip the cloth from the tree. *I'll throw it away myself—that'll stop this endless merry-go-round of grief.*

A dark shape moved just past her range of vision. It was about ten yards away, down close to the water. Her hand stopped in midair, and she shaded her eyes. *Too big for a sandpiper. Maybe a heron?* She wandered from the tree down to where the waves muddled against the sand. The figure loomed a few yards away. *Whaddya know, it's a person.*

Tall, broad shoulders. Pale jacket outlined against the milky air. It must be Daniel again. *What on earth is he doing way up here?* Beyond the wishing tree, Assateague was mainly wild, undeveloped land. *Wait—isn't there an old life-saving station not too far up? Pope's Island, right. Pope. Huh. As in Walter's family?* He did say he was raised in New Church. The hamlet lay only fourteen miles away off Route 13. She resolved to ask him when she saw him next.

I wonder how much is left of the station. The boathouse had been moved in the '60s, and the living quarters had been allowed to fall into disrepair. Maybe Daniel had found shelter there. She stared into the gloom, but he was no longer visible. She slowed, her mind occupied with a new consideration. If Daniel was here on the north end of Assateague, that would mean he wasn't camping on Tom's Cove after all. If so, who left the campfire ashes on the Hook?

Never mind that. What did he want with Nick? She weighed possible motives for Daniel's peace feelers. What did he expect to come out of a meeting with his brother? Did he intend to confess? Declare his innocence? Enlighten Nick as to his travel schedule? Too bad Peel showed up when he did. Was Daniel willing to do what Nick asked and turn himself in? *There's only one person who knows the answer to that question, and he's heading up the beach right now.* She started to run. With luck she would find him at the ruined building.

A few minutes later, the figure hove into view. He was walking very fast, almost as though he knew he was being followed. He picked up his pace, breaking into a trot.

She lost him in the fog again. "Daniel! It's me, Addison!"

As she bent over, trying to catch her breath, she felt a presence move into her sphere. "Daniel?"

"No."

Chapter Twenty

There is nothing which we receive with so much reluctance as advice.

~*Joseph Addison*

Assateague beach, Monday, March 31

She shot up. Her head banged into a solid object. "What the hell?"

Nick stood over her holding his chest. "Ouf! You give new meaning to the term 'hard-headed.' "

"Sorry. I…I…thought I saw your brother."

"Should I be jealous?" He gave her a half smile.

"No." She straightened and pointed north. "He was heading up there in a big hurry."

"Do you think he knew you were following him?"

"I don't know. I lost him in the fog."

He stared into the curtains of swirling gray. "Well, he's gone now."

"Nick? Is it possible he might have moved his camp up here from the Hook? There's a dilapidated rescue station on Pope's Island a few miles from here near the Maryland-Virginia line. It's empty country and would make good cover for him. After all, the Hook is just a sandy spit. He was easier to spot there."

"It's possible. The ashes at the campsite were still warm, but that was back on Friday. He does seem able

188

to stay one step ahead of everyone."

"Shall we go after him?"

He shook his head. "We'd never find him in this glop. Besides, he could have left the beach and climbed over the dunes anywhere." He stuck his hands in his pockets. "Might as well turn back."

They stayed close to the water as they walked. "You haven't heard from Daniel since the night he came to my house?"

"Uh-uh. I did hear about the Belarusian's death, though."

Addison tried to speak, but the words stuck in her throat. She finally managed, "Do you...do you think Daniel had anything to do with it?"

"I sure hope not." He stopped short. "If Vasilinak were his contact, that would explain why he abandoned the Hook site."

"Why?"

"His partner's dead. My guess is he's looking for temporary shelter until he can decamp."

Addison mused, "If Grigory were his contact, that means Daniel's a good guy, not a bad guy."

"And how do you deduce that?"

"I knew Grigory. He was no spy. He wanted to defect."

"He *what?*"

"He told me that he and the other Belarusians wish to request asylum in the United States."

Nick stared at her. "He told *you?* Why you?"

Addison, whose feet were becoming increasingly cold and wet, tugged on his sleeve. "Let's keep moving while I talk. He wanted to use my boat, but it's in storage. So Phoebe and Walter and I—"

"Phoebe...your cousin. Who's Walter?"

"Walter Pope. He's a security guard at the Wallops facility. They're sweet on each other."

"How heartwarming."

"He's a local boy. In fact, his family may have some connection to the Pope's Island station."

"Where you're postulating Daniel is hiding?"

"Yes. Walter would know what condition it's in. I'll ask him when we have our next planning meeting."

"Planning meeting? I have a horrible feeling you're going to tell me you hatched a plot to disgorge a gaggle of Eastern European scientists into the wilds of America."

"Why horrible?"

"Because you're not professionals. You're in way over your head. And you could land yourselves in the soup. At the very least."

Addison stuck her lip out. "I tried to get Agent Peel to do it, but he refused. He's too busy tracking down your brother."

"He doesn't think the Belarusians and Daniel are in league together?"

"He's not sure, but he's concentrating on identifying a second spy he claims is embedded with the biologists."

Nick was quiet. Finally, he said, "Addison, a man is dead. I think you and your friends should back off immediately."

"Well, *someone's* got to help them," she grumbled.

"It can't be you. Addison, if you persist, I'll...I'll—"

"You'll what?"

"I'll tattle to the authorities."

She knew it was an empty threat, but it seemed they were at an impasse, so she didn't argue. "Okay, we'll lay off." *For now.*

They were almost to the wishing tree when Nick said jauntily, "By the way, what are you doing out here in the misty mist and the dusky dusk?"

"Now we're quoting the *Wizard of Oz*?"

He grinned and ducked his head. "Unusual weather we're havin'."

"Ha-ha. I'm taking a break from Eliza."

"Eliza who? Are you two-timing me?"

She grinned. "In a way. She was a famous eighteenth-century English romance writer. I'm doing research on her."

" 'Research'? Is that what they're calling it now?"

Addison thanked God for the fog that hid her blush. "I'm toying with the idea of writing a book on English female authors. Eliza was one of the more prominent ones of the early eighteenth century, and I've been reading some of her books. They're pretty heady. After a few hours, you have to get some fresh air."

"Indeed. The experts all agree it's important to step back from porn now and then. They say it's addictive."

"Porn is a stretch. Her works are more of the swashbuckling hero and fainting damsel genre, but they do get the juices flowing sometimes." She snapped her mouth shut when she realized what she'd just said. "So...er...what are *you* doing out here?"

Nick didn't appear to hear—or at least to dwell on the double entendre. He held up his phone. "I'm trying to capture some evocative shots of birds. See?"

She studied the photo on his screen. It showed a black skimmer emerging from a low-hanging cloud to soar just above the waves, its bill open to scoop up surf fishes. "I love the stark contrast between his bright orange bill and his black body, set against the protean grays of sea and sky."

When she looked up, he was gazing at her. "Addison? Are you still? Are we? Could we—?"

She kissed him. When she opened her eyes, she caught a glimpse of an object flying past them. "What was that?"

"It came from the wishing tree." He ran toward the water and picked something up off the sand. "It's a piece of cloth." He brought it back to her.

Her heart slammed against her ribcage. *Could it be? Seth...oh Seth. Are you coming back to me?* She held her hand out. Nick gave her the scrap. She blinked twice. *It's not mine. Thank God.*

"Are you okay?"

She blinked again. "Um, yes. Shall we go?" She stuck the scrap in her pocket. She had to get home, be alone. She wanted to reflect on this novel reaction. *Am I finally surrendering the sorrow? Is it time?* It had only been a year. It wasn't fair to his memory. He was her husband. She wasn't supposed to slough him off like some hermit crab looking for a new shell. The familiar guilt sloshed over her. Then she caught a glimpse of Nick's profile, and her heart lurched.

He tentatively took her hand. "Was that...was that your token?"

"No." *Oh dear, I should have put it back on the tree!* She felt for the cloth in her pocket. *If I don't return it, am I altering someone's future? Smashing some young thing's dreams?* She peeked at Nick again and an unanticipated euphoria flooded her soul. *You know what? It doesn't matter. Whoever it is will find her heart's desire all on her own.* She held Nick's hand tightly as they walked back to the parking lot. She was getting into her Subaru when she noticed it was the only one in the lot. "Where's your Hummer?"

"I biked." He pointed to a rack by the visitor center.

Now's a good time to find out. "Where are you staying, by the way?"

He made a wry face. "I found a place through one of those online sites."

"Something wrong with it?"

"I should have read the description a little more carefully. Turned out to be the detached garage of this guy who runs a tour boat out of the Merritt marina." He shook his head. "He also owns the derelict launch from which I took a header."

"Not Jedediah Funt again? He's always trying to rent that run-down old shed. The chamber of commerce refuses to list it."

"Well, unluckily for me, he's discovered how easy it is to fudge on your Air Hostel posting. It consists of a cot, a chair, a shower, and a full set of truck tires."

She laughed. "When God gives you tires…"

"I know. Make a tire swing." He stood, rocking the bike handlebars back and forth.

"Well."

"Well." He threw a leg over the cross bar. "Better ride."

"Yes."

"You heading home?"

"Yes."

"See you there?"

"Yes."

****

Addison's house, Tuesday, late morning

"Well, I must say, your bed is far more accommodating than the army cot in Funt's garage."

"Faint praise." Addison rose and drew on a bathrobe. "I've got to feed Mopsy."

"The bunny? Peter's sibling?"

"No, the cat, so named because he looks like Beatrix Potter's rabbit. And he came from a litter of three."

"Let me guess: the others are Flopsy and Cottontail. Where are they?"

"Flopsy's in Old Town. Peter opted to stay with my brother's family."

Nick pulled on his pants and followed her downstairs. Addison went to the kitchen and poured some dry food into Mopsy's bowl, which he promptly knocked over. As she tried to sweep up the nuggets, he chased them around the floor, batting at them with a paw. "Stop that! I'm not giving you Fancy Feast. You're too fat as it is."

"Then you should let him play with his food. Good exercise." Nick opened the front door. "I see you subscribe to the local newspaper. I wonder if the police have discovered anything new on Vasilinak's death." He checked the headline. "It says 'Police Stymied by Closet Killer.' Editor-in-chief appears to have a sense of humor." He rattled the paper. "I guess that means they don't have a suspect."

Addison held onto the bowl to keep Mopsy from knocking it over again. The cat stalked out, tail swishing angrily. "It's got to be Olga, their KGB handler. I don't know why Leonard hasn't arrested her yet."

"Leonard?"

"Leonard Hogarth, chief of Chincoteague Police."

"I'm not sure he has jurisdiction. Wouldn't it be NASA?"

"That I don't know."

Nick helped himself to toast. "You're going on the assumption that this KGB person uncovered their defection plot?"

"Uh-huh. Olga must have figured out what they were up to when she saw me with Grigory."

"Tell you what: you seem to be on a first-name basis with the police. Why don't we ask this Leonard?"

"He's probably busy."

"Well, *yeah*. It's a safe bet if there's a homicide investigation, he'll be in the midst of it, if only to protect his turf."

"From whom?"

"From whom? The military? The state department? How about the county sheriff? They usually do criminal investigations. Or worse—from the FBI. That Peel guy. We need this Hogarth to keep us in the loop."

"I doubt very much whether any of them are willing to keep Leonard *himself* in the loop."

"Ah, but you're a witness. You can insist the only one you'll talk to is the Chincoteague police chief."

"Witness? I didn't see Grigory killed."

This only thwarted Nick for a minute. "Okay, but you may be the last person to have seen him alive. You told me you met with him. When was that?"

"Last Thursday. He asked me to meet him at the Assateague Inn."

"And that was the last time you saw him?"

"No—I visited him in jail on Saturday. There were at least five other people there. We all drove to the base. I left him with Director Klopman...Let's see...He also must have met with Walter to finalize their plans."

"Oh." He rallied. "Still, you were the one he confessed to. You were closest to him. The police will want to talk to you."

Addison didn't expect Leonard would agree but dialed the police station number. "Hi, Darlene. Addison Steele. Is Leonard in? Can I talk to him?" She waited. "Leonard? Oh, you do? All right. I'll be there in twenty." She hung up.

"I take it he wants to see you in person." She could tell he was dying to say "I told you so" but manfully resisting the temptation.

Good move, Nico. She started up to her bedroom. "Since Lenny brushed Agent Peel off, I seem to be his only friend. They're concentrating on Olga, but for some reason he wants to interview me."

"Probably suspects you had a hand in orchestrating the escape."

"Oh dear. Really?"

"Well, didn't you?"

Addison had no answer. She got dressed. After a brief discussion (read battle), she let Nick accompany her to the station. As they parked, an Accomack County sheriff's car left the lot, revealing Klopman's gray NASA limo idling at the curb. Addison glimpsed Eric at the wheel. He was frowning. As she watched, Klopman strode out of the building and jumped in the back of the car. It roared off.

Darlene led them to the door marked Captain

Hogarth and knocked.

"Come in." Leonard let Addison in and started to close the door on Nick, who stuck a foot in between. "I'm with her."

"Who the hell are you?"

"Nick Savage."

Leonard started. "Savage?" His hand went to the phone on his belt.

"Not that Savage. I'm Nick. His brother."

Leonard squinted at him. "You wanna tell me why you're here?"

"Later." He strode to the middle of the room.

Hogarth would have stood toe to toe with Nick were it not for the thick, protective layer of cellulose in his midsection. Instead, he sat down at his desk and groused, "All right. What do you want?"

Addison glared at him. "*You* summoned *me*."

Before he could answer, Nick jumped in. "First, have you taken Olga Zhuk—the KGB agent—into custody?"

"No, and don't get me started. The sheriff has assigned his new detective to the case, and the nitwit wants to do a full investigation. Believe me, the Wallops director was none too happy about it."

"Yes, we saw them leaving."

"Klopman is threatening to go over the sheriff's head if need be. According to him, Olga has diplomatic immunity."

Nick stirred. "She can be deported though, can't she?"

"One would think so, wouldn't one?"

At that moment, Darlene called from her desk in the outer room. "Lenny? Director Klopman's assistant

Eric is on the line."

Leonard picked up the handset. "Chief Hogarth." He listened. "Oh, really? Did you inform the sheriff? Okay. Thanks for letting me know." He didn't look like he meant it.

"What was that all about?"

"I thought Friedrich Klopman would go to the State Department or the FBI, but no. He went right to the top. The Belarus embassy."

Chapter Twenty-One

Encourage innocent amusement.

~Joseph Addison

Chincoteague police station, Tuesday, April 1

"The Belarus embassy! That doesn't seem kosher. If you'll pardon the expression."

Lenny was sanguine. "Not my call. According to Klopman, the ambassador had a little chat with Governor Dingus. Miss Zhuk stays."

"But she may have murdered Grigory!"

"Number one, 'may' is the operative word. We don't have enough evidence to charge her. And number two, we're not allowed to investigate her, so we'll *never* have enough evidence to charge her."

"You'd think the Belarusians would be happy to be rid of her."

"You'd think so, but they were adamant."

Nick leaned forward. "Really? What reason did they give?"

"The embassy asserts she is mandatory personnel. Every Belarusian citizen who goes overseas must have a KGB handler. I gather Belarus is independent of Russia but has a communist dictator running it. So it's just as bad as it was under the Soviet Union."

"That's true." When the other two looked at Nick,

he said quietly, "Lukashenkov has ruled Belarus with an iron fist since 1994. While the other former satellite countries are tasting liberty and capitalism for the first time, the poor Belarusians are stuck with a stagnating economy behind barbed wire fences."

"Well, it's not that they're ignorant of what's going on in the outside world." Addison didn't like the intimation that Belarusians were fine with the situation. "Vasilinak and his colleagues are fully aware of the joys of free speech and fair elections. Hence the desire to defect."

"You're right." Nick smiled at her. "And why Lukashenkov has been dealing with massive protests."

"How do you know so much about Belarus?" Leonard regarded Nick with ill-concealed mistrust.

Nick said mildly, "News junkie. So how come they couldn't simply replace Zhuk?"

The policeman dropped his gaze. "They claim there's a shortage of handlers—"

"Just can't get enough good spies these days, can you?"

Leonard didn't laugh. Addison did.

"Bottom line, she stays." The chief tapped a pencil on the desk. "Wallops is a federal facility. They have plenty of internal security to keep an eye on her."

Internal…"Lenny? We…uh…have a way to keep tabs on what goes on at the base."

"How?"

Should I tell him about Walter? "Er…I know someone who works there."

Lenny stared at her expectantly.

Nick shifted on the chair. "You mean Walter?"

Lenny turned to him. "Who's Walter?"

Ulp. "A security guard there. He's dating Phoebe."

"Huh."

Before Lenny could ask any more uncomfortable questions, Addison reverted to the subject of her protégés. "Speaking of security, what about the other members of the Belarusian team?"

"They're confined to quarters."

Nick asked, "And what have they done with Vasilinak's body?"

"It's at the district morgue in Norfolk. Now, if you'll excuse me." Leonard opened a file and pretended to read.

Addison wasn't about to be dismissed. "Lenny? Hello? You haven't told me yet why you asked me down here?"

The chief closed the file with a sigh. "I had planned to interview you on your contacts with the Belarusians—I know Vasilinak confided in you that they wanted to defect. But the whole thing seems moot now. Besides..." He picked up his keys. "NHL playoffs have begun. The Caps play the Bruins today. Puck drops at one." He got his hat from the hook and preceded them out of the station.

Addison brooded on the way home. "It's so sad. They were so close to breaking out."

"It's a dangerous game—defection."

"Yes. I know a hairdresser from Hungary. She told me the most harrowing tale of her escape. They hitched a ride with an American, and he drove them as close to the Italian border as they could get. They literally leapt over the wall under a hail of bullets."

Nick nodded. "Americans have forgotten—or don't learn in school—what life is like in communist countries. Young folks rarely ask the obvious question: if socialism is so great, why do so many people want to escape it?" He stopped the car in front of her house. "I've some research to do this afternoon before I head out to the refuge." He glanced at her out of the corner of his eye.

She felt a distinct lowering of temperature. *Quick, think of something!* "Er, how about a spot of lunch before you go?"

He perked up. "Good idea. I *am* a bit peckish." He turned off the engine and jumped out.

Amid the rush of pleasure, Addison recollected one little untimely detail. "Um...I don't have anything on hand. Maybe we could go to—" The lilting melody from "Heartbreak Hotel" broke into her sentence. She clicked Talk on her phone. "Hi, Phebes. What's up?...Walter does?...Oh, you do...Well, bring food if you're coming. Okay." She hung up. "Phoebe and Walter want a pow-wow. She'll bring lunch."

"Ooh, good. I get to meet the notorious Walter. Maybe he has news."

****

Addison's house, Tuesday noon

Phoebe held tight to Walter's arm. "This is Walter Pope." She glanced shyly at Nick. "Walter, this is Nick Savage, Addison's friend."

The two men sized each other up. Nick said, "I know what you're thinking, but we're twins."

Walter looked surprised. "Twins? Who are twins?"

Nick shot a look at Addison. She returned his look with as much meaning as she could without actually saying anything. *He's never seen Daniel.*

Nick accepted the six-pack of beer Phoebe held

out. "Er...So, Phoebe, what did you bring for lunch?"

Walter disentangled Phoebe's fingers from his arm and held up a paper bag. "I stopped in at that place near the campground and picked up grinders for everyone."

Addison fetched paper plates and plastic cups, and they took everything out to the deck.

Nick handed Walter a beer. "I understand you're a native of the Eastern Shore."

"Uh, yeah. New Church. Just up the road."

Now's the time to ask him. "Did your people settle Pope's Island over by Assateague?"

"Not much of an island, but yes, we owned some land there. Had to give it up when they established the refuge."

"What kind of shape is the life-saving station in?"

Walter looked blank. "Life-saving station?"

"At Pope's Island."

He shrugged. "Didn't know there was one. Must have been after our time."

A man poled by in a small boat. He raised his hat to Addison. "Mornin', Miz Steele. Your mama still doin' well?"

"She's fine, Mr. Tickell."

"Good to hear. Is that you, Miss Phoebe? Ike was just talking 'bout you t'other day." His glance landed on Walter. "Ah. Guess I'll tell him you's found yerself a live one."

Walter dropped the can of beer, and Phoebe gasped. Mr. Tickell grinned and poled on.

Addison picked up her sandwich and took a bite. "Mmm. I love Jed's meatball subs."

Nick popped the top on his beer. "So you're a security guard at Wallops, Pope?"

Walter opened his mouth, but Phoebe warbled, "And he used to work at the Spy Museum in DC! He knows all kinds of espionage stuff." She gazed at her boyfriend with pride.

Nick's eyes widened. "Really? Like what?"

"Oh, just enough to be able to answer visitors' questions." Walter's attempt at modesty lacked conviction. "You know, like Morse code and wiretapping and stuff."

Phoebe said loudly, "That's how we knew those flashing lights in Tom's Cove were in Morse code." She punched Walter on the arm, her gaze melting. "It was Walter who came up with the plan to spring the Belarusians. He procured the getaway car and everything."

Getaway...let's see if he confesses. "Walter, Grigory knew my name the day he arrived at Wallops. When he met me at the inn to ask about my boat, he refused to tell me who suggested he contact me. Was it you, by any chance?"

Walter didn't appear to hear her question. He picked up a roll of paper towels. "Can we use these as napkins?"

"Sure. Walter? Grigory?"

"Um. Yes." He wiped his mouth. "Actually, I was aware they were going to seek asylum before you told me. Vasilinak had...er...slipped me a note while we were waiting for the director. I'd heard of the Steeles and their big cruiser. When you two showed at the gate, I...uh...dropped your name to him. Sorry, Addison. At that point, I just wanted to shut him up."

"That was before we agreed to rescue the Belarusians." Phoebe was encouraging. "You're fully on board now. Right, Walter?"

Walter gazed at her adoringly. "Of course, Phebes. Whatever you want."

Nick stirred. "I don't understand why—"

Addison broke in before he could say something dismissive, or at least disparaging, about their activities. "Why don't we get settled, and we'll bring each other up to speed on the latest?"

When she had finished relating Klopman's insistence that Olga remain uninvestigated and in the United States, Walter paced. "If Olga had been placed in detention, we could have had a window of time when the scientists weren't under surveillance. We could have made our move. We'd have been heroes." He barked, "Why is Klopman putting up roadblocks? He's such a fool."

"He's just a bureaucrat. They always hate to rock the boat." Phoebe nodded sagely.

"Agreed, but that Eric...Eric Austen..." He paused. "Say, did he happen to be with Klopman at the police station?"

Nick answered. "He was driving the car."

"Aha." Walter scratched the stubble on his chin. "I don't trust that guy. I think he's filling Klopman's head with all kinds of rot. There's something sneaky about him."

"He's only an assistant, isn't he?"

"Yeah, but he turned up out of the blue when Klopman's long-time aide abruptly resigned a couple of weeks ago. Austen didn't go through any of the normal agency loops. I think he's a plant."

Nick whistled. "A plant? Another KGB agent?"

"Why not? I hear they prefer layers of security.

Someone to watch Olga watching the Belarusians."

Phoebe said complacently, "You just don't like him, Walter. He's not your type." She winked.

Nick sat down. "Plant or no plant, all the more reason to wash our hands of this whole thing." He tossed Addison an eloquent look.

He wants Phoebe and Walter to back off. Is he afraid they'll mess up Daniel's mission?

"But isn't there *something* we can do?" Phoebe crammed a large potato chip in her mouth. "Those poor Slavs...See that? Where I did that?" She looked for approval to Walter who gave a half-hearted snigger.

Addison moved the bowl with the chips out of Phoebe's reach. "Leonard says the team is sequestered. No visitors."

Walter grabbed a handful of chips and dropped them on Phoebe's plate. "They've been moved to a secure location—only Director Klopman knows where they are."

"Is Olga with them?"

"As far as I know. I haven't seen her."

Nick put his plate and cup in the trash. "I don't know why you guys are all a-flutter. The Belarusians are here to do biological research, I assume of global significance. We should let them get on with it."

The other three stared at him. Finally, Phoebe managed, "You're kidding, right? You don't think Addison is obliged to help after Vasilinak appealed to her?"

Addison wasn't sure she liked being singled out. After all, a man was dead because of their actions. "I don't know, Phebes. Somebody's playing for keeps. Maybe Nick is right—we should back off."

"Very sensible." Nick went to the door. "I have an appointment with the director of the refuge this afternoon."

"What for?"

"He's offered to let me see detailed maps of the refuge—I'm researching good camping spots for a certain someone."

Without thinking, Addison blurted, "Daniel?"

Walter seemed mystified. "Who's Daniel?"

Oh shit, do we tell him or not?

Phoebe said in a kindly tone, as to a toddler, "He's Nick's brother. He's lost."

Walter looked at all three faces in turn. "Wait a minute...Is your brother Daniel *Savage*? The spy?"

Chapter Twenty-Two

But now exposed, and shrinking from distress,
I fly to shelter while the tempests press;
My Muse to grief resigns the varying tone,
The raptures languish, and the numbers groan.
~Richard Savage, The Bastard

Addison's house, Tuesday, April 1

Addison fielded a look from Nick that clearly said, *No more information.* "No, no. That's a totally different Savage. No relation at all. In fact, I…uh…told Nick about the spy Daniel. He thought it was funny."

Nick interrupted to say genially, "To be honest, I thought it was an April Fool's joke."

When Walter looked blank, Phoebe nudged him. "You do know what day this is, don't you?"

"I…uh…"

Addison added quickly, "Not a joke. Nick's Daniel was lost at sea. Nick's down here seeking clues as to what happened to him."

Walter seemed even more befuddled. "If he was lost at sea, why are you scoping out camping sites for him?"

"Oh. Er. Uh. They're for me. I…uh…want to stay near the water in case he…washes ashore. *Anyhoo,* gotta go. Don't want to be late for my appointment.

Thanks for the grub." Nick left in a hurry.

They watched him go, then everyone started talking at once. Walter's voice rose above the women's. "Still seems kind of fishy—two Daniel Savages on the Eastern Shore at the same time. *Hmm.*"

Addison shot a warning glance at Phoebe. "Nick's brother only came down to fish a couple of weeks ago. Daniel Savage the scientist has been gone for almost two months, hasn't he?"

Walter still seemed distracted. "What's this Daniel do for a living?"

"Did. That is, if he is...you know. I believe"— *quick, Addison*—"he's...was...a...a travel writer. Yes. He was doing on article on deep sea fishing off the Virginia coast." She set her lips tightly, hoping that would be enough for Walter.

It seemed to be, for he said mildly, "Huh. Well, I've gotta split too—I'm on duty this afternoon. I'll see if I can find out where the Belarusians are being kept. Get word to them that we're still hoping something will work out." He clucked his tongue. "Doesn't look promising at this point."

"Oh, Walter." Phoebe's sigh of admiration was only slightly artificial.

"Uh, Phoebe?" Addison nudged her. "Didn't you tell me you had an appointment at school?"

She left off dreamily watching Walter's retreating back. "Oops. Yup. I have a teachers' meeting with the principal." She picked up the remains of their lunch and took it inside.

Addison followed her in. "Thanks for the subs."

"Any time. I came for the view." Phoebe grinned. "See you later."

****

Addison's house, Tuesday, early evening

"All clear?"

Addison looked up from her book. Nick was peeking in at the study door. "Clear of what?"

"The hangers-on. The posse. Walter and Phoebe."

"They're gone. Did you have your meeting?"

He slid into the chair by her desk. "I did. Director Dangerfield was most accommodating."

"Did you find anything promising?"

"I don't know yet. He's given me permission to take a dune buggy up the island to explore." He noted the title on her book. "*Tom Jones*? Delving into more salacious fiction?"

"Salacious isn't entirely accurate. In order to get it published, Fielding made every other chapter a sermonette on morals and marriage. You have to plow through a lot of preaching to get to the good stuff, and even then, anything salacious is implied, not overt."

"Why are you reading it, then?"

She snorted. "You're asking why I should bother with anything that isn't smutty? Just like a man." When he didn't laugh, she explained. "I'm comparing his style to that of the three women writers I told you about—the ones who were notorious for their lurid prose. I want to see if—or how—they influenced his writing."

"Better you than me. By the way, I've got an idea for a new travel article. Off-road camping in wildlife refuges."

"It won't be very long, since it's prohibited. Or is your target audience fugitives from the law?"

"A select few, to be sure, although police departments might purchase a few copies for their resource libraries."

Addison noted the fading light outside. The lighthouse would start beaming soon. She checked her watch. Five o'clock. It still got dark fairly early. "When are you planning to do your reconnaissance?"

"I was going to start tomorrow, but then I thought Daniel may move around during the day. If he has a campsite, he'll stay put for the night, and if he lights a fire or uses a lantern, it'll be easier to pinpoint his location."

"Good idea. I'll just get some gear together and—"

"Whoa. You're not coming with me."

"Of course I am. Daniel came to me for help."

"No, he didn't. He came to your house because he knew I'd be here."

"I'm going anyway."

The staring match lasted thirty seconds. Nick muttered, "I guess I could use another pair of eyes."

"Good. Have you secured the dune buggy?"

"It's in the employee parking lot of the refuge visitor center. Keys behind the wheel."

"Where do you propose to start looking?"

"We'll drive to the end of the island on the service road, then come back on the beach."

Addison was surprised. "You can only get to the service road via the loop trail, and that's closed after dusk."

"Ah, but when one has friends in high places, one is given the wherewithal to retract the spike strip."

"Director Dangerfield?"

"The mighty one himself."

"And he provided you with the key to the service road gate as well?"

"He did indeed."

She pounced. "Then tell me, my son, how a lowly travel writer merits access to parts of the park that are closed to the public?"

"My boyish charm?"

That was the only answer she could pry out of him. They ate a light supper and, when darkness had descended completely, made their way to the refuge. Leaving Nick's Hummer behind, they drove the little official ORV to the loop trail. Addison opened the gate to the service road. Nick drove through and stopped to pick her up.

They hadn't gone far when a side road opened up to their right. "Where does that lead?"

"I don't know. Let's take a look."

They drove about a quarter mile through the woods, the buggy's thick wheels kicking up sand and gravel from the road and spraying it into the open cart. The sky was starless and the wind chill. The pine trees had begun to close in around them, cutting off even the moon's pale light, when Nick whispered, "What's that?"

"Where?"

He pointed. "A light just flickered." He jumped out of the vehicle and set off on foot.

Addison struggled to keep up. She stubbed her toe on a rock. "Ouch." Then a branch whipped into her face. "Ow!"

Nick hissed over his shoulder. "*Shh.*"

A squirrel chattered behind her, upset by the presence of humans. Nearby an owl hooted. Nick was hurrying now. Addison stopped to catch her breath. As she bent over, panting, an arm slithered around her neck and a palm attached itself to her mouth. "*Mmph.*"

"Hush. I'm not going to hurt you."

Where have I heard that before? She dragged the hand covering her face away. "Daniel!"

"It is I."

"But…Nick."

"He'll come back when he realizes you're not behind him."

She couldn't see him in the dark, but she could smell him. Woodsmoke and a faint scent of clove. *Just like Nick.*

Lips brushed the top of her head. "Nice to see you again." When she pushed his chest away, he held up a hand in mock surrender. "Carpe diem, my dear. Ah, here he comes."

A low whistle pierced the gloom. "Addison? Where are you?"

"I'm here, Nick. And so is Dan."

Daniel turned on a flashlight and shone it in Nick's eyes.

He shielded his face. "What the hell are you doing?"

Daniel lowered the light. "Hey, bro. I see you've run me to ground."

Nick stood stock still, apparently at a loss for words.

Finally, Addison took the tiller. "Well, shall we adjourn to my house?"

A fierce "No!" issued simultaneously from two male throats.

She was firm. "Look, I live alone. No one will know Daniel is there, and he can get a shower and some home-cooked food." At Daniel's intake of breath, she smirked in the darkness. "Since he had to leave that lovely spaghetti behind when he shook off the long arm of the law."

"Um."

"Um."

She indicated the flashlight in Daniel's limp hand. "Why don't you get what you need and meet us back at the ORV?"

He nodded, turned swiftly, and went off.

Nick watched the light guttering through the trees. "Think he'll take a powder?"

"No. He wanted to talk to you before. Now's his chance."

"What about Peel? Does he have your house under surveillance?"

"*My* house? What for? Oh, because he thought Daniel was there last Saturday?"

"He probably has men monitoring every place Dan's been spotted."

"Makes sense. When we get close, I'll let you off and you can reconnoiter."

"Right. Here comes Dan."

They took the service road back to the visitor center, dropped the ORV off, and drove back to Chincoteague. Addison dropped Nick off at the turn onto Alder Island. Dan caught his arm. "Where do you think *you're* going?"

"To see if anyone's guarding the area." He was back in a few minutes. "No unidentified cars; just yours. No lights on anywhere."

"What about boats? There's a canal in the front."

"All clear. Come on."

Daniel bent double and ran between the other two

into the house. Addison checked all the rooms. "We're alone, but we'd better keep illumination to a minimum in case Peel *does* show up. He has a habit of charging in late at night." She took Daniel up to the guest room and opened the door to the bathroom. "There are towels in there. Let me know if you need anything else."

As she turned to leave, he clasped her hand. "Addison—"

Here it comes. "Dan, I'm not...available. I—" Her eyes went toward the stairs.

His gaze followed hers. "Nick? You don't think I'd try to horn in on my brother, do you?" He touched a blonde curl. "Even though you're one hot chick." When she took a step back, he held a hand up. "I only wanted to talk to you. That's a portrait of Richard Steele downstairs, isn't it?"

"Yes." *Where is this heading?*

"Did Nick tell you about our family's relationship to yours?"

So many events had intervened since that conversation that she couldn't remember the details. "I think he mentioned it."

"Did he happen to mention that every generation of Savages swears an oath to exact revenge on Richard Steele's descendants for what he did to Richard Savage?"

Revenge? That sounds familiar. "I...I think he said the feud was long over."

"Well, it's not. Savage died because of Steele."

"At his hand?"

"No, not exactly. See, my ancestor had an affair with a woman named Eliza Haywood."

"I know. She supposedly had a son by him."

"She did. According to the family account, she begged Richard to keep it quiet, but one thing led to another and he found himself forced to come up with a scapegoat. He chose Steele."

Addison was appalled. "What a monstrous thing to do!"

"Not at all. He knew Steele had such a sterling reputation that he could weather the storm, whereas Savage himself was nearly destitute and depended on his standing in literary circles to keep afloat."

"That's not much of an excuse. You don't use a friend that way."

Daniel pursed his lips. "I'm not defending his actions; I'm merely recounting them. Savage couldn't afford another blot on his reputation. Already, influential people were cutting ties to him. He'd worn out his welcome with his shenanigans, and once-generous purses had snapped shut."

"What happened?"

"Your ancestor not only denied the affair; he went after Savage. He publicly condemned him and renounced any association with him. Others like Samuel Johnson and Alexander Pope followed suit, and eventually Richard was down to his last penny. He died in a debtor's prison. His child—and Eliza's—swore eternal vengeance."

"Why are you telling me all this?"

He caught her arms and stared intently into her face. "Because my father swore me to the same oath."

Chapter Twenty-Three

Or Rashly deceived, I saw no pits to shun,
But thought to purpose and to act were one;
Heedless what pointed cares pervert his way,
Whom caution arms not, and whom woes betray.
                                   ~Richard Savage, The Bastard

Addison's house, Tuesday, April 1

Addison's throat constricted. "But...but..."

"Nick didn't tell you, did he?" Daniel let her go. "The feud didn't end with Richard Savage's death. It followed the families even to the New World."

"What are you talking about?"

"The Steeles screwed the Savages again, right here on Chincoteague Island."

Addison sat down on the bed. "I repeat, what are you talking about?"

"The land your house is on."

"You mean, Alder Island?"

"Yes. Your grandfather stole it out from under Hezekiah Savage."

"Stole it! Never." Addison's anger boiled over. "It was empty—undeveloped marsh."

Daniel sat down next to her. "If I may continue. The Savages had been here—fishing and working the land—since 1912."

She scoffed, "So? Steeles were already grazing cattle on Assateague in the seventeenth century."

"Yes, but when Sam Fields ran the settlers off in the 1920s, you left the area and didn't return for forty years. Meanwhile, Hezekiah had been busy building an empire. He operated a popular sightseeing tour bus and an ice cream shop. Then he decided to go into the oyster and clam export business." Daniel waved his arm. "He had his eye on this acreage for his shucking house, but before he could cobble together the down payment, some rich man from Washington, DC, swooped in and paid twice what Hezekiah had offered. Then the man built a house on it—a *vacation* home. On the spot where Hezekiah Savage had expected to make his fortune."

"Did it ruin him?"

Daniel hesitated. "No. Actually he found a better spot, partnered with his best friend, and shipped seafood to the A&P food stores for another half century. He...uh...did very well for himself." When she opened her mouth, he said harshly, "Still, the thirst for vengeance remained. When I found out who you were, I believed the time had come."

She cringed. "What are you going to do? Your brother is right downstairs. He won't—" An alarming thought struck her. *Nick is a Savage too. Would he protect me...or side with his brother?*

Daniel jumped up. "No, no! You misunderstand. Why do you think I'm telling you all this? I want to apologize."

"Huh?"

"When I met you, everything changed. The old desire for retribution crumbled, and I was finally free of what I now see is a family curse." He gazed admiringly at her. "You're beautiful, Addison. I confess I was very attracted, but—" He paused.

"But what?" *How do I get away from him?* She didn't want to reopen the rift between the brothers, but she couldn't let this go on.

"I can see that Nick cares deeply for you—maybe even loves you. I won't stand in the way."

Addison was floored. In a daze, she whispered, "Okay."

He turned to the bathroom. "Wow, I'm glad I got that off my chest. Think I'll go get that shower now."

She whispered again, "Okay." When he'd gone, she walked out to the landing.

Nick called. "Addison? Are you coming down?"

She rubbed her temples. "In a minute."

"Don't be long—I'll start to worry you're messing around with Dan." He laughed.

By the time Daniel reappeared, toweling off his wet head, Addison and Nick had finished their first beers. "PBR?"

"Don't mind if I do." He hung the towel on the door knob. "I've been subsisting on Kit-Kats, apples, and cherry cola for days." He sat down at the kitchen table and pulled the tab on a can.

"Comfy? Warm enough? Perhaps a pretzel to go with the beer?" Nick was suspiciously solicitous.

"I'm fine. Thanks, Nick." Daniel put the can down. "I suppose you're wondering why I've asked you all here."

Addison saw no reason to respond.

"Why, yes," returned Nick sarcastically. "Although I'm guessing after all these years you've come to your senses and joined the vast right-wing conspiracy. Have you finally found inner peace?"

Daniel didn't take the bait. "I deserved that. I'm sorry I haven't been in touch. I've been…in training."

Nick stood up and towered over his brother. "For what? An act of domestic terror?"

Addison sucked in her breath. "You're not going to blow up the NASA facility, are you?"

"Don't be ridiculous." Daniel waved his brother to his seat. When Nick had settled down, he resumed. "I see my brother told you I went to the dark side. Yes, I swallowed the leftist propaganda after I left college. Allowed those baser emotions of hate and covetousness to consume me. That's really all communism is—the world seen from the point of view of a toddler. You know: if I like it, it's mine. If you have it and I want it, it's mine."

"And if you won't let me have it, I'll get my big brother, aka the government, to take it away from you and give it to me."

Daniel grinned. "Exactly."

Nick took up the thread. "Capitalism is much fairer and more rational. At its core, it's simply a series of individual voluntary transactions for the mutual benefit of the two parties."

Addison got more cans from the refrigerator. "How do we get from two people doing a deal to an entire capitalist economy?"

Dan spoke before Nick could respond. "Let me put it this way. Say Mr. A needs a widget and makes it. Mrs. B wants one too, so Mr. A makes a second one for her. In exchange for the widget, Mrs. B gives Mr. A a sprocket. The widgets and sprockets prove to be popular, and other people offer other goods in exchange."

She laughed. "So pretty soon you have a house full of thingamajigs."

"Right." Nick hooked a pretzel from the bag and took a bite. "And everyone's content."

Daniel held up a finger. "It's when the government decides to intrude in that basic process that things get ugly. It can order Mr. A to give Mrs. B the widget in the name of 'fairness.' "

Nick observed, "As Thomas Sowell once remarked, 'What exactly is your fair share of what someone else has worked for?' "

"Uh-huh. Without reimbursement for his widgets, Mr. A can't buy new materials and he stops making them. Meanwhile, Mrs. B has already stopped making sprockets. She doesn't need to sell anything since the government is providing her with widgets 'for free.' "

Addison was beginning to see the picture. "Only they're not free."

"Bingo. So eventually we have no widgets and no sprockets. Since the government can't produce them on its own, the economy falls apart and everyone is left widgetless." Dan sighed happily.

Nick looked at his brother. "How long did it take you to figure this out?"

"Not as long as you think, brother mine."

Addison handed around second beers. "So what's your story? Did you steal the documents?"

"No! I'm not a thief. Well, I am, but—"

Nick leaned forward. "How are you going to wiggle out of trouble this time, bro?"

"I'm not what you think I am, *bro*."

"Oh, really? What *are* you then?"

Dan glanced quickly at Addison. "I'm a…travel writer. Just like you, Nicky." He winked.

Nick sucked in a breath and slowly shook his head. "This isn't about *me*, Daniel. Let's not go down that path. Just tell us the truth."

This isn't going well. Addison thought she'd better intervene. "How about I make us some sandwiches?"

"In a minute, thanks. I have to get this out." Dan took a deep gulp of his beer and put the can down. "Here it is: I work for the CIA."

Nick gurgled, "CIA? You?"

"Yeah, go figure." He saluted. "I was inserted at the Wallops facility because the security chief—Kermit Olson—had reason to believe that a spy had infiltrated the scientific team."

"The Belarusians?"

"No—they hadn't arrived yet. Classified documents had gone missing, but they were of such a general nature that it didn't point to any particular culprit." He seemed thoughtful. "Although Olson tells me files have been disappearing at a faster rate in the last few days. *Hmm.*"

"What did Director Klopman say about it?"

"He refused to believe anything was going on and forbade the chief to request outside assistance. Olson finally went behind his back and contacted a friend in the CIA. They sent me in unofficially and under cover."

Nick snuffled. "They didn't make you a scientist, did they? You flunked chemistry twice and barely squeaked through algebra."

"As a matter of fact, they coached me enough that I sounded like your average run-of-the-mill biologist.

Scientists are an introverted lot; no one asked questions after the initial inquiry about my area of expertise."

"And what is that?"

"I worked on the management of payload experiments. You know, coordination between the scientists and the engineers. Monitoring progress. Enforcing regulations. Really just a desk job. I never had to set foot in a lab, thank God."

Addison asked, "You admitted you were a thief. If not the documents, then what did you take?"

"Records of which documents had been taken. We wanted to evaluate what the spies were accessing and maybe glean what they intended to use it for. Also a sleeping bag and some whiskey." At Nick's expression he drew back. "What? It's cold on the beach at night. A man's gotta keep warm." He rubbed his shoulders.

Addison dropped her elbows on the table. "Tell me, how did the FBI get wind of your presence?"

Daniel fidgeted. "You know, I am a bit peckish after all. Do you have some peanuts? Anything to munch on?"

"I'll see what I can do." She fixed a plate of crackers and cheese dip and a bowl of olives. "You were answering my question."

"Question?"

"About the FBI. When or how did they get involved?" She waited while Daniel visibly plumbed his brain for a plausible answer.

He must have settled on the truth, for he finally muttered, "Someone on the base outed me." He scowled. "I only wish I knew who."

"One of the scientists?"

"I've no idea. I'm certain I deleted all trace of my

searches." He paused. "As I said, it couldn't be the Belarusians, since I was long gone when they appeared."

"Maybe it was the janitor."

"The janitor!" Daniel scratched his chin. "Funny, I never would have suspected him. Sort of like the butler did it, eh?"

Addison added, "He was the one who found Grigory's body in the closet, you know. No one should be above suspicion." *Oh dear, I sound like one of those officious TV detectives.* She peeped at Nick, but he was focused on Daniel.

"Found? Body? Whose body?" Daniel seemed totally at sea.

"That's right, you wouldn't know about the murder."

Dan folded his hands. "I'm listening."

They told him about Vasilinak's plea to Addison, about Walter's escape plan, and the subsequent tragic events.

"Wow. I go off campus for a month or so and all hell breaks loose."

"It only happened two days ago."

"I guess that's the excuse I'll give to my boss." Daniel's smile was wry.

Nick broke a cracker in half and dipped it in the cheese. "You were telling us how Peel entered the picture."

Addison added, "It was Klopman who notified the FBI, right?"

"So I gather. Whatever the snitch told him, he was furious. He called them and claimed I was a spy."

"He didn't disclose Chief Olson's warnings?"

"No—he conveniently forgot. Like I said, Olson never told Klopman about his contacts with the CIA. When Peel showed up, I had to make myself scarce."

Addison remembered Phoebe's remark. She grinned. "I hear everyone calls him Klippety Klopman."

"Yeah, I know. He's one of those super-naïve ivory-tower people. He refuses to believe there are bad guys out there who might use the research for other than peaceful purposes. He makes a point of being apolitical. As if that were possible."

"That's right." She recalled the conversation at the police station. "He wouldn't let Grigory seek asylum because it would cause an international incident."

Nick rubbed his temple. "I don't understand. Why would the director bring in the feds then? What better way to draw attention than to assert there's a spy in the facility?"

"You're right—he knew a big investigation would hobble the lab's work, and he couldn't have that. That's why—according to Olson—he contacted Peel directly."

Nick raised an eyebrow. "He didn't go through regular channels?"

"No. Olson only discovered it by accident."

"So Olson's never spoken to Peel?"

"No." Daniel peered at Nick. "Is this the first you're hearing about this? I assumed by now you'd have been briefed—"

Nick stood up quickly. "No one tells me anything." He moved around behind his brother, tapping him briefly on the shoulder. "Another beer?"

Dan jerked. "Uh, thanks." He eyed Addison. "Where was I? Oh, yeah. We were hoping I could evade Peel's clutches, but then Klopman tipped him off that I'd been seen near the records room. Peel immediately zeroed in on me. He's typical FBI—"

"Says the CIA guy."

"Damn right. FBI agents are like beagles. They get a scent, put their heads down, and follow it to their quarry without ever looking up. Which means sometimes they miss what's right above their heads, or on the right or left. And run smack into a telephone pole."

Nick dropped a can in front of Daniel. "How does Klopman know Peel? I can't imagine they run in the same social circles."

"That's an interesting question."

Addison thought it was time for a recap. "So Peel concluded you were the spy, and that's all he needed. He was unaware—"

"As was Klopman—"

"That you were CIA. Why not just tell him?"

"You forget—I'm deep undercover. Technically, the CIA can't operate on US soil. If I reveal myself, the real spy may get wind of the affair."

"I see. So now we have to hide you from the FBI. This will not look good on my record."

"Yup." Nick patted her cheek. "When they slap that third point on your driver's license, you'll be off the roads."

"Only if you're caught." Daniel brought them to earth. "That's why I have to disappear."

Chapter Twenty-Four

Women were formed to temper Mankind, and sooth them into Tenderness and Compassion; not to set an Edge upon their Minds, and blowup in them those Passions which are too apt to rise of their own Accord.
                                                        ~Joseph Addison

Addison's house, Tuesday, April 1

Nick said sharply, "No! You can't disappear."

Daniel raised an eyebrow. "Why not?"

"I'm not losing you again, Daniel. All this time I thought you hated me—or that you were dead. No, you stay. I propose we regroup tomorrow morning and plan our attack."

"Attack?"

"Well…make plans."

Daniel slumped on the chair. "All right, but I have the final say on what we do."

Addison rose. "You can stay in the guest room."

He brightened. "That would be very nice. Is it on the same floor as your bedroom?"

Nick growled, "What's it to you, Dan?"

He said cheekily, "Why nothing, Nickie dear. Just asking for a friend."

Addison made up Daniel's bed and left him heading to the bathroom. She expected Nick to take his leave, but he waited for her at the top of the stairs. Her face tinged pink, she whispered, "Do you think it's appropriate for you to stay here with your brother in the house?"

"Absolutely."

"Why?"

"Because I don't trust him."

Addison gulped. "Daniel won't try anything. He...uh..." She shut her mouth with a snap. *Heaven forbid I admit the truth about Dan's behavior in Alexandria. Or disclose our recent tête-à-tête.* Dan had promised he would lay off now that he was aware of Nick's feelings.

"Try anything? You mean to escape again? No. He values his comfort too much to go back to the wilds of Assateague. I'm not worried about that."

Uh-oh. "Then what are you worried about?" She crossed her fingers behind her back.

"That he's not who he claims to be. When Dan latches onto an ideology, you can't shake it loose from him with a wrecking ball. He's also the kind of guy who harbors a grudge forever."

Harbors a grudge forever? Was Daniel bluffing? Am I still in danger?

She was toying with the idea of coming clean when Nick blurted, "I just can't believe he went from banshee anarchist to clean-cut patriot that quickly."

"A banshee anarchist? What are you talking about?"

"It's a long story. Later."

She persisted. "Do you think he's working for the good guys or the bad guys?"

"There's one way to find out. I'll pay a visit to the security head at Wallops tomorrow. Alone. What was his name?"

"Olson, I think."

"He'll be able to tell me if he called the CIA."

"What if he refuses to talk to you? He may feel it's too dangerous to give an unofficial person that information."

Nick grinned. "Maybe I'll go as Daniel."

****

Addison's house, Wednesday afternoon

"Where's Daniel?"

"He went back up the island to retrieve the rest of his gear."

"Ah." Nick dropped into the easy chair. "Do you have any beer left?"

She got two from the refrigerator. "What happened with Olson?"

"Well, all our worries that he wouldn't open up to me were for naught."

"Why?"

"He's gone. Klopman fired him."

"Fired him! That's not fair. Olson was the one who tried to root out the spy."

"That was the problem. Klopman blamed Olson for forcing him to bring in the FBI."

"Surely he was more upset about Olson's unauthorized dealings with the CIA?"

"It's not clear Klopman was ever privy to that information." Nick put his hands on his knees. "Whatever the reason, I still don't have proof that Daniel's the operative."

"What more do you need?" They turned at the voice. Daniel stood on the deck, his hands filled with fishing gear and a backpack.

"For starters, when did you join the CIA?"

He dropped the gear and opened the sliding door. "We've had no contact for five years, Nick. What did you think I was doing?"

Addison interrupted. "Time to own up. What's the bad blood between you two?"

They were both silent.

"Well?"

Reluctantly, Nick spoke. "It was a woman."

Addison's heart contracted. "You fought over her?"

Daniel answered. "Yes, but it's not what you think." He glanced at Nick. "Nick didn't approve of my choice for a wife." Nick remained silent. "Sadie was a beautiful girl. I met her when she was a sophomore in college and I was about to graduate. She came from a small town in Connecticut. Her folks were decent, God-fearing people who ran the local tavern."

"That doesn't sound bad."

Addison pulled out another beer and handed it to Daniel, who cracked it open and took a long gulp. "Thanks, Addison. That hits the spot."

She sat down. "You were saying about Sadie?"

"Unfortunately, she wasn't quite ready to be on her own. She…she fell in with a far-left group. They filled her head with crazy ideas and turned her against her family."

"Gullible. Easily swayed." Nick spit it out.

Dan's expression was a mixture of anger and pain. "She encouraged me to participate, and I did. Nick couldn't understand why I'd espouse their hate-filled rhetoric, but at the time I believed a lot of it. However, as the group became more and more vocal about adopting violent tactics, I began to reel back, worried that they were going to extremes. Sadie and I wanted to get married, but the pack didn't trust me. Then Nick got involved and that tore it."

"I could see the path Sadie was going down. She would have dragged Daniel with her, and it could only end badly." Nick swallowed. "I'm so sorry, Dan."

Daniel ignored his brother. "She was furious. She cut both me and her parents off, and moved in with the gang in a house in Providence."

"Did this gang have a name?"

"They called themselves the Che Warriors—they idolized Che Guevara, the communist guerilla soldier."

Nick interrupted again. "Sadly unaware that Guevara wasn't this heroic freedom fighter, but a bloodthirsty bully who beat up women, tortured his prisoners, and murdered his rivals."

"Ignorant, yes. They were also pawns. See, the gang was backed by a secretive organization based abroad, which provided them with money, weapons, and supplies. Our foreign masters were big on toeing the line and regularly pulled Che members in for 'rehabilitation,' aka brainwashing. When their chief heard I'd been voicing doubts about the direction we were taking, he ordered me to appear before a kind of star chamber, to answer for my 'crimes.' I refused to go and was ousted from the Warriors. I tried to keep the lines of communication with Sadie open, but she was fading fast. Then…" He stopped and shut his eyes tightly.

Nick said quietly, "She and another member were trying to assemble a pipe bomb in their garage. It exploded prematurely, killing her." Daniel turned away and gazed out over the marsh.

"That's when Dan took off for Europe. I assumed he'd changed his mind and was ready to meet with the sponsors of the Warriors...to be reeducated." Nick stared at his brother's back. "He went off the radar, and I heard from a mutual friend that he'd...he'd died."

"I don't understand." Addison looked from one to the other. "Nick was right about her. Once you had proof, why would it come between the two of you? Why wouldn't it bring you closer together?"

Nick answered. "Daniel blamed me. He always said if I hadn't interfered, he could have saved Sadie."

Daniel turned around. "I stopped blaming you a long time ago, Nick. I just couldn't bring myself to apologize. Instead, I joined the CIA, and I've been working ever since to root out terrorists like the Che Warriors, together with their financial backers."

The two men stood four feet apart. Suddenly they lunged toward each other. "Dan, I'm so sorry about Sadie."

"Me too." They hugged quickly, then stepped back, shuffling their feet and bobbing their heads.

Addison smiled. *Men.* "How about another beer?"

"Sounds great."

"Thanks."

They sat around the kitchen table, chatting about the past, catching up. After half an hour, Addison felt it was time to get organized. "All right, what now? Who do we think is responsible for the document thefts? Olga?"

"No. She's KGB all right, but her job is to handle the Belarusian team. She's not stupid—she knows she'd be the first person the authorities would seize upon. No, it's got to be someone else."

Nick drew in a breath. "Wait—didn't you say the thefts began *before* the Belarusians arrived? So the culprit must be someone who's been at the base for longer than that."

"Right."

"Do you have a time frame?"

"Only that Olson became aware of it in early January."

Addison joked, "Maybe it's the janitor who found Vasilinak."

Nick chuckled. "We seem to be blaming the janitor for everything—outing you, stealing documents, murder...If we're not careful, he might sue us for defamation of character."

"Only if we're wrong," Daniel said more soberly. "Actually, the idea has merit. Nobody would pay attention to a cleaning person."

"No one—except anyone who's seen at least one spy movie. They're always hiding in laundry carts."

"Still—"

Addison broke in. "You also said the *frequency* of thefts increased after the Belarusians came. How do you account for that?"

"He could be working with one of the scientists now and the operation is more efficient."

Nick nodded knowingly. "He has greater access to the files."

Addison was still fixated on Olga. "Even if she's not the document thief, Olga would know who it is, right? She'd have to coordinate with him."

"Not necessarily. Her assignment is to keep the biologists in line. The spy's identity may be on a need-to-know basis."

Nick clicked his tongue. "We can't assume he's Belarusian. It could be anyone there. I believe scientists from some five different nations are detailed to the Wallops facility now, including Iraq and China. None of them are friendly to the US."

"But according to Peel, the Morse code messages were in Russian."

"Well, that makes it even less likely that the perpetrator is Olga. I understand she's Belarusian." Nick stood.

Addison held up a finger. "So what? Russian is an official language of Belarus."

Daniel slapped a palm on the table. "I have to get back into the facility somehow. I heard you say Klopman fired Olson. Without him, I have no inside source."

Nick mumbled something. "What was that?"

"I could go."

"You mean as me?"

"Uh-huh."

Addison interjected eagerly, "He can change his eye color just the way you did."

"Wouldn't fly. I'm already *persona non grata* there. Klopman would kick me—or you—out the minute I showed up."

"Well, what do you propose?"

Daniel said quietly, "I'll go in."

Addison blinked. "Didn't we just rule that out?"

"As Nick. Looking for information on my brother Daniel."

Nick was thoughtful. Finally, he said slowly, "It's too dangerous. If you're caught…"

"Not as dangerous as it would be for you. Look, I know the layout of the base. Plus I know what I'm looking for."

"What? What are you looking for?"

"The security videotapes. When I arrived, Olson took me into their computer room and gave me the passwords. Whoever killed Grigory Andreyevich Vasilinak is probably the agent I'm after. He must be one of the scientists. There could be film of him sifting through the files."

"Wouldn't the police have examined the tapes already?"

Addison added, "Or the spy could have erased them."

"I'll have to take that chance." Daniel faced the others. "It's too late tonight to do anything. We'll regroup tomorrow. Trust me, this is a good plan. You've got to let me try."

Nick took a deep breath. "Yes, let's sleep on it. I want to be damn sure it's foolproof. I can't lose you again, Dan. I have a couple more jokes I haven't told you."

Daniel grinned. "If they're as bad as your usual puns, I won't be missing anything."

Chapter Twenty-Five

All well-regulated families set apart an hour every morning for tea and bread and butter.

~*Joseph Addison*

Addison's house, Thursday, April 3

"Daniel, could you tell Nick breakfast is ready?"

"You can tell me yourself."

Addison spun around. "Nick?"

"At your service."

Addison was about to kiss him, when another Nick came in from the deck. "Hey, keep your chap stick off my girl's lips."

"Damn. I almost got lucky." Daniel gave his brother a jaunty grin, but Addison caught a gleam of desire in his eyes before he turned away.

She studied them. *It's no use. I can't tell the difference.* "Okay, you've proven your point. While you're in my house though, no pranks."

Nick trilled, "You mean you don't recognize the love of your life? I'm crushed."

" 'Love of my—' Don't be absurd. Now, the one who's Daniel—put a mark on your forehead or something."

"That was Cain, not Daniel."

"Well, pretend it's Ash Wednesday."

"Daniel was Old Testament. Pre-Ash Wednesday."

Addison threw up her hands. "If that's how it's going to be, I'm not speaking to either one of you. Get your own breakfast."

Unchastened, the brothers filled their plates, elbowing each other and snickering. As one of them poured coffee into a mug, she noticed a scar on the back of his hand. She whirled and grabbed the other man's arm. "Ha. Now I know how to tell you apart." She kissed the first one. "You're Nick."

"Huh. How'd you guess?"

She pointed at the scar. "Daniel doesn't have one of those." She cocked her head. "How did you get it, anyway?"

A spasm crossed Nick's face. Daniel said ruefully, "That's what happens when you fool around." He glanced at Nick. "We should have learned by now." He took a bite of egg. "When we were kids, we used to fill in for each other a lot."

Nick grinned. "We'd play tricks on the Sunday School teacher or the babysitter, but mostly on poor Dad."

Addison buttered her toast. "I take it the scar is the result of one such trick?"

"Indeed."

"You tell it, Dan."

"See, Dad loved to build bird houses and was forever roping one of us in to help. He claimed it was only so we'd learn how to handle power tools."

"I see." Addison had a feeling she knew where this was going.

"So Dad is droning on one day about the proper way to use a reciprocating saw." Dan glanced at his brother. "I saw Nick out in the yard and sent him the cue."

"It's a low whistle." Nick demonstrated. "We always told him it meant we were fascinated by whatever he was teaching us."

Dan continued. "While Dad was rummaging in his tool box, Nick skips in, and quick like a bunny, I'm outside."

Addison finished her toast. "So what happened?"

"Well, Nick had missed a crucial part of the instructions, and I had no way to warn him. He stuck his hand out to steady the board just as Dad lowered the saw. Sliced right across his hand, almost to the bone."

Nick said crisply, "Needless to say, there was a lot of blood and cussing, and we never switched places again. At least at home."

Daniel put his napkin down. "Okay, let's get moving. Is everybody down with the plan?"

Nick recited, "You, posing as me, pass through the gate and ask to see the Belarusians. While the guard goes off to get permission from the director, you slip into the building and head to the security offices. You snatch the video tapes and come back just as he returns. Then, if Klopman approves the visit, you go make small talk with the scientists for a few minutes and leave."

Addison dropped the fork she was holding. It landed with a clatter on the plate. "Oh dear, I just thought of something. What reason would Nick have to want to speak with the Belarusians?"

Nick interrupted. "Yeah—I thought I was supposed to ask about Daniel?"

"Ah, see, I'm not sure that works, because you'd

have to admit that Daniel Savage, the scientist and thief, is your brother."

Nick nodded. "Which would open up a whole new can of worms."

Addison objected. "Peel already knows you're Daniel's brother."

Nick had the answer. "Yes, but nobody else does."

"*Hmm.*" Daniel played with his eggs, swishing them around on the plate. "Houston, we have a problem."

Addison refilled her coffee cup. "Anyway, aren't the Belarusians still sequestered?"

"Oh right, I forgot."

"Maybe *I* should go. If Walter's on duty today, he'll let me in to go see them."

"And what if he's not on duty?" Nick pressed his lips together in frustration.

"I'll text Phoebe." Addison clicked some keys. A second later she got a reply. "She says he's on duty at the front gate today." She stood up. "So I'll go."

Daniel pulled her down again. "That would be great, except you don't know where the security room is, and if you found it, you wouldn't know what to look for."

They were quiet, mulling over possibilities. Nick slid the uneaten egg from Daniel's plate to his own. Daniel didn't seem to notice.

"Okay, I think I've got it." They all looked at Nick. "We go back to the original plan. I'll ask to see the scientists, yes, but it's because Addison has a message for them."

"We still have the same problem—you don't know the layout. No"—Dan shook his head—"it has to be me

239

posing as Nick."

"Okay. But say you have a message from Addison. She…uh…is indisposed and couldn't come herself."

"Agreed." Dan stood up. "We take two cars. I'll drive the Hummer; you, Nick, take Addison's Subaru. You'll have to stay out of sight—stop somewhere far enough away from the gates that the guard can't see you."

"Saddle up."

****

Wallops main base, Thursday midday

Half a mile from the gate, Nick and Addison pulled onto the verge. The Hummer kept going. Nick put an arm around Addison's shoulder. "If anyone stops to check on us, we'll be necking."

She removed his arm. "Great idea. So after Dan finishes his mission here, he can spring us from the hoosegow when we're run in for PDA."

"PDA?"

"Public Display of Affection. Frowned on here in the Bible Belt."

"Oh. Well." Nick stuck his hands between his knees.

Addison uncapped a thermos of coffee, and they shared a cup.

It seemed like an hour but was really only twenty minutes when they heard a vehicle approaching from the base. From the sound of it, it was burning rubber. They looked at each other. Nick said grimly, "This doesn't bode well. We'd better hide." They hunkered down under the dashboard.

The vehicle passed, its tires squealing. Addison risked a peek. "It's not a car at all. It's a school bus.

What the—"

"Must be a field trip. We should report the driver for speeding. There aren't any safety belts on those buses."

"It's not really our business, is it? We're not parents. We don't even live here."

While they argued about picking one's battles and the pluses and minuses of busybodies, the Hummer hove into view. Behind it rode a NASA security cruiser. They pulled up by the Subaru. Daniel got out of the Hummer, and Walter emerged from the cruiser. The guard swaggered over to them. "What are you doing here, Addison? Conducting a covert operation?" He started to laugh, but just then he noticed Nick. His eyes opened wide. "Who the hell are you?"

Nick quickly brushed his hair into his eyes and sat up. "Hi, Wal…Officer. I'm Dan. Nick's brother."

"Oh, you're the *other* Daniel Savage. I've heard about you. Addison and Phoebe said you drowned." He looked him over. "You don't look much the worse for wear."

"I…uh…wasn't in the water for long. I managed to swim to shore. Nick found me down at the Hook."

"*Hmm.* Well, that's good." His eyes went from Nick to his brother. "You two twins?"

"You noticed!" Daniel kept a straight face.

Walter gave him a suspicious look. "That's what you meant that day I met you. Huh."

Addison thought she'd better change the subject quickly. "So why are you escorting Nick?"

Walter patted Daniel on the back. "Orders. He asked for permission to meet with the Belarusians. Rules are I have to check in with the director." He peered at Addison. "He said you'd given him a message for them because you weren't feeling well."

Quick, Addy. She coughed and cleared her throat. "I'm much better. You were saying?"

"What? Oh, yeah. When my back was turned, he snuck through the gate and hightailed it to the Range Control Center. Found him in the corridor near an area off limits to civilians."

Daniel pulled a wry face. "I misunderstood you—I thought I was free to enter the grounds. The building was open, and I didn't see any sign saying I wasn't allowed in." He produced a facsimile of sheepish contrition. "Then I'm afraid I got lost. That place is a warren of labs and offices and corridors. This gentleman was kind enough to lead me back to civilization."

"Gentleman? You being funny, Nick?"

Addison mouthed, "Walter," to Daniel, who raised an eyebrow.

"Yeah, my little joke, Walter." He turned back to the Hummer.

"Wait." Walter caught his sleeve. "I never had a chance to tell you. The Belarusians aren't at the facility today anyway."

Daniel spun around. "Oh, yeah? What about the murder investigation? Aren't they still on lockdown?"

"The investigation's continuing, but they've all been cleared. Everyone had an alibi for the time of death. Five were in the canteen having breakfast, and the other four were in the lab together."

"What about Olga Zhuk, the KGB agent?"

Walter shrugged. "It's out of our hands. We don't have the right to detain her or even to keep her from her duties."

"Let's hope she doesn't try to knock off another scientist. People would begin to notice."

Addison asked, "So if they're not on lockdown, and not at the facility, where are they?"

"Olga Ilyich took them to Ray's Shanty."

"Ray's *shanty*?" Nick snickered. "Is that where the B-girls and village floozies gather?"

"If you consider rocket scientists bar girls, yes."

Nick rolled his eyes. "Okay, what is it?"

Addison answered. "It's a local joint. NASA folks like to hang out there. They can unwind—get off the reservation for a bit."

"Ah." Nick turned to Walter. "Did they by any chance leave in a big yellow school bus?"

Walter laughed. "Yeah. It hadn't occurred to me till now, but it might be considered, well, *unseemly*, for a school bus to be seen parked at the local watering hole. Hope the cops don't report them to Klopman." He snuffled.

"Who was driving anyway?"

"Olga."

"Well, she went like a bat out of hell. They may not get there at all."

"Really?" Walter looked a little nervous. "I should probably follow her. Make sure she's not up to anything."

Daniel backed away. "Yes. That's a good idea. I'll just get in my little jalopy and head home. Thanks for saving me from the wrath of the Man, Officer…Walter."

At the main road, Walter's cruiser went right, and the other two cars went left. They took the curve past the satellite field and drove the causeway to Chincoteague. When they reached Addison's house, Nick pulled beers out of the refrigerator while Daniel removed his colored lenses and changed his clothes. They sat on the deck watching a herring gull snatch a fish right out of the bill of a snowy egret. The egret—its yellow feet peeping from the mud—stood stunned as the gull slowly flapped off into the marsh.

"Well, I guess that was a bust. What'll we do now?" Nick looked at his brother.

"Bust? What makes you say that?" Daniel winked at Addison.

"Walter caught you before you could get into the room and nip the tapes. I don't think you can use the same strategy twice, especially now he knows we're twins."

"I won't have to. Your Walter caught me *leaving* the room, not entering it." He held up a manila envelope. "May it please the court, I have the tapes right here."

Chapter Twenty-Six

When a man has no design but to speak plain truth, he may say a great deal in a very narrow compass.

~Richard Steele

Addison's house, Thursday, April 3

"Well, that's the last video." Daniel exhaled and sat back. "I guess it was a bust after all."

Addison, who had been half asleep, rose reluctantly from the couch and looked over his shoulder. "So who came into the file room?"

"The only ones who entered the file room were security staff and a cleaning lady. Not a single scientist came in. I think we've hit a brick wall."

Nick came in from the kitchen. "No one else appears on the video?"

"Director Klopman comes in once, but all he does is chat a moment with Walter. Except…"

"What?"

"There are about two minutes of blank video at that point. I assumed it was Walter changing the tape, or moving the viewing angle, but I didn't actually see Klopman exit the room."

"Friedrich Klopman?" Addison was shocked. "The director of the whole facility? Are you suggesting *he's* the spy?"

Nick clicked his tongue. "It's not totally out of the realm of possibility. Klopman was awfully keen to keep the Belarusians from defecting. He said he wanted to avoid a diplomatic issue, but they could be acting as cover for his own activities somehow."

"If that's true, I'd like to know if he's also interfering with the police investigation of Grigory's death."

"Or at least impeding its progress. It's worth examining."

Addison rose. "We should bring our idea to Agent Peel."

"Peel? Not on your life. He's convinced I'm the spy. He'd think he was the luckiest cop on earth when his quarry waltzes into his office." Daniel closed the laptop.

"He can't lay a hand on you if we all go together. I'm sure when we clear the air…" Addison looked to Nick for support.

"It's worth a try."

Daniel made a wry face. "I'll think about it. Look, I'm a little beat. It's been a long day. Reckon I'll get some shuteye." He climbed the stairs to his bedroom.

****

Addison's house, Friday, early morning

The doorbell rang. Addison rubbed the sleep from her eyes and threw on a robe. She left Nick sprawled on the bed, a pillow over his head, and went downstairs. It was still dark in the house, although she discerned a coppery light coming from the east. When she opened the front door, she found Agent Peel and another man standing on the stoop. Between them sagged Daniel. Peel said, his voice bordering on jovial, "We caught him climbing out of your window. Care to explain?"

Addison checked the clock. "It's five o'clock in the morning, Agent Peel."

"And your point?"

"If you'd waited a few hours, you wouldn't have been forced to loiter on my property in the cold. We were all coming in to see you today."

"Well, we're here now."

She stepped aside to let them in.

He held up his free hand. "No, no. I only—"

Nick shuffled down the stairs, one shoe on and one shoe in his hand. He took in the scene. "We're not open yet. Come back at ten."

Addison gestured at the little group and faced Nick. "This is Agent Robert Peel of the FBI. Perhaps you've heard of him. And of course you already know *Dan*."

Nick said calmly, "Since you seem to have acquired my brother, we can all sit down and have a nice cozy chat. We'll bring you up to speed."

If Peel hadn't been a tough cop, his jaw would have dropped. As it was, he blinked twice and turned to his associate. "Take the prisoner to the car." Daniel didn't struggle. They left, crunching down the drive to an unmarked patrol car.

Peel faced the remaining two. "Tell me why I shouldn't arrest you both for aiding and abetting a known fugitive?"

Addison opened her mouth, but Nick jumped in. "If you'd let us get a word in edgewise, you'd see how wrong you are, Agent Peel. Daniel saw me exploring the north end of Assateague and followed me back here. He barged in and threatened us. We thought we'd talked him into giving himself up last night and were prepared to go to the station today. *At ten.*" He stood there, an encouraging smile plastered on his face.

Peel stared at Nick. "And you are?"

"Don't you know who I am?"

"Well, if I hadn't cuffed a man a second ago, I'd say you were Daniel Savage."

"I'm his brother, Nick."

Peel rubbed his forehead. "I've been looking for you. You're twins."

"Wow. You're a quick one, aren't you?"

Peel ignored the jibe. "Let me get this straight. You claim you're not working with him? We know you arrived soon after Daniel Savage disappeared from the Wallops Flight Facility along with several classified documents. Spell it out for me. Why shouldn't I assume you facilitated his escape?"

Nick shook his head. "I'm not working with him. We've been estranged for five years."

"Why were you searching for him then?"

"Our mother is dying."

In Addison's opinion, he said it a tad too quickly.

"When I got word that he might not have drowned, I came here hoping to persuade him to come home."

Addison kept her mouth tight shut. *At least he's telling the truth about the estrangement, but this is the first I've heard about his mother. Or is that another lie?*

Peel appeared unmoved. "Don't think I'm done with you two yet, but I have to go get Savage—Daniel, that is—settled. Don't plan to leave town. I'll see you later."

When he'd gone, Addison sat heavily on the sofa. "Your mother is dying?"

Nick's lips twisted. "I had to come up with

something fast."

"So she's all right?"

"She's fine. President of her Scrabble club. She's recently taken up clogging as well."

"I see." She studied him. "I wonder if I'll ever know which of your statements are true and which are lies."

He shifted uncomfortably. "Believe me—"

"*Excuse me?*"

"I mean, yes. There are certain facts I'm not telling you. All will become clear some day." He offered her a wan smile.

She took in the ringlet of coal black hair that had fallen across his brow. His indigo eyes glittered in the early morning light, and the white scar across his hand gleamed. *I guess it'll have to do.* She took another tack. "Now we definitely won't be able to switch you two off again."

Nick frowned. "Ya think?"

"It's up to us."

"Huh?"

"We have to find the document thief ourselves. It's the only way to exonerate Daniel."

"And how do you propose to do that?"

Addison dropped her chin into her hand. "How's this? The flashing lights. We pinpoint where they're coming from, go there, and nab the bad guys."

"I already found Daniel's campground. There was nothing there."

"*If* it was Daniel's camp, there wouldn't have been anything. Because he's not the bad guy. Try to keep up."

"You're suggesting someone *else* was camping on

the Hook? Surely Dan would have stumbled across him. And why was Dan there if he wasn't the one sending the beacon?"

"Did he actually confirm he'd camped there?"

Nick paused. "I can't remember."

"Well..." Addison tried and failed to stifle the yawn. "I can't think any more. I'm too tired." She gave him a come-hither look. "I didn't get much sleep last night."

Nick got up. "I'll let you go back to bed then."

"You're not staying?"

He kissed her fingertips. "I need to think."

Addison knew better than to ask what about. She watched the lights of the Hummer fade into the darkness.

****

Addison's house, Friday evening

"Addison! Open up!"

Addison sat bolt upright. It was pitch dark outside. *Is it still morning?* She clicked her phone. Five p.m. *I slept all day. Huh.*

"Addison!"

"All right, all right." She rubbed her eyes, threw on her robe, and tottered downstairs. She could see Nick through the sliding glass door. "Just a minute." She turned on a light and unlocked the door. "What is it?"

He skipped in and stood in the middle of the room, balancing on his toes. "I've *got* him!"

"Who?"

He threw himself into a chair. "Well, to be precise, I know where he is."

Now she felt not only groggy but cross. "At the risk of being redundant, where who is?"

"The guy who's flashing Morse code at the base."

"How did you get to the Hook? Whose boat did you take?"

"The Hook? Why would I go there?"

"Um. Because that's where the light is?"

He shook his head vigorously. "No, *that's* where you're wrong."

"But Phoebe and Walter said the lights originated from the Hook."

"Did they? Were they absolutely sure?"

Addison cast her mind back to their conversation with Agent Peel. "N…no. I believe there was some debate about whether it came from the Hook or Assateague Point…or maybe Gunboat Point? I don't honestly recall."

"Aha. That's because it's none of those."

Addison sat down next to him. "I'm waiting."

"You know I'm renting Jedediah Funt's garage down by the marina, right?"

"Yes, and you have yet to invite me to your castle by the sea."

"That's because it doesn't have a sea view. Or a bed—just a camp cot. And a ping-pong table. It does have a mini-refrigerator stocked with chips and beer. That's why he was able to get away with calling it 'all-inclusive.' Where was I?"

"Your pied-à-terre."

"Ah yes. It does have one perk."

"What's that?"

"It's a short walk to the Watermen's Memorial. From there you can see the Hook, Wallops Island, and what Funt tells me is called Chincoteague Point, even though it's an island."

"Right. I told you about it. It was part of Chincoteague proper until a storm sliced it off. It's separated from the mainland by what we call the Canal." The adventures of her childhood summers came back to her. "We used to hike there. There's a great view of the mainland from Hammock Point."

"The mainland...and the Wallops Island launch facility."

Addison was beginning to see the light. "Ah. You're positing that's where the flashes are coming from." She frowned. "Chincoteague Point can only be reached by boat."

"Funt tells me an old path or two remain on the island though. I propose we go see."

"Now?"

He looked out, where the sun was tossing a few last bursts of crimson over the trees of Assateague. "Maybe in a few hours, when it's dark."

"How about in a few *more* hours, when it's light?"

"You want to wait till morning?"

"Unless you prefer to run into an enemy spy in the dark—one who's undoubtedly armed." When he hesitated, she said, "Look, all we need is to find some proof—equipment or signs of human activity. We don't have to catch the guy red-handed."

He rubbed his jaw. "I suppose so."

Addison had been prepared for a protest and was pleasantly surprised by his accommodating mood. *Wait—that's not like him.* "I—"

He held up a hand and took stock of her flannel nightgown. "Looks like you're still dressed for bed."

"That's because I was *in* bed."

"Well, unless you made it before you came downstairs, we might as well use it again."

Ah. At least I don't have to go out in the dark.

Chapter Twenty-Seven

It has been a sort of maxim, that the greatest art is to conceal art; but I know not how, among some people we meet with, their greatest cunning is to appear cunning.

~Richard Steele

Curtis Merritt Harbor, Saturday, April 5

"Binoculars, check. Phone, check. Water, check. What else do we need?"

Addison closed her laptop. "Weather report says it's going to be unseasonably hot. We'll need mosquito repellent. Hats. Beer."

"Check, check, and check. Ready?"

"You have to carry the cooler."

"Why me?"

"Because you're a big, strong, manly man, and that's what they do."

"All right, then you drive the boat."

"Yeah, give the girl the easy job."

"Easy for you, maybe."

"Don't tell me you can't steer a bass boat? I thought you grew up in Rhode Island."

"I can sail like a demon; bass boats were my father's specialty. He was the fisherman of the family."

"So no fishing, or bird houses, or power tools—did

he pass *anything* down to you?"

"My good looks?"

They packed the car and drove down to the harbor. A grizzled old man in a cramped office rented them a small outboard skiff for an exorbitant sum. When Nick complained, he said huffily, "Hey, I'm giving you a discount 'cause Miss Steele's family has been here for three generations."

"Four, Bud. Four generations."

"Whatevah."

They motored down the Canal to the islet called Chincoteague Point and drew the boat up on the shore. Surrounding them were tall loblolly pines, sticking up like telephone poles among the mounds of greenbrier. The sun was almost at its peak, but the air was chilly under the trees.

Nick dropped the cooler on the ground. "We can break out the beer when we return in triumph, the fruits of our excursion in hand."

Addison, searching the woods, spied a narrow opening. "Oh, good. There *is* a path."

"You doubt the redoubtable Funt?"

They set off. Addison whispered, "It looks like it's been used recently."

"Damn. We'd better be careful. I forgot my gun."

"Your gun! You didn't tell me you owned one."

"It's just a .38 police special. It was my mother's. And yes, I have a carry permit."

Addison hissed, "Then you should have brought it, dummy. Who knows what we'll come up against?"

"*Shh.* I think I hear something."

"What?"

"You. Harassing me. Hush. It looks like we've

reached the other side of the island."

He pushed aside a bramble, revealing a small beach. Across the way, they could make out immense white structures lining Wallops Island. The sun beat down.

Nick shaded his eyes and surveyed the shore. He pointed. "Over there. See that little shack?"

"Uh-huh. Someone's been using it—there's trash in front of it." She pointed at the water. "No boat though."

"Hopefully, that means whoever's squatting here is off doing something else. Let's go investigate."

"Should we? They may be close by in the shallows or fishing in the flats. They could come back at any moment, and without your *gun*…"

"Lay off, will you? Come on."

They kept close to the tree line and, hunched over, zipped across the open space to the ramshackle building. A rain barrel filled with take-out food containers and empty soda bottles sat next to the sagging porch. Shards from the tin roof lay scattered on the sand. The wooden door hung on its hinges.

Nick whispered, "Stay here." He edged to the opening and peeked inside, then put a tentative foot down. "Floor's solid." He beckoned to Addison. She followed him in.

The interior held an empty gasoline jug, fishing gear, a camp stove, a rickety wooden table with two boxes for chairs, and some cans of food. Nick read the labels. "They're all chili with beans. Huh."

"You a bean man?"

"Not in mixed company."

"I wonder what that says about our hosts."

"For one thing, that it's not a love nest."

She giggled. "If it were, it wouldn't be much of one. No blanket. No melted candle wax on the table." She picked up an empty can. "Not even a bottle of drugstore champagne."

"So sad to see the romance go out of an illicit affair."

Addison nudged Nick. "Look." Two long, tube-shaped metal baskets, a coil of rope, and a heavy pair of shears peaked out from under a canvas tarp.

He poked at it. "What is all this stuff?"

"It's equipment for oyster harvesting."

He opened a big cooler and a rush of briny air assailed Addison's nostrils. "Lookee here. Oysters. Have we broken into an oysterman's hut?"

"There would be some kind of sign. You have to have a permit to farm—and anyway, I don't know any local oystermen who use this island." She picked up an oyster and said grimly, "No. I'm afraid what we have here are the tools for oyster poaching. Someone is robbing the oyster beds."

"That would be me."

They spun around. A young man in thigh-high rubber waders and a threadbare flannel shirt stood in the entrance. He was a little over five feet tall and scrawny, sporting a scraggly beard and hair that hadn't seen a comb since Genesis.

Addison figured Nick could take the kid easy, except for one thing: the shotgun said kid was aiming at Nick's chest. She whispered out of the corner of her mouth, "Now would have been a good time to have a gun."

"Yes, well." Nick gave their captor a big high-five

257

and said heartily, "Hey there."

The kid grunted.

"So…we'll just be moseying on. Didn't see anything. No, sir. Just trying to get out of the rain."

The man looked up. A ray of bright sunlight shot through a hole in the roof. "Rain. Yeah, right."

He continued to point the gun at them, and Addison despaired of coming up with an acceptable excuse. Finally, she said, "What are you going to do with us?"

He pushed the wad of chewing tobacco behind his teeth with a dirty finger and spat. "Angus'll know."

"Angus?"

"He'll know."

That was all they could get out of him. After a few minutes of awkward standing, the kid allowed Addison to sit on one of the boxes. Silence reigned. Finally, they heard the chug-chug of an outboard motor approaching the little beach. Addison—who had begun to toy with various means of escape—stiffened in fear. She threw a glance at Nick.

His eyes were riveted on the shotgun. He said, "Look, whatever your name is—"

"Spike."

Addison was pretty sure that wasn't his real name.

"Spike, we're not going to rat you out. We were looking for someone else—a very bad guy. You might be in danger if he finds you here."

"An' I s'pose *you* know what you're doin'?"

"We're from the government." Nick stated it ponderously, spacing out every word. "We know…how to deal…with spies."

Spike almost dropped his gun. His eyes huge, he

whispered, "Spies?"

Nick injected a little bluster into his voice. "Yeah. See, we're...FBI. We're on the trail of a Russian agent who's spying on the rocket facility over there." He indicated the doorway. "If you scram out of here quick, you won't get nailed for being a collaborator."

The boy started to back out and bumped into something. "Angus? We gotta vamoose, like *now*."

"Uh, actually, I don't think you're going anywhere."

Spike cringed.

Over his shoulder loomed a face Addison never thought she'd welcome in a million years. "Agent Peel!"

The agent deftly freed the gun from Spike's nerveless fingers and just as deftly clapped handcuffs on him. "In the flesh."

Nick cried, "He's got an accomplice—a guy named Angus."

"Big guy with a wart on his nose? Bad dentures?"

"We don't know. Spike here said he was on his way."

"Already nabbed him. You don't think I'd come out here without backup and unarmed, do you? Like the couple of amateurs I see before me did."

"Hey. How were we to know there were oyster poachers in the area?"

"Oyster poachers! Is that what these losers are? Now it makes sense. Let's go outside."

Pushing Spike before him, Peel and the others emerged into the boiling sunshine. Addison didn't complain. A patrol boat had been hauled up on the bank. Next to the outboard motor in the stern was a man in a black suit, cradling an AR-15 on his knees. Slumped in the bow sat a filthy, scowling man who could only be Angus.

Peel pushed Spike down on a log. The boy peered up at him fearfully. "Are you goin' ta take us ta the penitentiary, mister?"

"Huh? No. We'll drop you at the police station. Hogarth can deal with you."

Hands on hips, he glared at Addison and Nick. "Now tell me how you two found yourselves on a deserted island in the clutches of Sly McFox here."

Nick spoke quickly. "I was on a hill by the marina and saw the flashing lights. I realized they came from here and not the Hook. So Addison and I—"

"Took it upon yourselves to butt into a federal investigation and desecrate a possible crime scene."

"No!" Addison couldn't let that go by. "Daniel is innocent! We wanted to catch the real spy so he'd be cleared."

"I see. So you're merely lending a hand to the bumbling G-men. Well, for your information, we'd already determined this spot was the source of the lights. We're in the process of gathering evidence to prove Savage was here."

Spike muttered something. Peel ignored him. Addison thought she caught the word "nets." She touched his shoulder. "What did you say?"

The young man straightened and wiped his runny nose on his collar. "Um, iffin you let us go, mebbe I can help you."

Peel cast a contemptuous glance over him. "I doubt if you have anything to offer, kid."

"You're talking about lights coming from here,

right?"

"Yeah. Why?"

"Angus and me, we was using flashlights to find the baskets. We kept 'em real low to the water. Angus said that way the lights couldn't be seen from the channel."

"Baskets?"

Addison explained. "He means the mesh baskets used to raise the oysters."

"Yeah." Spike—obviously proud of his partner's ingenuity—spoke rapturously. "See, Angus figured if we only kept the light on for a second at a time, we'd be safe."

Peel stared at him. "Do I have this straight? You've been using a flashlight to find oyster beds? I take it you weren't chatting with each other using Morse code."

"Huh?"

Nick scratched his temple. "But Walter was certain it was Morse code."

Addison turned to Peel. "Yes, and you confirmed it, Agent Peel. Or at least you said you did. In fact, you stated that, according to your expert, the message was in Russian, but you refused to reveal the contents to me. Why?"

Peel said wearily, "I lied. Our decoders couldn't crack it either. We were shooting in the dark that it was Russian."

"Liars never prosper." Addison was prim.

"I think you mean cheaters." Peel took out his phone. "Get me the Chincoteague police…Captain Hogarth? Robert Peel here. We've snagged some oyster poachers for you. Yeah, we'll bring 'em in." He headed toward the boat, a protesting Spike in tow.

Nick hiccupped. "What about us?"

"You got yourselves here; you can get yourselves back. We left your boat where you parked it."

"And Daniel?"

"Nothing's changed. He's being transferred to DC. Oh, and by the way, I would gladly have arrested you for impersonating FBI agents, but you were so inept I would've been embarrassed to charge you."

Chapter Twenty-Eight

If you wish to succeed in life, make perseverance your bosom friend, experience your wise counselor, caution your elder brother, and hope your guardian genius.
~Joseph Addison

Dobie's, Saturday, April 5

"Well, this sucks."

"Shut up and drink your gin."

Addison, Nick, Phoebe, and Walter sat around a high-top in Cheyenne's Lounge. Nick had explained to Walter that his Morse code was not up to snuff.

He took it well. "I did say it was gobbledygook."

Phoebe stroked his arm. "You did your best. The FBI guys believed you. That counts for something."

Walter groused, "Doesn't say much for the FBI though, now does it?"

From the expressions on the others' faces, Addison was pretty sure everyone agreed with him. "So what do we do now?"

Nick put down his tumbler. "I have to find a way to prove my brother's innocence."

"Oh?" Walter raised a brow. "What's he done?"

Addison remembered too late that they'd told Walter Nick's brother was not the same Daniel as the spy. "We…uh…didn't tell you the truth before, Walter.

Daniel Savage is not a travel writer."

Nick twitched. "Is that what you told him?"

"It was the only thing I could think of. We didn't expect him to bump into the two of you in the same place."

Walter was glancing from one face to another. "The guy in the car when I escorted Nick out of Wallops was Daniel Savage the scientist? The guy Peel took prisoner? He's your brother?"

Addison started to explain that he'd escorted Daniel, not Nick, but a glimpse of the latter's expression told her that wasn't a good idea. *He'd think we'd enabled a spy to infiltrate the NASA facility.* "Yes. We were…we were…"

Nick jumped in. "We'd found him hiding near the base. We were taking him home to hear his story before we turned him in."

"So he had nothing to do with the Belarusians?" Walter seemed skeptical.

"Right. No. Nothing. Um. He just happened to be in the car."

When Walter's eyebrows rose, Addison figured she'd better distract him fast. "But that's neither here nor there. How do we get to the Belarusians now that they're locked down?"

Walter grew animated. "You can't, but I can. This is what I wanted to tell you. Klopman is still prohibiting any civilian contact with them, but as of today, he has renewed his permission for field trips. I think he's calculated that with the ringleader—Vasilinak—gone, they won't try anything."

"So what are you proposing?"

"I will volunteer to chaperone. I should be able to

get advance notice of a trip. When I do, I'll let you know, and you can arrange a car. Or a boat."

"That didn't work out so well for Grigory the last time."

"Grigory ran his mouth too much. I won't make that mistake. The scientists will be told only the minimum necessary and only at the last minute. Olga won't be able to winkle information out of them because they won't have any."

"So you take them to Ray's and get a free-for-all going. Everyone ends up in jail, where they can ask for sanctuary and Olga will be helpless to stop them. We're back to our original plan. Yay!" Phoebe raised a fist.

Addison said mildly, "You scotched that plan already, Phoebe. If Walter's an accessory to a brawl, he'll lose his job."

Walter had been tapping his foot impatiently. "Bar fight's a stupid idea anyway." He ignored Phoebe's snort. "It'd be better if they overpower me and escape."

"But won't Klopman blame you either way?"

Nick agreed. "Addison's right. Even if you're not canned, it won't do your career any good."

"I'm not worried. They're hard up for security guards. They keep quitting because Klopman's such a pr...jerk." He spit an ice cube back into his glass. "His assistant Eric doesn't help morale either. He's always sneaking around prying into people's business." His lip curled. "I'm keeping an eye on him—I still think he's KGB."

"Oh, for heaven's sake, you see spies under every bed. And anyway"—Phoebe appraised her boyfriend—"those Belarusians are weaklings. Nobody would believe they could beat you up."

He chortled. "Okay, how about this—you come in and punch me. Then you tie me up—"

Before Addison could laugh, Phoebe interrupted enthusiastically. "And gag you."

Walter gave her a wary look. "I guess. You stuff me in a closet and take off with the asylum seekers."

Phoebe mused, "You should say there was a whole gang. We were too much for you. That way you wouldn't look like a wuss."

This did not amuse Walter.

"And we'll make up your face to look like you have a black eye." She looked him over. "Maybe bang you up a little. For authenticity's sake."

Walter had opened his mouth to object when Addison spoke up. "There's at least one fly in the ointment."

"Only one?"

"Uh-huh. Olga. She won't let you take them anywhere by yourself. She'll insist on tagging along. And I'll bet she has a gun."

"She'd better not. She's a guest in the United States. I don't think foreign visitors are allowed to bring in firearms."

The other three stared at Walter.

Finally, Nick said, "I doubt she cares about the legal niceties. She shot Vasilinak after all."

"No, she didn't. She knifed him."

"That's true." Phoebe nodded. "Which means Walter could be right after all."

Addison wasn't ready to concede. "Alternatively, the murder was spur of the moment. She wasn't prepared, so she used whatever weapon was at hand."

"That makes sense—if it was premeditated, she

wouldn't have left him lying there for the janitor to discover." Walter shelled a peanut and popped it into his mouth.

"I can't see it. Olga's a professional." Phoebe's voice contained a hint of awe. "If she wanted to knock Vasilinak off, she would have had a plan."

Addison goggled at her. "Phoebe!"

Nick interrupted. "What makes you so sure Olga killed Vasilinak, Addison?"

"Who else? They'd just arrived here. She's supposed to keep them in line. She discovered his intentions and *boom*." She thought of the dented car. "She had already tried to run him over."

Phoebe shivered. "She is *not* a nice lady."

Walter snorted. "KGB handlers are not hired to be nice."

Addison gazed curiously at Walter. "How much do you know about the KGB?"

He reddened. "I learned a lot at the Spy Museum. And I've read all of John Le Carré and Martin Cruz Smith." He seemed to think that would silence them. It did.

Nick finished his whiskey. "There's another possibility."

"A different plan?"

"No, a solution to the murder."

Walter scoffed. "Do please tell us."

"One of the other scientists did it. A plant."

Phoebe cried, "*Another* KGB agent? Is the place crawling with them?"

Addison nodded. "It's not that farfetched an idea, Phoebe. Didn't Walter say it's normal procedure for the Russians to send a pair of agents overseas? One for backup? Or to keep each other honest? Walter?"

"Could be. I've been observing Eric Austen. So far I haven't seen him in any compromising situation. I might as well surveil all of them. If anyone seems furtive or I find him where he shouldn't be…"

"What will you do?"

Walter's nose rose in the air. "Take it to the proper authorities, of course."

"You mean Klopman? Wouldn't that be counterproductive?"

Walter deflated a little. "I suppose. How about Agent Peel? I could tell him."

Addison disagreed. "When I asked him to help us liberate the Belarusians, he said it wasn't his 'bailiwick.' " She thought about her meeting with Peel in Salisbury. "He did say they hadn't ruled out a spy among the Belarusians, but that his primary mission was to find and arrest Daniel." She added gloomily, "Mission accomplished."

"And if it's true that KGB agents are as thick on the ground as flies on a saltwater cowboy," seethed Phoebe, "he won't care if we dig up one more."

Nick ordered another drink. "Speaking of Peel, what do we do about Daniel?"

Walter hopped off his stool. "Nothing we *can* do. He's in the hands of the FBI now. We have no jurisdiction."

"But that's ridiculous. He's accused of committing a crime on NASA property."

Phoebe chimed in, "An *international* crime. The FBI is supposed to be restricted to domestic activities."

"Then let the CIA handle it. I've got to run." He pecked Phoebe's cheek. "Can you give Phoebe a ride home?"

Addison nodded.

Phoebe's lower lip protruded. "But, Walter—"

"Sorry, girl. I've got the midnight-to-six shift." He hotfooted it down the stairs.

Addison patted Phoebe's hand. "Maybe you shouldn't put all your eggs in one sandwich."

"Don't you mean one basket?"

"No—I'm saying Walter may be a little too hard-boiled for you."

"Ha-ha."

Nick brooded.

Addison leveled her gaze at him. "What's wrong?"

"You said Peel's mission is accomplished."

"So?"

"So what's he still doing here?"

****

Addison's house, Monday morning

Nick slammed down the phone. "Peel says Daniel is at a hidden location, and I'm not permitted to make any contact."

"Can the FBI do that? Aren't they supposed to allow him the usual rights?"

"I gather when it's an espionage case, they have different rules."

Addison put her newspaper down. "But surely the CIA will vouch for Daniel! They sent him after all."

"I'm guessing the CIA doesn't want its domestic activities exposed. Plus he was in deep cover. What do they call it? Plausible deniability?"

"No, that's not it…"

Nick got his windbreaker from a hook by the door. "I'm going to the refuge. I need some exercise."

Addison guessed a comment on the hours of exercise he'd recently engaged in in her bedroom would not be well received. *He's frustrated about his brother.* "I'll go with you."

They stopped at every trailhead—the Lighthouse, the Black Duck, the Woodland—and hiked. Addison was beginning to drag, but Nick kept marching on. He didn't even look up when she pointed out a tall hemlock frosted in great egrets, or the pair of pied-bill grebes feeding in the ditch. "Oh look! Hooded mergansers!" elicited no more than an absent nod.

They reached the beach parking. She nudged him. "I'm going to the wishing tree."

Nick stayed in his seat. "I'll wait for you."

"*Now* you're tired?"

"I just need to think."

"Okay." She climbed the wooden steps that bridged the dune. It was a warm day, and a few local families had spread blankets and set coolers on the gray sand. Toddlers were dipping toes in the still-cold water and running away, screaming in delight.

Addison tramped down the beach. Since she'd last visited, the tree had been embellished with even more shells, ribbons, and miniature toys. Her scrap of sailcloth still clung to the bark. *Where are you, Seth? Heaven? Hell? In a hospital bed suffering from amnesia? Or celebrating with bimbos on Paradise Island?* She sighed and searched her heart. *Is it possible I don't care anymore?* Nick's weary face, his blue eyes tinged with worry, rose before her. It seemed he had become a fixture while her mind was elsewhere. With little fanfare, he'd taken up residence on her floating rib, where he bobbed up and down, blowing kisses. She reached out and plucked the scrap from the tree, but then put it back. *As long as it stays here, Seth is gone and I don't have to face my feelings about either man.*

She turned around and marched back to the Hummer.

Nick was leaning against the car door. When he saw her, he waved both arms. As she approached, he yelled, "There you are! Hurry! We have to go!"

She went around to the other side and got in. Nick put the car in gear and roared out of the lot. "Why the sudden urgency?"

"It's Walter. He shot Olga."

Chapter Twenty-Nine

An evil intention perverts the best actions, and makes them sins.

~Joseph Addison

Chincoteague police station, Monday, April 7

"All right, Lenny, spill. And it had better be good."

The police chief indicated the two chairs in front of his desk. "Why don't you sit down?"

"But Lenny—"

Nick couldn't restrain himself. "Walter's a federal employee, isn't he? Do you have the power to arrest him?"

Lenny countered, "He's an American citizen, isn't he?"

"Yes, but…" Addison trailed off. Public employee union members had incredible protections—much more so than those in the private sector—but she wasn't sure they extended to assault charges.

"We're still working out the logistics. I'm trying to get Klopman on the horn. For now, I can at least hold him. He was in Accomack County when he killed the woman, so he's technically in our district no matter who ultimately deals with him."

Addison jumped back up. "He *killed* her? All we heard was that she was shot."

"When we called you, that was all we'd been told."

Nick asked curiously, "Why *did* you call us anyway?"

"Pope is asking to see you. Darlene's digging up a lawyer, but he said he wanted to talk to you ASAP."

"*Hmm.*" Nick tapped a finger on Lenny's desk. "Where exactly was he when he shot her?"

"From what he told Ike—"

Addison whispered, "Leonard's deputy, Corporal Tickell."

Lenny glared at her. "He told Ike it started on the bus."

"They were going on a field trip?" Addison and Nick exchanged glances. *He was supposed to tell us when they left the campus.* "Was the outing spur-of-the-moment?"

"That I don't know." Lenny sniffed sarcastically. "Evidently NASA takes their scientists on nature walks and to other local points of interest. Treats 'em like middle schoolers, if you ask me. But in this case the kiddies don't have to get advance permission from their parents."

"Local points of interest…like Ray's Shanty."

The captain gave Addison a funny look. "Yes. In fact, that's where it went down. How did you know?"

Nick smiled. "They've been there before. It's one of the few places on the Eastern Shore where you can get Russian vodka."

Addison added, "Ray's is on the mainland—technically New Church. Isn't that the sheriff's territory?"

"Yes, but he's busy with a big robbery-arson case in Wachapreague, so he asked me to deal with it. I'm a lot closer anyway."

Nick prompted, "You said it 'started' on the bus. What started?"

"The row between Mr. Pope and Ms. Zhuk. I gather it was conducted in some foreign language, so the bus driver had no idea what they were saying. He could only make out that Zhuk was angry with Pope over something."

"How about the other Belarusians? What did they hear?"

He shook his head. "They've clammed up. I'd say they were scared sh…to death."

"Okay, so Walter and Olga were arguing. Then what?"

"They all got off the bus at Ray's."

"Everyone? Including the bus driver?"

"Uh-huh. Zhuk and Pope stayed in the parking lot. They were still going at it hammer and tongs, so the scientists and the driver went inside. They'd just gotten their drinks when they heard a shot." He paused.

"And? Then what happened?"

Lenny consulted his notes. "Lessee. The bartender went to investigate. The bus was parked in a deserted lot in the back. He rounded the corner of the building to find Ms. Zhuk on the ground and Pope standing over her with a gun. Bartender called us on his cell phone and kept watch until we arrived and took Pope into custody."

"But what did Walter *say*?"

"Mr. Pope? He said the woman struck him first." Lenny stopped and wiped his forehead. "She sure was a *big* woman."

"Did she shoot him?"

"No. We found a gun in her pocket, but it hadn't been fired. He did have some scratches on his face consistent with fingernails. He says—" Lenny looked again at the form on his clipboard. " 'She lunged at me and scratched my face. She was reaching for the gun when I shot her.' "

"She was reaching for her own gun or his?"

Nick scratched his head. "And how did he know she had a gun if it was in her pocket?"

Hogarth pursed his lips. "You know, those are good questions to ask Pope."

Addison and Nick said in unison, "Can we see him?"

"Sure, but Ike has to stand outside the cell."

"That's okay."

The deputy unlocked the cell door, and they filed in. Walter sat on the same steel bench Vasilinak had occupied, his head in his hands. Addison called softly, "Walter?"

He looked up. His face was haggard. Twin scratches, still red and runny, stood out on his cheek. Addison touched his face. "Didn't they patch you up?"

His eyes were shiny with tears. "Doesn't matter. I just killed a person. Who cares about a little blood?"

She took a baby wipe from her purse and dabbed at the blood. He shrank back. "Ouch. That stings!"

"It's supposed to. Here." She gave him a tissue. "Press it on the cuts till the bleeding stops."

Nick sat down next to him. "Captain Hogarth tells us you were quarreling with Olga, and she attacked you. What touched it off?"

Addison bent down and whispered, "I thought we'd voted that script down."

He whispered back, "I didn't start it."

"Oh."

Walter dropped the tissue on the bench. Addison gently pressed it back on his cheek. "You say you didn't start it? What happened?"

"After the Vasilinak murder, Olga said she couldn't trust the men and grounded them for the next month."

"Who let them go off campus then?"

"Klopman. He didn't inform Olga of the excursion." He wrinkled his nose. "Probably asked *Eric* to tell her, but the little squirt was too busy digging into our personnel files. None of this would have happened if he'd done his job."

Addison couldn't decide if the jab was gratuitous or if Walter had proof of his accusation. *It's probably not important.* "So how did she discover they were leaving?"

"She saw me jogging toward the bus. I had just heard myself about the trip and thought I could head her off." He rubbed his arm, revealing a dark bruise. "Instead, she shoved me aside and climbed aboard."

"And you followed."

"Uh-huh." A ghost of a smile crossed his lips. "She wasn't pleased."

Nick stood up. "The bus driver said you were shouting at each other in a foreign language. Do you speak Belarusian?"

"Me? No way. We'd been talking in English, but when things grew heated, Olga lapsed into that hideous tongue. All hisses and shushes. I swear she was apoplectic. This little vein in the side of her neck kept vibrating. Even though I didn't understand a word she said, I could tell she was calling me all kinds of foul names."

"And this was happening while you were still on the bus?"

"Uh-huh. When we got to the tavern, the scientists tumbled out as fast as they could and ran into the bar. The bus driver followed them in. The two of us got off, and that's when Zhuk assaulted me." He took the tissue from Addison and dabbed at his face. "She hurled herself at me and raked my cheek with those long red nails of hers." He gazed at his friends, his expression a mix of terror and trepidation. "I saw this bulge in her pocket. It had to be a gun. I drew mine, and she went for hers. So I shot her." His face crumpled. "I…I meant to hit her knee—you know, disable her. I guess my training kicked in. They teach you to aim at the chest."

"Walter? Why did you have a gun?"

"I was on duty when I heard they were heading to the tavern. I didn't have time to ditch my service revolver before we left."

In the sudden silence, Nick patted him awkwardly. "Did Lenny—Chief Hogarth—tell you what's going to happen next?"

"Not a clue. I think they're debating who has say over my fate."

"Well, whoever does, it was clearly self-defense."

"With any luck, they'll see it that way. I can just hear Klippety Klopman squealing about another 'international incident' on his base."

"They haven't gotten hold of him yet. Let's hope Lenny finds you a lawyer before Klopman hears the news."

At that moment, a high-pitched shriek came from

the lobby. Addison checked her watch. "Uh oh. School's out." She grimaced. "That will be Phoebe."

The door to the cell block swung wide, and Phoebe rushed in. She was momentarily thwarted by the combination lock, but a clearly flustered deputy opened it for her. She landed on Walter like a lioness on a gazelle.

The rest looked on helplessly while he tried to fight her off without actually hurting her. "Phoebe! I'm all right. It's okay."

Phoebe finally drew back, which was when she glimpsed his face. "That...that *bitch*!"

His hand went to his cheek.

Phoebe jumped up and rattled the bars. "Ike! Lenny! Didn't you see Walter's wounded? What is *wrong* with you guys? Police brutality, that's what it is. Those cuts could get infected...Why, that woman— well, she's KGB, right? Don't they put poison under their fingernails? Walter could be a dead man walking!" She burst into tears and flopped on the bench.

Walter gave her a tentative pat on the shoulder.

Lenny came in, trailed by a man in a dark suit. When they saw who it was, their voices rose in a chorus of entreaties. Lenny lobbed eloquent glances at everybody before saying deliberately, "Dr. Klopman is here to take custody of Mr. Pope."

Klopman surveyed the upturned faces. "What are you all doing here?"

Nick said bracingly, "We're his backup."

The director glared at him. "I distinctly remember saying I wanted no international incidents."

A wave of giggles swept the room.

Klopman was momentarily disconcerted but

soldiered on. "The Belarusians have been secured." He ignored the rustle of disapproval. "But I'm still contending with this Turkish-Armenian standoff over access to the Destiny lab module. As if that weren't enough, Dr. Cheng is in my office every ten minutes complaining about Dr. Li, and Dr. Li pops in a minute later to insinuate Cheng is snooping on Li's work. And now we have a Belarusian national murdered by our own security guard."

"Hey! It was self-defense."

"Let's pray the Belarus ambassador sees it that way. At least for now, he's allowed me to take responsibility for you. I've assured him that justice will be done."

"Belarus ambassador?" Addison was puzzled. "Didn't Olga work for the Russians? I thought the KGB was a Russian agency."

Phoebe said impatiently, "I *told* you, Addy. Belarus has its own KGB." She faltered. "And…"

Klopman said impatiently, "She has—had—a Belarusian passport. Even if she were Russian, she was working for the Belarusian government."

"What will you do with her body?"

"The ambassador is sending the embassy's own physician down. He'll confer with the medical examiner here. Miss Zhuk will likely be transported back to Belarus."

Nick spoke up. "What about Grigory Vasilinak? He's at the morgue in Norfolk. Will they take him back to Belarus as well?"

Klopman, his tone petulant, muttered, "These foreign bureaucracies move at a snail's pace. They haven't finished the paperwork for Vasilinak yet.

Hopefully, we can get rid of—I mean, transfer—them both quickly."

"Will the university send another scientist?"

"Probably not. I presume they sent their entire contingent of microbiologists."

"What about a replacement for Zhuk?" Addison wondered if Nick were thinking what she was thinking. *Now's the time to help them escape.*

"The ambassador said he has to confer with the university and the Belarus foreign ministry. Rest assured, a replacement will be found." He helped Walter up. "Let's go."

They all trooped out of the cell and into the lobby. Klopman took Walter to a waiting car. Addison could make out Eric's profile in the gloomy interior. He was tapping his fingers on the steering wheel in time to the radio. The two men got in the back. As Eric began to roll up the windows, Phoebe put her hand on the frame. "Mr. Klopman, is Walter under house arrest?"

From the look on his face, Addison had the feeling Klopman hadn't thought that far. "Uh, yes. He won't be allowed off the base for the time being."

Phoebe clutched Walter's fingers. "I'll wait for you."

He grinned wanly. "If it takes forever?"

"Huh?"

Addison whispered, "It's a song, Phoebe. From the movie *The Umbrellas of Cherbourg*." She sang, "If it takes forever / I will wait for you / For a thousand summers / I will wait for you."

Phoebe seemed confused. "I only meant till they let him go—like the weekend or something."

Walter's face fell.

They watched the car drive away, tears streaming down Phoebe's cheeks. Once it turned the corner onto Deep Hole Road, she blew her nose loudly and marched to her car. "Lunch?"

"Phoebe!"

"What? He'll be okay. I'm sure he's got like diplomatic immunity or union protection or something. Come on, I'm in the mood for beef. Let's go to Jim's. His prime rib sandwich is to die for."

Nick cocked his head. "I could go for some seafood."

Addison gave up. "That actually sounds good. As for you, Phoebe, if that's your notion of how the anguished lover acts, you've been watching the wrong movies."

Nick led the way to the Hummer. "If Jim's serves oysters, I want confirmation they were legally harvested by someone *not* named Spike."

Chapter Thirty

Admiration is a very short-lived passion, that immediately decays upon growing familiar with its object.

~Joseph Addison

Addison's house, Tuesday, April 8

"He's free! He's free! Thank God Almighty!"

"Phoebe? Who's free?"

"Walter! The Belarusian embassy isn't going to press charges. I just got off the phone with him. I'm coming over."

"Aren't you in school?"

"School? I was done an hour ago. It's four o'clock!"

Addison gulped. She elbowed Nick and hissed, "Get up."

He blinked and wiped his eyes. "So much for afternoon delight." He rolled out of bed and reached for his pants. "I take it the accused has been unshackled? Was there exculpatory evidence or was it solely due to apathy?"

"I don't know. Phoebe can tell us. Here's your shirt."

He took a minute to admire her unclad form. "He sighs. You have too many friends, my dear."

She pulled the shift over her head as Phoebe's car roared up the lane and stopped, raising a cloud of dust. By the time Addison reached the living room, Phoebe was sliding open the deck door. "Isn't it *fabulous*?"

"Yes, yes. When did it happen?"

"This morning. Walter called me at school. He has to go home and clean up, but I'll see him tonight." She whirled around when a step creaked. "Oh, it's only you."

"What do you mean, 'only' me?" Nick stood at the bottom of the stairs buttoning his shirt, his features compressed in an inscrutable expression. Addison guessed he wasn't sure whether to be embarrassed or insulted.

Phoebe grinned. "A little hanky panky during siesta time is great for working up an appetite."

Addison sat down. "So give us the scoop. The Belarusians don't care that their handler was gunned down in broad daylight?"

"That's the point. They didn't want it to come out that she was KGB. I don't think it's allowed on American soil. At least officially."

"It's not like we don't know they're everywhere."

"I'm shocked, shocked to discover gambling going on here."

"So, her death means nothing." Addison didn't like the flippant tone of the conversation. "She was a human being after all."

Phoebe arched an eyebrow. "You feel sympathy for her? You didn't even *know* her. She killed Vasilinak, and she would have killed my Walter if he hadn't acted first."

Nick sat down on the sofa. "It's not certain she

killed the scientist. Nor do we know that she would have drawn her gun on Walter."

Phoebe spluttered, "You're taking her *side*?"

"No, no. I'm just pointing out that, while here in the States a person is innocent until proven guilty, to the communists, justice is more…elastic. Olga Zhuk was expendable."

Phoebe pouted. "The way I see it, justice was done."

"You're certainly entitled to your opinion." Addison got up and shut the glass door. "At least Walter isn't going to jail. I suppose he gets to keep his job too?"

"I don't know." Phoebe perked up. "But if Klippety Klopman remains true to form, he wouldn't want to cause an *incident* by firing him."

"Ha-ha." Nick headed to the kitchen. "Coffee, anyone?"

"No, thanks. I just dropped by to pick up my gray sweater." She took it off the hook. "Then I'm gonna go see if the consignment store has any new dresses." She plucked at her cotton shirtwaist covered in crayon marks and sticky handprints. "I want to wear something nice for my date tonight."

As she was leaving, Mr. Tickell poled by in his little punt. He tipped his cap. "Another fine afternoon, Miss Steele. Miss Phoebe."

"Indeed it is, Mr. Tickell. Are you going fishing?"

"Nope. I'm headin' down to Little Tom's Cove for a spot of clammin'. Mebbe put a pot in for crabs. That son of mine and the gal he married are finally ready to have his old folks over for suppah." He chuckled. "I figure we'll be needin' to bring our own food."

Nick said, "Tickell? Is your son Chief Hogarth's deputy?"

Mr. Tickell grinned. "That'd be Ike. We's ver' proud of him. Yessir. No, I meant our older son, Jesse. He married a Oates and all-a Shincoteague knows them Oateses can't cook for beans." He winked at Phoebe. "Ike's still a bachelor, bless 'im." He poled past them. A cormorant rode his wake, its neck arched like a queen parading in her carriage.

Phoebe flushed. "Why did Mr. Tickell wink at me, Addy?"

Addison smiled. "I think he's referring to how you and Ike were best buddies in the third grade. You even left a token on the wishing tree."

"Oh, yeah. It was a thimble from Mama's collection. Boy, was she livid."

"Ike told his father he was going to marry you when he grew up."

"Huh." Phoebe raised her eyebrows. "Well, I guess he forgot. And anyway, Mama made me bring the thimble back from the tree. She said the token had to be something that belonged to me." She shook herself. "I sure hope Ike's moved on...'cause I have." She flounced down the steps and rounded the corner of the house.

Nick watched her go. "I perceive *la donna è mobile*."

"Woman is fickle? You can hardly hold her to a troth pledged in third grade."

"Why not?"

Addison didn't bother to answer. She brought mugs and a plate of cookies out to the picnic table. A gull hovered overhead, then perched on the piling in front of them, eyeing the plate hungrily. "Whew! That sun's hot." She wound the umbrella open.

Nick watched her lazily. "I could sit here all afternoon."

Addison wished she could be as calm, but her mind was racing. "I wonder who they'll replace Olga with?"

"If they have to fly a new agent in from Belarus, it might take some time. I'm sure he'll need a visa."

"And a cover identity."

Nick sipped his coffee. "You'd think with the ton of spies already milling around, they could just promote one of them."

"He'd probably have to be Belarusian. Agent Peel believes there's another one already stationed at Wallops."

"Does he have any idea who it is?"

"No."

He tossed a crumb at the gull. "For all we know, there could be double agents mucking things up as well."

Addison had a frightening thought. "Daniel said he was CIA—could he in fact be a double agent—working for the Russians? And that's why they're letting him rot in prison?"

"God, I wish I knew!" Nick slapped his hands on the table. "Ouch." He sucked a splinter out of his palm. "I've got to find a way to contact Daniel."

"Where are they holding him?"

"All I know is he's unavailable. Didn't Hogarth say they were taking him to DC?"

"No, Peel did."

"I'm going to try calling Peel again."

"Worth a try."

Nick went inside. Addison had just picked up the last cookie when he returned. He sat heavily. "Our friendly neighborhood G-man is pissed."

"Why?"

He jumped up and crowed, his eyes dancing. "The CIA went over his head. Daniel is a free man!" Skipping around the table, he tripped on a loose board and nearly pitched into the canal.

Addison put the cookie down, uneaten. "That's fabulous news. Does Peel know where he is now?"

"He has no idea. The CIA didn't bother to inform him of their decision. He only found out when he called for an update. I caught Peel fresh from a bludgeoning by his boss."

"I suppose Daniel will have to lie low for a while. They won't let him come back here—he's compromised."

"Damn, you're probably right." He took Addison's hand. "I have so much to talk over with him, so many things to tell him."

"He'll find a way to get in touch."

"He'll try, but I don't want him to jeopardize his safety for me. I—" His phone rang. "Daniel! Where are you? I just got the news that you're out...I see....Oh? Okay. Let me know then." He clicked Off.

"He's coming down here?"

"Not yet, but he says he has news. He couldn't tell me over the phone."

"Well, if he can't come down and can't talk on the phone, how does he propose to convey this news to you?"

Nick scowled. "I...uh...forgot to ask."

Addison picked up the cookie again and finished it

off. "We'll just have to wait." She took the empty plate to the kitchen. "What do we do now?"

Nick brightened. "Finish our rudely interrupted siesta?"

She checked her watch. "There's an hour before the sun is over the yardarm."

"A touch of exercise before cocktails?"

"Don't mind if we do."

****

Addison's house, Wednesday afternoon

"I'm not so sure about Walter, Addison."

"Oh?"

Phoebe dropped her school bag on the floor. "What are you working on?"

"I'm looking for proof that Eliza Haywood and Richard Savage had a child together. Daniel told me they did—at least according to the Savage family annals. Apparently, illegitimacy was rampant in the eighteenth century and not anything to be ashamed of, but I still can't find confirmation."

"Why not?"

"Savage was a well-known reprobate who told all kinds of whoppers. The story goes that when Eliza broke with him, he thought he could palm his own progeny off on Steele."

"You'd think Miss Haywood would set it right."

"You'd think, but she was very mysterious about her background and private affairs. Strange when you think how open she was about her sexuality." Addison shut the laptop. "So how did your date go? Did you find a dress?"

Instead of answering, Phoebe went into the kitchen. She came out with a can of soda. "Where's Nick?"

"He had to go up to DC—he said he had a meeting with his publisher. He'll be back tomorrow."

"Funny, I haven't seen him writing anything."

"I think his book is only in the research phase."

Phoebe took a sip and remarked casually, "You mean, when he's done with the research, he'll leave?"

Addison gulped. "He...he hasn't said." *Why didn't that register? Of* course *he won't stay here.*

Her cousin said cheerfully, "Well, you won't be here much longer either, so it's moot, I guess. Where does he live?"

"I...I don't know. I only know he grew up in Rhode Island."

"Well, at least his publisher is in DC. When you're back home, I'm sure you'll be able to get together."

Addison wasn't so confident. "I don't know who his publisher is. Phoebe? I...I don't have any way to contact Nick."

"Then he'll find you. Chill, Addy." She tossed the empty can into the recycle bin. "You were asking about Walter."

Addison, lost in a funk, shut her eyes tight. When she opened them, nothing had changed. *Damn.* "No, you were *telling* me about Walter. What's wrong? Didn't he open the car door for you this time? Is he starting to take you for granted?"

Phoebe relaxed. "That's probably it. He was...I guess the word is preoccupied. Didn't talk much. Had a lot to drink." Her lower lip trembled. "Do you think he's lost interest? Did I keep him waiting too long for...you know?"

Addison said firmly, "He did just kill a person, Phebes. That would upset anybody." When Phoebe remained unpersuaded, she added, "I believe the adage goes that the longer they have to wait, the *more* interested they are. I've seen the way he looks at you, Phoebe. He wants you."

She grinned. "That's okay then. So, any news on the espionage front?"

Addison's hand flew to her mouth. "I'd almost forgotten! Daniel was released. The CIA took a hand and told Peel and the FBI he rode in on where to go." She beamed. "Evidently, Mr. Special Agent Robert Peel of the Federal Bureau of Investigation got his ass whupped by his boss."

Phoebe's jaw dropped. "The CIA took a hand? Why?"

Addison remembered that Phoebe wasn't present for Dan's revelation. "Dan is CIA. He's the one the security chief at Wallops called in."

"So he's not a bad guy?" Phoebe clapped her hands. "Fantastic! I'll tell Walter. He'll be so pleased." She picked up her bag. "Gotta go."

"That was quick."

"I have to find Walter. Maybe this will raise his spirits, and he'll be back to his old self." She blew Addison a kiss and ran down to her car.

Chapter Thirty-One

There is no greater sign of a bad cause, than when the patrons of it are reduced to the necessity of making use of the most wicked artifices to support it.

~ *Joseph Addison*

Addison's house, Thursday, April 10

Nick must have slipped into her bed while she was dreaming about Eliza and a masked lover cavorting in an English meadow. She was smiling in her sleep, enjoying the almost tangible caresses of Eliza's lover, when she woke up. "Nick?"

"Tell me, at what point did you realize they were real hands?"

She snuggled under his arm. "Does it matter?"

"It does to me. What if you were dreaming about, say, Daniel?"

She sat up. "What?" *Oh dear, did he pick up on Daniel's attraction?*

He pulled her back down, chuckling. "That wouldn't bother me—I'd just persuade myself that you had mistaken him for me. Now, if you were dreaming about Robert Peel...that would be different."

"Uh, yes." *Change the subject.* "How did your meeting go?"

There was a short silence. Then, "Oh, you mean

with my publisher?"

"Isn't that why you went to DC?"

"Yes, of course. It was fine. I asked for an extension of the deadline for the manuscript. I…uh…haven't had as much opportunity to visit the sites on my itinerary as I expected. I have yet to behold the lovely Assawoman."

She laughed. "But I'm sure you've visited *Horntown*."

"There is still much to enjoy here, little cricket."

"So…you're staying for a while?" She crossed her fingers.

"Uh-huh. Is that okay?" His tone was tentative.

Casual, Addy. Casual. "Of course. By the way, where do you live the rest of the year? Rhode Island?"

"I go back there for holidays when I can."

"You still have family there?"

"My mother. Some cousins." He pinched her. "An old girlfriend or two."

All right, fine. She'd let it pass. "Now that Walter knows about you and Daniel, you might confess to him that your mother is not actually on her death bed."

"I'll think about it." He kissed her. "Right now, I have things to do before I tell you about my trip."

"Oh, are you leaving?"

"That would make doing the things I have in mind a little harder. No, I think I'll stay right here."

She turned out the light, and for a while the only sounds were the murmuring of the tide coming in and a little heavy breathing.

****

Addison's house, Friday late morning

"Okay, I haven't told you everything that happened

while I was in DC." Nick refilled Addison's coffee cup. "I also hooked up with Daniel."

"You did! Did you rendezvous by a tree stump in Rock Creek Park? Or in an old abandoned warehouse?" She leaned forward eagerly. "Did you wear a *disguise*?"

"You've been reading too many thrillers. We met at a Dunkin Donuts. I wore a gray suit. Daniel was all in blue. He had a new haircut, if that helps."

"Well, that's something. How is he?"

"He's fine. We managed to lose his tail long enough for him to fill me in on what's happening at the base."

"How does he know what's going on? Walter?"

"No. Turns out there's another agent there."

"CIA?"

"Yes. He's embedded with the Belarusian team. His original mission was to keep an eye on Olga, but since Daniel departed, he's been hunting for the document thief." He poured a cup for himself. "And he found him."

"Wow. Who is it?"

"The agent wasn't able to pass his name on to the higher-ups and didn't want to share it with Daniel until he had. All Daniel knows is it's not one of the Belarusians."

"Why wouldn't the agent tell Daniel?"

"Um, maybe because it's a secret? These spook types don't give away information to just anyone."

"But Daniel's CIA! This was his mission. Surely he has a right to know."

"That's not how it works. Daniel is out of the loop now for a very good reason. If he reengages, he could blow the other agent's cover."

Addison was frustrated. *So close*. "Did he have any ideas about what we could do?"

"Other than sit tight? No." Nick watched a flock of glossy ibis winging over the grasses. "He says even the CIA is in a holding pattern, since the channel to their plant is now plugged. Klopman has confined the Belarusians to quarters and put a guard on them 24/7. He's determined not to have any more inconvenient events. He even took their phones away, so the agent has no means of getting his reports out."

Addison put her plate in the sink. "Do I have this straight? There's a good guy agent who's in detention, and a bad guy agent who's free to roam around the base. And we don't know who either one is."

"That about covers it."

"We need to reverse the order. Good guy out; bad guy in."

"We? Last I checked, we can't roam the base either, much less make a citizen's arrest of someone whose identity we don't know."

Addison tapped her fingers on the table. "I've got it. We tell Walter. He can arrange for a message to be smuggled in to the CIA man."

Nick pursed his lips. "Good idea. Oh, except for one problem. How does Walter contact an anonymous agent?"

"*Hmm…*" Addison brightened. "How about this? Walter pretends to forget his phone somewhere—say, in the canteen. Then, in the presence of the Belarusians, he announces that he can't leave his post to retrieve it because he's on duty. The agent gets the message, nips into the canteen, and uses Walter's phone to send his information out."

Nick stood up. "You know, that might work. As long as there's only one spy in the group, that is."

"Well, they can't *all* be spies. Klopman would notice if none of them had any scientific expertise." Addison rose. "Walter will know how to do it. Phoebe said he was on duty this afternoon. Let's go find him."

Nick caught her elbow. "Um, Addy? You might want to put some underwear on. And...er...brush your teeth."

Her hands went to her face, then to her bosom. "Ack! Be with you in a jiffy."

****

Wallops Flight Facility, Friday afternoon

A band of crows heckling a red-shouldered hawk flew over their heads as they crossed the causeway in the Hummer. "So Daniel says the real document thief is not Belarusian. He couldn't be an American, could he?"

"Let's hope not."

Addison harked back to the field trip with Phoebe's kindergartners. "What about Arabs?"

"Could be anyone. This is a NASA facility. It represents a gold mine of data to any country—China, Iran, Turkey...even France and Israel."

"Israel!"

"You didn't know every nation on earth is spying on every other nation on earth?"

Addison sat back. "Of course I did, but the only actual working spy we know is embedded with the Belarusians."

"Besides the file pilferer, that is."

"Should we take our information to Klopman?"

"Absolutely not. Remember the security tapes Daniel brought home? The missing two minutes when we don't know what Klopman was doing?"

Addison gazed out the window at the marshes. "I can't see Klippety Klopman as a traitor."

"Even if he isn't, he would never admit that clandestine activity is happening on his watch." Nick glanced at Addison. "I beg you to remember we're civilians, Addy. We shouldn't be injecting ourselves into any of this."

"Leave it to the professionals? How's that working out for you so far? Two people dead, your brother hamstrung, and a spy swiping highly classified data from a top-secret facility unchecked."

"Nonetheless. I want my objections to this whole caper on the record."

"Duly noted. We stick with the original plan. We find Walter and let him take it from there."

"Agreed." Nick made the turn to the main gate. "Klopman may listen to him if he won't listen to us."

They were stopped at the checkpoint. Nick leaned out his window. "We're here to see Walter Pope. He's a security guard. I believe he's on duty."

"Pope? Yeah. He just took a break." The officer pointed at a building. "He's probably in the canteen in Building N-1. Take these." He handed them plastic cards on lanyards. "You have to wear temporary badges while on the grounds."

They hung the IDs around their necks and, following the guard's directions, parked in a lot adjacent to an undistinguished single-story edifice with almost no windows. They found Walter sitting in a small room filled with Formica-topped tables and vending machines. He had a waxed cardboard cup of coffee before him.

"Walter?"

He looked up. "How did you two get in here?"

"We told the gatekeeper we needed to talk to you." Nick scanned the other tables. A few people in white coats sat in clusters, watching Addison and Nick curiously and whispering. One of them—a swarthy man with a heavy beard—openly stared.

Addison twitched. "Can we go somewhere private?"

"Sure." Walter led them to a small office. When they were inside, he closed the door and moved to the window. Addison took the sole chair. "I've only got a few minutes left of my break. What is it?"

Addison blurted, "We have information on the real spy—the one who's making off with the documents."

Walter straightened. "You mean Nick's brother Daniel?"

"No, no! It's not Daniel."

"I don't understand. If he's not guilty, why is he sitting in a jail cell in DC?"

"He isn't. Not anymore, anyway. He's been released. Didn't Phoebe tell you?"

"I haven't been in touch with her. I've been working a double shift."

Nick said, "Daniel is CIA."

Walter whistled. "CIA, huh?"

"Yes. Olson—"

"Olson? Our security chief? Former security chief, that is?"

"Yes, yes." Nick was clearly irritated by the interruptions. "He was concerned about the missing documents and notified the CIA. Daniel was sent here undercover, but somebody ratted him out."

Addison added, "Except that the informer lied to Klopman. He told him Daniel was the document thief. And Klopman told Peel."

Nick took up the story. "So Peel went after Daniel, who had to make himself scarce. He came to us for help. As luck would have it, Peel had Addison's house under surveillance and trapped him when he tried to take a powder."

"And you say Daniel's been released? Is he here?" Walter seemed only mildly curious.

Does he not understand what we're saying? "No, he's back in Washington, DC. We're on our own. That's why we came to see you."

"I see." Walter rubbed his chin. "First things first. How did you come by the information about the real spy? Legally, I hope."

"From Daniel himself. He didn't have specifics; the other CIA plant has the person's name."

Walter's eyes grew wide. "Oh, really. This place seems to be riddled with spies. And who, may I ask, is this second CIA agent?"

"We…er…don't know that either." Addison was beginning to wonder if this was such a good idea. They'd get the Wallops Island security team all up in arms with very little to go on.

"That's it? That's all you have?" Walter seemed, if anything, relieved. He moved around them to the door. "Look, let's forget we even had this little talk. I don't know what bilge your brother is feeding you, but there are no more spies here. We ran Daniel Savage to earth, and Olga Ilyich Zhuk has been…eliminated." He reddened. "That sounds awfully callous, doesn't it?"

Nick made a face. "It wasn't your fault. I guess

you're right. Sorry to bother you."

Walter slapped him on the back. "I must say, I appreciate your enthusiasm, but you'd better leave the sleuthing to us professionals after this."

"Agreed." Nick gestured at Addison. "Why don't we—"

The door flew open. A man Addison recognized as one of the Belarusian biologists stood on the threshold. He glanced at Addison and Nick, but locked his eyes on Walter. "So it's *you*."

Walter took a step toward him. "What are you talking about? You're not supposed to be out of the lab, Sergey."

"You're his accomplice."

"Whose accomplice?"

"Li Shun-yuan, the Chinese virologist. The spy. We knew he was working with someone who had access to every building. When I saw you take these two out of the canteen, I followed you. You came here to Li's office—the only place in the complex that isn't bugged." His eyes narrowed. "You thought they might be on to you. What were you going to do? Kill them too?"

"Don't be absurd. I—"

Sergey's hand moved to his waistband.

Addison saw the butt of a revolver sticking out. She cried, "Who are you?"

"Never mind." He spoke to Walter. "Leave them alone. Come with me."

Walter looked over Sergey's shoulder, out into the hall. "Dr. Li, why don't you join us?"

When Sergey spun around, Walter snatched the pistol. The barrel seemed unusually long. Addison guessed it had a silencer attached and wondered fleetingly if that were standard issue for Belarusian scientists. *Nah.* She craned her neck, but couldn't see anyone behind the Belarusian.

"There's no one—" Sergey turned, and Walter fired, hitting him in the chest. He toppled backward. Walter leaned out, looked up and down the hall, and dragged his victim back into the room.

It all happened so quickly that Addison was still sitting in her chair. Nick lunged at Walter, who swatted him away like a pesky gnat. He stepped over the corpse. "Shame about that. Would've let you go, but now I'm stuck with you. Gimme those." They took off the IDs and handed them to him. "Now come on." He gestured with the gun.

They passed him and went out into the hall. As Walter began to follow, Nick kicked back suddenly, hitting him below the knee. Through the mists of panic, Addison recalled that the move was supposed to incapacitate a person. *Nick is so clever.*

Her flirtation with optimism went poof when Walter straightened and shot Nick, who yowled, clutched at his arm, and staggered into the doorjamb. Blood seeped through his fingers.

Walter grabbed Nick's uninjured arm and pulled him upright. "It's just a scratch. Quit your caterwauling. Nobody can hear you—they're all at the director's meeting. Now get going, or I'll shoot Addison, and this time I won't aim wide."

They preceded him down the empty hall and out a side door. As they crossed a lane to the employee parking lot, an armed guard waved at Walter. He called, "You going home early, Pope?"

Walter stuck his pistol in Addison's back, using her as cover. "Just taking these hikers back to their car. They were a little lost."

The man laughed. "I guess they missed the big No Trespassing signs, huh." He pulled out his walkie talkie and walked away.

"Yeah." Walter surveyed the empty lot, then pushed Addison and Nick toward an old red Chevy in a far corner. He opened the trunk. "You. In there."

Nick climbed in.

Walter closed the lid and turned to Addison. "In the rear seat." As she bent down, he struck her on the back of the head with his gun. The last thing she saw was an empty vodka bottle.

Chapter Thirty-Two

Is there not some chosen curse, some hidden thunder in the stores of heaven, red with uncommon wrath, to blast the man who owes his greatness to his country's ruin!
~Joseph Addison

Addison's house, Friday, April 11

Addison woke to a pair of mud-colored eyes inches from hers. She tried to rear back but discovered she was tied to a straight-backed chair.

"You awake?"

"Of course I'm awake, Walter. Ow." She wished she could reach her aching head to rub it. "Where am I?"

"Don't you recognize the family plantation?"

She turned her head. *I'm in my own kitchen!* "Why did you bring me here? If Peel doesn't show up, Phoebe will."

"I happen to know Peel's in Salisbury catching up on paperwork." He rolled his eyes. "He's nothing more than a glorified apparatchik. Phoebe's primping for our date tonight." His face twisted in a wolfish grin. "Poor gal. She's going to be real disappointed. Her loving swain is skipping out on her."

So this is probably the best place to hide us. "What have you done with Nick?"

The voice came from behind her. "I'm here."

"I'll let you two gaze soulfully into each other's eyes while I find something to eat." Walter swung Addison's chair around roughly.

Nick lolled on the other kitchen chair. The only thing keeping him from falling were the ropes lashed tightly around him. A bandanna cinched his arm. It was red with blood. He made an effort to chirp brightly, "Hey, Walter. Tell you what: we'll wait here while you call 9-1-1."

At the sight of her lover in pain, Addison's fear evaporated and was replaced with fury. "You stinking rat, Walter. You tricked us. You lied to us. You're a...a..."

"Spy? Yes. I thought it was too funny when you all fell for the Spy Museum line. Ha-ha. No, I'm a genuine, fully trained espionage agent. I work for the Russian people, or rather, for their peerless leader, Vladimir Vladimirovich Putin. Let's just say I want to"—he snickered—"make Russia great again."

She wished she had the bad manners to spit on him. "What are you waiting for? Why don't you kill us?"

"Oh, I don't want to do that. Yet. Don't worry; I promise to make it quick and painless. It's time to finish the job and make my exit before that moron Klopman gets his act together."

"I'll ask again: what are you waiting for?"

"My ride. The eminent Dr. Li Shun-yuan."

From Nick's corner, they heard a weak snuffle. "Ah, the Dr. Li whose office isn't bugged. So he's the thief. You were working with him."

"A marriage of convenience. We discovered we had a mutual interest in NASA's activities. He wanted to steal the technology; I wanted to sabotage it."

"Those two ends sound mutually *exclusive*."

"Yes, well, Dr. Li will discover that when I lift the documents he stole from his lifeless body at the dock."

"Dock? What dock? Here?" The image of a corpse on her deck did not appeal to Addison.

"Now that wouldn't be smart, would it? No, Li's picking me up here. I'll take care of you two, then we'll go back to the lab. After I make the switch and gather supplies, we'll head down to Norfolk. Once there, I'll dispose of the eminent Dr. Li."

"So you used Dr. Li to get hold of the secret papers?"

"Let's just say I took advantage of his sticky fingers. We need the structural plans and readouts for the station."

Norfolk. "You're going to board a ship?"

He burnished his fingernails on his shirt. "The KGB spares no expense for their best operatives. I shall enjoy a relaxing voyage to Kaliningrad in a first-class cabin on the Liberian-flagged freighter *M. T. Poli.*"

Nick asked, "How long has Li been at this?"

"Six months. He's compiled quite a library of highly classified stuff. With it, China would be able to surpass the US within a year. That is, if they were to get hold of the documents. Which they won't."

"Daniel said the thefts increased after the Belarusians got here. Were they working with Li?"

Walter grunted. "Nah. When Li finally got rid of that meddling Taiwanese immunologist, he could get what he wanted without having to sneak around. That, and I told him"—here he sniggered again—"that I would let him bunk with me on the ship. He had to lay his hands on as much as he could in the limited time he had left."

This must be the part where we tie up the loose ends and the villain provides the solution to all the mysteries. Well, Addison was game. "Why did you help us with the defectors? Or were you going to report them to the Belarusian government?"

"Them? I could care less what happened to them, but it seemed a good cover—the patriotic American helping the poor devils who were seeking asylum from a communist utopia. Fools. Plus I could keep stringing Phoebe along."

That got Addison's attention. "Why did you need her?"

"She's got a big mouth. Blabbed everything you guys were doing. I could keep tabs on you without appearing too eager or showing up too often."

"You don't care for her?" *Poor Phoebe!*

"A broad who likes *tulips*? You kidding me? Little redneck brat."

Nick piped up before Addison could start swearing. "How did you know about the tulips?"

"Her life on Facebook is—pardon the expression—an open book." He sighed daintily and put a hand to his breast. "I jes' looove a man who opens the car door for me."

Addison tried to kick Walter but realized too late her ankles were bound to the legs of the chair. She toppled over, landing on her side facing away from the men. She heard an intake of breath from Nick, but silence from Walter. When nothing happened, she fumed, "So you're just going to leave me here?"

"I'm thinking about it."

"I might point out"—Nick's voice held a touch of humor—"that she's between you and the door, should you need to depart in a hurry."

"True. All right." Walter heaved Addison up. "Better?" He didn't wait for an answer. "So…you got any food around here?"

Addison went over the contents of her refrigerator. *Anything spoiled? Poisonous? How long has that milk been in there?*

"Never mind—I'll just have some crackers." He ripped the top off the box and munched on a few saltines, scattering crumbs on the floor.

Nick tried again. "So the only reason you encouraged the Belarusians to defect was to keep Phoebe interested?"

"Partly, but my orders were to keep tabs on them anyway. Their experiment in lactobacillus bacteria was my ticket to success."

"Russia wants information on gut bacteria? I doubt there's anything classified about that."

"You're right."

"Then what's this 'ticket to success' you're on about?"

He raised his eyebrows. "A weapon."

Nick frowned. "You plan to weaponize a *probiotic*?"

"Do I look like an idiot? No, see, they're assembling the materials for an experiment to determine the effect of zero gravity on lactobacillus. I intend to replace their bacteria with my own." He grinned slyly.

He did say he was planning to sabotage something. "What kind of bacteria?"

He winked. "Let's just say it doesn't improve your digestion."

Nick sucked in a breath. "That's diabolical."

"Indeed. If it weren't for that bitch Olga, the job would have been wrapped up already. They were planning to launch the rocket last Tuesday. After her death, they delayed it to tomorrow morning. I had to hustle to remove my substitute material before they rechecked the module. I was going to reinsert it today, but then you two showed up, putting yet *another* kink in my schedule." He slammed the back of Nick's chair, cracking one of the legs.

It sagged, pulling him sideways. Nick flinched and let out an oath.

"Oh, shut up."

Addison closed her eyes and counted out the seconds, waiting for the terror to subside. She fixed Walter with a hate-filled stare. "You murdered Olga."

"Well, of course I did."

"But she was on your side! Why didn't you just enlist her?"

"My side! Are you kidding? She's Belarus. Pain in the ass. She was going to report me—*me*—to Belarusian security. Get this: she actually thought she should *protect* her wards." He tittered. "You can't make this stuff up."

"Protect? From whom?" Addison stared at him. "You? Wait a minute: you killed Grigory Vasilinak too? But why?"

Instead of responding, Walter began to pace between his two prisoners, grumbling to himself. He suddenly shouted, "Damned satellites! Russia is better—stronger—without them. That's where

307

M. S. Spencer

President Putin is wrong—we don't need them."

"Satellites? Are you going to damage our satellites?"

"Huh?" He stopped pacing. "What are you talking about?"

She raised her eyes to the ceiling. "Communications satellites. In space."

"Space?" He grabbed her arms. "You've figured it out?...No way. Oh, I see." He let go. "No, I'm talking about satellite *countries*. Putin's like all Russian leaders before him. He wants to bring them all back into the Russian fold. To him, land—territory—is everything. He thinks a bigger land base gives us more power, but those states are more like giant vacuum machines that suck us dry of resources. We're the ones with the natural gas, the population, the industry. We can take on and defeat this American shithole ourselves, without having to *cooperate*"—he gave the word a vicious twist—"with yokels who don't even speak good Russian."

Wow. Talk about a confession. I only wish we could record this. Or live to tell about it. "But why kill Vasilinak? It only drew unwanted attention to Wallops."

Walter was still lost in his rant, muttering peevishly, "...trying to help the ungrateful bastards. Thought if I facilitated their defection I could purge a few disloyal Belarusians from the stock. How does Vasilinak repay me? He caught me fiddling with the canister in the lab. He—" Here he swung on Nick, seized his shirt, and shook him. "He threatened to report me to Klopman! What a buffoon."

"Fiddling with the canister? What canister?"

"The one they're sending up to the space station on the small launch vehicle." He snickered. "Those astronauts are in for a very nasty surprise."

Addison went over what Walter had said. A lot of it didn't make sense—it was as though he were speaking in code. Something about making the switch, and then a "module" and "substitute material." And a "station." *The space station*? "What kind of surprise?"

"Oh," he said airily, "a little anthrax where the lactobacillus bacteria are supposed to be." He closed his eyes, a smile playing across his thin lips. "I can see it now. They gather around the capsule, giddy with delight. It'll be like Christmas. They haven't received anything from home in over two months. The leader—I believe it's Chuck O'Henry. The most arrogant asshole in the space program. Karma's a bitch, ain't it, Chuckie?"

"You're going to poison the crew of the space station?" Addison couldn't keep the shock out of her voice.

"More than that. Don't ask me how it all works; I just follow the instructions. See, you place the anthrax inside a tube filled with natural gas. When it's opened in zero gravity, it explodes, raining deadly toxin down all over the station." He cackled. "It'll not only kill the humans, it will render most of the instruments inoperable. How I wish I could be there to see it!" His gaze went to Nick. "Ah, but then, I wouldn't be alive to bask on the porch of my new dacha in Kuntsevo."

Nick's brow creased. "I don't understand. Russians use the station as well. If you contaminate it, all *their* experiments and equipment will be lost too."

A cunning expression spread across Walter's face.

309

"I'm not supposed to know—privileged information. I was eavesdropping on the Belarusians and heard one of them—Vladimir Stepanovich Novik—boasting to his pals about joining the team for this hush-hush project in Russia. He spent two weeks in Moscow before coming to the US. He let slip that we're secretly building our own space station. It'll launch from somewhere in Siberia next year." He rubbed his hands. "No more sharing our experiments and our vodka with the running-dog Americans. Thank God for that new president of yours. We call him Mr. No-Balls in Moscow. He'll wet his pants—but he won't do anything."

Addison spoke suddenly. "Did Olga know any of this?"

He sniffed. "Not a thing. Too busy making goo-goo eyes at Sergey Pavlovich. She didn't have a clue he was CIA."

"Sergey? The man you killed in Dr. Li's office. So he is—was—the CIA plant with the Belarusians." She had a new idea. "You didn't know who he was until that moment, did you?"

Walter didn't answer for a minute, then shrugged. "Doesn't matter—he didn't have a chance to tell anyone about me, did he?"

Nick mumbled, "If Olga wasn't privy to your true mission, why did she attack you? Those scratches…"

"Scratches? The broad didn't get within a foot of me." He snorted. "KGB my ass. No training at all. Dispatched her with…uh…dispatch." He touched his cheek. "Did these myself so I could claim it was self-defense." He beamed. "Brilliant, don'tcha think?"

"But what precipitated the fight?"

"Vasilinak—the bastard—had somehow managed to get word to her that he'd caught me in the lab. Instead of confronting me alone, she decided to do it with an audience. If she thought that would be safer, she didn't reckon with my ability to think on my feet."

"Audience…you mean the Belarusians?"

He nodded. "She waited until we were all on the bus to make a scene. They began to catch on that I wasn't some simple security guard. And when the bus driver heard me speaking Russian, I had to do something quick or my whole mission would have to be aborted."

Nick interrupted. "But at the police station I asked you if you spoke Russian and you said no."

"Correction: you asked if I spoke *Belarusian*. Big difference. One of your many boo-boos."

Addison was trying to piece together the scene in her mind. "So you and Olga were arguing in Russian?"

"Yeah. That was a close one. I switched to English when I saw the driver staring at me."

"And he bought it?"

He nodded. "I pretended we were using high-tech speak—full of foreign terms."

"But the Belarusians were a different story." Nick shifted on his seat. "They understood what you were saying."

"Yeah, so I threatened them. Told 'em I'd hang Vasilinak's death on them. They shut their traps."

"Then what happened?" *Keep him talking.* She tried not to glance at the telephone. *Come on, Phoebe. Call me!*

"I told the driver to stop at the bar and offered a round on the house. I knew no one would turn down a free drink. Typical freeloading scientists."

"You got rid of them so you could kill her?"

For the first time, Walter looked a little uncomfortable. "That wasn't the plan. Once they were out of earshot, I tried to calm her down—get her to shut up before she exposed me. She seemed to understand, but then I saw the glint of a gun. Bitch was going to take me back to Klopman. So I shot her. *Bang*! No more fat Olga." He recovered his good mood. "And now, let's see how best to put you two out of your misery. I have to get back to my duties on the base soon, or they'll send out a search party." He laughed at his own joke.

Uh oh...what else can I ask? Come on, Addy. "Is Dr. Li coming here?"

He checked his watch. "Should've been here fifteen minutes ago. I hope he didn't have any trouble securing a car. We have to be in Norfolk by ten tonight."

"You're taking an official NASA car?"

"Only while we're close to the base. I have a pickup truck stowed down at Assawoman. *Hmm*." He stroked his chin. "That might be a better place to knock Li off than Norfolk. More empty country." He swung on Nick. "Well, I might as well get the gross part over with. There's no real need to wait for him." He raised his gun and pointed it at Nick's head.

"Did you get all that, Savage?"

Chapter Thirty-Three

There is no virtue so truly great and godlike as justice.
~Joseph Addison

Addison's house, Friday, April 11

Addison couldn't spin around at the unexpected but most welcome voice, but she could squeal in delight.

Walter did spin around and thus came face to face with an FBI agent and a CIA agent, both carrying wicked-looking Glock 19s. They were standing just inside the glass doors to the deck. "Drop the gun, Pope."

Walter carefully laid it on the floor.

Nick began to hum a tune.

Addison cocked her head at him. "What's that song?"

"Together again. Gee, it's good to be together again."

She hissed, "It's not the *Muppet Movie*."

He grinned. "Oh yeah?"

The two men crossed the living room to the kitchen, effectively blocking Walter inside it. Peel called over his shoulder, "Deputy Tickell? You can bring in your cuffs now."

"Coming, sir." They heard a crash and a grunt from outside the front door. A quivering voice yelled, "I'm okay, sir! I'll shake it off. Hang on." The door knob rattled. "It's locked, sir."

Daniel stepped back and tried to open it. "He's right." His eyes went to the dead bolt.

Peel shifted his gaze from Walter to Daniel for a mere second, which was all it took.

Walter slashed his wrist down on Peel's gun arm and kicked Daniel's pistol out of his hand. He picked up his Beretta and backed to the sliding glass doors that led out to the deck, which the agents had conveniently left open. He sneered, "So this is the best the vaunted American intelligence agencies can offer? In Russia, you'd be hauled off to Siberia for less."

He leapt outside. From the canal came a splash and a halloo. Addison ducked and peered through Daniel's legs.

By sheer bad luck, Mr. Tickell was trolling by the house. The sudden appearance of a man with a gun must have caught his attention, for he put the outboard in neutral and called, "Hey, Miss Steele, everything okay?"

As they watched in horror, Walter jumped into the boat, knocked the old man into the muddy water, revved the motor, and roared away.

"Well, here's a fine how-di-do."

"*Humph*. I like that, not so much as a kiss my grits or have an apple."

Nick growled at the two agents. "Levity is not a good look on guys who just blew it big time."

Peel growled back. "I might suggest you not engage in recriminations until the ropes are off."

"And you are brought up to speed." Daniel picked up his Glock and tucked it into his waistband. He pulled a handkerchief from the pocket of his blue work shirt and went out to help Mr. Tickell to the dock.

The old man accepted the handkerchief and wiped his face and neck. He gestured at the people inside and said loudly, "You go on in an' take care o' them. I'll be fine. Gotta go track down m'boat. Won't be far." He tottered around the corner.

Daniel returned, unbolted the front door, and went out.

Nick looked at Peel. "What are you going to do now?"

"I'm going to untie you two and call for an ambulance."

"For me?"

"For you."

"And for Ike too." Daniel came back in with Ike, his arm under the deputy's shoulders to support him. Ike hopped on one foot. "Addison, did you know you have a broken railing on the front steps?"

"I do?"

Ike groaned. "It must have been rotten. When I slipped on the gravel and grabbed for the rail, it came away in my hand. I fell on my butt and twisted my ankle. Sorry, Addison."

Daniel deposited the deputy on the sofa with his injured foot resting on the coffee table. Peel slipped the ropes off Addison and then Nick. The two agents stood by the front door conversing in low voices.

A siren wafted in from the lane.

Addison was still struck by their blasé attitude. "Aren't you worried Walter will escape? He was waiting for Dr. Li to pick him up. They could be long gone by now."

Nick added, "They were headed to Norfolk. Walter said he was booked on a freighter for Europe."

"Yes, to Kaliningrad. We know."

"How?"

Peel glanced at Daniel. "Dr. Li told me. I took him into custody right after Pope disappeared with you two."

"Robert was coming in the front door while you were going out the back door." Daniel laughed.

Addison rubbed her sore wrists. *So many questions.* "How did you discover Li was the document thief?"

Daniel answered. "Klopman, of all people."

Peel interrupted. "Well, to be precise, a Taiwanese immunologist named Cheng fingered Li. He suspected him of espionage and had been watching him for months. For his part, Li did everything in his power to get Cheng removed. When Cheng told Klopman of his suspicions, the director tried to dismiss them, blaming it on politics. Li finally succeeded in having Cheng moved to another building."

"According to Walter, there were a lot of Chinese scientists at the facility, and only one from Taiwan."

Daniel answered. "True, and unfortunately that fact diluted any leverage Cheng had with Klopman."

Nick burst out, "Klopman should be fired. He's a purely political animal. Espionage running rampant at a facility that's central to our national security, and he toadies to the Chinese. It's outrageous."

Daniel gave him an amused look. "Well, you're in a position to do something about it."

Addison twitched. "He is?"

Nick opened his mouth and shut it. "I don't know what you're talking about, *Dan*."

His brother made a show of locking his lips. "I...uh...I mean as a *concerned citizen*, of course. You can write your congressman and demand Klopman be removed."

Nick's eyes flickered. "I'll do that."

Addison hadn't finished with her questions. "So what made the director finally act?"

Peel answered. "One of the Belarusians is an immunologist, too—a Vladimir Stepanovich Novik. When Cheng was kicked out of Li's lab, Klopman put him with Novik. Cheng poured out his troubles to Novik, who in turn told the other Belarusians. They went as a body to Klopman and insisted he investigate. Friedrich relayed the information to me."

Addison had been thinking. "Why would Novik care about a Chinese spy? And why would he tell you?"

Peel shrugged. "He wants to defect to the US. I presume he's no fan of communists."

Nick rubbed his arm. "Did you hear Walter say he planned to kill Li when they got to Norfolk?"

"Uh-huh." Daniel was grim. "Peel, you'll have to make clear to Li how lucky he is. I'm sure he'll be very grateful."

Addison was only slightly relieved. "What about Walter? Shouldn't you at least be going after him?"

"He won't go far without Li. When he can't find him, he'll probably hole up to wait in his safe house. We know where it is."

"Is it on Assawoman? He said he had a pickup truck parked there."

"No. We'll track him down after we get our two casualties squared away."

Addison saw the crew off, the ambulance ding-donging merrily, while Daniel and Peel tooted their horns in response.

To Addison, it sounded way too much like a circus parade.

****

Addison's house, Saturday morning

Even with Walter on the loose, Addison felt a million times better waking up in her own bed. Beside her, Nick snored gently. She stretched. "I'm hungry."

She slipped out of bed and went to the kitchen. She was halfway through her eggs when she heard a step.

"Nothing for me?"

"How's coffee sound?"

"Good—if it goes with bacon and eggs. And toast with butter."

"How about some homemade marmalade instead?"

"The King sobbed, 'Oh deary me, I *only* want a little bit of butter for my bread.' "

" 'But marmalade is tasty if it's very thickly spread.' First Jim Henson, and now A. A. Milne? Did your poetry education stop at the fourth grade?"

"The best poems are those for children. Easy to memorize."

"Okay." She handed him a crock of butter. "How's your arm?"

"Much improved. Nurse Velma did a bang-up job with the Band-Aid, and Lenny gave Ike and me a ride in the chief's squad car."

"So the bullet just grazed you?"

"Uh-huh. Despite his braggadocio, Walter is not a crack shot. I blame Russian training." He took a big bite of toast. "I'm feeling awfully chipper. What say after breakfast we take a ride to the refuge? I hear there's a pair of wood ducks in that little pond in the bend of the road."

Addison checked the sky. "Looks like a lovely day. Let's do it."

They finished the meal and went upstairs to get dressed. "I can get the jeans on, but"—Nick held up his bandaged arm—"can you help me with my shirt?"

She carefully lifted a short-sleeved chambray shirt over his shoulders and buttoned it. "Shall I drive?"

"No, I can handle it." He went to the Hummer.

They drove over the bridge to Assateague, flushing a fleet of sandwich terns from the railing. The entrance kiosk was closed. Nick sailed through. "Why is it free?"

"It's still too early for the beachgoers, and they have an honor system for birders."

"I should think you'd have a lifetime pass."

Addison laughed. "Even better, as one of the original settlers, we've been great-great-great-grandfathered in—no Steeles will ever have to pay the fee. We do contribute to Ducks Unlimited and the Theodore Roosevelt Conservation Partnership. And of course, our tax dollars go to the Fish and Wildlife Service."

They drove slowly along the refuge road. The Swan Cove pool resembled O'Hare airport the day before Thanksgiving. Herds of northern shovelers grazed in the shallows. Flocks of blue-winged teal and pintails ebbed and flowed in the deeper water. Mute swans guarded their tiny hummocks of dry land, surrounded by feeding brants. Addison sighed. "Spring is such a wonderful time here. There's so much variety. And the birds stay longer since they're nesting."

Nick trained his binoculars on a pair of American

wigeons, which had just taken off. "So how far back does birding go in your family?"

"You mean bird watchers? That's relatively recent. My ancestors only watched birds in order to get them in their sights. Good hunting here. I still have the recipe for fried dowitcher from my great-grandmother's *Joy of Cooking*."

"I thought this was a refuge? Otherwise known as a sanctuary for birds. Isn't it illegal to hunt the migratory fowl?"

"Yes, it is." She waited, an impish smile on her face.

"Okay..." He typed something on his phone. "Says here the refuge was established in 1943. That's almost eighty years ago. Are you insinuating a stray uncle or cousin might've come home with a brace of snipe since then?"

"Let's just say, we ate well, but usually dined late." She giggled.

Nick attempted a remonstrative frown. "I'd heard that poaching is a formally recognized profession on Chincoteague, but I didn't believe it."

"Poaching of birds, yes, but not of oysters."

He pointed at a flock of ducks soaring over the pines. "Swear to me that you currently stick to watching them."

"*I* do. I can't speak for the rest of my family."

Nick passed the visitor center at Tom's Cove and went three-quarters of the way around the circle to park in the north lot. Addison was surprised to find it jam-packed with people. While the women—snuggled under blankets—read books with gloved hands, the men lined the shore, fishing poles bristling like fence pickets. "Fancy a walk on the beach?"

"Sure." She almost said, "I can check on the wishing tree," but stopped short. They had to pass the tree anyway, but she didn't plan to linger.

As she got out of the Hummer, Nick leaned over and took something from the glove compartment.

They were a few yards from the tree when she caught sight of a familiar figure in the distance. "Isn't that Daniel?"

"Yes, it is. He's still wearing the same clothes he had on yesterday. He must have been up all night searching for Walter. I wonder what he's doing here? You'd think they'd have gone to Norfolk."

"Maybe they lost him, and they're backtracking. Peel said they knew where Walter's safe house is. It could be somewhere around here."

Nick's eyes raked the dunes. "If so, you'd think Daniel would have discovered it when he was hiding up here himself."

"Daniel camped in the woods. I'm betting Walter's safe house is the old life-saving station on the beach."

"One way to find out." He strode up the beach to Daniel, who was staring north. "Fancy meeting you here."

Chapter Thirty-Four

Pride goes before destruction and a haughty spirit before a fall.

~Joseph Addison

Assateague beach, Saturday, April 12

Daniel started. "Oh, hey. I'm waiting for Peel. We're going to head up the island."

"You didn't catch Pope in Norfolk?"

"We had cops staked out at the ship, but he never showed."

"How about Assawoman?"

"The pickup is still parked there, so current theory is he had to retrieve something from his safe house before he left." His cell rang. "Savage. Oh? Well, hup to. I'm on the beach—about five yards north of that crazy tree with all the junk on it." He tucked the phone back in his pocket. "Peel's running late."

Addison tugged Daniel's sleeve. "You haven't explained how you and Peel hooked up, Dan. The last contact you had with him was when he captured you as you tried to run away."

Nick added, "Wasn't he tailing you in DC?"

"No. Well, yes. As it turns out, once he discovered I was CIA, he approached me. We've been working together—on the QT—since my release."

Nick shaded his eyes. "So, where's this safe house?"

Daniel pointed northwest. "There's an old shack just up there over the dunes. Must be a shelter for rangers who get stuck out here in bad weather."

Addison nodded. "It's the ruins of the Pope's Island life-saving station." She tried not to giggle. "I asked Walter if the island was his ancestral estate."

No one laughed. Nick said, "As I recall, he told you they had owned the land but gave it up when the refuge was established."

Daniel had been tapping his foot and checking his watch. "Peel had better get a move on. Walter has had plenty of time to get away. Typical FBI laggard."

Nick looked down the beach toward the parking lot. "How long did Peel say he was going to be?"

"Another twenty minutes."

Addison was worried. "How can you be so sure Walter is at the shack?"

"I'm not, but it's the most likely place. His car is still at your house. Last night Peel's men covered the mainland causeway, and I watched the road to the refuge. Half an hour ago, a motorcycle passed me on its way to the beach. It could only have been Walter."

"How do you know?"

"The bike had been reported missing from Dobie's parking lot last night."

"Did you find it?"

He shook his head. "No, but if he took the service road, he'll have hidden it somewhere in the trees. Peel is supposed to station a man to block the gate from the loop before he comes around to meet me. We figured it would be easier to get the drop on Pope if we come at him from the beach."

"He can't afford to stick around."

"Right. I'm betting he has false identity papers and money stashed in the building. He'll grab what he needs and make tracks."

Addison observed, "If his only mode of transportation is the motorcycle, he'll have to go back via the service road, won't he?"

"Not necessarily. It's low tide. He can drive the bike on the hard sand. When he gets to the parking lot, he'll blend in with the crowd. Dump the bike. Maybe steal a car."

"So why doesn't Peel leave another man at the main refuge entrance?"

"Not enough manpower."

"Well, that's just stupid. Did you call Lenny?"

"You mean the police chief? No. This is a covert operation, Addison. My cover's blown, but we still don't need every Tom, Dick, and Lenny on the case."

Nick added, "Because of the national security implications."

Addison reluctantly agreed. "Okay."

Nick took his brother's elbow. "Look, Peel's taking too long. We're all agreed we need to catch Pope before he escapes. Why don't you and I go on? We can at least hold him till the cavalry arrives."

"What about Addison?"

"We'll leave her here to apprise Peel of the situation."

Daniel gave his brother a long look and pulled the Glock from his belt. "He's armed."

Nick held up a .38 revolver. "So am I."

Addison gasped. "That's what you took from the

glove compartment. Did you expect to find Walter here?"

"It seemed likely. After Walter hijacked his boat, I overheard Mr. Tickell say he wouldn't have to go far to track it down. I took it to mean the motor was almost out of gas. If Walter were on foot, he'd head to his safe house."

"And you didn't see fit to pass that along?"

Nick shrugged. "To be honest, I didn't think much about it until this morning."

Addison was still irritated. "That's why you suggested a hike. Without bothering to tell me we might come across a murderous communist criminal."

"Uh-huh." He grinned at her.

Daniel asked, "What made you think he'd come here?"

"He couldn't resist using the Pope's Island place." Nick sniffed. "I'll bet he didn't see the irony in squatting on property that was appropriated by the State."

Addison was about to continue scolding, this time focusing on the gun, when a little voice whispered, "At least now he can protect himself." She already had proof that Walter wouldn't hesitate to shoot him, armed or unarmed. *"Humph."*

"Okay." Daniel turned to Addison. "You'll be all right?"

She deliberately faced south away from the men. "Of course I will." As they moved off, she peeked over her shoulder. Once they'd gone far enough, she pivoted to watch them. The resemblance between the two men was remarkable—even to their gait. *Ah, but one of them is…not like the other.* She hugged herself, savoring the nugget of happiness nestling in her breast.

Daniel and Nick trudged north up the beach a few hundred yards, then swerved and started to climb the dunes. A minute later, they'd disappeared. She sat down on the sand and leaned her back against the wishing tree. *How far inland was that shack?* She couldn't picture it from where she sat, having only passed it when she was on the service road. The land between the dunes and the woods was marshy and flat. *No cover. They would have to find a way to catch Walter off guard.*

A loud bang rent the air. Then two. *Oh my God, those were gunshots!* She leapt up and ran.

Where the two sets of footprints veered away from the beach, she began to climb. She was almost level with the top of the dune when she paused. *I could be a sitting duck too.* So how to see what was happening without exposing herself? *Maybe spring up and down quick, like a prairie dog popping out of its hole?* Instead, she got down on her hands and knees and crawled sideways, keeping her head down, until she reached a big tuft of saltgrass. She parted it carefully and immediately wished she hadn't.

Below her on an area of bare hardpan lay two bodies. Standing over one was Walter, pointing a 9-millimeter pistol at it. Addison stood up and plunged down the dune, beyond caring whether Walter shot her or not. He turned, but when he saw her he lowered his gun. She was within a few yards when she realized that one of the bodies was kicking. He was gagged and his hands were tied behind his back. The other one lay still, bleeding heavily from a wound in his chest, staining the blue shirt. *That's the shirt I helped Nick put on this morning.* "No!" She ran to him.

His eyes were closed, and he was taking shallow, rickety breaths. She knew he was dying.

"Oh my dear, my Nick. Oh God, oh God, don't take him from me. Please."

Walter pulled her roughly away. "I've had it with you people. Why couldn't you leave well enough alone? I was on the point of letting you live, Addison, but now I'm going to have to kill you all." Clasping her in a painful grip, he raised his gun and pressed it to her temple. She closed her eyes tightly, thinking miserably that it didn't matter anymore. Nick was dead. A shot rang out.

Chapter Thirty-Five

Zeal for the public good is the characteristic of a man of honor and a gentleman, and must take the place of pleasures, profits and all other private gratifications.
~Richard Steele

Assateague, Saturday, April 12

Addison unclenched her fists but kept her eyes closed. The side of her face stung. She felt light-headed. *Is this what death feels like? Like I can float free, nothing holding me down? But where's that white light they're always on about?* She felt oddly disgruntled and not a little disappointed. *Don't tell me all those angel stories were wrong!* She'd arrived at the part where she wondered if she'd see Nick in heaven when the voice that had been whispering in her ear grew louder.

"Addison! Wake up."

Okay, that sounds like Phoebe. Is she dead too?

"Open your damned eyes, Addy."

She did. Looming over her were the familiar gray eyes and red tresses of her cousin. She struggled to an upright position. "Phoebe! It *is* you. How did you get here?"

Her cousin sat on a log. Propped at her side was a Remington Fieldmaster rifle. "Dune buggy. Peel was diddling around trying to start it when that guy Eric—

Klopman's driver?—showed up, demanding to know what was going on. He and Peel got in this huge row. Looked like it was going to be a while." She pursed her lips. "*Men*. They're always fussing. I knew Walter was up here, so I took the buggy and crossed over the dunes to the loop and drove up the service road."

"How? I mean how did you know Walter was here?"

"I followed him last week. I had this hunch he was hiding something from me. I mean, he'd made no move to seduce me." At Addison's baffled look, she admitted, "Okay, it wasn't me who wanted to wait. I stretched the truth a bit. Call it foolish pride. But him? It didn't make any sense. I mean, *look* at me." Her smoky eyes sparkled, and her pixie mop shone in the sun. "I found the old life-saving station you were asking him about." Her eyes narrowed. "When I couldn't get hold of him for two days, I came out to the refuge. I wanted to catch him in the act—I was sure he was poaching ducks. Security guard, my eye."

"You didn't believe all that stuff about Morse code and the Spy Museum?"

"Nah. I looked up the Spy Museum website. No Walter Pope ever worked there. And get this: their staff training does *not* include Morse code."

Addison wiped the dirt off her hands. "Are you alone?"

"For now. If Peel settled things with Klopman's assistant, he should be along any minute." She tittered. "I'm guessing he's on foot, since I commandeered the buggy."

Phoebe's body blocked Addison's view of the others. "Where's Walter?"

Phoebe picked up the rifle and pretended to blow smoke from the barrel. "Gone to his maker."

"You *shot* him?"

"Should I have waited till he put a bullet in your brain?"

"No, no. I just didn't know you knew how to wield a firearm."

"Honey, I've been hunting since I was ten. Sporting clay state champ three years in a row. Remember old Cigar Oates? He used to take me and Bertie out to hunt rabbits and...other stuff." She grinned. "He knew all the spots the rangers didn't go."

"You poached?"

"Hey, it *is* a Chincoteague tradition."

"True. So why were you sore at Walter for doing it?"

"He's not a native. He's got no right. This is our land and our wardens. If he wanted to hunt, he could've gone on up to Boston and killed cats, for all I care. Just so long as he stayed away from our waterfowl."

"What do you mean, Boston? He's not from New Church?"

Phoebe patted her gun. "I guessed early on he wasn't from around here. He wasn't even from the Eastern Shore."

"What about Pope's Island?"

"Nothing to do with him."

"But he told us their land was confiscated for the refuge."

She shook her head. "Pope's Island wasn't added to the refuge until 1966, twenty-three years after it was established."

Addison eyed her. "Is that what made you realize

he wasn't who he said he was?"

Phoebe laid the gun down. "No, although that did rouse my suspicions. It was earlier, during that same lunch."

"Lunch?"

"Yeah, when we brought sandwiches for our pow-wow. He said he'd picked up grinders for us."

"You mean the subs?"

"Yeah. Now, you calls 'em subs, and I calls 'em subs, but only New Englanders call them grinders. I knew then and there he wasn't being honest with us."

"Huh." Addison wished she could soften the harsh truth. "He told us he was stringing you along—that he didn't like...didn't have feelings for you."

"Addy," Phoebe said equably, "Walter lied about everything. You know what I discovered when I started checking him out? His real name's Blake. It's true his family lived for a while in Chincoteague, but his great-great-grandfather ran away to Boston after he committed a crime."

"Blake? As in Jonah Blake? The man who beat up and robbed Little Dutch?"

Phoebe stared at her. "Oh my God, I forgot all about that story. That's right. Elmira Hopkins. Nana's tale of the wishing tree. She didn't tell it as often as she did the one about Jennie Hill. Small world."

Addison closed her eyes. "I always suspected that Jennie had another lover and that it was Jonah Blake."

"How could you possibly know that?"

"Her tombstone. The initials J. B. are carved on the back. They were contemporaries after all, and Jonah had a reputation for violence even before he assaulted Little Dutch."

"You're saying that Blake stole Jennie's heart from Tom and that's why Tom killed her?"

"No. I think Tom Freeman missed, and Jonah was the one who actually shot her. I told Nick…" She fell back and stared at the sky overhead. Tears brimmed. "Nick. Phoebe…Nick's dead."

Phoebe's eyes welled up. "I'm so sorry, Addison." She glanced at the prostrate form. "He's still alive, but it doesn't look good. He's lost a lot of blood."

"Alive? Why are we jibber-jabbering? Call 9-1-1!"

"Sit tight. Right after I shot Walter, I let Agent Peel know the situation and he called for an ambulance."

At that moment, a siren started up deep in the woods.

Addison inched over to the wounded man. His eyes were still closed. She laid her head on his stomach below the wound. "Oh Nick. It's not supposed to end this way. I…I loved you."

"You do?"

The voice was clear and deep. And a little too far away to come from the man beneath her.

She raised her head. "Nick?"

"I'm over here."

She rolled to a sitting position. Nick sat a few feet away, holding his hands in front of him.

Phoebe was busy untying his ropes. The gag lay on the ground. "Sorry, fellah, I had to make sure Addy was okay before I got to you."

Addison looked down. The same black hair, the same high cheekbones. *The same handsome face.* "Then this is…this is…"

"Yes. It's…" Nick's voice broke. "It's Daniel."

She turned back to the man lying so still. She bent

closer. "The scar. There's no scar on his hand."

Daniel's eyes fluttered open. They were already glazed with a thin film. "Nick?"

"I'm here."

Addison moved aside, and Nick knelt beside his brother.

Daniel made an effort to raise his chin. "Have to...tell you. Never was part of the gang. Always...always CIA. Undercover. Not able to explain before. Forgive me?"

Nick closed his lips tightly. "Forgiven."

Dan lifted one trembling hand and touched Nick's arm. "You still have the tattoo?"

Nick turned his wrist over, revealing the tiny plane and the letters DMB etched in blue. "You knew about it?"

He nodded. "Been following your career all these years. You've been pretty daring yourself. Who knew a desk job could be so exciting?"

"Yes. Well."

"I knew about everything—the foiled hijacking plot, the Indian affair, the suicidal astronaut. And the tattoo. Nick, I wanted so badly to get in touch. What I was working on...too dangerous even for you. I was always"—he laughed weakly—"in harm's way."

Nick whispered, "Don't try to talk. The ambulance is on its way."

Dan gazed up at his brother. "I shouldn't have left you, Nick. I shouldn't have abandoned you."

"It's okay." Nick's voice was hoarse. "I kind of suspected when your Wallops personnel file named me as your emergency contact. Everything else was fake."

Dan half chuckled. "Old habits die hard." He fell

back. "Hey Nick, now's a good time for one of your corny jokes. You got one?"

Nick took a deep breath and painted a smile on his face. "You hate my jokes."

"Give it a try. Maybe the millionth time's the charm."

Nick pressed his lips together. "Mom says hi."

"That's not much of a joke."

"Okay. How about this one? A ham sandwich walks into a bar. The bartender comes over and says, 'I'm sorry, sir. We don't serve food here.' " Daniel didn't move. "Get it?"

Nick's brother fought for a breath. His last words were "Ha-ha. That's a good one."

Chapter Thirty-Six

A lie is troublesome, and sets a man's invention upon the rack, and one trick needs a great many more to make it good.

~Richard Steele

Chincoteague police station, Monday, April 14

"So who the hell is Eric?"

Addison and Phoebe were sitting in Lenny Hogarth's office. Robert Peel lounged by the door. Walter's body had been taken to Norfolk, and Daniel's lay at Salyer's Funeral Home on Church Street. Nick was busy arranging for transport of the ashes. The chief had called the others in for a recap of recent events.

"A f...darned nuisance." Peel bit back the bad word. "I might have arrived in time to save Savage if he hadn't held me up."

Held him up...Oh no! "He wasn't in cahoots with Walter, was he?"

"Nothing so simple. He's from DHS."

"The Department of Homeland Security?"

Peel nodded. "Seems they got wind of trouble among the visiting scientists and decided they needed a man on the inside to observe. They sent widdle Ewic to spy on us spying on the spies." He glowered. "Man's just an obnoxious little paper pusher. Get this: he wanted the FBI to file a report with DHS on the operation! I told him I'd be happy to put my report where the sun don't shine."

"Is he still here?"

"For the time being. He announced his true affiliation in a meeting of the heads of departments at Wallops Island last Thursday. Caused a bit of a sensation. Klopman saw the writing on the wall and resigned then and there."

Lenny tilted his chair back, pencil between his teeth. "So, how about you brief us on the Chinese feller?"

"Li is squealing like a Peking duck."

Addison was curious. "Did you tell him Walter was planning to slip a package of anthrax onto the small launch vehicle and have it explode on the space station?"

Peel's jaw dropped. "You're kidding! My God, the damage would have been enormous. Billions of dollars in losses." He paused. "That puts a whole new light on things. Pope couldn't have worked for the Russians. He must have been a terrorist."

Addison cried, "You're wrong! Walter *was* KGB."

"That's crazy. The Russians have a huge stake in the station. Why would they destroy it?"

"Because they're secretly building their own."

Lenny and Phoebe gasped.

Peel took two swift strides to stand before Addison. "*What did you say?*"

"Walter overheard one of the Belarusians talking about it." She glanced at Peel. "You were hiding on my deck while he was telling us. How did you miss that part?"

He looked like he wanted to spit. "I was out front waiting for Deputy Tickell." He looked very grim. "Odd that Savage didn't see fit to relay such a significant piece of intelligence."

Dead silence reigned for a long minute. Then, as Lenny and Phoebe broke into loud chatter, Agent Peel left the room. After a while, the hubbub died down. The three in the office sat quietly.

Finally, Phoebe asked, "Where's Peel?"

Lenny shrugged. "I assume he's calling his superiors with the news."

Addison checked her watch. "He's been gone for fifteen minutes. Do you suppose they ordered him back to Salisbury? Or DC?"

Phoebe got up. "I'm going to look for him."

"I'm coming with you."

The agent's car was gone from the parking lot. Lenny came out, holding his phone to his ear. "Ladies? I've found him."

"Where is he?"

"He's being held at the Wallops facility."

"What do you mean, held?"

Lenny lowered the phone. "As in arrested. That was Eric Austen. Robert Peel is a Chinese spy."

****

Klopman's office, Wallops, Monday afternoon

The security guard ushered Lenny, Phoebe, and Addison into the director's office. Eric Austen sat at Klopman's desk. He said heartily, "Sit down, sit down."

Lenny looked around the room. "Where's Klopman?"

"He's finishing up his paperwork. He leaves tomorrow." He looked annoyingly smug.

"Are you filling in for him?"

"Me? Just for a week. An acting director is on his way."

Lenny harrumphed. "So where is Peel?"

"Locked in a windowless room down the hall. We were waiting for you, Chief Hogarth. Will you please take him into custody?"

The chief hemmed and hawed. "Yeah, I guess I have to, but I still think this should be handled by the feds."

Austen said acidly, "That would be fine with me, but we seem to be short on legitimate federal agents at the moment."

"I'd better call Ike then." He went out to the corridor.

While he was gone, Addison asked curiously, "So how did you discover Peel was a Chinese spy?"

"Couple of things raised my suspicions. He kept everyone else out of the room when he interrogated Dr. Li. It didn't ring true—I mean, most of these guys work in pairs. Then, when he refused to make his report available to DHS, I resolved to have a closer look at him."

"Is a report actually required?"

Eric hesitated. "Not exactly. But what was he hiding? So I checked with the FBI, and voilà: no Robert Peel on the force."

"But he showed me his badge!"

"Oh, that. Guess what? It was made in China."

Lenny returned, tucking his phone into his breast pocket. "Ike's on his way. What'd I miss?"

Addison sniffed. "Eric used his exceptional skills as an investigator to discover that Peel had his FBI accessories imported from China."

Austen treated her to a good glare. "When he showed up here today, he went straight to Dr. Li's office. We'd already detained Dr. Li, so I had Olson grab him."

"Kermit Olson? The former security chief? Didn't Klopman fire him?"

"He was at the facility to pick up his final paycheck. I made a command decision to reinstate him." Eric's concave chest expanded. "Since Klopman is on his way out, I had to take charge. Temporarily of course."

****

Addison's deck, Tuesday, April 15

"Wow. So Peel's a bad guy too?" Nick's eyes were huge. Phoebe handed him a can of Black Narrows lager. "What's this?"

"Local beer. Drink up; they'd like to make more."

Nick dutifully took a sip. "*Mmm.* Tasty." He put the can down. "Okay, Peel?"

"He's an agent for the Chinese Communist Party. His job was to facilitate Dr. Li's escape."

Phoebe ticked off her fingers. "Peel contacted Klopman using his FBI cover. When he arrived, Li told him Dan was CIA. To deflect attention from their activities, they pegged Dan as Olson's document thief."

Addison continued. "When the Belarusians informed Klopman that Li was in fact the thief, he passed it on to Peel. Peel realized they were compromised and pretended to arrest Li."

Phoebe grinned. "Peel warned Li to lie low while he helped Walter get away. He deliberately let Walter knock the gun out of his hand. Then he tried to slow us down at the refuge to give him extra time."

Addison popped the top on a can. "It wasn't until we were discussing the anthrax and the secret Russian space station in Lenny's office that Peel learned what Walter's real plans were." She remembered his change in demeanor. "He was definitely shaken."

Nick picked up the beer and drained it. "Actually, there's no way anyone could have suspected Walter."

The two women gawked at Nick. "How so?"

"We were all focused on the document thief. Walter's mission was so outlandish, so crazy, that no one could have foreseen what it was."

Phoebe took the empty cans to the kitchen and came back with a box of raisins. She poured several into her hand and started tossing them one at a time into her mouth. "Speaking of: did anyone ever disarm the poison-filled canister?"

Chapter Thirty-Seven

A woman seldom writes her mind but in her postscript.
~Richard Steele

Addison's house, Friday, April 18

"Is that all? It had better be, because your trunk is full. I'll have to put this one on the back seat." Phoebe picked up the suitcase and headed out the front door. "You sure you have to go?"

"They finished the library renovations, and I'm expected back on the job on Monday. I was lucky my boss allowed me a few extra days." Addison checked the car. "Is that everything?"

"Yeah." Phoebe took hold of her cousin's arms. "Addy, what about Nick?"

"He went home to scatter Daniel's ashes. He didn't say when"—*or if*—"he'd be back."

"I'm sorry."

She shook it off. "Do you want to get a bite to eat before I leave?"

"Can't. Have to get ready for my date."

"You have a date?" Addison raised an eyebrow. "It didn't take you long to forget Walter."

Phoebe made a face. "I was right all along about him and not just about the grinder thing. Lenny told me the FBI ran a full background check on him. The

Russians recruited him back in college. He was a commie for *twenty years*." She wrinkled her nose. "I *knew* there was something creepy about him."

"That's why you wouldn't go to bed with him."

"I can spot a phony a mile away."

Addison let that pass. "So who's the date with?"

"Ike Tickell." She blushed slightly.

Addison grinned. "He's been carrying the torch for you since elementary school, hasn't he?"

Phoebe rolled her eyes. "It's not that. He was impressed with my marksmanship."

"Marksmanship? You mean, taking Walter out?"

"Uh-huh. He said, and I quote, 'You don't see a perfect head shot from a hundred yards like that very often.' "

Addison took the keys from Phoebe's hand. "I'll be back in a week or so."

"You will? How come?"

"Let's just leave it that I have some unfinished business here." She didn't tell her cousin that she planned to go to the wishing tree and make her final farewells to Seth. *I have to stop looking backward and start looking ahead.* She had clung to him as her rock in a world in upheaval, but now the tide had risen, washing over him, and had finally and truly swept him away.

In his place was a waking dream, in which a figure was sitting on the sand where Seth had been, his back to her. She knew it was Nick, but she couldn't see his face. She wanted to call out, to touch him, but her limbs felt as heavy as tree branches weighed down with snow.

She hadn't heard from him since he'd said goodbye a few days before. He had seemed withdrawn then.

Unsettled? Off balance? Perhaps he was retreating to a different world and a previous life? She wished she knew where she stood with him. The past few weeks had been so fraught with perils and pitfalls. *Was that all it was, a coupling for safety?* Once it was over, did he believe the affair was a mistake? *Is he lost to me as well?*

Addison stifled the sob, got in the car, and started the engine. "Bye, Phoebe."

"Buh-bye. Let me know you arrived home safely." Phoebe stood in the driveway as Addison drove off, waving a white handkerchief, just as the Steeles had done for generations when any family member left the island.

****

District of Columbia, Monday afternoon

Even though the senators were still on their Easter recess, their staff kept Addison busy doing research for upcoming hearings and bills the members intended to introduce when they returned.

She had just given a stack of documents on the Colorado River Compact to a counsel for the Indian Affairs Committee when her boss walked in. "Hey, Addison, Chairman Gilley of the Commerce Committee just called. He's sending a staffer over to pick up the reports on their NASA oversight hearings from the last Congress. I guess he's upset somebody missed the memo about spies overrunning the Wallops Island Flight Facility."

"I'm on it." She headed to the section for the Subcommittee on Space and Science. "Just my luck they're on the top shelf." She rolled the ladder to the right spot and climbed up. As she was backing down, a batch of binders clamped between her chin and her chest, a man cleared his throat. She peeked over her shoulder and almost lost her grip. "Nick!"

He held up his arms and caught her as she touched the ground. The binders went flying, skittering across the floor. Nick regarded her solemnly before planting a tentative kiss on her lips. "Hi, Addison."

"Um…oh…" She gave up on finding anything else to say and mutely led him to her desk. He lowered himself onto the chair in front of it. After a minute, she sat on the other side. "How did you get in here?"

"What? No, hello? No, how have you been? Perhaps an 'I missed you'?"

"We'll get to that later. This library is for senators and their staff only. Who let you in?"

"I see. You want to verify my hall pass." He dug in his pocket and pulled out a badge on a long ribbon.

Addison bent down to read it. Under the blurry photo of Nick were the words U.S. Senate Committee on Commerce, Science, and Transportation, Staff. She looked up at him. "You work for the Commerce Committee?"

"That's right. My beat is oversight of the space and science subcommittee."

Her hand flew to her mouth. "You're the staffer the chairman sent over."

"In the flesh."

"But…you were *there*. On Chincoteague."

He had the grace to look embarrassed. "Yes. I was actually on assignment. My chairman had heard from a friend—an assistant secretary at DHS—about threats at the facility and sent me down to do a little quiet sleuthing."

"Threats?"

"National security threats. Contention among the foreign scientists."

"The Turk and the Armenian?"

"Yes, and the one between Li and Cheng. Gilley was worried about work interruptions if one of them were sent home."

"Did you perchance know Eric Austen was DHS?"

He shook his head in disgust. "No. Senator Gilley's friend didn't bother to tell him she was sending her own scout down." He chuckled. "Let's just say they had words."

Addison picked up a pencil and tapped it on the blotter. "So the travel writing bit was pure bunk?"

"Not at all." He flipped his ID up and down. "I do this while I'm waiting for my big break."

"You may have a modicum of talent. After all, your ancestor Richard was a writer—and a poet."

"I know. That's why I always use it as a cover. Despite his proclivities, he was a marvelous poet—even Alexander Pope thought so."

His words reminded her of the Savage family oath. "Were you aching for revenge on a Steele as well?"

Nick's face went rigid. "Dan told you about it?"

Suddenly Addison wished she'd kept her mouth shut. Nick and his brother had finally patched things up before Dan's death, and what she said now could ruin that reconciliation forever. "Dan told me he dropped the idea. He…he said he felt relieved of a heavy burden." She waited anxiously.

Nick was silent for a moment. Finally, he mumbled, "Daniel always insisted the vendetta was his duty. I condemned it as stupid and unhealthy. The dispute lay between us for years." He took a deep breath. "So that's that. I'm glad he was able to put it behind him." A brief smile wafted across his lips. "It must be fate that we crossed paths with you, Addison."

She tried to catch his eye, but he wouldn't look at her. *That's it. He's done with me.* The sudden pain shook her.

Nick raised his head, but when he saw the frozen look on her face, he dropped it. "I...uh...so..." He gestured at the floor. "Were those the reports I asked for?"

"What? Oh, yes." She gathered them up and piled them on the work table. He moved to pick them up, but she blocked him. "First, I want to hear the truth. How or when did you find out about the espionage?"

"When I contacted Olson—the Wallops security chief—to arrange my visit. He told me he'd found evidence of document thefts and had requested help from the CIA."

"I see." She rose and went into the break room. Nick followed her. "Coffee?"

"Sure."

She mixed them each a mug of instant coffee and settled at the tiny bistro table. "You still haven't told me where you come in."

"When Chairman Gilley learned of the CIA's involvement, he instructed me to go down to Wallops incognito."

"Why not go in your capacity as Commerce Committee oversight?"

"He wanted me to poke around, figure out who was really in charge, that sort of thing, before he made a stink."

She sipped from her mug. "Did you know Daniel was the CIA agent?"

"No! I thought he was still part of the Che Warriors."

"Then how—?"

"I was doing routine background on the scientists in residence at Wallops and saw his picture. I had no idea what to think. My brother a scientist? Or worse, a spy? Was he the one the CIA was after? I had to find out."

Addison watched Nick's face. "Why the song and dance about Daniel going overboard?"

He took a stab at chagrin. "I just blurted it out after you told me about Seth. Later on, it came in handy—I could safely ask around about Daniel without people wondering what my real motive was."

She sat back. "You're lucky I never ran into Captain Frank and asked about the accident."

He grinned. "Luck doesn't come into it. He was in Baltimore with his aged mother. I figured I'd better whip up a back story, so I googled 'boats for hire' in Chincoteague. He was the only one who was out of town."

"I see." A light sparked in her eyes. "So you live here?"

"I have an apartment in Del Ray. I just returned from Bristol, though." His blue eyes were moist.

"Bristol?"

"Rhode Island."

"Oh? Oh! Daniel."

"Yes. We scattered his ashes in the Atlantic." He attempted a smile. "So now he's officially lost at sea."

Chapter Thirty-Eight

One hope no sooner dies in us but another rises up in its stead.

~Joseph Addison

U. S. Senate Library, Monday, April 21

They were both quiet. Finally, Nick rose. "I'd better get back to the office."

She stood up quickly, knocking over her mug. Coffee spilled on the table, creating a large puddle. "Oh dear."

He waved her off. "I'll clean this up. You go get the reports."

"Okay." She walked unsteadily out of the room, her mind in a whirl. She hadn't expected to see Nick again. It upset all her plans to move on—first from Seth, and then from Nick. *That kiss. What did it mean? Does he care?* He hadn't said anything—hadn't responded—when she told him she loved him that terrible day on the refuge. *Well, after all, his brother was dying in front of him. The last thing he'd think about would be his feelings for me.* She marched to the table and slid her arms under the pile. The top few reports teetered, then slid off onto the floor. "Again? Sheesh."

She bent down, but a large hand with a white scar

running across it beat her to it and handed her the folders. "Do I have to sign these out?"

"Um, yes. Over here." She carried the materials to the checkout desk.

As he signed his name, he said offhandedly, "The chairman's leading a delegation next week to Mexico, and I have to go with him." His mouth twisted. "I haven't even unpacked from the Rhode Island trip yet. My cat doesn't recognize me."

"Oh, you have a cat?"

"Uh-huh. Sid's a Bombay—resembles a miniature black panther. Sleek black coat and huge round yellow eyes like topazes."

"What kind of a name is Sid for a cat?"

"Better than Mopsy. Mopsy, after all, was a rabbit."

She realized she was making endless small talk to keep Nick there. *You have to say goodbye some time. Get on with it, Addy.* "Er, do you need someone to watch Sid while you're gone?"

"No, thanks. My neighbor takes care of him." He gazed at her. "Well, I'd better go."

"Yes."

"Yes." He waited a minute, then, "Yes, well. All righty then." He went to the door. "I guess I'll see you when I get back." He didn't make it a question.

She jumped at it. "Would you like that?"

He blinked, his expression suddenly doubtful. "Would you?"

Now that he'd posed the question, she realized she wasn't sure at all. "I...I have to think about it."

He put the books down, stepped toward her, and kissed her lightly on the forehead. When she looked up, he was gone.

****

Addison's house, Chincoteague, Thursday, May 1

"You're back!"

"I told you, Phoebe—I have to get the house ready for Bertie's in-laws. They're coming in June."

Addison's cousin accepted a grocery bag and trudged up the steps of the house. "You're lucky I was here. I took a day off and thought I'd come over to feed Mopsy."

The cat came bounding downstairs and rubbed against Addison's legs. She picked him up and nuzzled him. "Did you miss me, you old growler?"

For answer, Mopsy licked her nose, then immediately struggled to be free. Addison pulled a bottle of wine from the refrigerator and got two glasses from the cupboard. "Fancy a drop of the grape?"

"For you, dear, sure. Normally I'd prefer beer, but I happen to know you're out." Phoebe grinned.

"Let's go out on the deck."

For a few minutes, they sat unspeaking. Addison drank in the familiar, beloved scents of marsh grass, fish, and brackish water. A flicker of bright indigo drew her eyes to a pair of blue grosbeaks courting on the berm across the canal. "Bit of a chop on the water."

"Uh-huh. It's the remnant of a big storm last Tuesday. Knocked over Noah Merritt's shack."

"About time."

They fell silent again. Addison was trying very hard not to think about the tall, lean man she'd last seen in DC. She was still in turmoil—unsure of her feelings toward him. At least she had made one decision in the last week.

"Oh, look, here comes Mr. Tickell." Phoebe waved.

The old man poled down the canal and pulled into Addison's dock. He looped a rope around the pylon. "Well, well, here's our Miss Addison back in our midst."

"For a short visit. Have you recovered from your dunking?"

"Oh, I'm used to it. I had five brothers after all." He rubbed his hands together. "Had m'revenge though, when that feller ran out-a gas half mile away. Found m'boat stuck between two pilings at Memorial Park." He raised his hat and scratched his forehead. "How long'll you be stayin'?"

"Just for the weekend."

"*Hmm.* You'll miss the festivities then?"

"Festivities? What festivities?"

Tickell looked from Addison to Phoebe. "You ain't tole her yet?"

"Told me what?"

Phoebe squirmed on the seat. "I haven't had a chance to, Mr. T. I needed to find the right moment."

Addison was totally bewildered. "What's going on?"

Her cousin's face went full scarlet. "I...I...uh..."

The old man chuckled. "She's a-tryin' ta tell you that she and my boy Ike are getting hitched."

Addison dropped her glass. The wine dribbled through the pine boards of the picnic table onto the deck. Mopsy slithered between Addison's legs and began to lick the puddle. "You're engaged?"

Phoebe nodded. She took a big swallow from her glass and coughed it up. When she'd recovered, she squeaked in a wobbly voice, "Ikey asked me a couple of days ago. We were at the range doing some target practice." Before Addison could respond, she said in a rush, "You're thinking it seems awful quick, but we've known each other forever and…it just clicked, Addy. I feel like it was there all along. We were meant to be together. You know?" She gazed breathlessly at Addison.

I wish…well… She gulped. "It's wonderful news. How lucky you both are!"

Phoebe continued to babble. "We don't have a date yet. There's no rush. We're—"

Addison glanced at Mr. Tickell. "So what are these festivities you're talking about then?"

The old man beamed. "The wife wants to throw an engagement party for them. Pull out all the stops. Maybe even have a tent inna backyard."

Addison felt the tears well up. "Oh, Phoebe."

Phoebe started to cry. "Oh, Addy."

****

Phoebe's house, Friday afternoon

"Okay then, what about *this* dress?" Phoebe slipped on a bright red shift with a slit up to her thigh and a plunging neckline.

"Perfect. It'll go great with those fishnet stockings and your four-inch stilettos. Some big hoop earrings should complete the effect. That is, if you *want* people to think you're a streetwalker."

"I take it that's a no." She took the dress off and put it back on its hanger. "Okay, I've shown you five dresses, and you've pooh-poohed them all. How about *you* tell *me* what's appropriate for an engagement party."

"Okay. It's going to be outside, so wear something comfortable." Addison wiped her forehead. "It'll probably be hot, too." She pulled out a dove-gray, cotton dress. "This will go beautifully with your eyes, and you can wear those pink flats for a spot of color."

Phoebe took it. "Ooh, and I have a matching ribbon for my hair." She looked at her cousin, her eyes glowing. "Thank you, Addy."

Addison stood up. "Okay, now that's settled, let's hit Dobie's for a drink."

The two women drove into town. As they slowed down to enter the restaurant's parking lot, a black Hummer exited. Addison watched it drive slowly down Main Street and turn left on Mumford. *Couldn't be.* She prayed Phoebe hadn't noticed the car. They climbed the steps to the lounge and settled themselves at the bar.

"What'll it be, ladies?"

"Gin and tonic for me, Toddy."

"Same for me."

He leaned over the counter. "So…when's the big day?"

"Big day?" From Phoebe's expression, Addison felt sure Toddy wasn't on the guest list. There was a moment of desperate silence while she tried to come up with an acceptable story.

Toddy's lower lip protruded. "You mean, I'm not invited?"

"Well, uh…"

"I have the perfect present. You know how she's always…um…keeping an eye on things. Well…" He pulled a small box from his pocket. "I found these teensy binoculars. She can keep them in her purse, and when she sees—"

"Uh, Toddy? Who are you talking about?"

"Cora Anne Jester. Aren't you throwing her a surprise birthday party? I was at Wrigley's and Bessie told me—"

The two women looked at each other and burst into laughter. When Addison caught her breath, she gurgled, "I guess we'll have to now."

Phoebe waited for Toddy to move away, then remarked casually, "So, did you notice that Hummer? Your Nick's not in town, is he?"

Damn. "He's not my Nick, and no, I don't think so. I...saw him in DC. Guess what? It turns out he works for the Senate! He was sent to investigate the spy allegations anonymously."

"Another guy with secrets." Phoebe pondered this. "Well, you're probably better off without him. All these people seem to be totally untrustworthy, or at least not who they say they are. Guess what I found out."

"What?"

"Walter's mission? The canister with the anthrax?"

"Oh my God—I'd forgotten about that! Was it ever disarmed?"

"Turns out it didn't have to be."

Addison sucked in a breath. "Anthrax is a deadly toxin—you can't just leave it lying around."

"They didn't. It was never in the module."

Addison set down her drink. "Explain."

"Walter told you he'd heard about the alternate space station from one of the Belarusians—a Vladimir something, right?"

"Right. Vladimir Novik. Come to think of it, he was the one who fingered Dr. Li too."

"That wasn't a coincidence."

Addison was feeling rather more than impatient. "Just tell me, Phebes."

Phoebe leaned forward and whispered dramatically. "Vladimir Novik is a spy!"

"*Another* one? Who does *he* work for?"

"He's a double agent—he partnered with Olga, but in reality he works for the CIA. He discovered the anthrax in the small vehicle launch lab and disposed of it, substituting baking soda. He said even with the anthrax, the explosion would never have done the damage Walter thought it would. He only spread the lie about a new Russian station to draw the culprit out."

"Whew. Walter never knew his sabotage had been sabotaged." Addison counted on her fingers. "That means at least six spies were gamboling about the halls of the Wallops facility."

Phoebe leaned over and pushed up one more finger. "Seven. There was one more white hat. Eric Austen."

"Austen! He seemed to be the worst of the lot."

"Not by a long shot." Phoebe handed her empty glass back to Toddy. "You know what he did? He arranged asylum for your Belarusian friends. They're sitting in a safe house somewhere in Maryland as we speak."

Addison clucked her tongue. "I wonder…"

"Yes, he was the one who tipped Vasilinak off about your boat. He had interviewed him when the Belarusians arrived in DC. Vasilinak told him they wanted to defect and needed a boat. He came up with your name."

"Eric was there when Klopman released Grigory from jail. Why didn't Grigory say something to him then?"

"The interview was by phone. They never met in person."

Addison visualized the little man-bunned fellow she still viewed as an officious meddler. "I must say, he looks so much like a rodent it's hard to believe he's a good guy after all."

Phoebe was philosophical. "They can't all look like your Nick."

"He's not my Nick. Say, you seem awfully up-to-date on the latest gossip. Since Walter's gone, who's your source for news of Wallops?"

"Ike. His best friend is the new security guard." Phoebe signaled for the check. "And I still think he's your Nick."

Chapter Thirty-Nine

Love is a second life; it grows into the soul, warms every vein, and beats in every pulse.

~Joseph Addison

The Wishing Tree, Saturday, May 3

Addison drove down Church Street to Chicken City Road and took a right on Maddox Boulevard. The entry kiosk at the refuge was still closed. She drove straight to the end and walked over the dune to the beach. It was empty at this early morning hour. The waves slithered over the sand, leaving a froth of yellow foam. Sanderlings and willets picked their way through the wrack, jabbing at mole crabs. The sky matched the dun-colored ocean, punctuated by darker clouds scudding in the distance, the remnants of the gale that had blown through the night before. She shaded her eyes and peered into the swirling spray. There—a pair of gannets shot through the clouds. A beam of light hit their bright golden heads, reminding her of tiny planets circling the sun.

Let's get it over with. She walked up to the wishing tree. Yup, there it was. The scrap from the mainsail on their honeymoon ketch. *I guess even last night's storm didn't dislodge it.* She summoned up that awful day of a year ago.

Seth was at the helm. The wind had just picked up, and he called to warn Addison they were coming about. A sudden gust knocked the boom loose, and the boat careened wildly. The wind tore into the sail and freed it from the spar. She ducked into the galley, grabbed the VHF radio, and called for help. Within seconds, the ketch heeled and capsized. The Coast Guard arrived and pulled her in, but Seth was nowhere to be seen. They searched all day and the day after. *If only he'd had his life vest on*…but Seth always refused. "I'm a champion swimmer, Addy," he'd grin. "And besides, why hide these great abs?"

The tears still wouldn't come. *Face it, Addy, it's always going to be an open wound.* She loved Nick, but feared her grief would hang between them forever, like a limp balloon left over from a birthday party. She touched the scrap. *Time to let go.*

Instead, she withdrew her hand and walked down to the ocean. The tide was going out, and as the water receded, she could hear the tinny *clack-clack* of dozens of coquinas slamming shut before burying themselves in the sand. A school of fish passed, churning the water. In their wake, a funnel rose out of the waves like Botticelli's Venus. It rolled past her up the beach, took a lap around the old oak, and picked up her token. The bit of cloth sailed, pitching and tossing, over her head and out to sea.

Huh. So…does that mean Seth's coming back? The thought did not bring her joy. Wait. How did the legend go?

"The guidebook says that if your token is carried away on the wind, your true love will find you."

She felt a hand on her shoulder. She didn't need to

turn around. *Nick.*

"I hoped to catch you at the Senate, but they said you were down here for another day. Something about an engagement." He peered at her, the question clear.

"Phoebe's. She's marrying Ike Tickell."

"Lenny's deputy? Good choice."

She twisted around. "You're back from the Mexico trip?"

"Yes. I would have come down sooner, but I had to go to Arlington Cemetery."

"Arlington Cemetery! What for?"

"To pick up Daniel's flag."

She knit her brows. "His flag?"

Nick smiled sadly. "The memorial service up in Rhode Island was private, and we didn't get a chance to arrange for military honors. The army offered to hold a separate ceremony to present the family with his flag."

"I didn't know Daniel was a veteran."

"Graduated from West Point. Made it to first lieutenant but then resigned his commission to be with Sadie."

"The woman who blew herself up."

"Yes."

"He was a true hero, Nick."

"That he was."

"I'm glad you two were able to make peace."

"Yes."

Impulsively, she blurted, "The trinket didn't actually have to blow away, you know. The girl's intended was supposed to remove it, keeping it until he was ready to propose."

"Ah."

They stood quietly for a minute. Finally, Nick said

softly, "I see *your* token is gone. Tell me, did your true love find you?"

Addison's eyes strayed to the horizon. The waves crashed, sending the salt spray roiling up, obscuring the sky. When she looked back, Nick drew a broken razor clam shell from his pocket. He went down on one knee.

"I found this on the wishing tree. Did perchance Maid Addison leave it there?"

She recognized the shell little Starlyn had left, it seemed so long ago. She started to demur but paused. *She'll have more and better dreams.* "Why yes, good sir. I did."

A word about the author…

Librarian, anthropologist, Congressional aide, speechwriter—M. S. Spencer has lived or traveled in five of the seven continents. She holds a BA from Vassar College, a diploma in Arabic Studies from the American University in Cairo, and Masters in Anthropology and in Library Science from the University of Chicago. All of this tends to insinuate itself into her works.

Ms. Spencer has published fifteen romantic suspense and mystery novels. She has two fabulous grown children and an incredible granddaughter and currently divides her time between the Gulf Coast of Florida and a tiny village in Maine.

http://msspencertalespinner.blogspot.com

Thank you for purchasing
this publication of The Wild Rose Press, Inc.

For questions or more information
contact us at
info@thewildrosepress.com.

The Wild Rose Press, Inc.
www.thewildrosepress.com